Beauty and Dread

Book 2 in the Troop of Shadows Chronicles

by Nicki Huntsman Smith

Published by NHS Marketing, LLC

COPYRIGHT NOTICE

Acknowledgements and Credits

I would like to thank the following:

Lori, my editor, proofreader, and grammar consultant extraordinaire. Thankfully, comma placement doesn't vex her as profoundly as it does me.

My beta readers, who provided advice, suggestions, and top-notch cheerleading. Al, your suggestions were especially helpful.

My friends and family, who have always accepted my eccentric interests and overt nerdiness with indulgent affection. If any of my children ever read my books, they will get mentioned by name. That's the deal.

Lastly and most importantly, my husband Ray, without whose constant encouragement, gentle nudging, infinite patience, and support on a million different levels, this book would never have been written. I owe him everything.

A Shadow

I said unto myself, if I were dead,
What would befall these children? What would be
Their fate, who now are looking up to me
For help and furtherance? Their lives, I said,
Would be a volume wherein I have read
But the first chapters, and no longer see
To read the rest of their dear history,
So full of beauty and so full of dread.
Be comforted; the world is very old,
And generations pass, as they have passed,
A troop of shadows moving with the sun;
Thousands of times has the old tale been told;
The world belongs to those who come the last,
They will find hope and strength as we have done.
--Henry Wadsworth Longfellow

Prologue

London

British Institute for the Study of Iraq

"Pity there's no one left to share this with," Harold muttered to himself.

Dr. Harold Clarke's final decoding of the seven mysterious Urak tablets had been gratifying and exhilarating; the pinnacle of his career, actually. It was the culmination of more than a year's tireless research, done first in his barricaded Twickenham flat, and then continued at the BISI housed in the British Academy Building in London. It had been a harrowing adventure making the pilgrimage from his home to London, but he had done it. It was vital to view the tablets themselves, not just pixilated photographs. Even more importantly, he needed to touch the cuneiform symbols chiseled into the stone, allowing the author's message to seep into his fingertips, travel along his body's nervous system, then find the appropriate neurons in his brain to explain what the fingertips had discovered.

Dr. Harold Clarke, brilliant anthropologist and world-renowned expert in ancient logophonetic languages, had a secret. Yes, he was a genius; his IQ was in the high 150 range. But he also possessed a hidden talent that had helped propel him to the lofty professional position he enjoyed before the end of the world happened. He had never told anyone about it. Not his family, nor his few friends, and certainly not his colleagues. His talent was something mainstream science would have ridiculed and dismissed. But because Harold was smart, he had used his gift to make himself a better scientist during his career, and again recently to decipher the ancient stone tablets before him. After weeks of studying them, touching them, coaxing from them their long-dead secrets, there had been a breakthrough, and it went beyond just the translation. He had connected, telepathically, with their author who should have died more than twelve thousand years ago.

Chapter 1

Liberty, Kansas

"What the hell do you mean, she's gone?" Maddie's pale face was flushed with frustration. Her red gold hair stuck out at odd angles, a follicular casualty of her recent head injury. After the necessary butchering, Pablo had said all that luxurious hair actually detracted from her beauty, and he meant it. But now, he had to bite his tongue to keep from laughing. She looked like a reject from a casting call of Peter Pan's Lost Boys.

"Jessie said she wasn't in her bed this morning, and she wasn't in the front or backyard. I'll keep looking though. Please, lie back down. In case you forgot, your beautiful noggin is still recovering. Getting upset can't be good for you."

A bright spot of blood blossomed on the white gauze bandage which encircled her shorn head, underscoring his concern.

Once he got her tucked back into bed, he would search for Amelia. But right now there was nothing more important than taking care of Maddie, making sure she didn't cause further harm to herself or the graphing calculator that was her brain.

Jessie stood in the doorway. He felt her presence there before he saw her. Those unusual sea-green eyes studied him, but he no longer found the child disconcerting. Somehow, Amelia had pulled Maddie through the devastation of a bullet wound in her skull, an injury that happened outside of Albuquerque the previous week. Jessie had been a witness to the doctoring, but Pablo had been banished from the room and would probably never know how Amelia had done it. Even more astonishing than Maddie's survival was the apparent lack of residual brain damage. So far the only side effect of the head trauma had been her newfound 'psychic' ability which had brought them to Liberty, caravanning with the other group of oddities which included the scary female warrior, the handsome guy, and the red-haired man, who died during the Hays mission.

That was a shame. He had liked the cheeky little fellow.

Pablo ushered the little girl out of the bedroom and closed the door behind them.

"You've searched all around the yard and up and down the street, Jessie? She can't have gone far."

The child nodded, but then remembered her agreement with Pablo. She must vocalize rather than gesticulate.

"Yes, Pablo." The singsong voice perfectly suited her. The elfin otherworldliness had diminished somewhat now that she was clean and communicative.

"Do you want to stay here while I go search? She's probably just exploring...chatting to the locals and whatnot. I don't think we have anything to worry about," he added when he noticed the distress on the child's face. They had all bonded with Amelia. Her easygoing nature, inherent wisdom, and tranquil demeanor had made her the perfect travel companion, and now, an invaluable friend.

"Yes, I'll stay with Maddie. Please go now."

"Okay, okay." He smiled at the child. "You're worrying for nothing though. I know she'll turn up any minute now."

For the rest of the morning and a good portion of the afternoon, he canvassed the surrounding area, returning every hour to check on the girls at their new home – a small ranch-style dwelling near the center of town where the community greenhouse was being built. Then later that day when he arrived at the meeting taking place in the former courthouse, he asked everyone he met if they had seen Amelia. No one had.

"Come on, people. Let's take it down a notch." Steven, Liberty's unofficial leader, raised his voice to be heard above the din.

Pablo hadn't yet decided how he felt about the man. He seemed insufferable at times, but little fault could be found with his decisions thus far. Sometimes exceptionally smart people were oblivious to their own pedantic natures; he had learned that lesson from his parents who had encouraged his creativity and supported his lofty literary goals but were quick to bring him down a peg when he complained about his less than articulate peers. So many people in his culture never embraced English, even though they lived in the United States. This baffled Pablo, who was a wordsmith in both English and Spanish. His parents had been proud of their son's exceptionalism but would often point out that nobody liked a *puto arrogante...a*rrogant asshole.

"Where the hell do you get off acting in direct violation of the vote, Steven?" The speaker's angry voice came from the row behind, but Pablo kept his eyes on Steven at the center of the room. "Is that how it's going to be from now on? Everyone has to abide by the rules except you? Is this what you bought with the food you shared?"

"The rescue operation was an exception, I promise. The circumstances demanded action and since we suffered no casualties, I think we should just let it go for now. There are more pressing matters to discuss. May we proceed?"

"Do we have a choice? You seem to be running the show now."

"We always have choices, but why waste valuable time and energy debating the semantics of government and majority rule when we won't make it through the winter with our current food supply levels?"

The man didn't respond.

Game, set, match.

"You're wrong about the casualties."

The voice came from a bench in the back row of concentric circles. The speaker was the intimidating young woman, Dani, and judging by the look on her face, she was either about to cry or kill someone. Maybe both. Pablo was glad he wasn't the one who had upset her.

"Of course. I misspoke. Your friend Fergus was a tragic loss, but also not yet a member of our town."

"No, but he volunteered for your dangerous, unsanctioned mission, and now he's gone. So there were casualties."

Steven tilted his head a degree, studying the girl. "You volunteered too."

"I had to. No one else on this planet could have done what I did, and clearly it was a job that needed to be done. As for all you assholes who voted against saving those women, fuck every last one of you. Sam, do you want to live in a town where half the people wanted to let those girls suffer?" She spoke to the Greek god sitting next to her.

Pablo watched Steven's face. Was he trying not to smile?

"Give us a chance. Let us prove to you that we're good folks. Scared folks, but good folks. You and Sam would be huge assets to our town, and we have a lot to offer in return," Steven said.

The girl opened her mouth to reply, but Sam reached for her arm and gently pulled her back onto the bench beside him. If any other person had tried that maneuver, he would have broken fingers now.

"We'll talk later, Dani. Candidly and with no sugarcoating, I promise. Now, Marilyn, what's first up on the agenda for today's discussion?"

Before focusing his attention on the spinsterish librarian, Pablo saw Steven wink at his sister, who sat with her strange companion in one of the front rows.

Now there's a human oddity, he thought, observing the wild blond hair and vacant smile of the person sitting next to Julia. Inspiration for a new poem came to mind as he covertly watched the young man.

Goodness is a notion in which all may not partake
Kindness is a choice not everyone must make
Be true to the nature at one's core
Love the dark things others abhor

Whatever dark things that nutcase might love, Pablo hoped never to find out.

Chapter 2

"**Y**ou're like a mother hen. Please don't fret so. I'm sure I'll be fine in a few days. These ladies are taking excellent care of me."

Julia stood at the bedside of her friend. The town had set up a makeshift medical clinic in the former Liberty Regional Hospital. There was no power, but plenty of sunlight streamed through the windows, and a kerosene lamp sat on a table next to a water cup and a plate with Thoozy's half-eaten lunch. He still didn't have his appetite nor his strength back after the morning she had found him barely conscious in his motel room.

"You must eat, old man. Come on, finish that tuna fish."

The dark-skinned face assumed the universal expression of disgust; the normally smiling mouth turned down in an exaggerated grimace. "It's just so fishy! If God intended for people to consume creatures that breathe water and swim in their own toilet, he'd have made them taste better."

"You big whiner. When I come back in the morning, I'll bring some land-based food. Steven has some canned pork and beans. How does that sound?"

"Sounds like I'll be able to entertain the nurses with my butt trumpet tomorrow night."

The warm grin was back to normal, but the haggardness around his eyes and the tight-lipped way he glanced at Logan hovering by the door bothered Julia. Something was deeply amiss with her friend, but it seemed there was nothing she could do to draw him out.

"Okay, Thoozy, we'll be back tomorrow bearing flatulence-creating, non-fishy-tasting gifts." She smiled at one of the women from the medical crew who had just breezed through the doorway. She remembered her name was Natalie, but that was all she had gotten from Steven about her other than some visibly discomfited foot shuffling. Her big-sister radar told her the two must have some history, but there had been no time yet for an extended conversation with her brother. She hoped to have one later once Logan and her nephew Jeffrey were in bed.

"One more thing, Doc," he said to her in a low, conspiratorial voice with another glance at the blond young man who was absorbed in studying the woman who'd just entered. Julia recognized that face: he was analyzing her 'colors.'

"Have you had a chance to talk to your brother about that thing we discussed in the car the other day?" The cotton ball head twitched in Logan's direction.

She read the subtext: *Have you told your brother about Logan? Explained his behavioral and psychological issues which could range from harmless Asperger's and manic depression to more dangerous disorders such as schizophrenia or psychopathy? And by the way, have you mentioned to your brother, in whose home you and your ward are guests, that your former traveling companion also exhibits savant-level abilities with firearms?*

She felt a flash of annoyance. This was her problem, not Thoozy's.

"Not yet, but I will, I promise. We had the town hall meeting this afternoon, and Steven has been busy preparing for it. See you tomorrow, Thoozy."

"When we can have a moment alone...just the two of us..." another head twitch in Logan's direction, "I need to talk to you about something. It's important."

She nodded, kissed the old man on the top of his Q-tip head, and hustled Logan through the door. A minute later they were outside of the hospital and walking toward their bicycles. A fierce wind gusted straight out of the north; the weak setting sun was no match for it. It would be a chilly ride back to Steven's house which was five miles from Liberty's town square.

"The nurse's colors weren't as pretty as yours."

"I saw you looking at her," Julia said, as they mounted their bikes. "It's good that you can do that, Logan. I believe it's quite a gift you have, but I wonder if it's something we should keep to ourselves. Some people might find it a bit off-putting." She noticed the sudden frown, his response when he didn't understand a word. "Unpleasant, I mean. It might feel to people that you can see inside their heads, which is not a comfortable feeling.

Most of us like our privacy, and we all have secrets, don't we?"

"Oh, yes. I think that's true. There's nothing bad about having secrets. My mom said so. She said I should not tell people about all the things I keep in my head. She said *oversharing wasn't good.*"

"I think your mother was a smart lady. What colors did you see, by the way? Around Natalie the nurse?"

"It was kind of weird. They kept changing. For a while they were yellow and orange, then they would get brownish. For a minute they were almost black, then they went back to yellow and orange again. Not pretty colors, like yours. Your colors are my favorite."

Julia laughed between the puffing and pedaling. She thought ahead to the talk with her brother and wondered if revealing all the details regarding Logan was necessary. Much of it was conjecture on her part. ..nothing more than amateur psychiatry. Having an interest in a subject and reading up on it doesn't make one an expert.

***

"Good grief, Julia. Am I hearing this right? You're saying that man upstairs, the one sleeping in my son's bedroom, could be a sociopath? How could you bring him into my home?"

"Steven, please calm down. You're overreacting." She splashed another ounce of amber liquid into his glass. "I'm just trying to describe the kinds of people that survived Chicxulub. Roughly fifty percent of all the survivors will have emotional issues of some kind, but only a small percentage of those may present with more troublesome symptoms."

"Troublesome? Shit. I consider sociopathic tendencies a hell of a lot worse than troublesome."

"Those would be rare cases. Please just hear me out. I've seen no evidence of psychopathy in Logan, and I've been with him for a week. If he were dangerous, I'd know it because I'd be dead now."

Steven frowned.

"And he's really just a boy in a man's body. I doubt his emotional and intellectual maturity is even at the same level as Jeffrey's."

"Not a good comparison. Jeffrey is a fifty-year-old in a fourteen-year-old's body."

"Well, you know what I'm saying. He is childlike in many ways. Who knows if I'd have made it here without him? Remember how he helped with those men at the Hays roadblock?"

"Yes, I heard the story of his shooting prowess. Not sure if that makes a constructive argument for your case though. Great, he's effective at killing people."

Julia's eyes narrowed. "You probably have a number of marginally dangerous people in Liberty even now. It's just the new reality of our world."

"They're not living down the hall from my son."

"Fine. If you want us to leave, we'll leave. It's not like there aren't plenty of houses to live in."

He knew that expression. He had pissed off his big sister and now she would slip into 'ice queen mode,' a term coined during their teen years. Nobody could do chilly reserve better than Julia.

"That's not what I want and you know it. You're much safer here than anywhere else. I just don't understand why you're so defensive of this young man whom you've only known a week. Please tell me there's not a Mrs. Robinson thing going on here."

He regretted the words the moment they tumbled out.

"Don't leave, I'm sorry!" he said to her backside as she stormed toward the stairs. "Come back and let's discuss this. I promise I will listen with my ears open and my mouth shut." It was their father's favorite directive; he had been a man with his hands full raising two gifted children who challenged him at every turn with logical and loud rebuttals.

She paused at the bottom step.

"I have chocolate." He waved a Dove Bar. He had saved a box for his sister whose love of dark chocolate was legendary in their family. "And there's more where this came from."

She turned, intending to scorch her little brother with her best go-to-hell look. Instead, she laughed. The goofy grin had the desired effect, melting her anger. She snatched the candy from his hand and plopped back down on the sofa.

"God, you look like dad now with that silver in your hair." She took a huge bite of chocolate. "I can't explain it. I admit, I've wondered the same thing. Maybe I got sucked in a little. When I first met him, he had just been injured, and he was so filthy I knew the wound would get infected. Then the more time we spent together, the more his childish innocence worked on me. It was almost refreshing in a way, I suppose, after hobnobbing with all the self-important blowhards at Stanford. Plus don't forget, I was alone for almost a year. I didn't realize how much I missed human companionship until I got used to Logan sitting next to me in the car. And," her voice lowered, eyes falling upon everything in the room but Steven's face, "I suspect there's some residual maternal instinct. You know, from before."

Steven nodded in understanding; pieces of a Julia jigsaw puzzle were snapping into place. He saw the pain on his sister's tired face. Was this a good time to mention her resemblance to the young woman who had been largely responsible for the success of the rescue mission? Probably not. Not yet.

"The baby you gave up for adoption back in undergrad school," he said.

"Yes."

"Of course that makes sense. Still," now it was Steven's turn to lower his voice, "I can't help that he gives me the creeps."

"I know. You're not the first person to have reservations about him." She thought of Thoozy back at the hospital. "But he's had a difficult life. He was a special-needs kids raised by a single mom. He got bullied and made fun of and has been shunned his entire life. I promised that Liberty would be a new start for him. Everything is different now, and there are so few people left. Most of them will also be special...in one way or another."

What Julia had just explained about the survivors made sense when he considered his personal experience from the past year. He had encountered a lot of smart people recently, as well as people with extraordinary talents. The mental capacity of some of those with remarkable abilities did seem lower than average, although not always, as evidenced by his son. Then there was Ed, who was brilliant at building and design but whose social skills were lacking, which could be attributed to Asperger's. He thought of Marilyn and Natalie, two very different women with exceptional intelligence, and Natalie's daughter Brittany, a musical prodigy who didn't seem especially bright. The intellectual disparity didn't stop Jeffrey from ogling the girl every chance he got though; she was beautiful. If surviving and keeping his son safe hadn't forced him to have tunnel vision, he would have realized sooner that something strange was going on. Now it all began to make sense.

Julia interrupted his thoughts. "There are no longer institutions and hospitals to stick these people in, or medication to alleviate their symptoms. No advanced placement classes or magnet schools for the gifted ones. We'll just have to figure out ways to manage them all."

Steven had an unpleasant thought.

"What about the men in Hays? What would have compelled them all to behave so despicably? How did so many of those bastards end up in the same small town?"

"I'm not sure. It could have been a combination of events. Suggestibility isn't an inherent trait, but if they had low self-esteem or borderline personality disorder, they could have been receptive to the influence of a strong leader. There's so much I don't know, and don't forget this is by no means my area of expertise. I think we could learn a lot by conducting a scientific study of the townspeople."

Steven nodded. "Yes, I'm sure you're right. I'm just not sure everyone will want to be put under your microscope."

"Well, there's no problem there. It got blown up along with all my data and other equipment."

"I meant figuratively, of course. Anyway, the bigger question is, how will people react when they discover the nature of some of the individuals they may be rubbing elbows with?"

"That's impossible to answer."

For the first time since Julia's revelation, Steven pondered the wisdom of sharing this newfound information with the rest of the townspeople. How would the social dynamic change if everyone were always wondering who was gifted, psychotic - or perhaps both? And more importantly, how would that altered dynamic affect their cooperative plans for survival?

***

Logan had very good hearing. His mother always said he could hear a pin drop on the other side of the house. He crouched at the top of the darkened stairwell and listened to Julia's conversation with her brother. He wasn't surprised to discover that Steven liked him about as much as he liked Steven, which wasn't very much at all. He didn't understand a lot of the words they used, like *psychopathy* and *sociopath*, but it didn't matter because Julia had stood up for him against her own brother. That meant a lot. Other than his mother

and Mr. Cheney, their neighbor who had taught him about duct tape and knives and how to trap stray animals, he'd never had a friend. Julia was his friend. She had just shown him that. And even though the Bad Thoughts said he should...*KILL HER! KILL THEM ALL!*...he wouldn't do it. Not yet, and never Julia. When the time came, though, he knew exactly who he would start with: that mean girl who always gave him the stink eye and who looked so much like Julia.

Chapter 3

"Sam, it's bullshit. I can see what's going on here. Steven is manipulating the entire town, getting everyone to go along with his ideas just because he gave them some food. And now that his sister is by his side, they'll end up running the show. This isn't a majority-rules democracy — this is a Stevocracy."

Sam laughed, then pulled her face toward his, kissing her slowly and deeply. When he was finished, Dani had almost forgotten what they had been discussing.

"I know what you're saying, but I guess I'm not too concerned about government stuff. I think Steven is a good guy and his sister is nice too."

He pushed away from the kitchen table and stood, smiling down at her. Late October sunshine spilled in through the windows, warming the room and transforming his beard from dark gold to fiery copper. She wasn't a fan of facial hair on men, but of course Sam could be covered in Yeti fur and still be drop-dead gorgeous. Very few men these days took the time to shave, but now that they were a couple, she had begun shaving her pits, legs, and the nether regions. She liked to be smooth down there, but he wouldn't care what kind of shrubbery she sprouted. He adored every inch of her body and was always happy to show his appreciation.

"Well, I don't like it," she said. "Yes, I get that they're nice, but Steven is a manipulator. He gets a lot of support from that hatchet-faced broad. What's her name? Marilyn? Marilyn the homely librarian?"

She gave an indelicate snort. Sam frowned. He hated when she made fun of people.

"Okay, I'm sorry. That was mean, and I actually kind of like her. She seems pretty damn smart. I just don't like the situation."

"So change it," he replied, as if the solution were obvious. He began his morning stretches, mindful of the healing wound in his abdomen. His recovery had been miraculously fast. If she hadn't witnessed it with her own eyes, she wouldn't have believed the circular puckering on the right side of his belly had been a gunshot hole a week earlier.

"What do you mean?" She had a good idea what he meant, but she wanted to hear it from him. For the first time since their arrival in Liberty, she felt a stirring of interest in staying put.

At least for a while.

"I know you love danger and thrill-looking, and you think you'll be bored if we stay here, but I think you could find plenty to keep you busy. And thrilled."

"You mean on their little security crew? Please. Their leader is a grocery store manager and two of their snipers are just kids."

"Have you seen them shoot? They're amazing. Better than us."

Sam was right. With his Springfield rifle, Steven's son Jeffrey could hit a target that she could barely even see. She and Sam were exceptional at hand-to-hand combat. He had taught her everything he knew about Krav Maga and other moves from various martial arts disciplines. They were a goddamn dynamic duo — Batman and Catwoman had nothing on them. But their firearms skills were merely excellent, not extraordinary like those of some of the members of the security crew. She suspected that new guy, the creepy blond with the freaky eyes who had arrived with Steven's sister, was better than all of them.

"You could get involved in the political stuff too. If you don't like what Steven is doing, let him and everyone else know it. Ruffle some goose feathers...make some whitecaps. You're great at that."

Dani smiled. Sam's massacred clichés always amused her. He had a point too. She might not be the best with guns — yet — but she was the best at everything else when it came to defense, logistics, and strategy. She contemplated Chuck; wondered how he would feel about abdicating his position. If she were going to participate in that aspect of Liberty's emerging society, she intended to spearhead it...and on her terms.

"What do you make of Chuck? The skinny dude who's in charge of security?"

Sam shrugged in mid-stretch. "He's okay. A little intense, but I think he's a good guy."

Dani had met just about all the residents in Liberty now, including the rescued women who were still in the hospital recovering from their abuse. Many of their wounds were emotional rather than physical. The rapists and misogynists that had comprised the male population of Hays prior to the rescue mission preferred their sex slaves unmarred. But they hadn't been finicky about cleanliness; she had seen (and smelled) that herself.

When she remembered the euphoric sensation of massacring all those fuckers, it brought a smile to her face. She would be hard-pressed to duplicate that kind of adrenaline rush, but maybe some stimulation could be found in defending the town and keeping it safe, as well as dabbling in its politics. For some reason, the idea of being a thorn in Steven's side appealed to her.

"You're a damn genius and I love you. I'll see you later." She swatted his backside as she left the kitchen and headed for the front door of the tiny house they had chosen to live in. She liked the smallness of it after the McMansion she had grown up in; it would be much easier to secure than her home in Texas.

"Hey, I'm not a side of cow meat, you know!"

Dani laughed as she skipped down the concrete steps and strode off in the direction of the town square, where the greenhouse construction would be well under way, despite the early hour.

"So you think you could do a better job than Chuck? Is that what I'm hearing?" Steven had been hammering nails into the wooden skeleton of the community greenhouse, but he slid the hammer into his tool belt and gave Dani his full attention. His to-do list was roughly the length of *War and Peace,* but he would always make time for Dani and her boyfriend. They were the good kind of 'special' that Liberty needed.

"Of course. I know he has some former military training, but his weapons skills aren't great, and he couldn't strategize his way out of a laundry basket. I've done a reconnoitering of the town's defenses and...holy shit...they suck. I've made some notes if you're interested," she pulled several sheets of folded notebook paper out of her black leather jacket and handed it to him. Steven scanned the bulleted lines scrawled in purple ink, barely concealing his growing admiration for the young woman. This one would be a handful, but worth the effort if he could corral her prodigious ego. Her critique of their current security measures were spot on, and her suggestions for improving them were excellent. Of course he would prefer someone with her capabilities managing the safety of their town, but he couldn't just fire Chuck.

"I know you're worried about how pissed that skinny dude will be when you replace him with me, but you'll be doing him and everyone else a favor. He's just not the best man for the job. End of story."

He grinned at the youthful naiveté. "Yeah, things are a little more complicated than that around here. It's been challenging, to say the least, getting people to cooperate, to perform demeaning jobs, to not kill each other. You know. Stuff like that."

"Well, that's your problem, isn't it? You signed up for the position of Grand Poohbah. All I want to do is keep everyone as safe as possible by shoring up perimeter fortifications and training the people who will be helping me. Maybe we'll get to kill some bad guys in the process."

Steven studied her, seeing her now in a different light after his conversation with Julia. She moved with the easy grace of a jungle cat – beautiful and deadly. Her intellect and martial arts skills made her dangerous even without the arsenal he knew she always carried.

And he couldn't blame her for that; everyone had weapons these days. "Open carry" was woven into the fabric of their new reality, which might become a point of contention if their town ever became the peaceful, organized, productive society he envisioned. It was a fine line they walked between taking steps to assure one's personal safety and engaging in Wild West intimidation tactics.

"I'm not joking about killing the bad guys, either. Just so you know."

Steven realized he had been staring at the girl too long. A hint of hostility was creeping into her demeanor.

"Sorry, I got lost for a minute. Yes, I don't doubt that you're quite serious about killing. You seem to have a taste for it." He didn't want to run this girl off, but he wouldn't take any crap either. He would be as blunt with her as she was with him.

Dani shrugged. "I don't see that as a problem, especially as head of security."

"I suppose you're right about that. Very well, young lady, I'll talk to Chuck. In the meantime, please keep this between us. The situation needs a bit of finesse and, no offense, but I don't think I saw 'diplomacy' on your resume."

Chapter 4

"I can't believe she would just leave. This makes no sense." Maddie had insisted on getting out of bed and sitting at the breakfast table. Her freckles looked less pronounced, which meant her color was improving. Pablo was not the nurse the absent Amelia had been, but he knew it was a good sign. This morning, Maddie appeared downright robust. Her cheeks were rosy and she gobbled the Dinty Moore beef stew like it might be her last meal. He watched in awe, feeling all that bottled up apprehension melt away.

She was going to make it. He wasn't going to lose the thing that made life worth living in this hellish place that had become their world.

"What are you staring at, Poet Fellow?" She had some gravy on the side of her mouth, but he decided not to put his fingers anywhere near those busy teeth.

"Just the most beautiful woman in the world, Angel Girl."

She paused between bites to give him one of her breathtaking smiles that felt like sunshine breaking through the clouds.

"You're not so bad yourself, my dear. So what's on the agenda for today?"

"Bed rest for you and work for me at the greenhouse. I also want to break ground on our own garden in the backyard. With winter approaching, it won't be much, but I can get some cabbage and spinach in and rig up a tent with plastic sheeting. Steven gave me some seeds from his seed bank. You'd think they were made of gold. Anyway, your job is to get well."

Jessie snickered at Pablo from across the table.

"What? What's so funny?"

"I'm not staying in that bed another minute. Jessie and I have a deal. We're going to get some things done together today. We'll keep an eye on each other, right, Jessie? She'll make sure I don't overdo, and I'll make sure she doesn't have to be alone again. Like in that place where we found her." She gave him a pointed look.

When he began to protest, she raised her hand to cut him off.

"No arguing. I feel good, and I think it would do wonders for my mental and emotional well-being if I got out today. As much as I love you, you're not the boss of me just because you have a p-e-n-i-s."

"I know I'm not the boss of you, but please be sensible. You've had a devastating head injury. It's a miracle that you're even alive. Who knows what that bullet did in there?"

"You mean besides give me mad clairvoyant skills?"

Pablo frowned. The vision Maddie had seen in Oklahoma was the reason they were in Kansas, but witnessing her in the throes of it had been a disturbing experience – one he hoped not to have again.

"You haven't seen anything else have you?"

"You worry too much. If I told you every time I had one, you'd freak out."

"Damn it, Maddie. When did they happen? What did you see? Why didn't you tell me?"

"For precisely this reason," she replied with a grin. "You're a worrier and a fretter, Pablo. It's cute, but it can be exhausting." She took an enormous bite of canned peaches. They had brought all their food with them, but it wouldn't last long. And the town was a picked-clean Thanksgiving turkey carcass; once their personal provisions were exhausted, he would have to go scavenging or beg food from Steven, a notion he did not relish.

"It's my job. I won't lose you again."

"You won't. Please just back off a little. I'm a big girl and did manage to survive much of this past year without you."

"I'm painfully aware of that."

"Don't read too much into that. I'm just making a point. I know my body better than you do, and at this moment it's telling me to gobble up everything in sight and get some exercise."

He couldn't deny the evidence of her renewed health; he had never seen her eat with such enthusiasm.

"Fine. I'll back off, but not too far. Now tell me about the visions."

"Alfred is dead. I saw him in a dream the night we arrived here."

He nodded. It wasn't an earth-shattering revelation. The old man with whom they had shared an evening in Arizona had been in his eighties or nineties. His food and water had been running low and when they ran out, he wouldn't replace them. *'That will be the end of Alfred,'* were the old man's words.

"Did he tell you he was dead in the vision?"

"No, I just knew. I saw him on the motel bed. He wasn't breathing."

"That's not too bad, right? We expected that."

She shook her head. "No, but it was sad. There's more though." Her face turned dreamy and the fork paused in mid-air, a dangling peach slice impaled on its tines. "He was dead, but his spirit wasn't gone. I could hear his voice in my head saying there was someone to fear. *'Malicious, malevolent, malignant, this one.'* That's what he said."

"He didn't say who it was?"

She blinked rapidly a few times, then continued the peach slice's journey to her mouth. "No, I don't think so," she said between bites. "I got the impression the bad guy was far away but not *that* far, you know?"

"That's pretty vague."

"I don't think psychic visions are inherently specific."

"Sorry. What else?"

"He said the man would rule the world or see it burn."

Pablo gave a low whistle. "That sounds ominous."

She shrugged. "Yes, but Alfred said I would know him when I saw him, so let's just tuck this away for now. Maybe I'll be able to feel his presence if he gets close. We can't fret about every little thing, especially if we can't control it."

He nodded, but his stomach churned. Now in addition to everything else, he would have to worry about some new-age Hitler wreaking havoc in their would-be ordered society.

"Anything else?"

She didn't meet his eyes when she shook her head. He knew dissembling when he saw it. There was something else, but she would not tell him when until she was ready. That was her way.

Jessie had been staring at Maddie with those huge green eyes. "Do you hear voices during the day when you're awake?" she asked.

"No, sweetheart. Just the voices in my visions, and mostly those happen at night when I'm asleep. Except for that first time."

The dark head nodded slowly.

"Are you worried about the monsters?" Maddie put her fork down and reached for the small hands.

"Yes, but not as much as when I was in the store."

"That's good. I bet over time those monsters will get quieter and quieter."

"Maybe," the child said after a long moment.

"I'm sure of it. Now let's not talk about scary stuff. It's a beautiful morning and we have errands to run." She winked. Jessie grinned and returned the wink with a cartoonish version. Pablo rolled his eyes in exasperation.

"If you insist on getting out, just be careful. Take your bag with the knife and stay where there are people around. Is it asking too much to expect you home before sundown?"

Maddie stood and gave him a peck on the cheek. "Not too much at all, my good man. We'll probably beat you home. We're going to need more water. We have enough bottles to last," a quick gaze up at the ceiling as the mental calculator worked the math, "six days. And only enough food to last two weeks. Less if I keep eating like a horse. Bruno and Curly Sue are almost out of Alpo. We'll have to feed them out of our own food soon if we don't get more. And there's only two more cans of tuna for the kitten."

"Duly noted. I'll talk to people this morning and see what the protocol is for procuring supplies. If we're going to live here, we'll have to adapt to their system. I think I'll sign up for the HG Crew."

"The hunter gatherers? That's cool. I think I'd like that too when I'm a little better."

Pablo bit his tongue. He was about to say, *"No way. It's too dangerous."* But he was learning. He would address the issue in a non-confrontational manner when the time came. In the meantime, he would encourage her to work in an area without such innate risk. Perhaps the medical or greenhouse crew.

The thought of their safety – Maddie's safety – was always at the forefront of his mind. Liberty seemed relatively safe considering everything. There were security measures in place that included a few strategically-placed battery-operated cameras which transmitted to a central monitoring station running off Steven's windmill power. The security crew also performed regular perimeter checks utilizing bicycles and a few Vespa motor scooters. Of course once the gas ran out, they would be forced to concoct some kind of alternative fuel for their combustion engines, or revert to horse power – the type that ate and pooped. Almost everyone except Steven's family had moved to homes near the cooperative greenhouse in the town square for reasons of proximity...a kind of wagon-circling. It was easier to protect people if they were close together.

Still, these measures seemed rice-paper thin when he thought about it. But would they be any safer by themselves on a farm in Oklahoma? Especially now that winter was almost upon them? In addition to the threat of ruthless, hungry people, they would need to stay warm and fed. There was safety in numbers and efficiency in distributing the labor among specialized groups rather than everyone doing all those countless mundane tasks for themselves. At the least, they would remain through the winter. Come spring, they would reassess the situation and decide where their future lay. He just wished the level-headed Amelia would be part of that process. He had resented her in the beginning, seeing her as a burden and an additional person with whom he must share his Maddie. Now he would give his last package of M&Ms to have her back.

Chapter 5

Central Kansas

Many hundreds of feet below the desolate flat terrain of a decaying wheat field, a small group gathered in what the surface-dwellers would consider a type of communal dining hall. The people, sitting or reclining on the objects which adapted for the comfort of the individual, shared a similar expression of anxiety. It was the face of an emotion that had changed little over the millions of years that humanoids had lived on the earth.

"Are you sure about this? It seems premature to be contemplating such extreme action." The man who spoke was small in stature, as they all were, and had almond-shaped eyes. He wore a frown between the sparse black eyebrows. None of the surface dwellers would have understood his ancient language.

A woman with gray strands woven throughout her long dark hair replied. "Yes. They chose to share with me since I had been so long among the current humans and could offer the detail they require." In addition to worry, fatigue was also evident on the brown-skinned face. Her body had not received the sleep it craved and required to rejuvenate itself.

"But there are many wondrous specimens amongst the survivors," the man continued. "We haven't had adequate time to recruit after the winnowing."

The woman's eyes were as sad as they were kind. "Yes, but there is an unexpected element."

"The savage ones," the man said.

"Yes. It was...unforeseen."

Everyone nodded in understanding. Most had spent time on the surface during the last earth-sun cycle and had seen the savagery first hand. The alarming, violent behavior of a portion of the surviving surface-dwellers had been a source of concern.

"But they're not all that way. Surely we must be allowed the time to separate the wheat from the chaff." It was an arcane term but an appropriate analogy, and it evoked another round of murmured agreement.

"I said the same, of course. They are taking it under consideration, but I don't think we have much time to convince them."

"Did they give you a date?"

"No, but I felt it was not too far. Their *scythen* implied as much." The word did not exist among the modern languages spoken above, but an approximation of its meaning could be conveyed through a combination of modern terms: *collective consciousness* and *telepathy*. Only the most ancient of all those who dwelled below had fully mastered the ability to *scythen*.

The almond-shaped eyes gazed at each of those assembled. The man smiled his mysterious smile and said, "It seems we don't have much time then. Are we in accord?"

All heads nodded. The woman with the grey-streaked hair sighed.

"I'd hoped to enjoy a long rest," she said. Her grin was equal parts weariness and determination.

Chapter 6

"It went better than I thought it would," Steven whispered to Dani as they stood in the courthouse, watching the security crew file in for the meeting.

She shrugged. Steven's earlier remark on her lack of diplomacy hadn't bothered her. She had told him diplomacy was just another word for compromise and pussyfooting, and neither were abilities she was interested in mastering.

"I'm sure you've all heard by now that Dani here will be leading your crew. I know she'll do a great job if her performance in Hays is any indication."

"I must have missed the voting process," a familiar voice said. He knew the speaker; he had changed his dirty diapers in another lifetime. Jeffrey was capable of producing children of his own now – a notion even more disturbing than the recent rebelliousness.

"It wasn't a voting situation, Jeffrey. I'm sure you all can understand that. Chuck," he gestured to the former grocery store manager, "feels he's not the best person for the job." The skinny man with the haggard expression nodded in agreement. "This young lady wanted it and provided compelling ideas and strategies for making us all safer."

His son shrugged, a gesture which was eerily similar to that of the girl standing beside him. The thought made him glance at his sister who had accompanied Logan to the meeting. They would need the odd young man's firearms prowess, but nobody seemed to like him much. Steven couldn't blame them. Those staring gold eyes and the vacant smile unsettled him.

"Let's get on with it then. Dani can explain the changes she wants to make. If you have a problem with anything, go to her, not me. I've got my hands full with too many duties as it is."

He sat down next to Julia and watched Dani take command of the room. Her boyfriend Sam would be a lieutenant of sorts, and nobody seemed to mind that the likeable young man would assume a role that put him in a leadership position too. Even Jeffrey didn't squawk about a 'vote.' The crew consisted of six people in addition to Dani and Sam; its membership had quickly become perceived as a kind of elevated status, but Steven was adamant about not changing its name from 'security crew' to 'police force.' Participants weren't obligated to do any other labor-intensive jobs, as were the rest of the townspeople. Their time was devoted solely to keeping everyone else safe, which required proven skills and exhaustive vigilance. Already a plundering attempt by a small group of armed thugs had been thwarted, resulting in the death of one attacker, and a knife wound to one of their own.

As the confident young woman before him outlined her plans for improving Liberty's fortifications, he felt a modicum of relief. She was well-suited for the role; her quick brain grappled with the logistics of offensive and defensive strategies like a four-star general. But what made her perfect for the job was her indifferent savagery. She wouldn't hesitate to destroy anyone who threatened the people she was in charge of protecting.

"I don't think they like me very much, Julia. Maybe I should be on a different crew."

"Nonsense, Logan. You're the best shooter of them all."

Julia was angry. Earlier, she had talked to Steven about Logan's rejection issues, and he assured her he would explain them to Dani. She didn't know if he had failed to do so, or if Dani's arrogance precluded her from kindness. During the meeting, she actually referred to him as 'creeper,' a nickname soon embraced by the other members of the crew.

"I don't think I like the name they gave me. Why didn't anyone else get a name?"

"They did, remember? They're calling the girl with the curly hair Annie Oakley. That's not her real name. Annie Oakley was a famous sharpshooter back in the Wild West days. See? Creeper is just a fun nickname. I think it means that you're stealthy."

He frowned.

"Stealthy means you can move about quietly so people don't see you."

"Oh, right. Yes, I can do that."

"I think it will take everyone a while to make friends. Just be patient. You proved how well you shoot the other day, didn't you?"

He nodded. "Yes, I'm very good with my guns. I think I like Creeper better than the name the guys at the range called me. The idiot part, I mean."

She had heard the story on the drive to Kansas from California. Logan's so-called friends at the gun range were probably accurate in their assessment, but 'idiot savant' was an archaic term and one Julia didn't intend to perpetuate.

"You're special in your own way, just as everyone else is in their way."

That's the understatement of the year, she thought as she considered Chicxulub's survivors. She and Steven had agreed not to tell anyone about her research findings just yet. Thoozy knew, since she had told him on the journey to Liberty, but he promised he would keep it to himself until they figured out the best way to present the information to everyone.

Logan wore his Ruger on one hip and his revolver on the other, western style. He carried his Sig Sauer tactical rifle in a harness that fit over his shoulders and down his back, keeping it out of the way but still accessible. He moved easily now that his shoulder was almost healed. The antibiotics she had given him had stopped infection from spreading, and the wound appeared surprisingly healthy – more like a month-old injury, not one that had occurred two weeks ago.

Perhaps the ability to heal quickly was another trait the remaining humans shared. She had observed that, generally speaking, the towns-people were rather more attractive than people had been on average before the plague. She had noticed it right away and was surprised nobody else had. But then she knew more about the survivors and their genetics than any other person on the planet.

Sometimes that knowledge threatened to overwhelm her. What would or could be done about it? How might they find a reasonable social balance between the fully cognitive gifted and the savants? What about those who had gathered in Hays? The men, and a few women too, seemed to enjoy their unspeakable acts of violence. She remembered the unfamiliar bloodlust she had felt that day after the young man, Pablo, explained the situation. She hadn't hesitated in allowing her vehicle to be commandeered for the purpose of blowing up a handful of the offenders. And she hadn't regretted it later when she heard the details of what had been happening in the small town. Had Hays been an isolated group, or were there more of these perverted individuals coming together in bands? The thought terrified her.

She glanced at Logan pedaling next to her on their way to the hospital. Her plate was full with her responsibilities on the medical and greenhouse crews. (Her brother had made it clear there would be no getting out of manual labor...they would set a good example for everyone.) But she must find time somewhere to conduct her study, and per Steven's directive, it must be done in secret.

Chapter 7

Oklahoma

"Geneneral, I think the natives are getting restless," the man said with a nervous smile. He hazarded a glance to gauge the reaction to his words; one never knew when a jest would be appreciated, or punished as insubordination. It was a knife's edge he danced on, being second in command. Nobody knew that better than he.

"How so, Lieutenant?" The honeyed voice was mellow today. Of course that could change as quickly as an axe falling upon a chopping block.

"The rations are getting smaller, and there is some grumbling about footwear."

The laughter, when it came, sounded like distant thunder during a warm summer rain. Martin knew better than to be lulled by it. It might be genuine amusement or the harbinger of a deadly storm.

"Do you know how the Roman legions moved about? Not the cavalry, of course, but the vast majority of the soldiers? On foot. They could march thirty-five miles in a day, and they didn't have access to Nike and L. L. Bean."

Isaiah spoke from the saddle of his Friesian. Martin rode a gelding of no impressive breeding, from what he could tell, but then he was no horseman – he was a goddamned software salesman when the world had ended. He preferred walking to the torture of putting his sore ass on that horse day after day. He kept thinking it would get less painful, but so far it hadn't. He suspected the animals were important to Isaiah more for the image they projected rather than for ease of travel. He had to admit, the General was magnificent on that giant black stallion, with his ebony skin glistening in the chilly sunlight and the movie star smile that somehow managed to both attract and repel. Horse and rider looked like a living statue carved from obsidian.

"Yes, sir. Those Romans were tough guys, I'm sure. The question I'm hearing the most is why we can't utilize automobiles. Some of them still work and we would make better time."

The brilliant smile widened. Martin held his breath.

"Because what they're accomplishing by walking is much more than just covering ground. They're becoming stronger, stauncher, sterner stuff. I'm forming them, fashioning them into hardened warriors, and the first step in that process is fortitude."

He found the general's wordplay exhausting. Why the man spoke in such a way, always using words that began with the same letter, had never been explained and he would never ask the why of it – he preferred to live. Besides, after being in Isaiah's army for several months now, long before leaving Texas, he had gained some insight into the nature of the man and come up with two probable explanations: First, it was an intellectual exercise – Isaiah was always working on his strength, both physical and mental. Secondly, it was a flamboyant affectation that made him more interesting. The man was consumed with his appearance. Martin thought often of a scene from an old horror movie where the bad guy, a clinical psychiatrist, gazed at a picture frame on his desk during sessions with patients. At the end of the film, the picture frame was revealed to be a mirror.

He knew a classic narcissist when he saw one.

"That makes perfect sense, sir."

"Of course, it does!" The smile expanded.

Here it comes. An oily, queasy feeling uncoiled in the pit of his stomach.

"Now, who were the grumbling ones?"

"Sir, it was just an undercurrent kind of thing. I don't know that I remember specifically who said what. I just thought you should be aware of it."

Isaiah reined in the Friesian and turned to face him. The Cheshire smile threatened to expand beyond the perimeter of the dark face.

"Think carefully, Martin," he said in a soft voice. "Mindful, meticulous, methodical. I shall ask again: Who were the grumbling ones?"

The lieutenant blinked once, swallowed the bile that had begun to rise in his throat, and said, "Javier and Brian, sir."

"Ah, of course. They're weak links. I knew it the moment I saw them. Bring them to me."

Martin would deal later with the guilt of throwing the two young men under the bus. Javier and Brian had said no such thing, but their names were the first that came to mind. He might have been just a mediocre salesman in his previous life, but he had always been a survivor when it came to corporate politics. This was essentially the same type of situation he had dealt with in his career, but with much higher stakes.

People were going to die today. Better them than him.

Chapter 8

Liberty, Kansas

Dani wished for the hundredth time that the quirky little man with hair like flames was still around. She missed the crude jokes and affectionate name-calling, but at that moment she needed his level-headed advice. She was in a dangerous situation and she knew it. If she lived through the next few minutes, she would get herself one of those *What Would Jesus Do?* bracelets, scratch out the *Jesus* and change it to *Fergus.* She had never had any use for religion or religious icons, but her friend had been a goddamn magician when it came to getting out of tight spots...literally. He could be counted on to pull any number of helpful objects out of that army-green coat he always wore: tampons for plugging bullet holes, night vision goggles, WWII era hand grenades. She had half expected him to pull a live rabbit out of it on a few occasions. The thought made her throat constrict, more than it already was by the strong hand that encircled it.

"You want to stop squirming. Don't get me wrong...I like a bit of a fight when I have my way with a sweet young thing like yourself, but information is what I need now. And once I've got all I can get from you, I'll take my time with that delicious slit between those long legs."

The man smelled of gasoline and body odor, and the whisky on his breath practically singed her eyebrows.

She had been out after dark checking on a glitchy camera at the eastern edge of town and had stupidly left her backside exposed when she reached toward the device which had been discreetly bolted to a corner of the *Welcome to Liberty, Pop. 4475* sign.

Also, stupidly, she hadn't bothered to tell anyone where she was going. Sam had been busy conducting his first self-defense class and turnout had been considerable, not only due to the townsfolks' desire to learn hand-to-hand combat, but also because of the eye candy Sam provided. Half the women in town were in love with him, and who could blame them?

"What are you smiling about, girly? You think I'm joking? Trust me. I'll ruin you for any other man. But first, tell me all about Liberty, Kansas, population 4475. Where is the food? What are the defenses?"

He was a hulking beast...probably six five standing, but at the moment his enormous bulk lay stretched out on top of her, pinning her to the ground. His goliathan hand gripped her throat like a vise. He might just be the strongest man she had ever encountered.

"Please, I can barely breathe. I promise, I'll tell you everything. Just let me sit up." She used the best 'weak female' voice she could muster and was satisfied with her degree of authenticity. Between the glowing three-quarter moon and the chilly, impersonal starlight, she could see the skepticism on the man's face. The cold asphalt seeped through the back of her jacket; she shuddered from the temperature as well as the first stirrings of genuine fear.

"Don't give me that bullshit. You're dressed like a warrior. I know bad acting when I see it. Start talking or I'll slice open your lovely swan neck by the light of this exquisite moon."

Dani was surprised by the words as well as the astuteness. Great. He wasn't one of the mouth-breathing window lickers.

"Okay, okay. There's a substantial cache of food at the library near the center of town. We're running a co-op of sorts. People keep what they need to last them a couple of weeks, but the remainder goes into the general provisions bank."

The man nodded. "Good. What about guns? Ammo?"

"Please, can't I just sit up?" She didn't bother with the helpless female shtick. "You've got me. I'm not going anywhere, and there's a rock in the middle of my back. I can't even think straight."

The man, who might have been a poster boy for creatine supplements and protein powders in his previous life, pondered her request.

"If you try to escape, I will catch you and I will hurt you. And when I say 'hurt,' I mean a ridiculously lengthy process that involves medieval torture techniques which have become fashionable again."

Dani's eyes widened as she thought of the Pear of Anguish she had mentioned to Isaiah recently. This dude was not to be trifled with. Intelligence gleamed in the bloodshot eyes, and that made him more dangerous than all the bulging biceps in a dozen Gold's Gyms.

"Agreed."

Her mind raced as the man released his grip and allowed her to sit up. He squatted a foot away on thighs the circumference of medium-sized oaks, watching her with what she just realized was amusement.

This motherfucker thinks I'm a joke?

The same cold, calculating fury she had harnessed in her confrontation with Isaiah made its way into her consciousness, a red-tinged miasma of single-minded focus and lethal determination.

She slowed her breathing as she positioned herself in front of the man and constructed a mental checklist of assets and liabilities, strengths and weaknesses. She formulated a few potentially successful maneuvers and discarded others that were inherently doomed to fail. Like murky water seeping through a sand filter, pristine drops of a plan coalesced in her mind.

She moved into a squatting position similar to that of Paul Bunyan in front of her. She spread her lips in a feral smile, anticipating her next move.

Suddenly, before she had even tensed her muscles in anticipation of the leap that would follow, the left side of the human megalith's head exploded in a fountain of blood, skull fragments, hair, and gray matter. The lifeless body of the man followed its viscera onto the pavement.

Dani hit the ground, her heart pounding. Was she next?

"It's okay! It's just me, Creeper!" The voice that called out from the dark sounded a good fifty yards away. When he trotted up to her moments later, she saw he carried an automatic pistol in his right hand; a revolver was wedged into a holster on his hip, and the tip of a tactical rifle poked out from behind his back.

Her mouth dropped open. "You made that shot with a fucking handgun?"

The grin disappeared and a frown took its place on the handsome, boyish face. "Was that wrong? Did I do bad?"

She barked a laugh, grabbing the strange young man in a fierce embrace as he stood with awkward arms pinned to his sides.

###

Sometimes things don't go as planned, but then actually turn out better. Logan loved the praise he got for saving Dani's life. They couldn't believe he'd made such a great shot without even using his Sig Sauer rifle with the Konus scope. He thought that was funny because he'd made more difficult shots before with the Ruger 9mm. He suspected before that it might be a magical weapon, and now he was sure of it.

He'd followed Dani earlier that evening when she left Steven's house. She had been looking at the monitors even though it was his turn to keep-an-eye-on-them. He was supposed to use the walkie-talkie if anyone other than people he knew appeared on one of the five screens. It was an important job, but it was kind of boring. It was late and everyone was probably asleep in their homes, so there wasn't anything interesting to watch. And there were never any cartoons on any of the TVs.

She had been standing behind him grumbling about one of the *camera feeds.* When she left, Logan was curious to know where she was going and also, the Bad Thoughts told him he might have an opportunity to kill her. Even though Julia tried to convince him that his new nickname was just for fun, he thought that when Dani said it, she sounded a lot like the kids at school when they had surrounded him on the playground. Those were mean kids for sure, and she was just a grown-up version of them.

Everyone thought he'd seen the big man hurting her on one of the TVs and then rushed to help her, but he was already nearby, using his invisibility magic so she wouldn't see him. He thought he might shoot her when she reached up for the camera, but then the big man came out of nowhere (he definitely had magic too), knocked her to the ground, then got on top her. He couldn't hear what they said, but the big man got off and she sat up. Dani's white face had been turned toward the moon and had been easy to see because of his x-ray vision. He wasn't sure what an x-ray was, but he knew he could see really well in the dark and for long distances compared to the other members of the security crew. Superman had it, so Logan thought that was what he had too.

When the Bad Thoughts said he should *SQUEEZE THE TRIGGER!* of the Ruger that was aimed at the white face, he hesitated. He didn't always have to do what they said, after all. Sometimes they had good ideas and sometimes they could be bossy, which he didn't like. He decided to take-a-minute-and-think-things-through, just like his mom had always told him. He struggled with something that would be impossible to explain even to Julia, since it wasn't something you could see, smell, taste, or hear. He called them daydreams and this one showed him how much everyone would like him if he killed the big man instead of Dani. They might call him a hero, because it seemed likely the big man was going to hurt her bad.

That's when he shifted the barrel a half inch to the left and shot the big man right in the head.

When Dani hugged him, it made him feel strange. He couldn't see colors very well in the dark, but he could kind of *feel* her colors when she had her arms around him, and they were exactly the same as Julia's.

The thought made him frown.

Chapter 9

"That's not an explanation, Amelia. Do you know how worried we were? Maddie was beside herself."

Pablo was exasperated. He couldn't decide whether to be elated by Amelia's sudden return or furious that the reason for her disappearance was so thin. A walkabout? Really? Isn't that something Australians do, not tiny Native American women with bad knees?

She was stubborn as hell too. She wouldn't even tell them where her supposed walkabout had taken her or what she had done or seen during her absence.

"I've missed you too, Pablo." The warm smile was reflected in the weary brown eyes. "But perhaps we should set some boundaries. I'm old enough to be your mother, and I don't think I should have to account to you or anyone else for my whereabouts."

He huffed in frustration. "So that's how it's going to be? You just come and go as you please? And what about Curly Sue? She whined for three days after you left." He realized the moment he spoke the words how ridiculous he sounded. He wasn't addressing a rebellious teenager; he was talking to a woman he trusted and appreciated for her insightfulness, wisdom, and wicked sense of humor.

And she had saved Maddie, a debt he could never repay. The least he could do was welcome her home without an interrogation.

"You're right. Of course, you're right. We were just all so worried. Jessie most of all, I think."

The little girl's eyes were like saucers as she followed the discourse between the grownups. She sat so closely to the small woman on the sofa that she might as well have been on her lap, and she clutched her growing kitten as if she feared it might also embark on a walkabout.

He felt Maddie's hand on his shoulder.

"That's enough of that," she said with a kiss to the top of his head. "Welcome home, Amelia. We couldn't be happier that you're back. We have some catching up to do, but we can get into all that tomorrow." Maddie gave the woman a wink. "Everyone to bed. It's late and I'm tired. Jessie and I covered a lot of ground today."

The bandage was gone and the red gold hair had been trimmed by one of the girls in town who was trading haircutting services for whatever she could get in return...extra food rations, clothes, soap, water. Maddie had traded a can of Amelia's Campbell's Chicken Noodle Soup in exchange for the haircut that made her feel more like her old self and less like the fragile invalid Pablo believed her to be.

The barter system was alive and thriving in Liberty. The daily forages by the HG crew had been particularly fruitful recently, and the stockpile of goods at the library was expanding rather than dwindling for the first time since Steven had donated half of his personal cache. Liberty's former librarian had assumed management of the town commissary, and performed the task with the same keen mind and no-nonsense demeanor as when she was dealing in books instead of food and the other necessities of life. In another person's less competent hands, it might have been a position that sparked resentment and anger. People were no longer starving, but they certainly didn't have everything they wanted. Marilyn had developed an efficient and fair system for determining everyone's bi-weekly allotments, and the criteria she used to tally all the incoming and outgoing items made Pablo's head spin.

He decided he liked her, once he had gotten past that stern expression. She had a turn of phrase as elegant as her physical appearance was not, and she loved poetry as much as he did. When he dropped supplies off at the library after the HG crew's excursions, she sometimes had a book of poetry for him, selected from her favorites. Mary Oliver's *Long Life: Essays and Other Writings* had been the first. It was one Pablo hadn't read for quite some time and experiencing it again had felt like sharing an intimate evening with an old friend. How serendipitous that she had chosen one of his favorite poets.

He had taken her latest offering, John Ashbery's *Some Trees,* to bed with him tonight. As he read the poems, considered avant-garde in the fifties when they were first published, he felt suddenly guilty. Did he really have time for reading, let alone writing poems, when there was so much work to be done?

"Do you think I should stop writing poetry?" he said to Maddie as they lay in bed. "It seems indulgent now. When it was just me and Bruno, I didn't worry about taking time off from surviving. Now that I have so many jobs and so many people counting on me, it feels like a luxury I can't afford."

"Hogwash," Maddie said, sitting up in bed. "Don't ever let me hear you talk like that again." Her eyes blazed in the weak moonlight. "It's more important now than ever before. If we don't keep making art, what's the point? We're meant to do more than just eat, shit, and squirt out babies. We're meant to create beauty in any form we can. We're meant to *feel* with every cell in our body, and not just happiness because we got laid or sadness because we lost someone we cared about...I'm talking about profound, complicated emotions that only we humans can feel. What do you want to use on your canvas, Pablo? The crappy four-crayon box they give kids at Macaroni Grill or a hundred tubes of Sennelier oils and the best sable brushes? That's what art does. It makes us feel complex emotions. It makes us experience life in ways we wouldn't otherwise, being so busy with the business of staying alive. When we read a poignant line of poetry or gaze upon a magnificent painting or hear an aria so exquisite it makes us weep, *that* is what it means to live. That's what it means to be human. Not this bullshit business of keeping our bellies full. Now shut the hell up and go to sleep.

"By the way, I love you, Poet Fellow."

Pablo smiled. "I love you too, Angel Girl."

"So you went to your real home?" Jessie murmured to Amelia from the bed where she had been sleeping all by herself like a big girl, down the hall from Pablo and Maddie. For the week Amelia had been gone, she had stared through the darkness to the empty twin bed against the other wall, wondering where her special friend had gone. She knew Pablo and Maddie were close by, but she worried the monsters' whispers would get louder when she slept all by herself. They were at their worst when she was alone and more so late at night. Sometimes they got loud even during the day, but not as loud as they had been at the store where her new family had found her.

"Yes. Remember I told you I might need to go there, and might not come back, but that there will always be someone like me to look after you."

"I'm glad it's still you that's looking after me."

"It may not always be so, my dear. If that time comes, you must be strong. Do you think you can do that?"

Jessie nodded, her hair rustling against the white pillow case.

"Good girl. And you haven't told anyone about what we've talked about, right?"

A shake of the dark head.

"Excellent."

"Did you come back to help Maddie's baby that's still tiny in her belly?"

"That's one of the reasons, but I realized I have more work to do here. Some very important jobs."

"Looking after me?"

"Yes, that is one of the most important jobs. Taking care of Maddie while the baby is still in her belly is also very important."

"What about the Smiling Man?"

Amelia frowned. "Who is the Smiling Man?"

"I can't see his name, but he has a pretty horse. His smile looks too big for his face. People are afraid of him but they do what he tells them to do. Sometimes they get killed anyway."

"I see. Is he near?"

Jessie rolled onto her back and gazed up at the popcorn texture of the small bedroom's ceiling. "Not yet."

"You mean he's coming here? Do you know why?"

"I think he's really mad at that Dani person. There's more but I can't see it. Maybe I will when he gets closer. Maddie sees him too."

"Did you tell her you see him?"

"No. I thought you might not want me to."

Amelia pondered something for a moment. "I have much to think about, child. You should try to sleep now. Everything will be fine, I promise."

The old-soul eyes didn't close the rest of the night.

Chapter 10

Steven felt something cold and wet on his cheek. He had been so absorbed with the task of getting the final work done on the greenhouse that he hadn't realized how chilly the weather had turned, nor had he noticed the slate clouds that had edged out the puffy white ones while he and the building crew nailed and tie-wrapped and Gorilla-glued the last board in place and the last bit of plastic sheeting onto the wood frame. The first incarnation of their community greenhouse was finished. He knew it would go through many changes and expansions as time went by. Their needs would increase as the population did...which was already happening. In addition to the Hays women, a handful of others had drifted into town and were allowed to remain after a thorough screening by the security crew. Julia had put together a list of questions to ask newcomers, and depending on their responses and their skills, some were invited to stay. As a result, Liberty's township had expanded to include a dental hygienist and her partner, who'd been a student of veterinary medicine minus the degree. Steven felt they had struck gold when the couple wandered up to the eastern checkpoint. Other new residents included a former senior manager for Wichita's main wastewater treatment plant who could turn brackish, bacteria-riddled water into potable water faster than any sand filter system, and a cantankerous old farmer whose knowledge of horticulture rivaled Lisa's and who also claimed to know blacksmithing. Steven had been delighted with all of them, or more specifically, with the addition of their talents.

It was the first snow of the season, and it had come early according to his almanac, but they were damn near ready for it. He stepped into the structure which took up a huge chunk of Liberty's town square, replacing much of the real estate that had previously been filled with tidy grass, quaint benches, and maple trees. It was sixteen feet wide and ninety-six feet long. Ed had modified his post-and-rafter design to accommodate the larger dimensions they had decided on, as well as the open trench system that would channel heated water throughout, raising the interior temperature during the dead of winter when solar heating alone would be inadequate. The well had been bored several days earlier, hitting the water table at a relatively shallow depth, then fitted with a PVC system of pipes, screens, and valves which would be powered by the unfinished windmill looming beside it. The cistern contained two valves and was ready to attach to the windmill the moment it was finished. One valve had been equipped with a commercial faucet for use by the townspeople, so everyone had easy access to clean water without having to haul it from Wilson Lake. The second valve had been fitted with copper pipe and connected to the boiler, a rusty but functional steel dinosaur that had been salvaged from one of the old government buildings. From the other side, warm water would flow down a wooden trough lined with more sheeting, warming the air as it traveled between the rows of vegetables. Gravity would do the work of circulating it on its journey through the greenhouse to its final destination: a collection reservoir that required a power source to channel the water back uphill to the boiler. The smaller windmill was already built and in place waiting for its bigger cousin to begin pumping water out of the ground. This part of the project had been hugely laborious, but during sunless conditions, it would save their food from freezing. The other options they had considered – Trombe walls and a heat exchange system using car radiators – had been nixed due to concerns about efficacy and sustainability. Their trench method was downright medieval, but it would work and it would last.

The walls and ceiling were polycarbonate sheeting made of a thermoplastic polymer; an insulating layer of horticultural bubble wrap was attached to the interior side. When the sun shone, they could expect an ambient temperature of at least fifty degrees, even if it was below freezing outside. When Mother Nature withheld her sunshine, or worse, sent one of the nasty blizzards she unleashed once or twice each winter, the heated water system would be utilized. Someone would keep the fire burning beneath the boiler; the fuel crew had stacked a cord of chopped oak and cottonwood nearby.

Lisa hadn't waited for the walls to go up before she had begun cultivating and preparing the soil in anticipation of the planting. The dozen or so members of the garden crew all reported sprouted seedlings from the peat pellets they had been nurturing. Now it was time to plant them in the raised beds or the prepared furrows, depending on the variety.

It was an auspicious moment. Steven wouldn't have made a fuss about it, but he knew the others had planned a celebration of sorts. Someone had provided champagne for the occasion, and everyone took a sip from the bottle.

"You've done a hell of a job," he said to Lisa and her staff.

The first crop would consist of spinach, kale, carrots, broccoli, and seed potatoes. The seedlings were handled with the reverence they deserved; these tiny plants would keep their town from starving when there was no more food to be scavenged. He hoped the timing of their first harvest worked out without an uncomfortable period when people wished they had used their resources for foraging.

That's what ants do, though. They plan ahead. Everyone should be ants.

Steven nodded. "I knew my seeds were in good hands, but the seedling crop your group turned out was better than what I could have done."

The frank brown eyes crinkled at the corners. "That's because you don't count on people enough. You're afraid to delegate important stuff. You think you're the only one who can do the task correctly. No offense, but you have to trust people to be smart enough to at least do the simple jobs."

Ouch. If she hadn't been dead on, he might have been offended...but she was right. The machinery of their small community would force him to change his ways.

"Duly noted. I'll try harder. I promise."

"Uh huh. I need to get to work. The windmill will be ready soon? If not, we'll have to hand pump the first watering."

"Yes, ma'am. I'm heading there next."

He stepped through the wood framed plastic door and out into the chilly overcast day. He could control a lot of things, but he couldn't control the weather. Since he had let his personal garden go fallow after the last harvest, he was as dependent as everyone else on the success of the cooperative venture. There hadn't been enough hours in the day for him and Jeffrey to keep up with it. Perhaps by spring, his communal responsibilities would abate and he could get back to work at his own household.

Ed and three workers were measuring, sawing, and hammering with fervor. Steven smiled. He knew Ed wanted the windmill finished more to impress Lisa than for any other reason. The meager snow flurries had petered out, but it was cold. They would need to get it finished and warm water running before nightfall, when the temperature could plummet. The seedlings were at their most vulnerable, and since there were no perfectly-coiffed meteorologists providing weekly forecasts on the six o'clock news, they must always be prepared for the worst.

"How's it looking?"

Just as Steven, Ed had a way of fixating on the task at hand to the point that everything else in the world ceased to exist. It was one of the many qualities he liked about the man. His construction knowledge was profound, and what he lacked in social skills, he more than made up for in tenacity. Giving Ed the task of windmill building was like setting a hound loose at a fox hunt – he wouldn't stop until the fox was dead and they were pumping water, even if it took all night.

It was interesting how jobs that might have been considered lowly or blue collar before Chicxulub were now given the respect they had always deserved. There was no need for art history scholars or law professors these days, but people who could weld pipe, knit socks, and create nutritious meals from Spam and kale would be valued in Liberty.

"Four hours. Five at the most. Does Lisa know we're close?"

"Yes, I told her we would have wind power to pump her water before nightfall. Don't make a liar out of me, Ed."

"No sir. We can do it."

"Good man." Steven clapped the bony shoulder, then turned as he heard the sound of his son's bike approaching.

"Dad, they want you to come to the hospital." Jeffrey skidded to a halt. As one of the youngest members of the security crew, he was often recruited to run errands. Only a few people had walkie-talkies which were reserved for emergency use only; batteries were too valuable for mundane tasks.

"What's the problem?"

"Natalie wouldn't tell me. She just said to come get you."

Steven frowned. Natalie had taken a position at the hospital, her master's degree in literature not being a useful commodity these days. He wondered how she was faring under the somewhat baleful eye of Cate, the nurse practitioner turned 'doctor.' These days Natalie seemed barely able to contain her hostility every time his path crossed with hers.

"Ride on back and tell them I'll come as soon as possible."

"I think they wanted you to come now."

"Damn it. All right." With a glance back at the nonfunctioning windmill, he pedaled after his son. Like batteries, gasoline was far too precious to waste just to get a person from point A to point B. It was saved for the HG, fuel, and security crews. Everyone else had to hoof it or pedal.

Father and son made good time to the hospital, only a few blocks away from the greenhouse. When he followed Jeffrey into the building, he was surprised by the progress since his last visit. Everything looked organized and clean, and a fair amount of weak sunlight filtered into the large lobby where the nursing station had been set up. Just like gasoline and batteries, candles and kerosene were precious commodities and were used sparingly...mostly at night.

Steven pondered his lengthy to-do list and considered whether he should move the mini power grid system closer to the top. It would be wonderful to get the lights back on in Liberty, but he knew it would be a herculean task. Hell, it might not even be possible. Better to stay focused on the necessities. Electricity was a luxury some of their great grandparents did without, and it could wait for now.

"We have a problem." Natalie was as lovely as always. Her hair was pulled back from her face in a tight bun and she was beginning to get some meat back on her bones. She would always be willowy, but at least she no longer looked skeletal. Despite the wave of animosity he always felt in her presence, he wished nothing but the best for her.

"What is it?"

Suddenly Cate appeared behind Natalie. For a large woman, she moved with surprising grace. And stealth.

"Looks like one of the Hays girls brought a case of measles with her."

"Measles? Who gets measles these days?"

"The children of people who oppose inoculating their offspring."

"Really? There are people stupid enough not to vaccinate their kids?"

"Apparently there were," Cate replied in the high-pitched voice that was at odds with her size. "The anti-vaxxers believed inoculating caused a number of maladies, including autism. No evidence was found to corroborate their beliefs, but was that because it didn't exist or that not enough scientific study had been done? And besides, why should the government force you to inject chemicals into your child's body?"

Steven studied the woman's face. The smirk was present, as usual, so it was difficult to discern on which side of the issue she stood.

"Because vaccinating is the reason we no longer have polio, tuberculosis, and small pox," he said.

The beefy shoulders shrugged. "Yes, but think about the explosion of autism and behavioral issues since the fifties. Maybe there is a correlation."

"Or maybe parents coddle their children too much."

"At any rate, we have a case of measles. Turns out the girl was home schooled and was never vaccinated for anything."

"But if the rest of us were, where's the problem?"

Cate snorted. "You're smarter than that, Steven. Vaccines aren't a hundred percent effective, nor do they last forever. They diminish in efficacy throughout our lives. Consider the newborns. If these diseases are present, they'll be sitting ducks. I expect infant mortality to revert to nineteenth century levels."

He nodded. Thank goodness Jeffrey had received every vaccination the public school system required. Laura had seen to it.

"We don't have to worry about that yet, I guess," he said.

"I suppose not, but it's just a matter of time."

"So what's to be done?"

"Not a damn thing. I'm just a country doctor, Jim. All we can do is isolate the patient and care for her as best we can. She'll either recover or she won't."

He smiled at the *Star Trek* reference and wondered if there weren't a lot more layers to this odd duck than just her strange voice and inexplicable bulk.

"How contagious is she?"

"Very. Unlike Ebola or HIV, the measles virus is spread through casual contact. You can be exposed by walking into a room that an infected person recently coughed in."

"Shit. What protocol are you following?"

"SOP as with any infectious disease. Only people who have been vaccinated," she indicated Natalie, "are allowed to enter the girl's room.

Latex gloves, paper masks, and eye protection. If it were something even more serious like SARS or TB, more extreme measures would be taken. Fortunately, the hospital is well supplied with gear."

"But no medicine, right?"

"Correct. Just like the Walgreens and CVS stores, the hospital's pharmacy had been cleaned out."

"It sounds like you have everything under control. We'll mention this at the next meeting."

"There's one more thing. We're also seeing some early cases of vitamin deficiencies. I think we may have some scurvy and pellagra showing up here in Pleasantville."

"Can't we just give them some Flintstones Chewables?" Steven was beginning to feel annoyed. He had more on his plate than he could get done in a year. Must he also deal with these kinds of issues that should be Cate's and the HG crew's responsibility?

Another noncommittal shrug. "They're not to be found. People must have been smart enough to stock up on them before the end."

"I'll talk to the HG people. See if we can make it a priority."

"Very well." The woman turned her back and walked down one of the darkened corridors. There was no "take care" or "see you later." She was finished with the conversation and didn't feel the need to offer the typical valediction expected in normal social situations.

Steven found it refreshing.

Natalie was staring at him. He could feel her hostility, but there was also something else.

"I need to talk to you," she whispered with a glance at Cate's diminishing backside.

"What's up?"

"Not here. Go outside and wait for me around the corner of the building next to the smoking area." Then she was gone.

I don't have time for this female drama, he thought, and then felt a minor pang of guilt. A couple of weeks ago, he'd had sex with her then kicked her out of his house. Other than some near tangible animosity, there had been little fallout. The least he could do was give her a few moments of his time.

He had been leaning next to the building for ten minutes and was about to leave when she arrived.

"So what's with all the secrecy?"

"I don't want Cate to hear. This is about her. There is something fishy about that woman. For one thing, why is she so well-fed when the rest of us are practically starving?"

"I don't think anyone is starving at this point, Natalie. You look better too."

"Thanks for noticing."

"I'm serious. I know everyone isn't eating as much as they'd like, but nobody is starving."

"Yes, I realize that. But isn't it suspicious that she's so...rotund? She must be holding out."

"Don't you think everyone is doing a bit of that? Did you donate any items to the commissary?"

"I didn't have anything to give," she said, the gray eyes slid away from his. "Besides, it's not just that. There's more. I saw her touching one of the girls the other day, when she was asleep."

"What do you mean? Like fondling?"

"No, no. Nothing like that. But it wasn't the way a nurse or doctor would normally touch a patient. I'm not even sure her hands were making contact with the girl's body. It looked like she was just sort of hovering them over her. She stopped doing it when she heard me at the door. It was just so strange."

"No offense, but this isn't your area of expertise. The woman has a master's degree in nursing, so she claims. Her medical knowledge seems to back it up, though, wouldn't you agree? The Hays women are recovering nicely, I'm told."

"Yes, she's knowledgeable, but I'm telling you that something is off about her. And if you don't want to get to the bottom of it, I will."

"I just don't know what you expect me to do. The last thing we want is to piss off our only doctor by asking why she's fifty pounds overweight. If you come up with anything concrete, let me know. Is there anything else you need? Is Brittany doing okay?"

Natalie scowled. "Yes, she's fine, thanks. You might want to find some condoms for your son, though. Those two are like rutting sheep. They haven't done the deed yet, but it's inevitable, and I'm too young to be a grandmother."

Steven wasn't surprised. The couple had been sitting together at the last town hall gathering, holding hands and exchanging covert kisses. He remembered what it was like to be a randy youth. He would speak to the HG crew about condoms as well as vitamins.

"I'll have a talk with him."

"Thank you. I'm sorry if I've been a bitch. I'm just working through some things. I'll see you later."

She turned and walked away. Steven smiled. That sounded like progress to him.

Chapter 11

"I'm sorry, but I can't let you do that." Pablo's voice sounded surprisingly calm. On the inside, his stomach was doing backflips.

"Who the fuck is leading this crew?" The man who spoke was short but compensated for his height deficiency with blustery intimidation tactics. Pablo had seen the same method used by playground bullies and low intellect supervisors his entire life.

He ignored the rhetorical question. "What you're proposing is inherently dangerous. Why would you subject your people to needless peril?"

"There you go again, using all those big fucking words. I've had just about enough of your smart mouth." The grizzled beard was so close, Pablo could identify dried clumps of the oatmeal he must have eaten for breakfast.

"I'll switch to monosyllabic. Don't do this. It would be bad." The reply flew out before he could stop it. Being a *puto arrogante* just might get his ass kicked today. The leader of the Hunter-Gatherers was short, but he was all wiry muscle and lightning reflexes. There was a reason he had been selected for the job, and it had little to do with book smarts.

"You smartass beaner."

And there it was. Funny how people still clung to their bigotry even after the world had ended.

"There is a vehicle parked behind the dumpster at the back. Until we check it out and at least confirm it's been sitting there for a year, we need to assume the person or people who drove it here are inside."

Ted squinted in the direction of the dumpster. The rest of the group, two men and one woman, stood in a semicircle next to their Dodge Ram. It was one of the two official HG vehicles. The other was a twenty-four foot U-Haul moving truck. So far, the only instance when its capacity had been required was at a restaurant supply building near the airport in

Wichita. The warehouse hadn't been fully stocked, but there'd been two pallets of canned peas, a dozen cases of beef consommé, and enough Scott 2-ply to fill a small house. The toilet paper was quite a boon; it was the new gold standard these days.

Ted's gaze returned to Pablo. The man's thoughts were so obvious he could have had English subtext scrolling across his forehead. The newest member of his crew was right, but if he admitted it in front of his people, he would lose street cred.

The situation was about to take a nosedive.

"Here's how this is going down," Ted replied. "We're going in. You can go with us, or you can sit your happy brown ass right here."

"Why don't you at least send one person through the back entrance? That way if there are hostiles in there, you can deal with them from two vantages. You could be walking into an ambush."

"I think he's right," one of the men muttered.

The short man spun to face the subversive, shoving the taller man in the chest with enough force to knock him to the pavement. "I'm in charge. I make the decisions. Let's get going *now!*"

The group scrambled to obey. Pablo watched them cross the parking lot to the front of the Kwik Shop, which was located in the outskirts of Salina, seventy miles to the east of Liberty. Almost every foray took them farther away from the relative safety of their town. This would be the third Kwik Shop of the day. The chain of convenience stores was as prolific here in Kansas as Starbucks must have been in Washington. The previous two had been picked clean. This location was on a remote secondary road, and for that reason, it might have escaped notice. That was Ted's reasoning, at least.

Pablo was no hero. He knew that about himself. He would put his life on the line for Maddie, Jessie, and Amelia, but he barely knew any of these people. Why follow Racist Ted into potential danger?

"Goddamn it," he grumbled, then jogged around to the back of the small building. He held his shotgun in one hand, and in the other, a Glock .380, given to him by Ted with smirk.

Know how to use that, taco head?

It's a handgun, not a Rube Goldberg machine...I think I can figure it out.

The blank expression on the face of the leader of the monumentally important Hunter-Gatherers had told Pablo the man had no idea what a Rube Goldberg machine was, and probably didn't know a lot of other things too.

He stopped at the corner of the building and peered around to the back. All clear. But the metal rear exit door had been propped open with a rock.

"Shit."

He crept toward the door then stuck the barrel of the shotgun in the opening. There was no answering blast of gunfire. So far so good. He stepped into the darkened stockroom and flipped on his flashlight. A quick scan revealed no occupants other than a stack of Pepsi six-packs, two large boxes with the Cheetos' cheetah printed on the side, and a small box with an M&M logo. Maddie's words echoed in his head: *You and your M&M addiction. You're such a girl.*

Instinct told him the dust-free pile had recently been assembled, which meant whomever had left their automobile by the dumpster and propped open the back door was still in the building. His ambush theory was probably correct.

Adrenaline surged into his bloodstream, priming his body for the confrontation his brain told him was imminent. He gave a soft push to one of the swing doors leading into the store, creating a three-inch gap. The glass windows at the front of the building allowed enough light to illuminate the backs of two people crouched next to a row of empty shelves. He could also see their firearms pointed at the members of the HG crew as they walked about.

Pablo shouldered through the doors, aiming his shotgun at the crouching man and the Glock at the woman next to him. They were so focused on the people at the front, they never heard him until he spoke from half an aisle behind.

"Let's not make this a bloodbath. No sudden moves. Stand up slowly, toss your weapons to the ground, and raise your hands where I can see them. More than anything, I do not want to kill either of you today, but I will to keep you from killing my friends."

The couple rose, the man's knees cracking and popping. The two exchanged a look as they stood. Critical information was sent and received in that brief moment. Even in the dim light Pablo could see a resemblance in the profiles of the older man and the twenty-something girl.

Please don't let them do anything stupid.

"What we got here?" Ted's nasal voice came from in front of the couple, who now stood with their arms in the air. They had yet to drop their guns.

"Just a man and his daughter. I don't think they want to hurt anyone."

"Is that so, taco head? You're a psychic too? How the hell do you know what these people want? If they're anything like everyone else left in this godforsaken world, they'd just as soon cut out your heart as look at you. Ain't that right, old man?"

Ted and his people carried an assortment of firepower, all pointed at the father and daughter. At that moment, he realized he was in the worst possible position if people started shooting.

"Come on. Don't be such a moronic dick."

The words were ill-chosen. He knew it the second he spoke them. Red splotches of rage blossomed above the grizzled beard.

The older man standing in front of him saw them too. With surprising speed, the father whipped his rifle down and got a shot off at the same moment Ted's .45 fired. Pablo had just enough time to dive to the ground.

It was a superfluous effort. Both bullets found their targets.

Pablo's Journal, Entry #417

For a man with such an impressive lexicon, I certainly screwed the pooch today. I can't say that my goading was responsible for getting Ted and the father killed, but I did see the fury on Ted's face as clearly as a snapping red flag next to the ocean. My calling him a 'moronic dick' sparked a riptide of rage that resulted in two deaths. If I hadn't one-upped him moments earlier, he might not have already been so violently fueled, and the daughter might still have her father.

Or perhaps if my happy brown ass had stayed in the parking lot as Ted had directed, all the members of the HG crew would have died at the hands of the pair.

We'll never know how the unrealized ripples of these non-events, the impact of those actions NOT taken today, might have affected the future. They're fascinating to contemplate...the infinite 'what ifs.' I find myself pondering them too much lately. It's an exercise in creativity but also futility.

In the meantime, more responsibility has been added to my considerable burden. The irony of being assigned the position of leading the Hunter-Gath-erers (after participating in the death of its former commander) isn't lost on me. I argued with Steven when he proposed it, but at the behest of the crew's remaining members and after another hour of gentle prodding from Steven, I acquiesced. I guess I'm susceptible to peer pressure after all.

Pablo lifted the pen from the spiral notebook. He gazed at Maddie in bed next to him. She slept like the dead these days, even with the two-hour afternoon naps. He might have been worried about her sudden need for so much sleep if she didn't look like a rosy-cheeked cover girl for *Health* magazine.

"I'm beginning to think that sleeping is your super power," he had said to her yesterday. She flashed him one of her dazzling smiles and replied, "I'm no super hero. I'm a Sleep Viking! And I can pulverize wakefulness with my mighty dream hammer!"

He smiled at the memory as he watched her breathing; watched the rise and fall, rise and fall of her chest. Ever since her injury, this had become a nightly routine he looked forward to. Nothing brought him more happiness and comfort than to see Maddie nestled in beside him, sleeping soundly. He leaned over and brushed his lips across a cheek as soft as the lamb's ear in his mother's flower garden, glanced at the shotgun next to him on the bedside table, then placed pen to paper again.

Tomorrow is a day of some import. I've given it considerable thought and decided that we're going to start focusing on the hunting rather than the gathering. I've no doubt there is still food 'out there,' hidden in remote, isolat-ed, or inaccessible locations; in places that require gasoline, time, and energy to find. But next week, we'll shift focus a bit. We'll look for items not packaged in boxes or shrink wrapped or canned. We'll search for those delinquent pigs and wayward cows Maddie and I discussed in Arizona. Perhaps we'll hunt the deer I've caught glimpses of in the forested areas outside of town. Maybe we'll take a few fishing poles to Wilson Lake. We'll need to find horses too at some point, but for now the priority is food on the hoof or the fin. Against my better judgment, I've requested the services of Logan for the week. He's quite the hero these days. The story of his one-in-a-million shot would be difficult to believe if I hadn't witnessed his talent firsthand in Hays. I think he will improve our odds of bringing burgers and bacon home to Maddie. She mentioned an intense craving just this morning...

Pablo slid open the bedside table drawer and tucked his journal away for the night. He was too tired to write anything more taxing than stream of consciousness – the latest poem would have to wait. He thought of Maddie's rant about creating art. *Art takes energy, of which I'm currently in short supply. Art will be postponed at least until tomorrow night.* He blew out the candle and was asleep in less than a minute.

Next to him, Maddie dreamed of a dark-skinned man. His eyes glowed like burning coals and his smile was beautiful and terrifying. He was the one Alfred had warned of in a previous dream; she knew that instantly. Unlike the nebulous quality of normal dreams, she could see him with surprising clarity – not crisp and colorful, but like an actor in an old black and white movie. If Pablo had been awake next to her, he would have heard her moan when the man's gaze fell upon her.

Down the hallway of the modest ranch house, Jessie also moaned in her sleep. She shared Maddie's dream movie, but her vantage was from behind the camera. She saw Maddie standing in front of the dark-skinned man who was sitting on a black horse. He held a sword. The beast reared back on its hind legs and when the hooves came crashing back to the ground, the long blade found its way to Maddie's belly.

The anguished dream scream woke up the corporeal Jessie. She rubbed her sleep-crusted eyes with a tiny fist. Amelia sat on the other bed watching her.

"Was it terrible? Do you remember what happened?"

A kittenish mewl escaped her throat. She covered the cherub mouth so more wouldn't follow.

"It's okay if you feel like crying. Crying doesn't mean you're weak. It means you're human," Amelia whispered. "What did you see?"

"The Smiling Man is getting closer. I think he wants to hurt Maddie's baby. I think he wants to hurt everyone else too."

"How would he know about the baby?"

A shrug of the small shoulders. "I don't know. Maybe he has dreams like Maddie and I do."

"Do you think he was having the same dream tonight that you were having?"

Another shrug. "I don't know. I think he might hear the monsters though. Like I do, but more. More often. I think he likes the monsters."

"Did he see you? Did he look at you?"

A shake of the bed-tangled hair. "No. He could only see Maddie. I was hiding behind a tree."

"Ah. Good girl. Listen to me carefully, child. This is important. Are you ready to listen?"

"Yes, I'm ready."

"The next time you dream of the Smiling Man, find a place to hide. You must always hide from him. Search for another tree or dig a hole in the ground and cover yourself up with dream dirt. Do you understand why?"

The child nodded. "Yes. So he can't find me in the real world."

"Yes, that's it exactly. Perhaps he'll never find out about you."

"But he knows about the baby."

"There's nothing to be done about that now. At least not in the dream world."

"What can we do about it in the real world?"

The expression Amelia wore now was one Pablo would have recognized. It was the same slipping of the Amelia mask he had seen the day Maddie was shot. There wasn't a different person beneath the mask, there was just more showing of the woman than was normally visible. Jessie was used to it now.

"We'll have to find a way to kill him."

Jessie nodded. The answer made perfect sense.

"Would you like to go to the hospital with me tomorrow? There's someone I'd like you to meet. His name is Abraham but most people call him Thoozy. I think you'll like him very much. He's like us."

Chapter 12

Dani stepped back to survey her handiwork. In addition to gigantic piles of road-blocking debris, they had posted signs on all the roads leading into their town:

STOP. YOU ARE UNDER ARMED SURVEILLANCE.
PLACE ALL WEAPONS ON THE GROUND BEHIND YOU.
WAIT. YOU WILL BE APPROACHED AND ASSESSED.
IF WE LIKE YOU, YOU WILL BE ALLOWED TO STAY.
IF YOU MEAN US HARM OR CAUSE TROUBLE, WE WILL KILL YOU.
WELCOME TO LIBERTY, KANSAS.

"I think it's perfect. What do you think?" She glanced over her shoulder at the ribbon of blacktop that was Interstate 70. Sam stood with crossed arms on the yellow stripe that stretched beyond him to the horizon. The flat topography made the curvature of the earth appear a thousand miles away.

"Did we have to use red paint? It looks like it was written in blood."

"Yes. It's supposed to be a subliminal warning."

"Did you have to say that part about killing?"

"Yes. Again the sign is meant to be a warning. We may be in Kansas but this isn't Oz, and the people out there aren't adorable munchkins. They're more like flying monkeys."

He laughed. "You're a flying monkey." He wrapped his arms around her waist and buried his face in her hair.

"I'm no flying monkey. I'm the goddamned wicked witch that's going to keep this town safe."

He smiled as he pulled away, studying her with the adoring expression he always wore when he gazed at her. She never tired of seeing it. There had never been anyone who looked at her the way Sam did.

"Does this mean what I think it means? We're staying?" he asked.

"Yes, at least for now. These people need us. They're sitting ducks without us. Think about it. What they're building here is going to be the envy of every scavenger, marauder, pillager, and plunderer. Liberty might as well have a giant bullseye painted on the plastic roof of that greenhouse. And if word gets out that we might get the power back on, it'll be worse. So far the people that are coming here have been fairly benign...well, except for the Incredible Hulk."

Sam frowned.

"We got him. No harm, no foul," she said.

"But it could have gone the other way."

"But it didn't. Let's drop it."

"All I'm saying is you need to be more careful. You took a chance that night coming out here by yourself. I don't think you were thrill-looking, but it was careless."

Both pairs of eyes gravitated to the oily-looking patch on the blacktop – the residual viscera of the man who'd planned to do a lot more to her than just make her talk.

"I promise I'll be more careful."

He kissed her on the forehead. "That's all I can hope for."

She glanced up at the camera, which had been moved from the sign-post to a hidden spot in the pile of debris. Nobody would see it, therefore nobody could mess with it and hinder the ability of Liberty's security crew to monitor the activity at the edges of town. If the hunter-gatherers could locate more equipment, they could put more eyes out there in addition to the five locations currently monitored. The more eyes, the safer everyone would be. She would mention it at the meeting that was scheduled for later that day.

"How are you doing, Logan? Are you comfortable?" Dani yelled, turning away from Sam and shifting her attention to the young man camouflaged in the junk. It was Logan's turn to stand guard at the eastern checkpoint. He sat in an armchair placed behind a door-less refrigerator. A hole, large enough for a rifle barrel and scope to fit through, had been bored through the back of the massive appliance. From the other side of the rubble, the direction from which outsiders would approach, the fridge appeared innocuous – just part of a mountain of junk. Their attention would be drawn past the manmade hill of rusting automobiles and kitchen appliances, to the corrugated tin shed off to the side. It was a decoy, intended to look like a guard station and draw scrutiny away from the Frigidaire where a sentry would be at all times. That is, if she were allocated more staff.

Similar structures had been constructed on the western edge of town and also northern and southern checkpoints positioned on State Highway 40. Liberty's perimeter was reasonably secure in terms of paved ingress. Dani had given serious thought to transforming their real estate into a walled city of sorts, like medieval Carcassonne in France – a place she had visited with her parents one summer – but of course that wasn't within the realm of possibility...yet. The debris piles had been put together in only two days. They were intended to be a stop gap measure and would be replaced with prison-quality fencing and razor wire when there was time to do so.

It was a more effective and efficient system than Chuck had come up with. The former head of security had abdicated his position without any arguments. Word on the street was that he had his hands full with his crazy-ass son. Chuck was still a member of the crew, though, and followed Dani's orders without resentment. Perhaps he had been relieved to lose the burden of leadership, an alien notion to her.

"I'm comfortable, Dani!" Logan hollered back. She couldn't see him from where she stood, which was what she wanted. She also couldn't pinpoint the spot from where his voice emanated, which meant no one else could either.

"Do you remember what you're supposed to do if strangers approach?"

"Yes! I use the walkie-talkie to tell everyone."

"That's right. Let's have a drill. Pretend that Sam and I are strangers and we're walking toward you. What do you do?"

Using his right hand, Logan sighted the girl with his Konus scope. Her face, which looked like Julia's but without the worry lines, appeared in the cross hairs. With his left hand he gripped the walkie-talkie. He didn't push the button on the side because this was just pretend. Dani had explained earlier about *drills*. They were just playing a practice game. He hoped that he wouldn't have to wait too long before he could shoot somebody for real. Pretending wasn't nearly as much fun.

"Stop! Hands in the air! Drop your weapons! Okay, I have the walkie-talkie in my hand but because this is just a drill, I won't push the button."

"Very good, Creeper!"

Logan still wasn't sure that he liked his nickname. At least the way Dani said it now no longer reminded him of the mean kids on the playground. He thought back a few days ago to when he'd made his one-in-a-million shot. He was proud of it, even though he didn't think it had been that special, but he was more proud of the decision he'd made to kill the big man instead of Dani. He had become an Important Person. Word had gotten out about how he'd saved her life, and he enjoyed how everyone smiled at him and patted him on the back. Julia had also been proud of him. That was the best part.

He had always felt alone, even when his mother was still alive. Now, he thought he understood how the popular kids at school had felt. What was the word? Oh, yes. He felt that he *belonged.* He was right in the middle of things rather than watching from a distance. He'd never been accepted into any group before. The guys at the gun range weren't truly his friends, even though they had also patted him on the back. He could tell when someone was being phony. That was a word Mr. Cheney had taught him. It meant when people pretended they liked you but they really didn't. He'd known lots of phony people in his life. Julia wasn't phony, but her brother sure was. Steven acted like he smelled something rotten every time Logan was around.

He set the walkie-talkie down on the pavement and sniffed under his arms. Kansas was colder than California, so he didn't think he sweated as much here, which should mean he didn't stink too much.

The Bad Thoughts still talked to him, but now it happened mostly at night. He'd been so busy during the last few days moving junk around, watching the TVs, and standing-guard-at-his-post (even though he didn't actually stand but sat on the comfy chair), that they hadn't been bothering him too much. At night though, before he fell asleep, they got loud. Lately they had been asking: *What are you waiting for?* And then they would say: *Kill them! Kill them all!*

He knew he didn't have to do what they told him, but they got pretty mad when he didn't.

"Logan! Did you hear me?"

Dani's yell snapped him back to the comfy chair. He realized he'd been daydreaming again.

"I'm sorry. What did you say?" he yelled back.

She didn't answer but he heard her and Sam coming back to his side. He hoped he wasn't in trouble for daydreaming when he should have been listening to her.

"I asked if you remembered what you're supposed to do if the people don't stop."

Dani could be scary when she wasn't happy. She was wearing her unhappy-but-not-really-mad face. Julia had one of those too. Ever since Logan had shot the big man, he and Dani had sort of become friends. Still, it bothered him that her colors were exactly the same as Julia's.

He could see the purple and green all around her now as she stood next to her boyfriend. Sam's colors were the prettiest he'd ever seen. There wasn't just one or two either; every color in the rainbow and about a million more were all around Sam. Logan smiled because he thought it was funny that a boy's colors were so pretty.

"Creeper, snap out of it. Quit ogling Sam. What do you do if they don't stop?"

"Oh, I'm supposed to fire a warning shot…in front of them. I should aim for the road. Then I press the button on the walkie-talkie again and tell everyone to *hurry-the-hell-up-code-yellow-at-the-eastern-checkpoint*."

She nodded but didn't smile and didn't say anything. That meant she was waiting for him to keep going. He was learning to read her like he'd learned to read Julia. His mother had tried to explain this before…reading people like they were a book without words and pages. It had confused him at the time – how the heck could you read a person if they didn't have words and pages and lots of pictures? But now he thought he understood what she had been trying to teach him.

"Then I yell *THE NEXT SHOT WILL BE IN YOUR SKULL MOTHER FUCKER!* Is that right?"

She nodded again. There was the smile now. She was pleased with his answers.

"Yes. Now do you remember about a code red?"

"Yes. I say *code-red-at-the-eastern-checkpoint* into the walkie-talkie when there are more than five people."

"Do you remember why that is?"

"Yes, because I might not be able to handle more than five people, although I'm pretty sure I could shoot a lot more than that."

She laughed, which made Logan smile.

"Of that, I have no doubt. But it's a good number for the rest of us, so we'll just keep it at that. Simple rules that apply to everyone and that everyone can understand. Right, Creeper?"

"Right, Dani!"

"Okay, we're out of here. You're on until ten tonight, right?"

"Yes," he said, glancing for the hundredth time at his new digital watch. He needed it for his job now. Of course he had always known how to tell time, but there hadn't been any need to since he no longer worked at the doughnut shop.

"And who is relieving you?"

He gazed up at the clouds that looked so low he might be able to touch their bumpy gray bottoms if he could jump just a little higher.

"Annie Oakley!"

"Good. Remember to be vigilant and use the Folgers can if you have to take a leak. No wandering off for privacy."

"Got it!"

She clapped his shoulder, then got on her bicycle. Sam got on his, which was even better than Dani's. Logan wondered how many people he would need to kill to get one as nice as Sam's. Logan's bicycle had a basket on the front, which made it look like it might belong to a girl. It didn't look like a bike someone with x-ray vision would ride.

Maybe he could just shoot Sam and take his.

He watched them pedal away and pondered how he might go about doing it.

Dani could tell Sam was deep in thought. She let him take his time as he worked through whatever was troubling him. The light was fading and a frigid wind blew dozens of icy porcupine quills into the exposed skin of her face. Sam's replacement bicycle for the one abandoned in Oklahoma was a sleek, ultralight racing machine. He didn't need an all-terrain version here in Liberty. On his new Fuji Altamira, he could jet about Liberty almost as fast as when they rode the Vespas. The man was a damn Olympian. She struggled to keep up with him, knowing her slowness would be the reason they were late to the town hall meeting.

Two blocks from the municipal building, he came to an abrupt halt.

"You took one of the scooters from Steven's house to the eastern checkpoint? That night when the camera was glitchy?"

"Yes. I didn't feel like getting a workout in the middle of the night. They can take the gas expense out of my paycheck."

She stopped next to him on the street, forcing herself to be patient with his thought process. In the interim, she basked in the nineteenth century feel of the downtown district, with its Victorian streetlamps and tidy red brick streets. Downtown Liberty was polar opposite from the opulent, nouveau riche, history-less suburb where she had grown up.

"How long were you out there before the guy came at you?"

"Just a minute or two. I surveilled the area when I first arrived, but not well enough, obviously."

"How long did he have you...pinned...before Logan shot him?"

She could see how painful it was for him to talk about the danger she had been in.

"I don't know. Five minutes? Ten? It's weird how time kind of slows down when you're in a situation like that. Couldn't have been more than ten minutes tops, though. Why?"

"How long do you think it takes Logan to ride from Steven's house to the eastern checkpoint?"

"Sam, we're going to be late."

"It's important, Dani."

"Well, I know how long it takes me, but then I'm not you, Lance Armstrong. Let's say fifteen minutes."

"Right. So if he saw the guy on the monitor and came to help, how could he have gotten there so quickly?"

"I don't know. Maybe he pedaled extra fast. What difference does it make? We need to get going. I'll be lobbying for more worker bees today."

She left him sitting on his Fuji Altamira, wearing an exaggerated frown that did nothing to mar the handsomeness of his face.

Chapter 13

"Let's come to order." Steven was exhausted and in no mood to waste time. He wondered if cold weather affected people the way it did dogs. The population of Liberty, which had burgeoned to more than eighty souls last time they had counted, were acting downright frisky. At this rate, the afternoon would turn into evening before they finished with all the bulleted items on Marilyn's legal pad.

"Please, let's all take a seat and get started."

Everyone continued to mingle and talk in raised, excited voices. It occurred to him that some might be inebriated. Booze had not been on the requisition lists, so if anyone was holding out, they were within their rights to do so. The decision had been a split-second one; he knew better than to try to pry alcohol out of the hands of people it belonged to.

A shrill whistle echoed through the courtroom. All heads turned to the young woman who stood on one of the wooden benches. The warm glow of the kerosene lanterns softened the sharp angles of her face – a kind of archaic Photo-shopping which airbrushed the harsh beauty into something softer...more delicate.

He knew better. There was nothing soft or delicate about Dani.

"Thank you. Let's get started. Marilyn, what's the first item?"

"Some matters regarding the commissary crew." The bifocals perched on the tip of the hawkish nose turned the librarian into a caricature of her former occupation. If she pinned her hair up in a bun, the picture would be complete. The bulky sweater she frequently wore had been replaced with a fitted version in a deep crimson that suited her.

"We prefer the original title," Pablo said from the second row. "'Hunter-gatherers' sounds capable, tenacious. Primal even. 'Commissary crew' could be a geriatric social club that does grocery shopping on Sundays."

The young man's smile was self-deprecating and quite likeable. His staff respected him, and his recent rash of successful forays had scored points with Liberty's residents. Just this morning they shot a two-hundred-pound hog which had been butchered and was being smoked over hickory logs in Ed's massive homemade smoking contraption. Steven caught whiffs of the scintillating aroma on the way to the meeting. They had also captured five feral piglets, the fate of which would be discussed next.

"Marilyn, would you please change it in your records? Back to the HG crew it is. Will you be raising the piglets or butchering them?"

"We're going to raise them. Butchering them now is like eating our seed corn," Pablo said.

Ah, we have another ant in our midst. He liked the young man even more now.

"Anyone have a problem with that?" Steven asked the room.

"I don't mind feeding the pigs from which we'll get more food in the long run," Natalie said from the last row. It was an odd place for someone who seemed to crave the limelight. "What I do have a problem with is taking food from the mouths of humans to feed cats and dogs...unless we plan on eating them too."

Steven's mouth opened but nothing came out. At his house alone, there was one of each. Maggie had been part of the family for years and Julia was quite attached to the orange tabby she had brought with her from California. He hadn't anticipated this being a sticking point. What kind of person would suggest forcing people to starve their beloved pets?

"I realize that makes me sound like a monster, Steven. You really should work on your poker face." Natalie stood and walked toward him. Her grace and beauty were on display tonight, as if she had expected to be on stage. And of course, she had.

"What are you suggesting?" He pushed the words through clenched teeth.

"Not what you might think. Now pull that stick out of your backside."

The lovely smile charmed the room, and the remark evoked a wave of snorts and snickers. She had an effect on people. Was it because she was truly that charming, or did people agree with her assessment of him? Either way, the woman was movie star stunning now that she had put some meat on her bones, and she possessed the poise and self-confidence typical of those used to being in front of a camera.

"What I'm proposing is that people may keep their furry companions, but if they do, they must feed them from their own rations. They should not receive extra unless the animals benefit the community, ergo pigs. Cattle and horses too, if we ever manage to capture any."

He saw Pablo's eyes narrow. Pressure to obtain livestock had intensified. Everyone craved the milk and cheese cows would provide, and horses would be needed when they could no longer find viable gasoline. Pablo crossed his arms, refusing to take the bait. Good for him. Steven remembered there were several pets in the young man's household, and the expression on the intelligent face told him Natalie had just gained an enemy.

She continued, "It's just common sense. Yes, we're not starving but who knows what the future holds? What if the greenhouse fails? What if provisions can no longer be procured? The food we're allocating for these animals might be what saves our lives at some point. What's more important, people or dogs and cats?"

"Dogs *are* people," Pablo said. "They're better people than some people I know."

Natalie deflected the barb with a musical laugh. "You're probably right about that. However, there is still inequality in the allocation system. People who don't have pets are getting cheated. It's not fair."

More than half the crowd murmured in agreement.

"What a bitch," Maddie said, making no effort to whisper.

"You've made your point, Natalie. We'll vote on this later. Marilyn, please make a note."

All eyes watched the graceful departure from center stage, back to her seat next to a tall, middle-aged man with intense eyes and a dark, neatly-trimmed beard. Liberty's newest citizen was a Baptist minister who claimed to have a degree in pharmacology; his alleged medicinal knowledge was the reason he had been allowed to stay. His claim hadn't been put to the test, but Steven decided he would make it a priority.

"Next up is the hospital," Marilyn said, drawing attention back to the meeting.

"Right. People, we have a situation. Nothing too grim but it needs to be addressed." He took the next five minutes to describe the measles outbreak, which had spread to a second person: a child who'd been too young to be inoculated prior to Chicxulub.

"They're both stable for now," Cate said from the back of the room. No one sat near her. "But if anyone is holding out on antibiotics, now would be the time share."

"I didn't think they worked on measles." Chuck, the former security crew leader, stood next to his son, who outweighed him by fifty pounds. The boy was Jeffrey's age but could have been a defensive lineman for Kansas State. Chuck usually left the boy at home, and now Steven remembered why. He had been diagnosed as bipolar, and along with antibiotics and every other useful medicine, antipsychotic drugs were no longer available at the local Super Value Pharmacy.

"Of course antibiotics don't cure measles. They stave off secondary bacterial infections, like pneumonia," Cate said as if speaking to a child.

Steven didn't offer a comment, even though all eyes looked at him. He had donated half his Fish-Mox and Fish-Flex to the hospital. The medicines, marketed to aquarium owners, were identical to the Amoxicillin and Cephalexin prescribed for humans. The only difference was in the packaging and their over-the-counter ease of purchase. He had stocked up before the end, and he would not part with any more. Someday his son or his sister might have need of them.

Yes, I'm the prepper. I'm the ant. And I've given you people all you're going to get from me.

Cate continued, "We have some antibiotics, but they're too valuable to use as a preventative. We'll keep them for life or death situations. Do you agree with that, Steven?"

There was the amused smile again. He thought about his conversation with Natalie. The woman's inexplicable weight and strange hand-hovering behavior should be addressed, but how?

"I agree. In addition to the vitamins we discussed earlier, what else should the HG crew be on the lookout for?"

"You mean besides condoms?" Cate barked a laugh, eliciting a few chuckles throughout the room. "We have a minor STD case. One that antibiotics won't cure anyway." She kept her eyes carefully on Steven. He was grateful she didn't pinpoint the patient with a glance. "But it brings up the issue of those STDs that, if left untreated, can be serious. Chlamydia, gonorrhea, syphilis. People, if you're going to have sex, wear a damn condom. We have a few boxes at the hospital, but not many, so also use restraint. This applies to everyone, not just the horny teenagers. It will be difficult enough treating people for injuries and ailments – STDs are preventable. I'm surprised that I even have to bring this up."

Steven felt blood rushing to his cheeks and was thankful for the low light.

"We have some," Maddie said. "We'll be happy to donate them. Don't worry, Pablo. You'll still get laid."

The young man was visibly embarrassed by the eruption of laughter.

"Thanks, Maddie," Steven said with a grin. "I'm sure everyone appreciates your generosity."

"Everyone except Pablo!" The remark brought another round of laughter.

"Back to business, people. At this rate we'll be here all night. Cate, any other hospital or medical issues?"

The stout woman shook her head.

"Next up, Marilyn?"

"Dani would like to say a few words."

Steven found the young woman in the crowd again. Her boyfriend Sam sat next to her along with a few members of the security crew. He assumed the rest of her staff were at their posts. He locked eyes with her and nodded, receiving a nod in return. Like Natalie, she moved with confident, fluid grace to the center of the room, but her movements seemed to deflect attention rather than demand it...a sinewy shadow cast in a darkened room. Steven thought of midnight assassins.

"We need more recruits," Dani said abruptly. "You people want to snooze soundly at night? Give me more bodies. Armed guards are posted at all four checkpoints twenty-four seven. We have someone monitoring the cameras at all times. That barely leaves eight hours for sleep, let alone fortifying the perimeters. Which reminds me, Steven, we need some of your construction people. I have ideas for turning this town into fucking Fort Knox."

"We can spare a couple, but we're working on windmills and wells now. Plus, if we ever want to get the power back on, I'll need workers for that."

"What's more important, lightbulbs or not getting your throat sliced in the middle of the night?"

"That's a bit disingenuous, but I see your point. I'll take a look at the labor situation and see what can be done."

She studied him with crossed arms and a tilted head. He could see she had found his answer inadequate.

Dani turned her back on him and spoke directly to the residents of Liberty. "So who wants to be one of the cool kids? Our team gets state-of-the-art weaponry and top-notch ninja training from Sam."

Two female arms shot up, and at least four belonging to men who were building windmills and digging wells – Steven's laborers.

Goddamn it. I need those guys.

"Look Dani, we can't take all these people away from their existing jobs. What's the minimum number you need? Be reasonable."

The predatory smile was back. He had his hands full keeping her in line, but there was no doubt their town was safer because of her. How old was this ferocious young woman? Twenty-one? Twenty-two? How many years ago had Julia given up her baby? Should he mention the resemblance to his sister? What would be gained? More importantly, how might that knowledge create problems within the community?

"A reasonable number is six. A scarcely adequate number is four. A number that will exponentially diminish our chances of keeping our throats intact would be the two you mentioned."

"How about four part-timers? You mainly need checkpoint sentries, correct? You people who are interested, would you be willing to work two part-time jobs instead of one full-time job? That might mean some twelve-hour days."

Sam appeared at her side. According to Julia, his effect on most women was like sunshine on a pat of butter.

"Like Dani mentioned, our people get cool weapons and training in Krav Maga and Russian Systema, with a little Jiu Jitsu thrown in," Sam said to the room. "It's a system of fighting I came up with over the last year. Dani and I have worked really hard on it. I don't want to draw too pretty of a painting here – recruits need to be in good shape and able to handle pain. It's very physical. You won't make it if you can't take some punches and falls." The slow smile softened the words. Several females in the crowd bit their lips suddenly, and there was a steely glint in the eyes of the men who had also raised their hands.

He's working the crowd. Using his sex appeal on the females and a macho challenge to the men. Steven decided he might have underestimated the Sam half of the dynamic duo. Together these two young people could take over the world.

He might need to keep a closer eye on both of them.

"If you're interested in part-time work for the security crew, talk to Dani and Sam after the meeting. Agreed, Dani? Four part-timers?"

He acknowledged the young woman's curt nod, then Steven had the floor to himself again.

"Marilyn, what's next?"

"The gasoline conundrum."

"Oh yes. So the hunter-gatherers believe that finding good gas should be the fuel crew's job, yet the fuel crew's allocation of gasoline is just adequate for getting them back and forth to the wooded lot west of town, plus what they need for their chain saws. So the fuel crew should either be given extra gasoline so they can go *find* more gasoline, or the task of finding more gasoline should be included in the HG crew's regular supply forays rather than separate expeditions, which means less time looking for food. Do I have that correct?"

"That's it." Marilyn's smile was just for Steven, and it was a doozy. In the flattering lamplight, she was downright pretty. The brilliant mind behind the smile made her, in Steven's opinion, just about the sexiest woman in town. He felt the color rise in his cheeks again.

"We'd just as soon let those guys do it." The fuel crew's leader looked like the quintessential lumberjack he actually was. He never removed his black beanie, even in the body-heated room, and his biceps threatened to burst through the red-checked flannel at the slightest exertion.

"We're not great at knowing where to look for stuff," the man continued in a slow voice that resonated like a bass violin. "We know how to cut down trees and turn 'em into heat for y'all's homes. That's what we do. But wandering around looking for gasoline just don't seem like it should be our job."

Finding, chopping, and delivering firewood wasn't something that required Steven's intellect, so his conversations with the man had been few. He knew little about the gentle giant other than his name and that he was from Arkansas.

"Billy Ray, I tend to agree with you. What do you say, Pablo? You guys are out there anyway." Steven swooped his arm in a vague gesture indicating the world beyond Liberty, Kansas.

Pablo sighed. Maddie snickered beside him. "He'll do it, but he won't be happy about it. Sucking gas is just about the worst thing you can ask Pablo to do, other than telling him to use a double negative or end a sentence with an open preposition."

Everyone who knew Pablo even superficially laughed at his expense.

"Why do I feel that I have a target on my back tonight?" he said with a grin. "Fine. We'll do what we can."

"Can't ask more than that." Steven smiled at the young man who'd been building quite a favorable reputation, not just for the successful forays, but for the storytelling sessions he and Maddie hosted. With the help of Amelia, the Native American woman with the quick smile and wise eyes, those events were the hottest ticket in town. Two nights every week they opened their home to anyone interested in stories and poetry. He hadn't been to one yet, but he decided to make the effort soon.

He studied Pablo and his firecracker girlfriend with affection. These were the kind of people Liberty needed.

"Next up, Marilyn?"

"The sanitation situation."

Steven rolled his eyes. "Oh yes. It seems some people are still inclined to...um...go outside. I understand that it's not always convenient to find a toilet or carry flushing water for said toilet, but the last thing we want is an outbreak of giardia or cholera. Now that we're using well water instead of lake water, we must be vigilant about our waste. You people that have septic tanks are fortunate. You won't have to worry about the main sewer lines backing up. Everyone else, it doesn't seem to be a problem yet, but if it becomes one, you may have to move into a home that has a septic system. We have Frank monitoring the situation, and he'll tell us if that time comes. Right, Frank?" He spoke to a short man with thick Clark Kent glasses. As a former manager at Wichita's largest wastewater facility, his job assignment had been a no-brainer.

The man nodded.

"Are we all in agreement about pooping and peeing inside?"

It was absurd that the issue even needed to be addressed, but when he noticed Logan sitting next to his sister, he remembered for the hundredth time that some of the residents of his town were 'special needs.' At that moment, he decided to delay Julia's explosive revelation until the next meeting. He knew withholding the information bordered on duplicity, but the machinery of civilization had been chugging along so well; he wouldn't throw a cog in the gears now. When everyone discovered there might be psychopaths in their midst, mayhem would ensue.

"Greenhouse," Marilyn said when he glanced again in her direction.

"Lisa, how are we doing?" Steven asked the ponytailed dynamo in the second row. "I know people are getting hungry for some fresh produce. I certainly am."

"We should have our first crop of baby carrots and radishes in two weeks. Then the kale and spinach. Everything is going well so far. We had to keep the fire burning last night on the boiler. The temp in the greenhouse was dipping too low for my peace of mind, so I made the call. Probably will have to do the same thing tonight. Other than tending the fire, there's not much else to be done at the moment. We're utilizing every inch of the interior space."

Steven noticed there was no hardwood visible on the bench between Lisa and Ed. If the relationship had progressed to the point this detail implied, he was happy for his friend.

"Are you saying you're overstaffed?"

"I'm hesitant to say yes, because I'll need every able-bodied person I can get my hands on come spring. But for now, yes. I can spare a couple of my people for other jobs over the winter. Ed and I have worked up some plans for a second greenhouse, which we'll need if the town keeps growing like it has been. Plus I've found a field for our first wheat crop. I rode along with Billy Ray yesterday. It's close to the acreage where they're getting our firewood. The area will be good for corn too, which needs a lot of space. Once the last chance of a freeze has passed, I want to cultivate the entire town square for spring planting...more vegetables and berries. Turns out, the soil is perfect. I won't need to do much other than turn it over. When that time comes, I'll be asking for more of those precious seeds, Steven, and my hired help back. Between our two seed banks and what we can gather from fallow fields, we'll be able to grow just about everything we could want that works in the 5B hardiness zone. Which reminds me, I'm available for consultation on the victory gardens. People can come talk to me after the meeting. We can use the cold weather down time to start designing the layouts and getting the fence work done. Deer and rabbits will be a problem, so ten-foot fencing is recommended."

It had been Lisa's idea for everyone to start their own gardens, just as the British populace did during World War II. Steven knew a lot about gardening, but his knowledge paled in comparison to the woman's horticultural expertise. Liberty was damn lucky to have her, and Jeffrey and his Springfield rifle were to thank.

"Marilyn, what's next?"

The question had just been asked when one of the courtroom doors opened and a small dark-haired man with almond-shaped eyes emerged in the doorway.

"Good grief, Tung! Where the hell have you been?" Steven blurted out. A wave of relief washed over him. After the Hays mission, the man had disappeared. Nobody knew where he had gone, and everyone had suspected the worst.

"I needed to get away. Clear my head a bit. Sorry I didn't leave a note or tell anyone."

All heads swiveled to face the back of the court room. The warm glow of the kerosene lamps revealed neatly trimmed hair and clean clothes. Tung hadn't been roughing it since his departure, but now was not the time for rapid-fire questions.

"Well, we're glad you're back. There's been talk of some projects where your talents would be invaluable, specifically making fuel that will burn in our vehicles. Ethanol? Biodiesel? Grab a seat and we'll get together later."

The small man nodded and selected the empty space on the bench next to Cate. Pablo saw the burly woman's eyes narrow as she watched the new arrival; she continued to study him long after the attention of everyone else had returned to Steven.

Pablo studied him too. He pondered the coincidence that Tung and Amelia had both disappeared about the same time. Amelia had been back for a while, and this man had just returned, but the timing of their departures and the vague reasons for going AWOL in the first place were puzzling in their similarity. Was there a connection between them? It seemed unlikely, and it might be worth the risk of annoying Amelia to find out.

Chapter 14

"Are we going to visit Thoozy today?"

Jessie was attached to the old man. Ever since Amelia had taken her to the hospital, she hadn't gone a day without seeing him. Now that he lived in the house next door, she could visit him as often as she liked.

"We'll see. I'm not sure if he went to the town hall meeting. It must be running long tonight since Pablo and Maddie aren't home yet."

Amelia stood in the living room of their house, stirring something in the big pot that hung from a metal stick in the fireplace. She said the pot was called a *Dutch oven* and the metal stick was an *andiron,* and that people had used them for cooking before electricity. Jessie thought it looked fun, but she wasn't old enough to get too close to the fire. Amelia said in another year or so she could. Everything the grownups cooked tasted delicious compared to the stuff she had eaten back at the Circle K where she had been all by herself for so long. She especially liked something called *hominy.* She had never eaten it before in her life because her dad never made it for her. Maddie said it was something southerners ate, and since she and her father were from Arizona, she figured that's why. Pablo had found tons of it – *pallets* they said, whatever that meant – and everyone in town was eating a lot of it.

"What are you cooking?" Jessie asked.

"Spaghettio Stew."

"You don't like Spaghettio Stew? You're making that face."

"No. I think it's quite revolting, but it has calories, and I'm tired of hominy."

"Can't we mix some hominy into the Spaghettio Stew?"

Amelia laughed. "How about I put some just in your bowl?"

Jessie nodded with a grin, then asked, "How old do you think Thoozy is? He says he's the oldest man on the planet. Do you think that's true? I saw people on TV...before...that looked older than him. Do you think all those old people are dead now?"

"I don't know, but it's likely. He is not the oldest person alive, but he is quite ancient. You know that word, yes?"

Another nod.

"He is one of the oldest people I know. He was born before me, and that was a long time ago too. But there are people at my home who are even more ancient than me. More ancient even than Thoozy."

"You mean your home under the ground?"

"Yes." Amelia sighed.

"Do you miss your home?"

"Very much so, but the work that must be done here is more important than missing my home."

"Keeping me safe?"

"Yes, and getting you ready to go below when it's time. There's something else that's also quite important."

"What is it? Killing the Smiling Man?"

"We just might have to do that. You didn't dream about him again, did you?"

A shake of the dark head.

"Good. Yes, if he comes here, we'll have to kill him. Killing is a terrible thing, Jessie. Do you understand that?"

"Yes. Daddy said so too. He had to kill that man back at the store. The one that I piled rocks on top of. But only because the man was going to kill us first. He said that made it okay."

"That's why we must kill the Smiling Man if the time comes, only because he is bad and will kill everyone else if he gets the chance."

"I think that too. His smile isn't the good kind. It's the kind that looks like there might be worms crawling around in his head, and the worms are itching his brain, and that tickles him and makes him smile."

Amelia stared at the child for a long moment, then continued. "Anyway, there's another even more important task I must do before we can go below. I have to convince those very ancient people, the ones that are more ancient than Thoozy and me, not to destroy the world."

###

"Julia, I'm sorry," Steven said. "It was a last-minute decision. Everything is going so well...I just couldn't bring myself to watch all that progress go sideways. Think about what we've accomplished in such a short time. It's remarkable."

She was giving him 'the look.' He had hated that look when they were kids and he hated it now. His big sister disapproved. No matter how he might try to dismiss the qualms the disapproval evoked, he couldn't get rid of them altogether. He had sought her approval his entire life, whether consciously or subconsciously.

"Please don't look at me like that," he continued. "You know I can't stand it. We're rebooting civilization...no minor task. Let's just get a little further before we risk crashing the hard drive."

"Nice analogy." Julia shook her head and sipped at her scotch. Even after weeks of being in Steven's home, she still marveled at the ice cubes in the glass. Her little brother was extraordinary. "Fine. But for the record, I don't know how much longer we can keep a lid on it. Thoozy knows."

"Yes, but you made him promise not to tell anyone."

"That doesn't mean he hasn't. I don't think he has though, or we would know by now."

"Yeah. We would know because half of the town would want to put the other half in padded rooms."

"Your numbers are off, but yes."

"And we couldn't blame them," he said, glancing at the top of the stairs where his son slept down the hall from Logan.

The meeting had run long, and as soon as they had returned, Jeffrey had passed out from exhaustion in what was now their shared bedroom, since Julia and Logan occupied the other two bedrooms. His son's full-time job with the security crew, plus the training with Sam, was a man's workload. Steven was damn proud of him for taking it all on.

The other person sleeping upstairs was a different matter. When Logan was in the house, he felt on edge. Despite Julia's claims that the young man was harmless, Steven didn't trust him.

"I'll talk to Thoozy again," she said quickly, following her brother's gaze. "I doubt he'll approve. He's one of those straight arrows."

"Yes, I got that impression as well. How is his health? Is it time to assign him a job?"

"Not yet. He's quite elderly. He won't give me the exact number, but

I suspect he's in his late seventies, early eighties. You need to give him something easy."

"No problem." He would do just about anything to erase that disapproving expression from his sister's tired face. "How are things going at the hospital?"

"Cate is working me like a field hand. I have to say, I'm not terribly fond of emptying bedpans and changing linens. I'm not trying to shirk my blue-collar duties, but perhaps I could be put somewhere better suited to my talents."

"The molecular biology lab down the street is on hiatus."

"Right, smartass. I was thinking of setting up a clinic. I'm no shrink, but I did a lot of reading on psychiatry during my down times at the university, and of course I did tons more after the Chicxulub DNA test results came in. I know some of these people are struggling with depression, mood issues and other maladies, and there's no medicine to alleviate their symptoms. Maybe I could help? We could have group therapy sessions. Letting people talk about their anxiety and stress is better than nothing."

Steven snorted, imagining the old Peanuts cartoon where Lucy sat under a scrawled sign that read 'Psychiatric Help 5¢, Doctor is IN.'

Julia frowned.

"I'm sorry. I wasn't laughing at you. Actually, I think it's an excellent idea." He paused. "Do it. You're hereby relieved of bedpan duty."

"I don't want people to think I'm not carrying my weight."

"Can you put in some extra hours at the commissary? Marilyn is struggling a bit. She has a demanding job, but she's averse to letting too many people get their fingers in the commissary pie. Something tells me she wouldn't have a problem with my sister, though."

It was Julia's turn to laugh. "Oh listen to you, you smug bastard. You're so convinced of your own appeal. Have you seen all that gray hair sprouting from your ears? Good grief, you look just like dad."

"Shit, I thought I was doing well just keeping up with the nose hairs. Nobody told me staying this dead sexy would take so much work."

Steven rubbed his bearded jaw, smiling at his sister. He thought about his son sleeping upstairs, about Julia who was finally safe after all those months alone in California, and finally, he thought about the date he had scheduled with Marilyn the following evening.

Life had gone on for a handful of people...would continue to go on.

How fortunate that two of his loved ones were here with him now, sharing his journey. He took another sip of whisky and tried to stay focused on what Julia was saying, but his mind kept wanting to contemplate tomorrow night.

Three people stood in a bedroom with pink walls and frilly white curtains. The blinds had been drawn. It had hosted a child at some point but was now the setting for meetings nobody else in Liberty knew about. Candlelight flickered on the faces of Amelia, Thoozy, and Tung. Those weren't their real names, but ones they had chosen for themselves because their actual names would have raised eyebrows, and the last thing these three wanted was to stand out. As an additional safeguard, they spoke in a language no one else could understand. It was the dialect of their home, and these clandestine gatherings were the only time they allowed the indulgence of speaking in their native tongue.

"How are you feeling, old man?" Amelia smiled at her friend. She had come close to losing him on his road trip from Colorado. Weeks earlier, he had shared the details of Logan's attempted murder. She still found it abhorrent to be in the young man's presence even now, despite her friend's return to good health.

"I feel like a puppy with two peckers." Thoozy grinned.

"You sound like Fergus," she said with a sigh.

"You're missing that rascal, aren't you, my dear?"

"More than words can express."

"Me too," said Tung. "I think he's in Pensacola now. My *scythen* sent me an image. He looked happy."

"He had probably just bedded some female." There was no trace of anger or animosity in her voice – only warmth and love. The concept of jealousy was one only the surface dwellers embraced. Those who dwelt below did not subscribe to that destructive construct; did not allow that negative emotion in their consciousness.

"I suppose we should get to it," Amelia said. "The child is everything we thought and more. If the Ancients want confirmation that there is worthwhile life here on earth, hers is the brightest star amongst all the other stars I've seen."

"From what you've told us, I tend to agree," Tung said. "Her *langthal* alone makes her perhaps the most valuable human left on the surface." There was no translation for the word. It conveyed an ability to heal or cure...a dynamic force which abided, inert, until it was stirred to life by the touch of an afflicted person. A handful of Japanese Reiki masters could produce a similar effect, but on an infinitely smaller scale. If Reiki were a lit match, *langthal* was a flamethrower.

"It's what saved Fergus. And Maddie too, of course," she said. "But is one extraordinary child enough to stop the Ancients from another earth cleansing?"

"While there are surely other societies forming around the world, this place...these people feel exceptional," Tung said. "Perhaps that's why our *scythen* drew us here. And the location so near our home cannot be a coincidence. I suspect an energy conduit."

Both the braided head and the white cotton-tufted one nodded.

Tung continued, "I know time is short. I just wish we knew how short. Will you be making another journey below soon?"

"I thought I would try to gather more evidence first. Also, Pablo gets grouchy when I disappear," Amelia said. She had become quite fond of her new little family. They were all gifted. Not to the degree that Jessie was, but in their own right. She loved them. More than anything, she did not want to see them perish in a great flood or die of starvation as a result of an artificial winter.

Thoozy had grown quiet during the exchange. In unison, the two others turned to him and waited. He liked to take his time with his words. It was his way.

"I know how you both feel about another earth cleansing, but I have to admit, I have my doubts about the people that remain. That Logan fellow is downright scary. I've also caught glimpses with my *scythen* of that other one. The Smiling Man, as Jessie calls him. And what about all those bad people in that little town? You know, the ones that the 'good people' destroyed," Thoozy said.

Tung nodded. He remembered a conversation with Steven prior to the rescue mission in which they had discussed the justification for committing murder.

Amelia frowned. "You know what those terrible men were doing. They needed to be exterminated, just like one would put down a rabid skunk or a mad dog."

"Your reference is charming and smacks of this world. No point in getting all worked up about it though. We've had the same conversation a thousand times over the millennia. All I'm saying is I'm not as convinced as you two that these people have earned a reprieve. I would like more time to study and watch. For now, I'm sitting on the fence."

"You've picked up some interesting jargon yourself this time." Amelia said with a grin.

"And you are just as beautiful as you always were." Thoozy kissed the brown cheek. "Now, about that Smiling Man business. What's the latest news?"

"Neither Jessie nor Maddie has dreamt about him in a week. Perhaps we'll get lucky and he'll head off in another direction." She spoke the last words without conviction.

"Not likely," Tung replied. His was the strongest *scythen* of the three. "I received an impression a few days ago. I think there's no deterring him. I believe he is bent on revenge, if I'm reading him correctly. I think he also would like to be king of the world. It's not the first time we've seen that."

Tung's smile was bitter. The other two nodded. Three pairs of eyes filled with sadness, evoked by ancient memories.

"It will be difficult for us not to interfere, if that's what the residents want to do, but we must remember to let them initiate. We are not vigilantes." The last remark was directed at Amelia. She didn't respond.

"Do you have any sense of when this monster will make his appearance in person?" Thoozy asked.

"No. The images are amorphous. Perhaps your prodigy can help, Amelia?"

"I'll see what I can do. I don't want to expose her. That creature will be even more determined to get here if he knows about the child's gifts."

"Agreed. Is there anything else?"

"No. I'm exhausted," she said.

"Me too." Thoozy yawned as he stood and stretched. "Thankfully, I only have to walk down the hall to crawl into my bed."

"Yes, and I have to sneak past two dogs, a cat, and several humans to get to mine."

Tung smiled at his friends. He doubted sleep would find him that night. He had much to think about.

Chapter 15

A small house sat apart from its neighbors on the outskirts of town. The peeling paint looked gray in the moonlight, but had been many colors at various points in its lengthy history. The wraparound porch had entertained seven generations of iced tea sippers, beer guzzlers, rambunctious children, and white-haired old people who rocked away their final years on its wood plank flooring.

It was the women who lived the longest. That's because the familial gifts were passed from female to female. Theirs was a matriarchy, and for good reason. The power resided with the women; always had. Even during the dark tumultuous years of burnings and hangings, when it had been especially dangerous for mundane types to discover their secrets, the legacy had endured.

Until now.

Cate worked in the cellar by the light of a single fat candle. Even in the summer, the cinderblock was chilly to the touch. Now that winter had arrived, the temperature in the room hovered just above freezing. Perfect for the items that were stored there, and not uncomfortable for the woman who spent much of her time in the large space; its subterranean walls extended well beyond the perimeter of the house overhead. She rarely felt the ill effects of extreme heat or cold. It was one of the gifts she had received from her mother, passed to her mother by her grandmother, and her great-grandmother before her, all the way back to Constantine, so the story went. It weighed on her that the end of the bloodline was her fault. Her supreme failure. After all those generations, hers would be the last. She hadn't menstruated in months, and male suitors weren't knocking on her door asking to fertilize any remaining eggs her ovaries might have hoarded.

Even before the plague, boyfriends had been a rarity. She had always loved growing herbs and reading medical books and honing her craft, much more than kissing boys and allowing their rough hands on her body. As a teenager, she was ridiculed for her weight – the result of a minor thyroid issue, but also, if she were honest, an obsession with sweets. It wasn't until her late teens that she realized she liked girls in the way that most girls liked boys, a fact she had never shared with her mother. It was fine that she did – there was little bigotry in her family in matters of race, religion, or sexual orientation – but it was unacceptable not to procreate. Just prior to Chicxulub, the pressure to become pregnant had reached levels that rivaled living on the bottom of an ocean. She often wondered if she had known then what was going to happen, would she have done anything differently. And while the loss of her mother still felt like a hot stone in her belly, she didn't miss the tight-lipped frowns of disappointment.

She had decided months ago that she could bear the burden of failure as long as she could continue her work. Serendipitously, Steven had given her that opportunity when he had asked her to be Liberty's doctor. She hadn't attended college, let alone earned the advanced degrees required to legitimately claim the title of 'nurse practitioner,' as she told everyone. It didn't matter that she had lied; she knew more than most six-year medical students, and she believed the townspeople were in qualified hands...literally. Hers could bring about spontaneous remissions, and melt artery-clogging cholesterol. They could stimulate the healing platelets and fibroblasts in a wound faster than nature left to its own devices; the same for chondroblasts when there was a broken bone. Many of the burns she had treated in the past barely scarred at all. She was convinced she had cured one of the Hays girls of chlamydia with nothing more than the focused energy of her hands.

Of course there had also been plenty of failures over the years.

The tricky part was corralling the energy. Too little and it didn't help the patient. Too much and it could kill them. That had happened in the past as well, and was the reason she had been fired from her last three home healthcare jobs.

Oh well. You can't win them all.

While she worked her pestle and mortar, crushing the dried St. John's wart with a pinch of fox glove, she realized how happy she was. She could make a difference in this new world, and she was resolved to do so. Since the legacy would end with her, she would make it all count; all those generations of exceptional women the world had never known existed, outside of fairy tales.

She hummed as she toiled in the chilly space. It was a trifle mean-spirited, but she had to admit she was relieved that those awful children – the ones who'd called her *Witch!* and egged her house every Halloween – had perished in the scourge. Those who remained knew nothing about her or her past mistakes, and she intended to keep it that way.

"Calvin, give me a boost," Natalie said to the tall man standing next to her.

In the weak light, his intense blue eyes appeared gray, just like the peeling paint of the house beside him. Without a word, he grabbed the shapely calves and hoisted her up. This was the only room in the house in which the blinds hadn't been drawn. A kerosene lantern glowed from the fireplace mantle, revealing a tidy living room crammed with mismatched threadbare furniture and dozens of dainty crocheted doilies.

"Ugh. It looks like Grandma Moses threw up in here."

"Did you find what you were looking for?" The man's deep voice resonated in the crisp air. The cultured clip of the consonants and intentional drawing out of the vowels suggested the speaker was not only used to talking from behind a pulpit, but knew how to sway crowds.

"No, damn it. I'm not seeing anything out of the ordinary."

"What did you hope to find?"

"I don't know. Evidence or clues, I guess. A treasure trove of food and a sex slave tied up to her bed. Something is just not kosher about that woman. I feel it with every fiber of my being."

The man slid Natalie's body down the length of his until both feet were back on the ground. He didn't release her.

"Thank you, Calvin," she said with a gentle push to his chest. "I appreciate you coming out here with me."

He gazed at the lovely woman, an achromatic movie star in the gloom.

Slowly he released her, but held one of her slender hands, fingering the delicate bones with their fragile covering of soft skin. He smiled down at her, then raised the hand to his lips, brushed the back with a kiss, and let her go.

It took a few moments for her pulse to return to normal. She couldn't tell if she was titillated or terrified.

"I would think you'd be feeling mighty smug right about now," he drawled.

"I'm pleased with the result of the vote, if that's what you mean. If people choose to keep pets, they should be the ones to make sacrifices, not me. It isn't fair. You can't deny that."

"I can't deny your logic, but I am curious about your motives."

"Fairness. That's my motive. Equity. Nothing else."

"I see."

"Anyway, it's over now. I wonder how difficult it would be to pick that padlock on the cellar door."

"I have many skills, my dear, but lock-picking isn't one of them. And besides, what if the lady is down there? How will you explain your burglary to the other residents of the town?"

"It's three o'clock in the morning. She's on duty at eight tomorrow. Why in the world would she be up so late? Unless she's doing something nefarious, in which case, you'll be my witness."

"I have a better idea. Let's come back when you know for certain she's not at home. When is her shift at the hospital?"

"Coincidently, it's the same as mine. Guess who's in charge of the schedule."

"The lady in question, no doubt."

"Correct. Although I could take a long break tomorrow. Tell her Brittany is sick at home and I need to check on her."

The man said nothing, but the corners of his eyes crinkled with amusement.

"That's what I'll do," she continued. "And I'll bring some bolt cutters with me."

"Will you be seeking my help in this clandestine enterprise?"

She flashed her most charming smile.

"If you don't mind. I'm not sure I have the strength to cut the lock."

"Very well, but I'll need something from you in return."

"I'm not going to sleep with you, if that's what you're thinking. Not yet, at least."

The amused grin stretched to a full-blown smile. Moonlight glinted off perfect teeth and illuminated a face that was well known in Georgia prior to Chicxulub. It had appeared on billboards throughout the Bible Belt but was most famous in Atlanta, home of the Whitehaven Baptist Church. Their Sunday sermon was televised locally and viewed through syndication in five southern states.

"You'll sleep with me when you're ready, which will be sooner than you think. But that's not what I want in exchange for my bolt-cutting prowess, my silence, and my complicity."

Her eyes narrowed. "What do you want?"

He took his time before answering, a smile still hovering about the corners of his mouth. When he finished, Natalie was also smiling.

Chapter 16

"Holy shit, Sam. I told you not to do that."

Dani had woken under the weight of a heavy down comforter between cozy flannel sheets. Her head rested on a pillow that felt like it was stuffed with marshmallows and fairy dust. With her eyes closed, she marveled at the decadent comfort of sleeping under such conditions. The town had her to thank for it too. Courtesy of her security measures, the residents of Liberty could reasonably expect to wake up every morning not dead. When she opened her eyes, Sam was gazing at her from five inches away.

"I can't help it. You're air-suckingly beautiful."

She laughed. "Yes and so are you. Good grief, how many women are in your harem now?"

"You mean my self-defense class? I think I'm up to nine. Plus the two going through the security training. Those girls are tough too. Not as tough as you, but pretty darn tough."

The notion of him having admiration for any other woman would have caused jealousy to flare in the heart of the old, chubby nerdy Dani. The new and improved version – Dani 4.0 – didn't bat an eyelash. It wasn't in Sam's nature to stray, but it was her supreme confidence that kept any would-be jealousy at bay; confidence gained from self-educating, from the grueling martial arts sessions with Sam, and from victories, both small and large. They were starting to add up now. It would be impossible not to feel the tiniest bit smug. She knew that characteristic rubbed some people the wrong way, and she didn't care.

Results were all that mattered, and she was getting them. Just look at what she had accomplished in such a short time with the help of her crew, which had already become fiercely loyal to her. Hell, even the Creeper seemed to like her now. At least he had stopped doing that weird oblique staring thing. He replaced it with occasional direct eye contact and his trademark creepy grin. She would take that grin over the tilted head, unblinking sideways stare any day.

His oddness was irrelevant. He had saved her life, and he was the best shooter they had. He had earned her loyalty with the first and her respect with the second. It wasn't any more complicated than that, which is the way she liked it. Black and white. Gray areas were for people like Steven.

"I'm glad they're tough," she said. "That's what we want. No shrinking violets or crybabies allowed. Are you working them as hard as the guys? Like you did me?"

Sam's golden beard tickled her neck where he nuzzled that spot that drove her crazy.

"I'm not working them like this, if that's what you mean." She could hear the smile in his voice.

She grinned, guiding his face lower, down to her breasts. Her fingers brushed the top of his forearm where Isaiah's 'brand' had healed with much less scarring than hers. Sam never brought it up anymore because it infuriated her – that psycho bastard had made a permanent mark on her body. Nobody had the right to do that. If she ever got the opportunity, she would tie him up and carve her brand all over his body. Then she would kill him. She contemplated the design of her brand, then considered the odds that she would ever see the lunatic again. It was unlikely.

Sam's gentle, slow kisses had progressed to her belly button. All thoughts of Isaiah vanished as his tongue found its way between her legs.

"Sir, our scouts discovered a large house with well water and a manual pump. It would be a good place to set up camp for the night. There are four bedrooms in the main house and a lot of floor space. There's also a big stable but no horses, and a small barracks of sorts. Probably for the ranch hands. It's all in good shape. Another house down the road was demolished. They said it looked like a tornado went through there."

Martin could not get a feel for the mood of his general today. He had been quiet and aloof since morning, yet had ordered no executions. The man was either exuberantly happy or exuberantly bloodthirsty. There was no in between. Until now. The change was unsettling.

"Mother Nature is a cold, capricious cunt, isn't she lieutenant?" Isaiah replied. His tone seemed distracted, another new development. Martin had never known him to be anything but laser-focused on the topic at hand.

"She is that, sir."

"It seems to be a universally female characteristic. Flighty, fickle, frivolous. Do you think that's because of the heavy burden they bear?"

"What burden is that, sir?"

"Procreation, of course. The greatest burden of all. Yes, it takes a man to fertilize a womb, but one squirt and his job is done."

Isaiah smiled at the crudeness of his own joke – another rare event. The man's verbiage was downright chaste most of the time.

Martin chuckled, careful to achieve what he hoped was the correct balance of respect and appreciation for the jest. He was in new territory now.

"The women," Isaiah continued, "theirs is the true power. The power of life itself. Is there any greater? My own dear mother died in the process of giving birth to me. I've only seen her in photographs and dreams."

"I'm sorry for your loss, sir."

"None of that, please. I'm a product of my life experiences, like tempered steel pounded and doused and forged until the resulting blade is magnificent, mighty, matchless."

"You are certainly all those things."

Isaiah glanced at his lieutenant, as if seeing him for the first time during their conversation. "Martin, don't be such a suck-up."

"Yes, sir."

The wide grin in the dark face looked genuine for once. The lieutenant didn't know whether to be relieved or shit his pants.

"You know, I often wonder how I would have turned out if she hadn't died. Can you fathom the difference having a mother makes in the life of a child? Did you have both parents?"

"I did, sir."

"Your mother, was she kind?"

The terrified man nodded.

"You were lucky then, in some ways. Not so much in others."

"How so, sir?"

"From great suffering comes great strength. I imagine your mother coddled you, fed you, bathed you, kissed your boo-boos...all those things mothers do. That nurturing made you weak because you didn't suffer. Did you realize that?"

"I'd never thought of it in those terms. That's an interesting perspective."

Honeyed laughter bubbled up from the muscled chest.

If he lived through the day, Martin promised his frayed nerves two ounces of the Bacardi he had stashed in his saddlebag. He would probably need to make use of the clean underwear the bottle was wrapped in, as his bowels threatened to turn to liquid at any moment.

"It's the truth, as ugly and as beautiful as it may be. Suffering made me the person I am today. Do you know what my father did for a living?"

"No sir."

"He was a police officer. During his thirty-year career, he received three medals of valor and five commendations for exceptional bravery in the line of duty. I know this because they were proudly displayed in our house. He would show them to me every time I fell short of his expectations. After he forced my small fingers to trace the engraving on the metal stars and touch the glass where the certificates were hung on the wall, he would beat me. I often passed out from the pain, I'm sorry to say. I was still being forged then, you understand."

"How old were you sir? When he beat you?"

"He always beat me. My earliest recollections were of him beating me. Right up until the day I killed him. I was fifteen years old. It's one of my fondest memories."

Martin tried to swallow, but his mouth was lined with sandpaper. His body's moisture seemed to be migrating south at the moment.

"Do you appreciate the irony? His brutality spawned the very thing that would vanquish it forever. Me." The smile this time was back to normal. "Sublime, stupendous, superb me."

Isaiah reached down from his stallion to give him a playful punch in the shoulder.

"I don't regret a thing. Not one bruise, not one bloodied lip, not one broken bone, because they produced the man you see before you today. And you have to admit, I'm breathtaking."

When the laughter came again, it made Martin think of how hot magma oozes out of volcanic fissures just before an eruption.

"Do you think she senses me? Sees me in her dreams, as I see her?"

"You mean the girl, sir? Dani?"

The smile vanished.

"Of course I mean the girl. Who else would I mean? Martha Stewart?"

"Sorry, sir."

"I see her," Isaiah continued, his eyes, like smoky quartz marbles, had taken on a misty quality. "I see her standing next to a sign that I can't quite make out. I know the name of a town is on that sign, and I know the closer I get to it, the more legible it will be. She taunts me in those dreams, as she taunted me that day back in Texas. I underestimated her then. It won't happen again. She's a worthy adversary, that one. Fierce and formidable. And female. So the bitch has that going for her."

Martin raised his eyebrows at the vulgarity.

"All that power, in addition to martial arts training and a quick mind. I don't think I've ever encountered her equal."

"She'll be sorry for what she did, sir. You'll make sure of that."

"Indeed, and in ways that give me pleasure to contemplate. Now about that house. How far out are we? I'm feeling rather peckish."

The exuberance was back. Martin decided to wait until tomorrow to tell his general about the massive roadblock the scouts had also spotted, positioned on I35 between them and Kansas, where they were headed. He wondered, briefly, if tonight wouldn't be a good time to cut and run. He knew there were spies within their army; Martin was the highest ranking spy of all. Informants were paid in favor and extra food rations for the intelligence they shared with their general. He suspected the newest member of his own quad was, in fact, a spy.

Isaiah was crazier than a shithouse rat, but he was no fool. He had anticipated a desertion problem. The solution was to have his soldiers inform on each other, and make it appealing to do so. To ensure nobody slunk away during the night, everyone was assigned three people with whom to sleep – sleeping quads. If someone needed to take a leak, one of their quad mates had to accompany them. Sentry duty was conducted in pairs, as were scouting missions. People were moved about frequently to deter friendships.

Nobody went anywhere or did anything by themselves, because any person seen alone at any time was shot on sight.

It was a brilliant system, and so far it had been effective in keeping him at Isaiah's side. Their army had burgeoned to nearly a hundred and fifty members. Some had volunteered, lured by the appeal of violence; others had been conscripted. The conscripted were usually the ones executed.

It felt like he had been on a roller coaster ever since the day Isaiah had incised Martin's forearm. His had been the second such surgical branding, just after the general had carved his own arm. Since that day, he felt as if he had been sitting in the front car of that metaphorical roller coaster as it had been clicking, clacking, clicking along for months, slowly and relentlessly ascending a rusty track. There was no safety bar to hold onto, and loose bolts barely held the metal runners to a scaffolding of diseased pine. Something told him they were close to reaching the apex of the ride. When that happened, the inevitable plummet would be terrifying and bloody. The question was, should he stay aboard and hope to survive the crash, or risk jumping off before? Did he have the balls to attempt an escape? Because anything less than success meant certain death.

And just as Isaiah, neither was Martin a fool.

Chapter 17

"Logan, we've talked about this. I think it would be helpful to everyone else if you would participate."

Julia gave him her stern look. It usually worked, but not today. Logan sat next to her in the circle of folding chairs. He seemed to be fascinated with a speck on the freshly-swept carpet of the hospital's conference room where Julia had hung her virtual "Psychiatric Help" sign. It was her second group therapy session, and all seats were occupied. People were struggling with mood and behavioral issues, depression, anxiety, and insomnia. She spent her free time in the library/commissary with Marilyn, reading everything she could find on the subject of psychiatric therapies.

The recommended treatment usually included a laundry list of pharmaceuticals – not an option these days. So she was making do with patience, empathy, and gut instinct.

"Logan, use your words, please."

A long moment later he raised his head, seeming to just realize where he was. He studied a few of the faces in the circle, and skipped over others. Finally his gaze came to rest on Julia. She realized how tired he looked and wondered if Dani was pushing him too hard. Yes, he was physically a man, but he was still a child in all the ways that mattered. She knew from their road trip together that he required more sleep than an average adult, and she knew he was getting less than eight hours a day.

She would talk to Dani about that.

"Sometimes I wish it was just you and me, Julia. Remember how much fun we had in Yellowstone? Then sometimes I think I might need to go away and be by myself again. Like I was before I found you at your house, when your car wouldn't start."

"Yes, I remember that day, Logan. But you're much safer here than you were by yourself."

The messy blond head nodded. "But I did okay back then. I got to shoot my guns more than I do now. I had Twinkies too, and they don't have any of those here."

"Maybe we can ask Pablo to look for Twinkies."

"I bet he won't find them. I think everybody likes them as much as I do and they've eaten all of them up."

Chuck's son snickered. Logan's blink-less stare shifted to the large boy. Julia recognized the expression; she knew what was coming next.

"You're black and orange. Nice! You're Halloween colors! I've never seen that before. I love Halloween."

"What the hell are you talking about? My shirt is blue. Don't you even know your colors? That's baby stuff, like numbers and shapes." It wasn't a man's voice yet, but was in that discordant, in-between stage.

Julia's heart sank when she saw Logan smile.

"You sound funny. Like a cartoon boy."

"Eat me, dipshit." The light eyes narrowed to slits of chipped ice.

"That's enough, Bradley," Chuck said, placing his hand on the boy's shoulder. Julia noticed how small it looked there.

"Let's shift gears," she said quickly. "Let's talk about anxiety and the ways in which we can address it. I think just about everyone here is dealing with that, right?"

All but two heads nodded. Julia had been surprised to see Natalie and the new man, Calvin, show up at her group therapy session. Neither seemed to be struggling, but hers was an open-door, no-questions-asked policy.

"There are several things you can do when you feel anxious, or when you feel a panic attack coming on. First, take ten deep breaths, slowly breathing in through your nose and exhaling out through your mouth. Let's practice doing that, shall we?"

For the next minute everyone was occupied with the process of breathing. Julia saw Thoozy wink at her from across the circle. She appreciated his offer to be here during these sessions. He seemed to have a calming effect on people, herself included. He could always be counted on for helpful advice, even when it wasn't asked for.

She winked back.

"I know I feel better. Meditation is also an excellent tool. And of course talking to others about your feelings is one of the best things you can do, so kudos for everyone's attendance tonight. I'm glad you're all here. Just remember, there's no shame in sharing. Saying what's troubling you, and expressing your fears doesn't make you weak. It makes you feel better. And better is stronger."

"I think that young man over there is plenty strong enough," Thoozy said with a grin, indicating Bradley whose expression remained hostile as he continued to glare at Logan.

Appreciative laughter was interrupted by the squawk of Logan's walkie-talkie. A male voice emerged through the static.

"Code red, western checkpoint!"

Logan launched himself from his chair and toward the doorway. Chuck, who was also on the security crew, was right behind him.

As an afterthought, Logan yelled over his shoulder, "Don't worry, Julia! I'll be careful!" The next moment he was gone.

"What's that all about?" the new man, Calvin, asked.

"It means there is a group of at least five people approaching the western barricade. That was a call to the members of the security crew who are not currently on duty."

She had helped Logan go over the protocols many times. She did not want him to fail the town, but even more, she did not want him to fail Dani. Something about that ferocious young woman resonated with her. She found herself sitting up straighter in her presence, as crazy as that sounded.

"Perhaps I should go see about helping." The man's voice was cultured and southern, evoking images of cigar-smoking gentlemen in white suits and sun-hatted ladies sipping mint juleps, or whatever it was those southerners sipped.

"I wouldn't advise that. The security crew is capable. Dani has systems in place to deal with just about any contingency."

The man's smile blazed from within the neat dark beard. "I'm certain that's true, Miss Julia. She seems quite exceptional, despite her manners."

Julia arched an eyebrow and gave him her full attention now.

"But she is just a girl," the pleasant voice continued. "She can't be much more than twenty. I wonder about this onerous responsibility resting on such young shoulders."

"Her shoulders are stronger than you realize," Julia snapped. "And it was my brother who wisely placed that responsibility with her. She could massacre you at chess and kill you with her bare hands. At the same time."

The man's laughter managed to sound contrite.

"I apologize, ma'am. I'm new here. Just trying to get a feel for the lay of the land. I mean no disrespect to you or the young lady in question. Is she a relative of yours? I can't help but notice a resemblance."

Julia's eyes narrowed. "No relation, but you'll find we're a close-knit group here in Liberty, much like a family. And while we sometimes welcome *newcomers*," she gave the word a delicate emphasis, "we tend to rely on those with proven skills and unquestionable loyalty."

"Calvin, please don't go starting trouble now," Natalie interjected. "You're the new guy here. Be respectful of that."

Julia heard the patronizing tone in Natalie's voice. She had yet to make up her mind about the woman, and she hadn't been able to pry any information from Steven. She knew something had happened between them, but Steven was taking the gentlemanly path; if there'd been kissing, he wasn't telling.

"We'll end the session early tonight," she said as she stood, dismissing both Natalie and her apparent beau with a turned back. "I would advise everyone to go home and stay alert. If there's a problem, you'll be notified via the town crier."

"Town crier? Oh my!"

"Calvin!" Natalie punched his arm.

Julia had started toward the door, ushering people on their way out. She turned to address the source of the amused laughter, stopping a ruler's length from the man's chest. She was a tall woman. Their eyes locked at roughly the same latitude.

"I don't know what your experience has been since the world ended, sir, but here in Liberty we've been reduced to nineteenth century technology. We're making the most of what resources we have: elbow grease combined with the considerable intellects of some very gifted people. We're doing better than everyone else left out there, I'd bet. We have food and clean water and we stay warm at night in the relative safety of our beds. If you want to remain here and be a part of that, I suggest keeping your rude comments to yourself and wiping that smug expression off your face."

The smile blazed again from within the dark beard, but Julia saw a flash of something in the eyes. Something that made her think of euphoric tent revivals and the handling of snakes.

"Again, my apologies, ma'am. I assure you it won't happen again."

"Come on, Calvin. Let's go. Sorry, Julia. I think he's been on the road too long. We forget how barbaric it can be out there."

Natalie pulled the man's arm and dragged him out of the room.

Julia realized her heart was racing and her hands were shaking from a surge of anger-fueled adrenaline. Bradley, Chuck's large son, paused and spoke in her ear just before he left.

"That man is an asshole," he said in a low, cracking voice. "If you need any help with him, you let us know. Dad says we have ways of dealing with jerks like that."

'We' was the security crew, of course. Julia contemplated the subtext of the boy's statement, then wondered if Logan had told her everything that went on at their meetings.

Chapter 18

"Jeff, you cover the three gorillas on the left. Creeper, you have the four on the right. Got 'em?" Dani's whisper carried a plume of vapor in the night air.

"Yes."

"Got 'em covered!"

Logan was more lucid and animated than she had ever seen him. The thought made her smile. Knowing these two sharpshooters were at her side deepened her confidence in the outcome she envisioned.

People were going to die tonight. But they wouldn't be her people.

She stepped back from the junk pile that was the western checkpoint and pressed the button on the side of her walkie-talkie.

"Sam, you copy?"

The response was instantaneous. "Copy. It's just like you said. I see two trying to flank us here on the east. Annie Oakley and I have them in our sights. I don't want to shoot anyone unless we have to."

She swallowed down the knee-jerk annoyance. "Wait until you hear from me. Chuck, you copy?"

"Copy that. No activity at the southern checkpoint."

"Excellent. Winston, you copy?"

One of the security crew's newest recruits was a forty-year old tax accountant who could shoot a tin can off a tree stump from two football fields away.

"Copy. All clear in the north. I'm moving out now."

"Good deal. Stay frosty, everyone. The shit's about to hit."

She walked around the mountain of rubble and into the line of fire of the seven people who had taken up defensive positions fifty yards in front of her. They had received the obligatory warning shot and the shouted speech, after ignoring the threatening sign.

That mistake was about to bite them in their collective asses.

"Hey stupid fucks! Can you not read, or do you have a death wish?" She felt the follicles on the back of her neck tingle as she was sighted in multiple crosshairs.

"Don't even think about it. The second your finger begins squeezing those triggers, my guys will blow the tops off your skulls."

This was the weakest part of her plan. Of course she wore Kevlar under her leather jacket, but it wouldn't protect her from a head shot.

"I just want to have a chat. Be nice now. Why have you come to our little burg, brandishing weapons and ignoring every attempt we've made to dissuade you from forcing your way in? We're reasonable people. If you'd followed the simple instructions on the sign, the situation would be different now. More's the pity. I'm interested in your motivation and the confidence in a strategy that compelled you to select force over polite conversation."

A snicker wafted through the still night air. Seconds ticked by. Despite the forty-degree temperature, she felt dampness in her armpits. *Just another couple of minutes...*

"Hi, Dani! Long time, no see!"

She couldn't see the speaker, but she recognized the voice. It was melodic and affable, just as it had been that day at the Best Western when she had recruited Dolores's help for the rescue mission. She pictured the unfortunate face with its asymmetrical features, and the keen intelligence in the lopsided eyes.

There was nothing dumb about Dumb Dolores.

She had convinced Dani she was on her side, then ratted her out to the misogynist who ran the town. Why she had done so was still a mystery, but the betrayal had almost cost Dani her life.

Dani narrowed her eyes, trying to find the girl with marginal help from the moonlight.

"I bet you're wondering why I betrayed you that day." The singsong voice floated out of the gloom.

"I was just now pondering that very thing."

"The guy who ran the town was my pa. Jacob was my brother."

Oh shit. She hadn't seen that coming.

"I thought you said your pa kept you in a woodshed? Didn't let you go to school?"

A snort wafted over the heads of the invaders. "You're kind of gullible for such a smart girl. You trusted me way too soon. You thought being friendly and touching my bad hand would make us instant friends. We might have been too, if it hadn't been for you killing my family."

As unexpected as the Dolores development was, it wouldn't change the plan. She just needed to stall for another few minutes.

"They were doing horrible things to those women. Why were you a part of that?" Dani replied.

"Because they were my kin."

She could hear in the tone that 'kin' should have explained everything. Family was a bond strong enough to compel an intelligent girl's complicity in despicable, heinous acts against other females.

"That's a damn shame. I wish I could say I'm sorry it ended the way it did, but I'd be lying."

Her walkie-talkie burped static. She didn't know it, but she now wore the predatory smile almost everyone in Liberty had come to recognize.

"I think you're going to be sorry quite soon," Dolores hollered.

I think you're going to be sorry in about half a second.

Her left thumb on the hand that had been hiding the Motorola pressed the squelch. Three rifles fired at the same moment, two from behind the debris and one from the northern side of the highway. While Dani had been stalling for time, Winston had utilized a recently-cleared path through the dead cornfield to flank their adversaries. They had been prepared for a frontal assault, not an additional one from behind.

She didn't bother hitting the pavement because she could see that all seven were down. She hoped to find an eighth body farther to the west.

"Sam, what's your status?" she said into the walkie-talkie.

"We have the two in custody. There doesn't seem to be anyone else coming. You're okay?" She could hear the relief in his voice even through the tinny transmission.

"I'm fine. Chuck?"

"Still clear here."

"Alice?"

"Still clear in the north. Did Winston make it?"

"Yes. Keep your eyes peeled, Alice. Winston, you stay put. We need to make sure nobody else is out there. Creeper, you come with me," she said to the junk pile. "Jeff, stay in position." She had promised Steven his son's safety would be given top priority, as long as it didn't compromise a mission. Julia had tried to wrangle the same deal for Logan, but with no luck. All bets were off when it came to the grownups, no matter their mental age.

Logan was beside her the next moment.

"We're going to proceed with caution," she told him. "I'm pretty sure they're all dead, but someone could be playing possum."

"Got it," he said, matching her whisper.

The Sig Sauer was relegated to its back harness and Logan held the Ruger handgun now. She had seen him in action with that thing and knew she was about as safe as she could be, under the circumstances. She reached behind her back, sliding the filigreed revolver from her belt. She was good with the Cattleman, but she was no match for the weirdo walking beside her.

Bodies lay sprawled on the asphalt. She squatted seven times to check seven pulses, knowing it was a superfluous effort. Five men and two women were dead, thanks to her sharpshooters.

There was just one more body to find now.

"You out there, Dolores? Might as well give up. It'll go better for you."

Dani's voice rang out in the cold air. Her ears felt preternaturally tuned to the sounds of the night. She could imagine them swiveling forward, wolf-like, to the hoot of an owl from a leafless oak up ahead. Then toward a crackling of dead cornstalks beside the highway.

"That you at three o'clock, Winston?" she whispered into the walkie-talkie.

"Yes," came the reply. "Sorry. I had to pee."

She and Logan proceeded another hundred yards.

"Dolores, you're only making this harder on yourself. I can have twenty people here in five minutes, beating the bushes for you. If I have to do that, I'll be more pissed than I already am, which won't end well for you."

She breathed in the wintry air, processing the scents of earth, decaying vegetation, blacktop tar, and something else...faint and unpleasant.

The next moment she identified the odor: an unwashed female body. She remembered Dolores's stench from the Best Western. She also remembered her words: *I'm very fast. Nobody even saw me. That's because I can be invisible.* And her own thought at the time: *The girl moves like a ghost.*

"Fuck. She's gone. If I call in the cavalry, people will be irritated when we don't catch the little bitch."

Logan didn't respond. He continued scanning the area, waiting for a directive from his boss.

"Let's call it, Creeper."

"You want me to keep looking? I don't mind. I can go on up a bit farther."

"No, it's okay. Julia will get butt-hurt if I send you out on your own. I think she hauled ass through the fields. That girl is Flo Jo. And quiet too."

"Do you think that's her super power? Maybe she has magic. I think a lot of people do these days."

She patted him on the back with a grin. "Maybe she does. That would explain how she got out of Hays. Come on, let's go get some chow. I'm famished."

"I think I'm famished too!"

"We're not going to execute them." There was steel in Steven's tone, just below the fatigue. The two captives from the eastern barricade, a man and a woman, stood in his living room with their hands tied behind their backs. Their clothing was tattered and filthy, and they wore identical insolent expressions; an easy task since they were siblings. Fraternal twins, the same age as Steven himself.

"That's your call, but you're asking for trouble. They'll just gather new recruits, hook back up with Dolores, and try again. But now they'll have more information about our town," Dani said between huge bites of canned potatoes, eaten directly from one of Steven's mason jars.

"They didn't see much. We had them blindfolded like you asked," Sam said with a frown. He stood close to the prisoners, exuding a protective air. Dani rolled her eyes.

"More importantly, we're not murderers," Steven said.

"Oh, right. We're not murderers when we storm into a town with our guns blazing because it's a 'rescue mission.' You're splitting hairs. Consider their execution a preemptive strike. It's only a matter of time before they try again."

"And was it necessary to kill those seven other people?" Julia asked, standing from her seat on the bottom step of the stairwell.

Dani set down the jar, and swiveled to face her.

"And what would you have done in my place? Subdue them with harsh language? Deter them with a stern look?"

Julia held the defiant gaze with a similar version.

"I wasn't there, so I can't answer the question of what I would have done," Julia said. "But it seems to me they could have been wounded rather than killed. Our intent should be to incapacitate, not annihilate. There's been so much bloodshed, and yet we're supposed to be the good guys. At least that was my impression." She glanced at Steven, who didn't respond. "Cooperation. Compassion. Mercy. These are the qualities of an advanced civilization. If we don't emphasize these things, embrace these ideals, then we're no better than those people in Hays."

Dani's eyes narrowed. "We're not raping anyone. We're not enslaving anyone. We're not trying to expand our empire through subjugation. I think we're doing pretty fucking great considering everything."

Steven watched the confrontation with fascination. Dani stood in front of his sister; barely two feet of carpet separated them. Both pairs of arms were crossed. The girl had to look up a few inches; Julia had her in height and outgunned her in the education department, but Dani had probably never lost a battle of wills in her life.

"But we can do better. We can always do better," Julia said. "If we just accept murder as the status quo, I don't think I want to live here."

"Then don't let the door hit you in the ass."

"That's enough for now," Steven said. "I won't second guess your decision, Dani. You're keeping us safe, and that's what you were hired to do." His smile didn't reach his eyes. "Julia, you're tired. You were worried about Logan. And Jeffrey too. Your nerves are on edge, just like everyone else. We can have a discussion about this after we've all slept and aren't so emotionally wrung out."

"What about these two in the meantime?" Sam said to nobody in particular. "I could take them a few miles out of town and let them go."

Dani made a disgusted sound. "Do what you want. I'm going home."

The next moment she made good on her statement.

"Well, that didn't go so well." Steven's remark was directed at his sister.

"She's a remarkable girl," Julia replied, "but I meant what I said. I don't want to live in a society that sanctions executions based on threat assessment. Do you realize how abhorrent that is? Good god, what's next?

Internment camps? Genocide? You, more than anyone else, understand the implications." Her eyes were like laser beams as they bored into him.

"Enough, Jules. We'll talk about that later." There were people in the room who didn't know about Chicxulub's survivors. Thoozy did, but he was merely observing the speakers like they were actors in a melodrama. He hadn't spoken a word since his arrival. Sam still stood beside the captives, and Logan watched from the stairs where he perched like a tousle-headed gargoyle a few steps above Julia.

"This isn't the end of it," she said. "I'm going to bed. Thoozy, can you get home by yourself? Do you want Logan to escort you?"

"No, ma'am. I'll be fine. Don't worry your head about me. You got enough on your mind without fretting about my old black hide." His warm grin had the effect it always did; everyone seemed to relax a bit.

When Logan and Julia had retreated upstairs, Steven turned to Sam. The expression on the handsome face was a caricature of dismay; goodness practically oozed from the pores of the young man. If Sam had been put in charge of security, there would be fewer casualties – but greater peril.

As was oftentimes the case, the issue was as clear as mud, and no outcome was perfect. In this instance, though, it wasn't a difficult call.

"Sam, take one of your people and drive these folks to Salina. You can borrow the fuel truck from Billy Ray. Leave them there with some food and water. Will you do that?"

"Yes." The relief was evident in his voice.

"As for you two," he addressed the captives, "don't come back. Ever. If you do, I'll unleash the kraken on you. I think you know who I mean. Got it?"

The heads of the middle-aged siblings nodded in unison.

The next moment Steven had his living room to himself except for the old man. Steven was exhausted, but Thoozy appeared quite comfortable in Steven's favorite chair, giving no indication he intended to leave anytime soon.

"I could use a stiff drink. Care to join me?"

"I never pass up the opportunity to share a beverage with good people."

Julia was fond of this character, and Steven could see why.

"Oh my. That hits the spot," he said after taking a sip of Steven's second best scotch. The twenty-six-year-old Glenfiddich was still nestled in his cellar, waiting for an occasion more momentous than this.

"It does indeed."

The old man had something on his mind. Steven waited, enjoying the heat that had begun to spread from his belly to his toes. Thoozy's eyes gleamed in the light of the kerosene lamp that rested on the coffee table between them. With a backdrop of flame-licked logs in the fireplace, he looked like a benevolent demon. The thought made Steven smile. The old guy in the Denver Nuggets sweatshirt and baggy jeans probably posed less of a threat than any other person in town.

"It's a tough job you have here. The responsibility weighs you down from time to time, I bet."

"That may be the understatement of the century," Steven replied.

"I imagine it's not so much the worry about keeping everybody fed and healthy that troubles you the most. I think a big chunk of your worry has more to do with the...special...people here." A gnarled oak of a hand waved the glass in the direction of Liberty proper. "And the ones that are still out there." The glass swung in the opposite direction.

The rest of the world.

"You could say that. I know Julia shared some information with you. And I know you agreed to keep it to yourself."

"I did. My word is as good as it gets, son. It's pretty much all I have left now that my pecker doesn't work so well." The golden grin. Steven found himself being charmed and decided not to fight it. The whisky and the company felt good.

"I think something else that troubles you is the kind of situation that happened here tonight." Thoozy took another sip of the amber liquid, smacking his lips in appreciation. "It's a conundrum, isn't it? Are we justified in taking one life to save our own or that of another? I have a feeling that question has vexed us hominids since the beginning of time."

"I think you may be right about that. And we're no closer to answering it."

"Perhaps what's important is the manner in which we address the question rather than answering it."

"You're talking about our humanity, aren't you?"

Thoozy's response was a smile.

"It's not the destination but the journey, I suppose," Steven said. "I'm not a religious man. I doubt there's anything on the other side of this life other than a nice long sleep. So every second matters. Needs to count for something. Never before have so few humans had so much influence in determining the continuation of the species."

Thoozy's grin broadened.

"Our decisions and choices have never been this important. Have never had such an impact. The ripples we create now, in this decimated world, are like tsunamis. I'm aware of that fact from the moment I wake up in the morning until I go to bed at night. So yes, I guess you could say it weighs me down."

"Might it be better to kill off all the bad people? Before they can harm the good people? Perhaps that young woman has a point."

Steven didn't know if he were being baited, or if the old man shared Dani's preemptive strike philosophy.

"Don't think I haven't considered it. I even thought about sending armed caravans throughout Kansas to find them and eliminate them before they get to us. Don't mention that to Dani, by the way. That girl doesn't need more bloodthirsty seeds planted in her head than are already sprouting there. But of course we won't do that. Because of our humanity. Because we're fundamentally good. Even those who aren't good can change. Nurture versus nature, right? But those types, even the awful ones, serve a purpose. They make the rest of us better than we are, better than we would be if they weren't around to cause trouble. They inspire us to new heights of bravery and honor – qualities that are uniquely human."

Steven paused, considering his summation. Thoozy watched him, the ancient eyes crinkling a fraction at the corners.

"What I'm trying to say is, there can be no light without darkness."

The old man nodded in understanding. He wore the warm grin that his sister declared worked on everyone like a Valium.

"You're a good man, Steven. I'm honored to know you. Thank you for this fine whisky and your company. And thank you for everything you're doing for these people. I think most of them appreciate you, but if they don't, just know that I do."

The mahogany hand extended over the coffee table. Steven grasped it, registering the warmth in its bones and sinew.

"I'll let myself out. Be sure to lock up after me." The old man winked.

"You sure you don't need some help getting home? Won't you be cold?"

Thoozy waved him off. "A useful aspect of being old is there isn't much flesh to get cold. I'll be fine. You just take care of your family and don't worry about me. Good night, sir."

Steven watched him amble down the driveway, turn left at the road, then disappear into the gloom. He closed the door against the night.

A shadow detached itself from the tree against which it had been leaning and glided to the road where the old man was shuffling past. Thoozy had much on his mind at the moment; otherwise, his *scythen* would have alerted him to the presence. He thought about Steven's words, allowed them exclusive space in his head like a cache of rare pearls placed a distance away from other precious gems. Then he thought of Julia. He had become fond of her these past months. She and her brother were extraordinary, but not in the way that recruits must be. Next he pondered the dangerous young man whom Julia had taken under her wing. He sighed. He was old, but he still felt the gamut of human emotions: frustration, dismay, joy, heartache, longing, love.

And fear.

"I wondered if we would meet again under such circumstances," Thoozy said to the night. He was relieved to hear strength in his voice. There was no hint of old-man quaver.

"I think your magic has gotten weak. Your colors look different now."

"You may be right about that. So what happens next? You gonna shoot me or strangle me?"

Logan paused, contemplating both options.

"It wouldn't be smart to shoot you. People might hear."

"True. So it's to be strangling then?"

Thoozy turned to face his opponent. Light from the moon gleamed off Logan's Cheshire cat smile.

"Maybe there's a third thing I could do."

A blade shimmered in the gloom. The next moment he felt the metal between his ribs, then a burning sensation in the place it had just been. Then he was lying on crumbling asphalt.

He had suffered many physical injuries in his unfathomably long life.

He always assumed he would die someday, but he hoped his demise would be meaningful; a bit grand, even. Perhaps there would be time to give a compelling speech to a respectful gathering of his peers. He didn't imagine it would end like this, with nobody around to bear witness except the deranged young man sitting beside him.

"Does it hurt?" Logan might have been asking about a paper cut.

"It doesn't feel like a walk on the beach." Damn. There was the old man quaver now. Hearing it made him sadder than knowing he was about to die. Perhaps it was just as well to go out this way, where no one he loved could hear the infirmity in his voice.

"I didn't want to kill you, but I knew I had to after what happened that night when I thought I had killed you but didn't."

"Why did you try to kill me that night? Did the voices tell you to?"

"Yes. You know about them? They were really loud back then and sometimes it's just easier to do what they tell me to. They're not as loud now though, so that's good." The handsome face tilted toward the night sky, frowning from complex thoughts. "I don't think they want me to be liked by people. Real people, I mean. They don't come into my head as often now. Sometimes when I go to bed at night, I think they're already asleep."

There would be no compelling speech to an appreciative audience, but Thoozy's last words could have long-reaching effects – ripples that might become tsunamis.

"I'm happy to hear this. Do you know that these voices are bad?"

Logan shifted his attention from the star-washed sky back down to the earth and the old man who lay dying upon it.

"Yes. I know they are."

"Do you want to be bad like them, or do you want to be good like Julia?"

"It's fun to be bad sometimes. Like when I kill things, I know it's bad but it feels good to do it. At least it used to. It didn't feel good to put that knife in you. Well, not as good as I thought it would. It feels good to be liked by everyone too. That feels really good."

"Yes, of course it does. You must listen very hard to what I'm about to tell you. Julia's life depends on it."

The messy blond head nodded in the darkness.

"You have to make a choice. You can keep killing people, or you can be liked by everyone, especially Julia. Which feels better? Having friends, right? Isn't that wonderful? Doesn't it make your heart sing to know that people like you?"

"I don't think my heart can sing. Only my mouth can sing. Is that your magic? Does your heart have a voice box? I always wanted to see what one looks like. I think it might look like those ballerina boxes that little girls have. The kind that has a key that you wind up and it makes the ballerina dance."

Thoozy felt a flicker of impatience, and also more tired than he had ever been. He didn't have long.

"Imagine yourself standing on a beautiful mountain. On one side of you is a very long drop down to where a river is flowing. There are jagged rocks in the river. It would be terrible, just awful, to jump off the mountain and into that cold water.

"On the other side is a lovely meadow. It's filled with beautiful wildflowers and there are pretty deer grazing in the tall grasses. Birds are singing and the sun is shining. It would feel so nice to walk over there. Are you picturing it?"

Logan's eyes were closed. He nodded.

"Now here's the part that you must pay attention to. This is a type of story called a parable. Parables teach lessons, like being in school. The mountain represents where you are in your life at this moment. The cold, awful river symbolizes your decision to keep killing people. The beautiful meadow is your decision not to kill people and have everyone like you and have lots of friends. Which will you choose?" Thoozy barely had the strength to ask the question. His life was down to seconds now. He must make them count.

Logan stared at the old man on the ground. Saw the lifeblood seeping out onto the road, an ever widening pool of spilled ink.

"Can I shoot the deer in the meadow? I'm very good with my guns."

Thoozy's eyelids were so heavy now. He had to let them close. Memories began flooding into his head, pushing out the urgency of his message to the young man beside him. People he had loved and lost in his time on earth came to him. They were smiling and welcoming him. The love of a thousand lifetimes, ten thousand lifetimes, was all around him. The last movement of his ancient body was to smile.

He was home.

Chapter 19

"Do you think he'll come back?" Jessie's enormous eyes glistened with tears. She had let her spoon fall into the oatmeal in front of her.

Amelia had already cried herself out. She felt as dry as the dead corn husks in the fallow fields outside of town. She knew last week that he had passed, but of course had hidden that knowledge from her adopted family. She felt the loss in the night seven days ago. His presence, his spirit, the essence of who he was had been so strong that the black hole of its absence had fluttered her *scythen.* Tung felt it too. They had shared their anguish in a night-long vigil together, remembering Thoozy's contributions to their people, laughing at his jokes told in any number of languages, and marveling at the wisdom that was even more ancient than their own.

"No, child, I don't think he'll be back. He was very old. I guess it was just his time."

Jessie nodded, the movement spilling more tears onto the damp cheeks.

"I really miss him."

"I do too."

Maddie was weeping now too. Pablo squeezed her hand.

"It's sad that he's gone, but at least he doesn't feel pain any longer," Pablo said. "You know old people have a lot of aches and pains. Now he doesn't have to feel all that. When a young person dies, it's tragic, but when an old person dies, it's natural. It's just part of living."

"The end part," Jessie whispered.

Pablo smiled. "Yes, the end part. I have an idea. We could write another song...one for Thoozy. Like when we wrote *Arizona in the Rearview Mirror.* What do you think?"

The child nodded. "I think he would like that. Don't you Amelia?"

"Yes, I'm certain of it."

"So they still haven't found the, uh, remains?" Pablo asked.

"No. Just the puddle of blood on the street a block or so from Steven's house."

Pablo nodded. "A wild animal then, I'm guessing. We've been seeing more coyotes lately. And even though Steven claims mountain lions have been extinct in Kansas for a long time, I swear we saw one in Great Bend that day we found all the hominy. Maybe they're expanding their territory now that so few humans are left to run them off."

"Perhaps," Amelia replied looking down at her bowl.

"You need to be more careful then," Maddie said.

"I'm always careful, my love." He kissed her cheek.

She wiped the tears from her face with a dishtowel, took a deep, quivering breath and said, "We're going to have a baby."

Pablo sat motionless, allowing Maddie's words to fully register. Then he leaped from the breakfast table, knocking over a kitchen chair in the process. He scooped her into his arms and swung her around in circles.

"Stop! I'm going to puke!"

He gave one more *whoop* of joy, then set her back down.

"When? How far along are we?"

"We think the due date will be in May," she said. Her freckled ivory skin had a greenish cast now. "Ugh, I hope I don't throw up all that oatmeal. That would be wasteful." She swallowed quickly several times.

"I'm sorry, Maddie. I'm just so happy!" He looked at Amelia and Jessie. "You both knew?"

Two braided heads nodded in unison.

"Why am I the last to find out? Oh, never mind. It doesn't matter. What will we call her? Or him?"

"We can have that discussion when my stomach settles down."

"Amelia, you've examined her? Everything is normal?"

"Yes, everything appears as it should."

"Our world is so primitive now. What if there's a problem? Does she need a special diet? Will she be able to deliver without medication for the pain? What if she needs a C-section or the baby is breach? She's so slender! What if it won't come out on its own?"

He was beginning to hyperventilate.

"Pablo, get a grip. This is why I haven't told you before now. Take deep breaths and put your head between your legs. There you go. In through the nose, out through the mouth."

Maddie and Amelia exchanged smiles across the table as they watched him struggle to control his panic attack.

"You're amazing," she continued. "Every day you go out there in that scary world and you deal with all kinds of dangerous situations. You stay calm. You evaluate your environment and make smart decisions. You bring back food and supplies that keep this town afloat, and you never get freaked out or even flustered. Why can't you do that with me? You lose your s-h-i-t when it comes to me."

He lifted his head, his face flushed from the gravity of blood flow.

"It's because if something happened to you, I couldn't go on. I lost you once. I thought you were dead back at that Walgreens store. We weren't even a couple then. We were just friends and I barely managed to survive it. Then I almost lost you again when that happened." He touched the place in her short hair where the scar was fading more every day. "I couldn't bear it. It would kill me."

"It's imperative that you live. You have a child. Our child. You must keep yourself safe so you can be a father. It will be the most important job you've ever had. Now stop being a damn girl. Everything will be fine. I'm in perfect health...Amelia said so. Also I had Cate check me out and she said the same thing."

"That's good. I'm sorry I'm being such a wimp. I'll try not to let that happen again." He kneeled on the linoleum floor at Maddie's knees. "I promise that I will be a good father, and I will never leave your side. Figuratively, I mean," he added hastily.

"What else?"

"I promise I will not lose my s-h-i-t every time you tell me something that makes me worry about you."

She smiled. "What else?"

Pablo thought for a moment, then said, "If you have a craving, I will fetch Rocky Road ice cream from 7-11 at three o'clock in the morning. I will massage your swollen feet. I will rub cocoa butter on your ballooning belly. Later, I will change the poopy diapers as happily as I change the pee-pee diapers."

She laughed. "Excellent. Who knew it would be so easy getting you to do my bidding. All I had to do was get knocked up."

He gripped her pale-skinned hands in his darker ones, kissed the knuckle of each finger and gazed up into the beautiful face. "And I promise that I will share my M&Ms with you, even the greenies, as long as I get to pick out the name."

"Oh you're a wily one. I'll agree to that providing I have veto power."

"Agreed. I love you, Angel Girl."

"I love you too, Poet Fellow."

Chapter 20

"You think there's a need for this? You never struck me as the religious type before."

Steven watched her graceful movements as Natalie stapled a sheet protector containing a hand written flyer to the wooden telephone pole next to the greenhouse. It had become Liberty's message board. People who offered services or products with which to barter posted their ads here.

NON-DENOMINATIONAL WORSHIP SERVICE
TOMORROW AND EVERY SUNDAY
ONE HOUR AFTER SUNRISE
TRINITY UNITED METHODIST CHURCH
WE NEED GOD MORE THAN EVER BEFORE!
ALL ARE WELCOME!

"There's a lot you don't know about me. Unless you plan on obstructing our religious freedom, I suggest you give us one hour every Sunday to do something other than the jobs you've assigned us."

He considered a reply; discarded it. "I'm guessing your new beau will be giving the sermon?"

"That's correct. He's quite good. I think people will want to hear what he has to say. They need sustenance for their souls as well as their bodies."

He laughed at the parrot-like delivery. These weren't her words. They were Calvin's.

"If you say so," he said with a smile. "Maybe I'll attend. I haven't been inside that church since I was a kid."

"This isn't a joke. You don't need to be there if you're not interested in the spiritual message."

"I can't watch the show for secular entertainment? That doesn't seem fair."

"Keep it up, Steven. You'll offend the true believers and alienate your minions."

He felt the sting of her word choice. "I don't have minions. This is a majority rules democracy."

She snorted, diminishing her beauty exponentially.

"Right. What's that old chestnut? Whoever has the gold makes the rules? Your food cache and antibiotics bought your position."

There had been some grumbling along this line, but he had dismissed it. Anyone could speak up during town hall meetings. All complaints were addressed, despite how trivial they may be. Every significant issue was put to a vote. If people didn't like the job he was doing, let them step up to the plate and take over. Carrying the burden of a hundred daily decisions and taking responsibility for them when they fizzled, would probably cost him a few years on the back end. Marilyn had remarked how much grayer his beard was now.

It occurred to him who might have instigated these rumblings of discontent.

"What my generosity bought me was less food for my own family. You think you can do a better job, Natalie? It's yours for the taking. Just understand that you'll get about half the beauty sleep you require and a lot more gray hair. I don't see you making those kinds of sacrifices."

He knew the last comment was childish, but it slipped out before he could stop it. She was baiting him and he gobbled up the worm even though he should have known there was a barbed hook inside.

"Interesting that you feel that way. While I don't find the idea of supreme leadership appealing, there might be others who do. Enjoy your day, Steven." She flashed a smile that could have graced the cover of a celebrity magazine, then glided down the street toward the hospital. Her body language told him she knew he watched. He turned his back in annoyance.

The plastic sheeting of the greenhouse was dewy with condensation. He stepped through the opening that had been reinforced now with an actual glass door, and into the humid, warmish interior. Several people were bent over greenery; watering, tending, scrutinizing every leaf for signs of disease.

"Steven! Come take a look at these bad boys," Lisa hollered from the far side of the structure.

When he stood beside the diminutive blond, he saw the source of her excitement. Dozens of neat rows of fernlike sprouts filled the raised beds. Below the feathery leaves, orange shoulders poked up from the black soil. Steven's stomach rumbled.

"Are they ready to harvest?"

She grinned. "Yes. I'm hungry for them too. Normally we would only take what we can eat at the time. Carrots can stay in the ground for many weeks after they're ripe, as long as it doesn't freeze. But we'll pull these guys up, and plant more seedlings. They'll need to be stored somewhere dry and cool. Since the commissary is heated, I don't think that's the best place. What about your root cellar?"

He shook his head. "I think that might send the wrong signal."

She nodded in understanding. "I'll figure something else out. I saw you out there talking to Natalie. Don't listen to her. Most everyone thinks you're doing a great job and are grateful for your leadership, no matter how it came to be."

So there was more to the grumbling than he had assumed. *Never underestimate the ingratitude of the masses.* Of course his contributions earned him some deference at first, but wasn't it his knowledge and talent that kept him in charge?

"Do you think we should have an election? Make it more official? I don't want it said that I bought my position."

"The same people who said that in the beginning are the ones who are still saying it. I don't think that's the general consensus. Don't worry about it," she gave him a crooked grin. "But because you're Steven, you will worry about it. So have an election if it will put your mind to rest. You'll win by a landslide, then people won't have a damn thing to complain about. But of course they still will. We'll always have a few bad apples."

He nodded, distracted. He was considering how the process would be done and tallying the votes he knew he could count on. It might not be the landslide Lisa predicted. He realized something about himself at that moment: despite the lack of sleep, the endless decision-making, and the weighty burden of responsibility, he loved being at the helm of this community. In hindsight, his life with Jeffrey for those first months had been a hollow existence. Their physical needs had been the focus, not their emotional and intellectual well-being. He would miss his prominent role as the keystone of the society they were building, if he were to lose it.

And he wouldn't give it up without a fight.

Chapter 21

"Do you know she's instructing her people to report any dissident behavior? I'm not talking about new residents either. I mean the people who have been here from the beginning," Julia said.

"I don't have time for this. I want to be at the church before the sermon begins," Steven replied.

"I've been trying to talk to you about it for a week. Ever since the night that we lost Thoozy."

"Then it can wait for a couple more hours, right?" Steven tugged on his boots and tied the laces while his sister watched with annoyance.

"You've decided to get religion? Please. I know you better than that."

"I need to make an appearance, and I want to get a better feel for that bible-thumper."

"How disappointing. My brother, the pragmatic, plain-talking, forthright guy, is now a spying politician."

"That was harsh. Why are your panties in such a wad? Dani is keeping this town safe and I'm trying to keep it from imploding. That preacher is in cahoots with Natalie. I think the two of them have cooked something up together. World domination, probably. Or at least Liberty domination."

"Why do you think so?"

"Call it a gut instinct. So can we talk about this later, please?" He shrugged into his jacket and glanced back at his sister. The expression she wore was an older but equally fierce version of one he frequently saw on Dani's face. An idea popped into his head. One that would accomplish two things: getting Julia off his back about Dani, and coming clean about the resemblance between the two. He should have mentioned it long before now.

He stepped back into the warmth of his living room and took his sister's hands in his own. Her eyes opened wide at the sudden shift in mood and demeanor.

"How many years ago did you give the baby up for adoption?"

"What? Why the hell are you asking me that question?"

"Please, this is important. How many years ago?"

"Twenty-two years and three months." Her lips were pressed into a tight, thin line. "You're an asshole. You know how much that hurts."

"Did you know that Dani was adopted? Have you thought about how similar you and she look? Do you even realize that despite the slight Texan accent, her speech pattern is just like yours? Have you noticed the way you both stand with your arms crossed too close to whomever has just pissed you off? The other night it was like watching a young Julia arguing with the current Julia. The similarities are too uncanny to be a coincidence. I thought you might have seen it, but I think it's that forest-trees thing."

Her mouth was half open, but nothing came out. Steven kissed his sister on the cheek and pulled the door shut behind him.

"Brothers and sisters, welcome! What a joyous day this is. Finally we shall get to work on healing our spirit. Of course it's important to keep the body healthy, for it is the vessel which houses our immortal, sacred self...that part of us which, through God's grace, allows us to live forever. But what has become of our souls in these trying times?"

An unintentional snort escaped Steven. *Trying?* An abysmally inadequate word choice. Several heads turned in his direction then swiveled back to face the charismatic man at the pulpit. Calvin's appearance was impeccable. The white shirt unbuttoned at the neck was pristine, a near-miraculous accomplishment in a world without electric washing machines. Of course, the clothing, the perfect hair, and the freshly shaven face (another anomaly these days), had been planned and orchestrated to achieve one goal: to acquire admirers and followers. It was so contrived, he had to stifle another disdainful snort. What man took the time to fuss over his clothes and his hair when their very survival was on the line?

"I'll tell you what has happened to it. It has atrophied like an underused muscle. Like a rose desiccating in a bone-dry vase, your spiritual being has been neglected and is also withering away. It is dangerously close to shriveling up and dying. But it's not too late, brothers and sisters. It's not too late to water it with God's word, to feed it with God's love, and to resurrect it with God's mercy. I'm here to tell you that we have stopped the patient's bleeding just in the nick of time!"

Steven rolled his eyes at the cornball metaphors, then swept a covert glance across the room. From the pews of the Trinity United Methodist Church, thirty faces were gazing at the speaker with universal expressions of joy. Steven's smirk faded. He leaned back against the uncomfortable wooden bench and crossed his arms. His eyes narrowed as he watched the preacher, then narrowed further as he glanced at the back of Natalie's head on the front center pew.

"We are here for such a short time, yet the actions we take and the behavior in which we engage while we are here on this earth will determine whether we enter the kingdom of heaven. And it makes for some tough choices, folks. I won't sugarcoat it. Sometimes a sin feels justified at the moment. It seems like the logical thing to do for a million different reasons. But that's just Satan's little trick of muddying the waters...of clouding your thoughts. A sin is a sin is a sin. God made them crystal clear for us when he directed Moses to carry those tablets down from Mount Sinai. How many of those Ten Commandments have we honored? All of them? Some of them? None of them? Do you even remember what they are?"

The eyes blazed. The indulgent smile was gone, replaced by a frown that managed to convey both disappointment and affection; the face of a father whose children have misbehaved.

"Let me recite them, in case you've forgotten, being too distracted with the business of keeping the physical vessel alive."

A tight knot formed in the pit of Steven's stomach as he studied the enthralled faces of a significant number of Liberty's citizens. His citizens. His people.

"You will not take God's name in vain. You will honor your parents. You will not kill." The blazing eyes rested on Steven for a heartbeat before continuing. "You will not commit adultery. You will not steal. You will not bear false witness. You will not covet your neighbor's wife, nor your neighbor's possessions. You will remember to keep the Sabbath Day holy. And now folks, the most important commandment of all: you will worship the Lord your God and will serve only him. You will put no other before him. And if there is one who would ask that you do so, who would suggest that you put someone or something before the Lord your God and his commandments, then you must know that creature is the instrument of Satan."

Natalie was also studying the congregation, taking their measure. When her attention came to rest on Steven, she paused, then smiled.

He had never hit a woman in his life, but at that moment, it seemed well within the realm of possibility.

"Thank you for coming, Steven. I realize this," an elegant gesture encompassed the church and the would-be parishioners who were exiting through the open doorway, "is not your forte."

Steven had waited on the stoop to get a word with the preacher himself, standing in line for the honor; the delay did nothing to improve his mood.

"You could say that." His smile felt phony even to himself, whereas Calvin's actually looked sincere. "But I like to keep tabs on everything that goes on here in our town. Well, at least the important stuff."

"On that we agree. What could be more important than the well-being of our immortal souls?"

Steven bit off a tart retort, aware of the eavesdropping crowd. He pondered the words he wanted to say to the preacher, allowing a few seconds to mentally smooth some of their rough edges – gritty river rocks orbiting in a polishing tumbler. The gems that emerged were infinitely lovelier than what first went in.

"You're new here, sir. If your intentions are as honorable as I'd like to believe, then you are welcome to stay. I think you're correct about one thing and that is what is at stake in these perilous times. You call it a soul, I call it humanity. Despite the difference in verbiage and the ramifications of our actions on a so-called afterlife, what we do now is crucial. It has been my job to keep these people alive, and we've done that. We'll continue doing that, as long as we all cooperate. I understand the importance of keeping everyone physically healthy. Soon after arriving here, my clever sister Julia realized that our emotional and psychological health also needed to be addressed."

"Yes, indeed. I've attended one of her sessions. She's quite a woman, and I applaud her...efforts."

"I think you could be helpful in achieving our goal of a robust, flourishing, and humane society."

Steven extended his hand. Calvin grasped it in his own non-calloused one. Before releasing his grip, Steven leaned in close to whisper into the ear of Liberty's new religious leader.

"If you fuck with me or what I've accomplished here, I will have you dropped down a hole so dark and deep, you will never see the light of day again."

When he pulled away, Steven's smile was as genuine as the preacher's had seemed moments earlier.

Chapter 22

"Just a few more minutes. I want to make sure this place is as abandoned as it appears." Pablo whispered.

The five members of the HG crew squatted next to an immaculate, cherry-colored barn. Most manmade structures were beginning to deteriorate, being denied the necessary upkeep from the ravages of Midwest weather. Weeds had forged new avenues of ingress into the blacktop of those roadways linking the towns and cities of Kansas. There were no Sunday drivers, no vacationing families, and no long-haul truckers to keep them squashed down; no Department of Transportation workers to splash hot tar into their cracks. Snow and ice resumed the work the summer weeds had begun. Paint flaked off the sides of buildings and houses in ever-widening patches. Triangular shards of glass clung to window casings like glittering vampire fangs. Everywhere metal was rusting and lumber was rotting. Nature was reclaiming that which had been hers all along, having evicted the majority of her most troublesome tenants.

The nearby farmhouse was much less pristine than the barn. It would seem that rural Kansans put the comfort of their animals before that of their own families. Still, Pablo didn't get the sense it was empty. There were no obvious signs of habitation; no smoke curled from the lopsided chimney and no footprints were visible in the inch of snow that had fallen the night before. But something told him they were not alone on this parcel of farmland which lay about a hundred miles northwest of Liberty. It was the farthest they had ventured so far. He knew a day would soon come when their morning-to-evening forays would evolve into overnight excursions, and then weekly missions, as the surrounding countryside became as depleted of useful items as the cities had.

That's why capturing the Holstein and her calf was so important. Worst case, it would mean milk right away, then cheese and butter soon after. Best case, if they could also find the bull that had knocked up the spotted bovine and produced the calf currently scampering twenty yards away, they would officially be in the ranching business. Livestock and crops were true sustainability, not this increasingly difficult job of picking through the bones of a dead world.

"Good thing we brought the trailer," someone whispered. "We'd be kicking ourselves if we hadn't."

Pablo nodded, distracted. Bringing the livestock trailer had been a calculated risk. The precious extra gasoline required to tow the hulking beast had been remarked upon by a number of Liberty's more vocal citizens. But like Pablo, Steven understood it as an investment in their future – one that hadn't paid off so far. They had lugged it along on the last seven outings and no hooved animals had returned in its belly.

Today might be the day, though. All they had to do was catch the mama and the baby would follow. But first, he needed to make sure the area was secure and his people were reasonably safe. Cattle rustling was an offense punishable by death back in the Old West. And so it was again, as evidenced by the healing buckshot wound of one of his people.

"Come on, let's get 'er done. I don't think there's anyone in that house." The person who spoke was a grizzled, scrappy man in his sixties. He was a fearless little fellow with an intellectual capacity well below average; but he could lasso a tree stump or a sprinting feral piglet ten times out of ten. He was remarkable.

"Festus, that kind of thinking is what put those holes in your backside."

"Who the heck is Festus? I'm Zane."

"I know. It was a joke. Didn't you ever watch *Gunsmoke*?"

"Oh, right! Yep, I sure did. Marshall Dillon, now there's a tough sumbitch. I remember that gimpy little guy now. What was his name? Fescue? That show was on way before your time!"

Pablo smiled. Despite the intellectual disparity, Zane was his favorite crew member; amiable, friendly, and as quick to follow orders as he was to offer a kind word or a happy grin, the effect of which was not diminished by all the missing teeth.

"Reruns. Anyway, I just have a feeling. Let's stay here a bit longer and watch."

"Okay, boss. Your feelins is usually right, but if them cows get away, you're gonna take some heat overn'it."

"Wouldn't be the first time. Won't be the last." Pablo kept his voice low and his focus on the farmhouse. They had done a cursory check of the barn and found it empty of anything edible. Broken, rust-eaten shovels and rakes were piled in a corner amongst scattered hay. Intact but dust-covered farm implements and garden tools hung on hooks in tidy rows on one wall. They would load those in the trailer before leaving.

Pablo's instincts told him anything of interest would be in the run-down house. The barn almost felt like a misdirection. Its sanguine paint is what had caught their attention from the farm-to-market road they had been driving down. The tiny shotgun house with the sagging roof looked decidedly unpromising, so much so in comparison to the barn that its dilapidation felt intentional. What do you do when you know the magician wants you to watch his left hand?

You keep your eyes glued to the other hand.

As Zane had said, Pablo's feelings were usually right. He had become adept these past weeks and months at not only securing food, but keeping his people safe in the process. His success rate was vastly superior to that of Ted, his predecessor. Since then, nobody had been killed, a fact of which he was more proud than the largesse of the forays. He had a sixth sense about danger that had saved their hides on several occasions during his stint as leader of the HG crew.

Pablo leaned his head back to whisper a directive to the four people huddling behind him. If he hadn't, the bullet that whizzed past his ear would have smashed into his skull instead.

"Everyone down! Lock and load!" He no longer bothered to whisper. They had been discovered and were under attack. The shot came from a copse of trees to the west of the house, a three o'clock position to the house's high noon. He dug binoculars from the pocket of his fleece-lined pants. Another bullet zinged over the top of his woolen beanie.

"Into the barn!"

Pablo was the last to scramble inside, staying low to the ground and somehow managing to evade the additional five shots fired upon them during their retreat.

"Everyone okay?" He asked, his rapid breaths spewing vapor in the chilly interior as he peered through a knothole in one of the wooden planks.

"I got winged, boss. Ain't no big deal. Just a little scrape."

Pablo rushed to the older man, who sat on the earthen floor against the far wall.

"Let me see."

Zane pulled a bloodied hand away from his abdomen. Pablo's heart sank. A gut shot rarely ended well these days.

"Lie down. I need to look at it," he said, his voice gentle as he peeled back the older man's clothing. Blood as bright as the paint on the surrounding walls oozed from a section of pale, hairy skin just next to the belly button. With unsteady hands, Pablo reached around the skinny torso to feel for an exit wound. There was none.

"It's still in there."

"I know, boss. I can feel her."

"Get the kit, Missy," he said to the curly-haired woman squatting beside him.

"Right here." She handed him a thick gauze pad, then continued to rifle through their first-aid supplies. "I'm looking for the Quick-Clot."

"Good." Pablo sniffed at an unpleasant odor as he pressed the square of woven cotton against the bleeding dime-sized hole.

"Looky here, boss. You need to tend to that shooter. He's prolly on his way over right now. We're sittin ducks here."

The other two members of the HG crew – a slender quiet young man with sad brown eyes and surprising strength, and his twin brother – had taken up positions near two of the three windows of the barn wall facing the copse of trees. The monozygotic twins were physical carbon copies of each other, but their dissimilar personalities made it easy to tell which one was Bobby Kennedy and which one was Jack. They were known in Liberty simply as The Twins. It had taken Pablo a few weeks before he could address them by their names without thinking of dead presidents and American dynasties.

"Boss, I think I see someone coming," said Bobby, whose gregarious personality didn't match his mournful eyes.

"Make that two someones," his brother muttered. Jack was a stoic. He doled out his words grudgingly, a starving man made to share his few morsels of food with someone not nearly as hungry.

"Get the binoculars. There on the ground. Rifles?" Pablo asked as he removed the blood-soaked gauze and sprinkled Quick-Clot into the bullet wound. The zeolite beads slowed the blood flow, but did not diminish the fecal odor. He knew what that meant.

"Yes," Bobby replied as he pressed the field glasses against the filmy glass pane. "Two dudes. One is carrying a Bushmaster, I think. The other has a Colt. Both semis."

"Jack, look out the other side."

The young man peered through the window on the opposite side of the barn.

"Damn. Four more coming from this direction."

"We're in a world of trouble," Zane said, grabbing Pablo's arm to get his attention. "I'm a goner. You know it and I know it. I know the smell of shit as good as the next feller. That there bullet nicked my, what do ya call it? Colon? I call it a poop bag. All that shit's circulatin in my blood already. Septic tank, I think is what it's called when that happens. Anyways, ain't nothin can be done about it neither."

"Wrong. Antibiotics will help," Pablo replied. He would not lose a man. Not on his watch.

"Boss, listen. Even if you get me back home in the next couple of hours, it'll still be too late. That's even if we can get that chubby broad to give me any pills. In the meantime, those fellers out there are a'comin for us. Now go tend to that. I mean it."

Zane gave him a weak shove and pulled the bloody shirt back over his belly.

"Go on now!"

Pablo sighed then scrambled to a third window.

"How fast are they coming?"

"Slowly. They're being cautious."

"Same on this side. Careful. Not exposing themselves," Jack said. "They're dressed in camouflage. They're fanned out and moving through the trees toward us." The young man paused then added, "They don't move like hayseeds with guns."

Pablo's mind raced while he scanned the interior of the barn, looking for anything that might spark an idea for escape. His gaze slid over the earthen floor for the fourth or fifth time. Finally, something that his subconscious had been trying to tell him found its way to his conscious mind. The floor was compacted dirt, tidy and level. The entire building was immaculate in a way that seemed odd. Now, the pile of strewn hay and broken garden tools that were concentrated in a corner seemed even more out of place. Everything was so clean and neat, except that area. Pablo darted toward it. He used the toe of his boot to kick away the straw but when it connected with a rusted hoe, it wouldn't budge. It had been nailed down, as had the rest of the surrounding items.

"Missy bring me that broom from the wall!"

Moments later, the straw had been swept from a rectangular wooden surface, three feet by four feet. He yanked on an exposed eyebolt, pulling up the trap door and revealing concrete steps that disappeared into inky blackness. He clicked on a flashlight but nothing could be seen in the circle of light other than a packed dirt floor at the bottom of the steps.

"We go down there, we'll really be sitting ducks," Bobby said.

"Yes," Pablo replied, distracted. "If it's just a cellar or storm shelter, that's true." Something told him it was more though; that same something that had kept his people alive for weeks, and himself alive during the violent crumbling of society.

"You all get down there," Zane said. "I'll cover it back up and tell 'em you hightailed it outta here."

"I can't let you do that."

The older man struggled to his feet and shuffled over to the group who now circled the open trap door.

"I'll take out as many as I can first though," he continued. "I got my bowie and my Smith and Wesson. I may be dyin but I can still pick a fly off a shit truck from twenty yards with either of 'em. You youngsters got lotsa life left to live. I'm done in. Now get on down there."

"I can't let you do that," Pablo repeated, with less conviction now. Zane was right. He was dying, and his willing sacrifice just might save the others. The problem was, what if Zane didn't kill all their assailants, and the stairs lead to a dead end and not the tunnel Pablo's gut whispered of? The remaining adversaries could weigh down the door from above and they would be trapped down there, left to starve to death.

But something told him it was indeed a tunnel; perhaps his instincts had been fine-tuned these past months. Maybe when they had been outside surveilling the area, he had noticed a detail but hadn't yet processed its significance. Hell, maybe some of Maddie's newfound psychic ability had rubbed off on him. Wherever it came from, he knew they were looking at one end of a passageway that lead away from the barn.

"They're gonna be here any second now." The kind eyes were pleading.

Pablo grabbed his friend, gathering him into a hug and getting blood all over his coat in the process. The other three took turns doing the same.

"Everyone down the stairs. Zane, I don't believe in heaven, but I still hope that's where you end up."

"It's okay. You don't have to believe in Heaven. I believe enough for both of us. I'll see you on the other side, boss."

Pablo watched from the steps as Zane closed the door on himself and the daylight. They could hear him shuffling around above, replacing the swept hay. The flashlight beam revealed a wooden plank ceiling held in place by cinder block walls spaced five feet apart. The walls didn't widen to become a room, but extended into darkness as far as the light could reach.

A tunnel.

It smelled like damp earth and fresh lumber. This was not an old smuggler's tunnel left over from Prohibition, nor an ancient section of Underground Railroad used during the Civil War. It was newly built, and its purpose was something about which Pablo could only speculate.

"I don't have a good feeling about this," Missy said, her eyes owl-like in the gloom. "What's on the other end of this could be worse than what we might be facing with those guys."

"I know what you're saying. But there were six of them against five of us. Four and a half with Zane not at full capacity. They could have waited us out. Let us freeze or starve. That's if they didn't just rush us from all directions."

"I agree, boss," Jack said. "Something about those guys, the way they moved felt, I don't know, soldierly. You know what I mean?"

"Yes. We don't know what we're dealing with here, but I think this tunnel wasn't meant to be found by us. I think our odds are better taking our chances with it rather than waiting for them to come to us. Agreed?"

Three heads nodded in unison.

"Let's go then."

Pablo preceded his crew down the claustrophobic passageway. He held the flashlight in one hand and his shotgun in the other. It had served him well all this time, and he had no intention of upgrading. Besides, he was no sharpshooter. His contribution to the group was his intellect.

"Looks like there's a wall up ahead. The passageway goes left and right."

The next moment they stood at the T-intersection. The air smelled different here; top notes of something pleasant mingled with the fragrance of earth and lumber. Pablo had a flash of Sunday afternoons at his abuela's casita – plates of cabrito, heavy with cumin and other Mexican spices placed around the dinner table. He inhaled deeply, noticing an underlying aroma of something else...something that evoked unwelcome memories of the time shortly after Chicxulub.

It was the smell of death.

"Which way, boss?" Bobby asked, pointing his flashlight down the left passageway while Pablo's beam illuminated the right. Nothing but more tunnel could be seen in either direction.

Faint sounds of gunfire echoed from behind.

Four people exchanged knowing expressions. With his own life, Zane was buying them the precious gift of time. They damn well better make the most of it.

"You smell that, Missy?"

"Yeah. It smells like stew. Beef or goat, maybe. Something else though, too. I can't place it. There's also wood smoke...hickory? Might be apple. Not sure." In Missy's former life, she had been the youngest Michelin-starred chef in the country.

"Can you tell which direction it's coming from?"

The petite woman stepped from behind the men and walked several feet into the tunnel on the left, then into the one on the right.

"It's hard to tell. There's something bad too." She closed her eyes and repeated the process, lifting her freckled nose upward like a bloodhound.

She opened her eyes and said, "Dead bodies on the left. Stew on the right."

"That means we go right, right?"

Pablo hesitated, struggling to interpret the meaning of the disparate aromas. There were too many unknowns; both brain and gut were drawing blanks.

"We're splitting up," Pablo said finally.

"No way," Bobby said. "We're a team."

"Think about it. If one door is the Lady and one door is the Tiger, then at least two of us will survive."

Jack nodded in understanding. "I remember that story. Makes sense, boss."

"Who gets the stew and who gets the dead bodies?" Bobby asked. A thin ring of brown surrounded his dilated pupils. The eyes were no longer sad. They were unhappy and afraid.

"I think first we need to decide teams."

"What do you mean? I'm staying with my brother."

Jack shook his head. "We gotta split up, bro. We're the best shooters," he said. He had grasped Pablo's logic.

"That's right. Missy is safer with one of you two than she is with me."

"Hey, I'm right here. I resent the implication that I need to be protected."

All three remaining members of the HG crew began talking at once. He gave them exactly five seconds before cutting them off.

"That's it. Time's out and the decision is made. Jack, you take Missy down the stew tunnel. Bobby and I will take the other. This isn't a democracy. Now let's hurry the hell up. If you escape, go back to the truck and hide somewhere in the surrounding area where you can keep an eye on it. If the others don't show up within an hour, go get reinforcements. That's the plan."

A minute later, Missy and Jack were out of sight, gobbled up by blackness.

"The smell is getting worse," Bobby said from behind him. The lug soles of their boots made no sound on the compacted earth.

"Yes, it is. There's another turn coming up."

It was an L-intersection this time. No decisions to make other than going forward or backward. When they rounded the corner, the stench of death intensified; they walked into a miasma of putrefaction tinged with sulfur, ammonia, and feces.

He heard Bobby slide the clip out of his handgun, then clicked it back into place.

"Full mag?"

"Yep. Twelve rounds in the Glock and twelve in the Remi."

"Good." Pablo himself carried a dozen shotgun shells in the pocket of his down jacket. He could get to them quickly there. "Stairs up ahead."

The next moment they tiptoed up the cinder block steps. He aimed the flashlight's beam on a second trap door, identical to the one in the barn.

"Ready?"

"Ready, boss."

He pressed against the rough wooden surface. It lifted. Nothing was weighing it down, nor locking it in place. He peered through the two-inch opening. A scene from the goriest of slasher films awaited him.

Meat hooks lined two sides of a ramshackle structure. Enough dust-moted sunlight slivered through the weathered boards to illuminate the dangling carcasses. He identified a cow, four deer, a goat, two tusked feral hogs, and several large dogs. Flesh had been neatly removed from some; others were intact. None of these were what drew Pablo's attention.

Three carcasses at the end of one of the rows were human.

As with the animals, they were in various stages of being processed; the genitalia revealed two females and one male. Thankfully they were all adults. That fact was what kept Pablo's breakfast in his stomach.

"What do you see?" Bobby whispered from below.

"Your worst nightmare."

He raised the door a few inches farther and stuck head and shotgun through the opening. In addition to the carnage hanging from hooks, there was a large wire cage in one corner. He couldn't see what was inside. He pushed the door the rest of the way open and stepped onto the floor of the death house; the soil was fouled and mucky with viscera, urine, and shit.

If there was indeed a hell, it wasn't at the center of the earth. It was right here in Concordia, Kansas.

Bobby stood beside him now, silent and horrified. A mouse-like stirring came from the cage. Both firearms swiveled toward it. Pablo clicked the flashlight on.

Two pairs of eyes gazed back at him.

"Close the door and stand on it. I don't want anyone coming up behind us. Keep your gun on the other one." He indicated a large double door on one side of the building, its wooden planks appeared to be a new addition to the ancient structure.

When he got closer to the cage, the occupants crawled to the farthest corner. The original tenants might have been chickens, but the door was heavily reinforced with barbed wire. A length of chain and a grimy padlock secured it well beyond the requirements of containing poultry. He stepped a few feet away to vomit, wiped his mouth with the back of a hand, and shined the light upon the two blinking humans huddled there.

"We're here to help," he said, clenching his teeth against a rebellious gag reflex. He could make out their ragged clothing now, sadly inadequate to protect against the cold weather, and hair so matted it was impossible to discern its color. The most disturbing detail was their size.

"My name is Pablo. What's yours?"

"Are you here to eat us?" The child's voice was strong. Defiant even.

"No. We're here to rescue you."

"If you're here to eat us, there's not much meat on us. You'd be smart to wait a bit longer. Let us grow up and make more meat."

Pablo felt hot tears coursing down his cheeks. "What is your name, child? Is that your sister? I promise we're not here to eat you. We're here to save you."

Even through the layers of filth, he could see a transformation on the small face: the dawning of hope.

"I'm Rebecca and this is my big sister, Tiffany. She doesn't talk any more. If you mean it, about the rescuing, you better hurry. One of them comes to bring us food about this time of the day." The wide eyes darted toward a patch of sunlight on the mucky floor, an improvised sundial.

He studied the padlock, wondering how he would get it off.

"The key is above the door. See that ledge? You may need to get something to stand on. The guy that usually gets it is the tallest one. I think he might be a giant."

He found a rusted metal bucket by the door that would serve as a stepstool, then ran his fingers along the ledge until they connected with an object. The padlock key.

He fumbled with the lock on the cage door, snapping it open after several attempts. His hands were shaking, making him clumsy, and his eyes were blurry with tears that he didn't have time for.

The children crawled through the opening, the shorter girl leading the taller one by the hand. Tiffany looked about twelve-years-old; Rebecca, no more than eight. Despite the height and age difference, she was the one in charge. The big sister didn't look at him, but rather through him, with the vacant stare of someone who had shut down.

"She hasn't said anything in a long time," Rebecca said. "I miss her talking, but mostly I miss her singing. She has a beautiful voice. Well...had. The problem is going to be the big door. They take that key with them."

"We could go back down the tunnel, boss," Bobby finally spoke up. His face was wet too.

"Whatever you're going to do, you need to do it soon." She might have been commenting on a school bus rounding the corner.

Pablo tried the latch handle of the double door. It was locked. The heavy-duty hardware displayed *Schlage* embossing at the top. "They could be coming up the tunnel," he said.

"Yeah, or they could be twenty feet away from that door," Bobby replied.

The smaller child watched the discourse between the adults, then blew out an exasperated breath.

"Just kick through one of those boards in the wall. They can't be very sturdy. See how old this building is? But you need to hurry up. If I was big enough, I'd do it myself, but I'm just a kid."

Pablo grinned, despite the horrific circumstances.

Three minutes later, he broke through a segment of weathered lumber. All four squeezed through the opening into a thicket of winter-bare cottonwood trees. He could the red paint of the barn fifty yards away.

"This way, girls." He took off in the direction of the pickup, followed by the children and Bobby bringing up the rear. "Stay close to the ground and be as quiet as possible."

"Duh," Rebecca whispered.

A half hour had passed waiting in some brush, and still there'd been no sign of Missy or Jack. Pablo felt exposed here. He could only hope that Zane had been successful in taking out most of the hunters. Otherwise, it was just a matter of time before they were discovered hiding next to the pickup with the attached trailer.

"Boss, we gotta go back."

"You know that wasn't the plan. If they're not here it's because they're in trouble. If they're in trouble, it's because they couldn't handle the situation themselves, which means we should go get help. We'll bring back a dozen people armed to the teeth and eradicate these abominations from the face of the earth."

"And in the meantime, they could die. Jack is alive now. It's a twin thing …I can feel it in my bones. It's a four-hour round trip back to Liberty, plus the time it'll take to gather everyone up. My brother could be murdered any minute. Or worse." The brown eyes glanced in the direction of the death house, no longer visible from the farm-to-market road.

Pablo understood the young man's urgency. If it were Maddie, he would feel the same way. But he had a responsibility as the leader to make logical, non-emotional decisions, especially when it came to their safety.

"Going back down that tunnel would be reckless. We don't know how many of those guys Zane got, nor how many are still out there."

"You don't have to go into the tunnel," Rebecca said between bites of the shoestring potatoes and bean dip Pablo had given her. Her sister sat silently on the ground, wrapped in a blanket and oblivious to the food.

"What do you mean?" He squatted down to the child's level.

"If they went down the other side of the tunnel...the one that doesn't go to where we were, then they're in the house. The one where all the food gets cooked." She swiped two small fingers in the can and stuck them in her mouth.

He tried not to think about how filthy those fingers were. "You mean the one with the crooked chimney and the sagging roof?"

The matted head nodded. "Yep. It looks nicer on the inside than it does on the outside. I was in there once just for a minute. It smelled really good. There were ladies cooking all kinds of stuff on two big stoves that had blue fire coming out of them. I've never seen stoves like that. The one we had at home had the rings that turned orange when they got hot."

"What about the men, Rebecca? Do you know how many there are?"

"I didn't see any men in there. Just the ladies. The only men I saw were the ones who caught me and Tiff and took us to the meat house. That's what they call it."

"So you didn't enter the cooking house through the tunnel?"

"Nope. They took us through the back door, but then we went down the tunnel later to get to the meat house. That's also how the guys bring us food. They use it as much as possible, I heard them say. It's to keep from being seen. Anyway, they wanted the ladies to look at us first. I didn't know why they felt all around our bellies and squeezed our arms and legs...and pinched our bottoms too. But I know now. They were checking to see how much meat we had on us."

Pablo's stomach lurched.

"Pretty awful, huh?" she said casually, as if noticing a broken shoelace.

"Yeah, pretty awful."

"I had a lot of time to think when me and Tiff were in the cage. I figure these people are like the witch from Hansel and Gretel. Except there's more of them, and that house sure isn't made out of gingerbread."

"I think you're right. What else can you tell us?"

The bean dip-covered fingers paused in the can while the child pondered the question.

"I think if you want to find this guy's brother and that other girl, you better not wait. I think the witch people will have them up on hooks in no time."

"If we go back to the barn to see about Zane and find out how many of those bastards he got, we could trip the same motion detectors, or whatever they're using, that told them we were there the first time. We should go straight to the cook house."

Pablo nodded, distracted. He was trying to think through all the possible scenarios, but there were just too many. Cannibalism wasn't terribly surprising given the food shortages now that more than a year had passed since Chicxulub. But the systemization of it, from the initial luring and trapping of humans, to their grisly demise in the meat house, and then their final resting place in a stew pot, was unfathomable.

Good god. How could people be so evil?

"Bobby, I hate to say this, but I think we should split up. One of us should go back to the barn, then through the tunnel. The other flanks the barn, giving it a wide berth, and hits the back door of the cook house. That way they can't get us both at the same time and the other still has a chance of saving Jack and Missy."

The young man nodded. "I agree. Which are you taking?"

"You're better with firearms. You take the house."

Another quick nod. "Good luck, boss. I hope to see you soon."

The next moment he was gone. Pablo squatted down beside the girls where they sat on the cold ground. The older child gazed serenely at a spot above his head, never tempted to make the journey two inches down to his face. Julia would have her hands full with this one, assuming any of them got out of there alive.

"Rebecca, you two stay here and stay hidden. If none of us come back in an hour, take your sister and run as far away from here as you can. Will you do that?"

A bob of the filthy head. "Got any more food? I'll try to get Tiff to eat something."

He removed the keys from his pants and pressed them into the small, grimy hand. "Be quick about it. Every second that you're near that truck, you've got a big target on your back. Do you understand that?"

"Duh. I know what a target is."

"Take care of your sister, then. We'll be back as soon as we can."

As he trudged off in the direction of the barn, he heard a melodic child's voice.

"Are those two men going to eat us?"

The little sister replied, "No, I don't think so. I think they're good guys."

The melodic voice again, "I don't think there are any of those left."

Soon he was out of earshot. He shifted focus back to the dangers at hand, dismissing thoughts of the two huddled children and the horrors they had endured. Dismissing thoughts of the baby – his baby – that Maddie carried inside her. Dismissing thoughts of what he would do to anyone that hurt that baby or its mother. He needed to concentrate on the task at hand: saving his people and keeping himself alive for his family.

But if he found any of those cannibals still breathing, he would not hesitate to execute them.

###

Five minutes later, he was back at the barn. The door stood open. The pungent scent of gunpowder mingled with the metallic tang of blood. He squatted next to the door for a few seconds, took a deep breath, then charged through the opening.

Zane had done a thorough job.

Five men lay spread out on the compacted dirt floor. A quick check revealed they were all dead. A bullet hole in the forehead of four of the men explained their demise. The fifth sprouted an enormous bowie knife from his chest. Vacant eyes stared back at Pablo as he went from body to body. When he reached Zane slumped against a wall in the corner near the trap door, he could see a barely perceptible rise and fall of the skinny chest. He touched the hand that still clutched the Smith and Wesson. Eyes fluttered open.

"I done it, boss."

"You sure did. You saved our lives. You know something else? There were two little girls on the other end of that tunnel that you saved too. They're out waiting by the truck."

"Ah, that make me happy. You know, I think I done a pretty good job just now. Maybe I'm more like Marshall Dillon than Fescue. At least I was today."

The next moment the eyes closed. The chest didn't rise again.

Pablo laid his friend out on the ground in a more dignified position, then reached for the bolt ring and clicked on his flashlight.

He was down the steps and at the T-section of the passageway in seconds. Without hesitation, he turned right. Again the image of his grandmother's casita flashed through his mind as a pleasant aroma flowed over him, but this time the nostalgia was tainted. Thoughts of the meat that was in those stew pots stirred something to life...summoned an uncoiling from its place deep within the aggression-controlling amygdala part of his brain. Cold rage ejected the nausea from his belly, replacing its weak siblings – logic and restraint – with ruthless determination. With every placement of boot heel on dirt floor, it grew.

The man that flew up the concrete steps at the end of the tunnel and through the trap door wasn't the Poet Fellow Maddie knew.

The first sight he encountered as he sprang from the tunnel was two women and a man in a cramped kitchen. He glanced past their surprised expressions to see Jack and Missy gagged and tied in the space beyond. His shotgun pumped buckshot into the people standing next to the huge stockpots.

The man reacted quicker than the women, diving behind them into the adjoining room. Blood jettisoned from the females onto the yellowed wallpaper; chunks of bone and tissue splatted onto roosters and teapots. He stepped over their bodies as he followed the escaping man. When Pablo emerged into the room, the man was crouched behind Missy, holding a knife to her throat. Jack sat two feet away, his wrists and feet bound. A blood-stained rag covered most of his lower face.

Pablo lifted his shotgun again.

"You do that and you kill her too."

He hesitated.

"Yeah, that's what I thought." The man was enormous. Even squatting down, he seemed to fill half the room.

"You must be the giant Rebecca told me about."

"Oh, you've met the girls then?"

Pablo felt the adrenaline coursing through his veins, demanding action *NOW!* He ignored the directive, forcing his body to remain still. The last thing he wanted was to lose another crew member.

"Yes. They're safe now."

"No worries. I'll find more. Once you've eaten the tender flesh of a prepubescent girl, it's tough going back to other types of humans, let alone stringy goat." The giant grinned.

"You'll be doing it on your own. All your buddies are dead in the barn."

There was a flinch of emotion, then it vanished and the grin was back.

"I'll find more of them too, then. Right after I deal with you people. This female feels pretty good...not too muscle-bound like some of them get. The best way to soften them up is to keep them caged without any exercise. Just like veal. I'm telling you, once you've tasted it, you're ruined for any other kind of meat."

Pablo knew he was being taunted. Knew the man wanted to get a reaction from him so he could take advantage of anger-evoked carelessness. Two could play that game.

"Something tells me you have a taste for cock even more than little girls. Perhaps the reason the girls are saved for the stew pot is because the boys are tied up in a bedroom." He saw an angry spark in the man's eyes and the blade pressed deeper against Missy's throat.

"Look, asshole. You have a shotgun. There's no way you're going to use it in tight quarters like these. You know it and I know it. We'll make a deal. Set the gun down and I'll put the knife away. You all can just walk on out of here and go on about your business. I'll go on about mine. No harm, no foul. What do you say?"

"Right. We're just going to pretend you don't have human flesh simmering on the stoves in there?"

"Why should that concern you? You didn't know them. And besides, you killed my women. And my buddies in the barn, if what you say is true.

I don't think you have the moral high ground here." The man grinned again, pleased with his little speech. He had hit on a nerve, though; something in Pablo's demeanor must have given it away. "You're one of those self-righteous fucks. Is that it? Too goddamned high and mighty to stoop to eating people, yet you're willing to commit murder."

"Self-defense isn't murder."

The man's booming laughter filled the small space. "Yeah, the women were threatening you with a soup ladle...is that it?"

Jack stirred, drawing Pablo's attention away from the man for a split second. Next, three events occurred simultaneously. One would haunt him for the rest of his life.

Jack shifted from a sitting position to lying flat on the stained rug.

At the same time, something smashed through the window of the small living room striking Missy's captor in his right temple.

But what would be branded into Pablo's memory was the image of the shiny blade sliding across Missy's throat, then the white gap that followed just before her life's blood rushed to escape through the opening, turning it crimson.

The front door of the small living room crashed open. Bobby ran to his brother who lay unharmed on the carpet.

Missy and her assailant slid sideways onto the floor together in a grisly embrace.

"You did everything you could, Pablo. Please don't keep beating your-self up about it." Maddie pressed her lips against his, willing him to forgive himself. He would do anything for her – anything for his Angel Girl – but not that. He turned on his side, away from her, and pulled the heavy wool blanket over his head. He didn't want her to see the tears of a weak man.

Soon he felt her breathing regulate, deepen. He was thankful that she had fallen asleep early tonight. He wanted to watch her sleep. Wanted to see the rise and fall of her chest. Wanted to know that, for the moment, she was safe. He turned over so he could witness the dream emotions flit across her face: a quick grin, then a furrowed brow. A faint moan escaped the barely-parted lips. Pablo held his breath, then released it when the moans turned to soft snores. Better to watch Maddie than to close his eyes and see the face of a dead girl.

Down the hall, Jessie whimpered as she dreamed. Amelia was awake instantly. Ever since losing Thoozy, her slumber had been troubled and non-restorative. It was no hardship to leave it. If she survived this ordeal above ground, when she returned home she intended to sleep for a decade. She turned on her side and studied the child in the gloom, thinking about her conversation with Tung a few hours earlier; they had engaged in numerous discussions since the passing of Thoozy, yet they were no closer to gathering enough compelling evidence to justify the continued existence of human life on the planet. If anything, after hearing of Pablo's experience with the cannibals, they had lost some ground. She almost wished Tung hadn't needed to be told of that development because it nudged him more in the direction of advocating for humanity's obliteration. But there were few secrets between their kind. Their *scythen* directed the most important thoughts not only to each other, but down to the *Cthor* – the Ancient Ones. The details would be delivered in person when they were summoned below for a full disclosure of everything they had seen and experienced these recent months. And since Fergus was who-knew-where and doing who-knew-whom, she sometimes felt like humanity's solitary champion.

It was a tremendous burden and one she could have born more staunchly if she could get some decent sleep.

Jessie moaned again. Amelia slid her feet out from under the warm covers and sat down beside her. She brushed the tousled hair away from the elfin face and cooed in a language the child would not have understood.

Moments later, the eyelids fluttered open. Even the sepia tones of moonlight couldn't diminish the brilliance of the sea-green irises. They practically glowed...a lighthouse beacon reflecting off tropical waters.

"Were you dreaming of the Smiling Man?" Amelia whispered.

"Yes. I thought he saw me at first, but I think he was looking at someone else."

"Is he still coming?"

"Yes. He's closer now, but not so close that he can see where we are. Not yet."

"That's good. I wonder how much time we have?" she said more to herself than the child.

"I don't know, but I saw a sign on the side of a road. I think I was seeing it through someone else's eyes. I think his name is Lootinent Martin. Anyway, the sign said G-U-T-H-R-I-E."

"Guthrie? As in Guthrie, Oklahoma, no doubt." She drew her flannel robe tighter around her small body. "What else, child?"

"There are a lot of people with him. Some of them are bad people and some are just scared people, but they do bad things."

"How many people?"

"I don't know. I couldn't really count them," Jessie said, squirming under the intense gaze.

"Think about the space those people would fill up. Don't worry about counting them. Just tell me, if all those people were squished together in one room, what kind of room would it be? The size of the living room?"

"I think those people would need ten living rooms. Is that bad? What does it mean?"

The soulful eyes lifted toward the moon framed by the window casing. "It means it will soon be time to tell Steven. Before too much longer, we'll need to start preparing for battle."

Chapter 23

Martin sat next to his general on the cold ground. He studied the sleeping face of the man who held the power of life and death over himself and everyone else in the army, which had burgeoned since the massacre at the barricade near Norman and the subsequent conscription of two dozen survivors. Now the I35 corridor was open to whomever had the desire to pass through.

Nobody would stand in the way of Isaiah and his reckoning.

Martin watched the firelight lick the contours of the chiseled features; planes and hollows carved from obsidian. Lips so full and eyelashes so thick, any female would be envious. Only a few of Isaiah's most trusted followers were given the privilege of guarding him while he slept. He bestowed the honor upon individuals as a reward for their unquestioned loyalty. But in this instance, as in all others, Isaiah was no fool. Martin wasn't the only person in attendance. He flicked a glance at the creature sitting a coffin's length away. Lily's ascent had been the swiftest so far. Besides himself, there was no one Isaiah trusted more. Martin often wondered if that trust were well-placed. For him, not an hour passed without thoughts of escape, freedom, even mutiny. When he observed Lily watching the sleeping Isaiah, all he saw on the homely face was adoration. Was it an act, or did the strange woman truly love him? He couldn't be sure, and he certainly couldn't ask.

And therein lay the brilliance of Isaiah's system. Executions weren't a daily occurrence, but not a week went by without one or two people shot while trying to escape or hung from a nearby tree for treason. Treasonous acts might be as minor as grumbling about latrine duty or a hungry belly, so who in their right mind would risk confiding in another person? Not him, that was for damn sure. If he were going to escape, it would be a well-planned, meticulously orchestrated party of one. And because of the rule about never being seen alone, it was a formidable problem.

Martin darted another covert glance at the woman. They had picked her up at the ranch house where they had camped recently; she had been living in a heap of tornado-ravaged debris just down the road. She dressed in rags and carried a collection of knives in every shape and size, tucked away in hidden pockets throughout the tattered layers of clothing. She looked like an animated pile of dirty laundry, but she moved like a spider...unseen, unnoticed, until you felt a sharp pinch above your collar bone and realized your carotid artery had just been nicked. And the doll she carried with her at all times added to her overall creepiness factor.

In her way, she was as terrifying as Isaiah.

Martin watched as her absorbed focus shifted away from their general and toward him, as if just now sensing his presence. Irises, twin bottom-less pits set far apart in the pallid nondescript face, latched onto him like tractor beams. Tiny hairs stirred on the back of his neck. His rectum puckered.

"He's dreaming." The whisper was gravelly, rusty and rough from lack of use. "Think it's one of *those* dreams."

The closer to their ultimate destination, wherever that ended up being, the more frequent and detailed Isaiah's clairvoyant dreams became. At least that's what he claimed. Martin wasn't convinced it wasn't just more grandiose posturing.

"Let's hope it's a clearer picture of where we're going," he muttered.

The bottomless pits narrowed.

"Not that I'm complaining, mind you," he hastily added. "I just think our general will feel better and rest easier when he's able to pinpoint the location. I think it distresses him, don't you?"

Flames from the campfire reflected in the black, unblinking orbs. She seemed to be pondering his words, weighing their sincerity on some inner lie detecting scale. He held his breath.

"Yes, I think that's true. The woman vexes him. He will have his reck-oning."

"Yes, yes. He deserves it too." He breathed a sigh of relief. He noticed the woman slip a knife back into whatever pocket it had come from – it had materialized into her hand seemingly from thin air. In its place was the doll now, immaculate against the grimy fingers. She began stroking the curly synthetic hair.

Perhaps there was an opportunity here to gain the woman's confidence.

"Lily, that doll must be quite special to you. Was it yours before? I mean from your childhood?"

"She's not a *doll.* She's my baby. Come near her and I will skewer your eyeballs, roast them in the fire, and eat them with hollandaise sauce."

He turned away from the woman and gazed into the dwindling flames of the campfire, swallowing hard several times.

Honeyed laughter came from the direction of Isaiah's pallet. When Martin turned around again, he could see the whites of the man's eyes in the darkness.

"I guess she told you." The perfect teeth flashed in the moonlight. "A smart person would keep his distance from Lily and her baby. I suspect they don't need anyone in their world but me. Isn't that right, Lily?"

The dirty laundry pile nodded. "Did you have one of your dreams, dearest General?"

Nobody else spoke to Isaiah with such familiarity; it was not prudent to do so. But Lily did and had done so practically from day one. Isaiah tolerated it with an air of kindly indulgence.

"Yes, as a matter of fact I did. I hovered above their town, crept through their streets, peered into their bedrooms like the Angel of Death. Seeing the remarkable progress and knowing the girl is allowed the privilege of living under such cozy circumstances further fans the flame of my fury. But it also made me realize that our task ahead is multi-pronged. Not only will we pluck the girl from her warm bed and bask in the glory of her painful demise, we'll take the town for ourselves. They've done all the work for us...all that's left is to move in – after we've disposed of every man, woman, and child in residence there, of course. Think about it Martin," Isaiah sat up, excited to share his new plan, "Sleeping in your own bed every night, drinking fresh water that isn't crawling with cooties," he giggled at the silly word. "Eating vegetables instead of the garbage we've been consuming these months. They have a greenhouse. It's beautiful! I saw it in my dream. And a well that pumps clean water and runs on windmill power. Brilliant, really. The man in charge must be quite extraordinary. I may consider letting him live. Anyway, that will give the troops a morale boost. We're not just marching north to kill a girl, we're going there to establish a stronghold for what will become a new world order – Rome of the Great Plains. From that location, we'll branch out in all directions, expanding our dominion and rebuilding the fabric of society in a way that is practical and orderly. We'll have none of that democratic nonsense of our former government."

These ramblings weren't a new development. Isaiah had always planned to create an empire, but until the girl came into their lives, Texas was to be the epicenter.

Martin's disappointment was profound. He hated cold weather. If he ever did manage to get away, he knew exactly where he would go. He liked to imagine himself sitting on a beach, his feet covered in golden sand that made them look like catfish dipped in cornmeal ready to slide into a deep fryer; squinting from the sunlight sparkling off the turquoise sea and feeling the warmth on his body that would turn it first red, then eventually a delicious leathery bronze. Screw skin cancer. He would rather die from melanoma than at the end of a noose.

"Martin, did you hear me?" The general's sharp tone sliced through his reverie.

"Yes, sir. You said Rome of the Great Plains. Will we call the city Rome, or will you name it something else?"

Isaiah frowned. Martin felt a sickening rush of nausea. It was never good when he frowned, and it was very bad to be the cause of it.

"That's a good question. Unfortunately, I was not able to see the name of this mecca. Not yet. But soon. I feel it. Whatever its current moniker, we shall change it to something worthy of its importance. You've given me food for thought, Lieutenant."

Martin's smile trembled at the corners. "Very good, sir. Will you be making an announcement to the troops in the morning?"

Isaiah nodded, yawned, and lay back down on his pallet. Lily scampered over to cover him with a blanket.

"Yes. I want to get an early start tomorrow. Get everyone up before dawn and ready to march by seven. Any lollygaggers will be shot."

"Understood, sir."

Moments later he heard gentle snores. For once, he was glad to have been given guard duty. He would get no sleep that night, but he would have a few hours before sunrise to work on his escape plan.

When he glanced at Lily, she was staring at him with those black, un-blinking eyes again. He hoped that mind-reading wasn't included among her near-preternatural talents.

Chapter 24

"So invite her over for tea," Steven said to Julia.

She knew he hated seeing her like this. His normally calm, stoic big sister had been a bundle of raw emotion ever since he had mentioned her resemblance to Dani. The boyfriend confirmed that Dani had been adopted as a baby. Her age fit with the date Julia had given up her baby. There were no longer labs performing genealogy services, no online 24-marker DNA tests to buy, and her lab equipment had been blown up outside of Hays the day she arrived.

There would never be a way to empirically prove Dani was her daughter, but she felt on a level she could only think of as 'maternal instinct,' that she was. Julia had analyzed their prior conversations, studied her during any excuse to be in her presence, watched her movements. Everything she did reminded her of a less-filtered, younger version of herself. Except for the savage streak. That must have come from the young man with whom she had been briefly infatuated all those years ago, but who had become tired of taking a backseat to her true loves: science, academia, and career. She never even told him she was pregnant; their relationship had run its course by then anyway.

The conundrum was what to do now. Every time she envisioned the scene where she revealed her suspicion to Dani, it always played out like an episode of *Dr. Phil*. Was there anything to be gained from Dani knowing? Would the young woman be better off if she didn't? Would she hate her biological mother for giving her up? That was the worst part of all the imagined scenarios: enduring her newfound daughter's scorn and loathing.

"I just don't know. When I think about talking to her, I get butterflies in my stomach. Maybe it's not the right thing to do."

"Nothing ventured, nothing gained," Steven replied, distracted by the scrawled words on the legal pad next to him.

"You're no help."

"Sorry. I'm writing my speech for the town hall meeting tomorrow afternoon. About the election."

Steady rain pattered on the roof and against the window panes. So far, winter had been mild and wet, but they still had a long way to go before spring planting. If it weren't for the Dani angst, Julia would have been curled up on Steven's couch with a book. Sundays had been designated as a secular 'day of rest,' a motion Steven had presented to the citizens as a preemptive strike. She knew he was worried about Reverend Calvin and his rapidly-growing following. Not everybody in Liberty attended Sunday services, but many non-religious and agnostic types did so for the sheer entertainment. These days, a good performance of any type was appreciated and embraced as a way of breaking up the work week. Everyone had jobs, many of which entailed physical labor and long hours. Without movies and television to provide a reprieve from the demands of daily survival, people found whatever else would do the trick. The popularity of Pablo and Maddie's poetry-reading and story-telling gatherings had outgrown their modest living room, so the courtroom where the town hall meetings were held became the new venue. The bi-weekly event had expanded to include musical numbers, sing-a-longs, and recently, a poignant interpretation by Pablo of Hamlet's famous soliloquy, done in contemporary language rather than Shakespearean. It had brought the house down.

"You're a shoe-in, so why worry about it?" Julia asked.

"Never underestimate the gullibility of people in the thrall of religion."

"You think he's going to make a run at you?"

"Of course. I think it's been his plan all along. With Natalie at his side spewing feel-good scripture every chance she gets, they're quite the power couple these days."

Julia nodded, her turn to be distracted. She needed to make a decision about Dani soon. This limbo state was driving her crazy.

"So back on my problem. Do you really think I should talk to her? It could back-fire on me."

Steven set his pen down and gave his sister his full attention. "It very well could, but if you don't, you'll continue to wallow in misery and self-doubt forever. Just do it and get it over with. Let the chips fall where they may. That's my advice."

She chewed a fingernail. "I think I will. Speaking of uncomfortable revelations, when do you plan on broaching the subject of my research findings?"

He plucked the readers from his nose and rubbed his eyes. "I haven't forgotten. I just question the wisdom of it. What's to be gained from people knowing their neighbor could be a sociopath? It's more likely that neighbor isn't, so why plant the seed in people's minds? Unlike your situation with Dani, I just don't see any positive benefit of it getting out."

"I see. So you've made the autonomous decision to keep it between us? Do you think that's ethical?"

Steven gave her a thoughtful look. "I think it's pragmatic. So that's what I'm going to do and so are you. Now that Thoozy is gone, there's nobody else who knows. Maybe when things are a bit more stable, we can share the knowledge. Let's just get through the winter, then revisit this in the spring. Agreed?"

"I don't like it, but I'll agree. For now. But I'm telling you, Steven, this is too monumental to keep to ourselves. People have a right to know."

"Why? Why do they have a right to know?"

She gave him a thoughtful look in return, then said, "Because very little good comes from a few people at the top deciding what the masses should and shouldn't know when it concerns their welfare. I'll give you until May, but no longer."

"Fair enough."

Logan eavesdropped from the top of the stairs, as he often did when Julia and Steven were having one of those conversations where they used a lot of big words. He thought he understood most of what they were saying though. He still didn't like the brother, but he knew that Julia did, which is one of the reasons he hadn't killed him. He knew it would make her very sad, and he hated seeing her sad. Ever since that night with Thoozy on the dark road, he felt...different sort of. Changed maybe. He was a little mad at the old man for telling him that story right before he died. The story that was more than a story. He thought the word was *parable*, but he wasn't sure. It was a word he had never heard before.

Anyway, ever since that night, Logan thought about that story. Thought about the choice of jumping into that cold river which was very far down, or walking over to where the deer were playing in the pretty meadow. Thoozy had said he would lose all his new friends and people wouldn't like him any longer if he kept doing bad things. That doing more bad things was like jumping into the river. But Logan didn't get that part. It would probably hurt and it didn't look like it would be fun, but bad things *were* fun, and he hadn't done anything bad since the night he'd stuck the knife into the old man.

He was starting to miss doing them.

Julia thought Dani was her daughter. He had heard her and Steven talking about it a couple of times now. Before, he had intended to kill her, but now he sort of liked her. She had been nice to him ever since he saved her life. But he was very jealous of all the attention Julia had been giving her lately. And of course there was the problem of the colors. Logan knew the second he saw that Dani's colors were identical to Julia's, that there was something between them. Even before Steven suspected it.

Logan really enjoyed how important he had become to the other members of the security crew. And because they all liked him, everybody else in town were nice to him too. Back in the old days, nobody but his mom and Mr. Cheney had ever really been nice to him. He might lose that if he killed Dani or someone else, so maybe that's what Thoozy had been saying. But what the old man didn't mention was a third option, which was somewhere between the cold river and the pretty meadow.

Maybe he could keep killing but just make sure not to get caught.

Chapter 25

"You're fucking kidding me, right?" Dani's clenched jaw barely allowed the words to escape. She had been sitting on the sofa next to Julia, listening to her lengthy backstory, while Sam watched wide-eyed from his favorite chair. She had wondered how long it was going to take her to get to the damn point. What the hell did she care about the woman's teenage years, the grueling college classes, all those advanced degrees? Why was she telling her all this?

She soon had the answer. Julia talked about getting pregnant at an inconvenient time in her life. A time that was the same year Dani was born.

"Of course, we'll never have proof, unless I can get my hands on a DNA sequencer." The older woman gave her a shaky smile.

Dani's head was swimming. Too many emotions were hitting her at once, but the prominent one was outrage: she had been abandoned because she was an inconvenience. A tiny voice inside her head said, *Can you blame her though?* Julia had been a goddamn rock star in the science world. She had been top of her class; wooed by corporations, universities, and governments before she had even finished the thesis for her master's degree. That was when the '80s era EPT test had shown a dark circle instead of a blob at the bottom of the glass vial.

"At least you didn't get an abortion. Otherwise, we wouldn't be having this conversation," Dani said, leaning back on the couch and closing her eyes.

"That's right. I could have, but I didn't. I think that's the best solution for some people in some circumstances, but it wasn't for me. I chose a career over raising the child I gave birth to, and that was all the guilt I could handle at the time." Silent tears streamed down Julia's face, but her voice was steady.

Dani opened her eyes and studied the woman for a long moment. "I've wondered about you my whole life. Imagined what you might be like, what you were doing at some random moment, wondered if I'd gotten my brains from you or the guy who donated the sperm. Did you look like me? Did you talk like me? Did you snort when you laughed, like I do? Were your pinky toes an inch shorter than all your other toes, like mine are? Did you hate cabbage but adore Brussel sprouts? When you were a little girl, did you fall in love with Narnia and crawl to the back of your closet, hoping to find a magical entrance?" An impatient hand brushed away a single tear. "I wondered what my life would have been like if I had been raised by someone like me, rather than the generous, indulgent, loving, *average* people who were my parents. The only parents I ever knew."

"Don't feel that accepting me, on any level, is a betrayal of them. It's not. I remember how wonderful they sounded on paper. They included a heartfelt essay with the adoption application. That's why I selected theirs over all the others, even though I never knew their names, nor where they lived. You and I can have a relationship, whatever kind you're comfortable with, and I think that would make them happy."

Dani stared at the tear-streaked face of the person who was likely her biological mother, noticing for the first time how similar the features were to her own. It was a moment she had thought about often in the past, especially that first year after her parents had given her the 'you're adopted' speech. She had been six-years-old at the time; young for most children to be told such an earth-shattering revelation, but not so for her. She had begun to question why her hair was dark and her eyes were blue, when both her parents had light hair and brown eyes. They had already had her tested and knew she was gifted. Knew she would understand far better than most children her age, that while they were her parents – would always be her parents – in one significant way, they were not.

She had understood, but it hadn't kept her from wondering about the people who made her. She had filled that void with figments; their incarnations influenced by whatever book she was reading at the time. There were fantastical stories of a swarthy seafaring father and the lovely pirate queen who captured his heart. A wicked sorceress who changed her evil ways after falling in love with a handsome, kindly woodsman. Her favorite was the shape-shifting alien who mated with a human female, but then had to return to his planet, which would explain why she was so different from all the other children. These inventions continued throughout her youth until the day she turned sixteen and decided to put away such childish fantasies.

And now one of those fantasies was here in the flesh, asking to be let into her life.

"You need to leave. Now." Dani stood, walked to the bedroom, and slammed the door behind her.

A small moan escaped Julia. Sam was at her side the next moment. He reached for her hands, then held them in his warm, calloused ones.

"You need to give her some time. Dani is the best. I love her more than anything in the world, but she can be a little stubborn. Especially if there's some hurt mixed in with her anger. I think there's a lot of hurt mixed in right now, but it'll get better the longer she has time to think about it all."

She nodded, sliding a hand away from Sam's so she could wipe her dripping nose with a tissue.

"You know her. What do you think my chances are? Eventually, I mean."

He smiled. Suddenly Julia understood why all the females in town were so smitten with him. It wasn't just his movie star face or muscular body. He exuded compassion and empathy with every gesture. His frequent grin was beautiful, genuine, and inclusive. When Sam smiled at you, you felt its warmth almost as a physical embrace.

"I think someday, if you play your checkers right, you will get to be her friend. I don't think you'll ever get to be her mother. She already had one of those. She won't want to lose another one."

Chapter 26

Cate returned Steven's intense gaze with her usual smirk.

"Yes, from what I can tell, his credentials are legit. He seems to know about pharmaceuticals."

"Is he a benefit to the hospital?"

She shrugged her brawny shoulders. Steven had corralled her and ushered her to a quiet corner of the courthouse.

"He would be if we had access to more drugs, but the medicine cabinet is pretty bare now. Someone with knowledge of natural and homeopathic remedies is far more useful these days. Like me."

The smug grin was disconcerting, but he couldn't be bothered with the oddity that was Liberty's resident doctor. Not at the moment. The election was about to take place and all the mayoral candidates would be allowed fifteen minutes to convince the residents of Liberty why they were the best person for the job. The voting process would be a straight popular vote…whoever got the most votes got to be mayor for one year. The town had decided if they voted in a bad apple, they didn't want him or her in a position of power for too long.

As the incumbent, Steven had the advantage, but it was also a disadvantage. Everything that had gone wrong these past months could be attributed to him, draped around his neck like a smelly albatross; even messes he hadn't created. The other candidates could promise the moon, with no prior 'governing' history that could bite them in their asses. He would not resort to cheap personal attacks even if it cost him the election, but he would use any legitimate information he uncovered. He had hoped to discover that Calvin's alleged pharmacological degree was bogus, that his credentials had been fabricated to gain admission to their town. Then Steven would present his findings in such a way as to diminish the man's reputation.

"Has he been putting in his hours?"

The grin expanded. "If I didn't know better, I'd say you were trying to get some dirt on your biggest rival. Isn't that sort of thing beneath you?"

He frowned at the criticism. "Yeah, not very honorable, is it?"

A spindly cackle bubbled up from the depths of the woman's ample bosom. "No, it's not. But I understand. He's probably doing the same thing. Catch you later, Steven. Good luck. You have my vote, by the way. That preacher gives me the willies."

Steven watched her amble down the corridor, remembering his conversation with Natalie about Cate's eccentric behavior: the strange hand-hovering business with the patients. He had barely given it a thought though. And when Natalie had mentioned as a follow-up concern that the woman was probably a *lesbian* (whispered like a dirty word), he had become angry. Who gave a rat's ass about the woman's sexual preference?

She was odd, though. There was no denying it. No matter who won the election, he resolved to find out more about the person who held the power of healing their sick and wounded in the palms of her hands.

"Let's quiet down, people. Marilyn, please draw a name from the fishbowl."

There were five squares of notebook paper, folded in an identical manner, visible through the clear glass of the bowl. The order of speeches would be random, so any benefit to going first or last would be left to chance.

"Billy Ray."

It was absurd to think of the large man from Arkansas, with his terrible grammar and plodding thought process, taking on the role of Liberty's mayor. He walked to the center of the room, stopping at the small table which held a pitcher of water and six glasses.

He cleared his throat, then said in his deep voice, "I know I ain't an educated man. Not like these other fellers and lady." An enormous hand indicated Steven, Calvin, the dental hygienist Isabel, and the Kennedy brothers who were running as a team on a joint ticket. The candidates were all seated together in an area reserved for them. "But I'm an honest man. A good man. A strong man, for sure." He flexed a gigantic flannel-covered bicep for emphasis and winked at the crowd. Everyone who was physically able and not on guard duty was in attendance, and their laughter was genuine. But there was no way in hell Billy Ray could run the town. Most people knew that, if not the man himself.

Steven smiled, then switched the ongoing speech to a mental back burner while he mulled his own.

The next names to be called were the twins, even more well-liked in the town after the cannibal rescue, but not a serious threat. They were too young and lacked the maturity necessary for the job. In a few years, he might have to worry about them, though. They were good, smart boys. When Bobby finished with a bawdy joke, Steven knew their popularity couldn't save them.

He held his breath for the next name to be called, then released it. Isabel was intelligent and compelling, but also abrasive. Her overt feminist message fell on many receptive ears, but she had missed the mark. Gender mattered little these days when life and death were on the line daily. And while he agreed that their future society should not be gender-biased, it was more important right now to keep everyone's bellies full.

As it turned out, he and Calvin – the forerunners – would be speaking next to last and last. Suspicious to some, perhaps, but the fishbowl nor its contents had been rigged by him in any way.

That was confirmed when Marilyn called his name next. He shot a covert glance at his rival, seeing only benevolence on the preacher's face.

He approached the table with what he hoped was a calm demeanor and a smile plastered on his face, even though it felt like a grimace. He was more nervous than he ever remembered being in his life. Tung had told him he was a natural speaker...good at getting people to do what he wanted. While that had been a revelation to him at the time, in hindsight he knew it was true.

But in the public speaking arena, Steven was outgunned by the man whose speech would follow his. He had to be flawless.

"Good evening, everyone. The smoke-free lighting for this evening's meeting is brought to you by the Hunter Gatherers and their recent score of high-quality paraffin oil. Great job, guys." Steven made eye contact with Pablo in the second row. On the right of the young man sat a recently married husband and wife from Nebraska, the replacements for Missy and Zane.

"Thanks to Pablo and his people, and Lisa and her gardeners, we're eating better than we have in months." Steven sought the blond ponytail in the audience, acknowledging her with a nod. She sat next to her beau Ed, who had been working minor miracles with his construction team. Many residents now had fencing around their gardens that would dissuade all but the most persistent deer. A few had requested smaller versions of the huge community greenhouse, and he had been tireless in assisting them. Ed and his people had also installed a second well next to the hospital, saving the backs of the medical staff from hauling water for blocks.

"I'd like to take a few minutes to thank everyone for all their hard work. Ed and his crew for helping everyone get their fencing put up and the million other projects they've been working on. Cate and her staff for keeping us healthy. Frank for working out the kinks with our waste and sanitation. Dani and her group for making sure we're safe." He found the girl sitting next to her boyfriend in the last row. Her face was a careful mask of indifference. She ignored his acknowledgement, but Sam's smile was an acceptable proxy. "Marilyn and her excellent distribution system at the commissary. My sister and her work with those who are struggling with some emotional and psychological issues." Julia sat on the opposite side of the room from Dani. Her pale, unsmiling face didn't convey much support for his cause. Logan was beside her, having just finished his shift on the eastern barricade.

"We couldn't have come as far as we have without everyone working hard, working smart, and most importantly, cooperating. Think about where we were just a few months ago. We were fragmented. Some of us were starving, many were ill. But we came together as an organized society. We assessed our strengths then utilized them. Discovered our weaknesses, and shored them up. This ability to function as a whole, like a hundred cogs on a wheel...each one as important as the next, is why we've achieved what we have. I wonder how many societies out there have come close to accomplishing what we have. It's quite remarkable. But does that mean we can rest on our laurels? Of course not. I have big plans. Plans to expand our current agricultural endeavors to include grain crops and orchards, and plans to build an electrical grid for our town. Think about that. Not only will we eat better...grains for bread and fruit for cobblers, but we'll be able to enjoy them in our brightly-lit kitchens." This was his trump card. He was the only person in town – perhaps even the state – who had the expertise to get the power back on.

"You all know that I'm a stickler for detail. I call it being anal-retentive; others might call it being a jerk. But that sort of attention to detail is what's required in this job. Without it, stuff falls through the cracks, and a little problem becomes a huge problem very quickly. As a mechanical engineer, I'm uniquely qualified to see these tiny fissures and recognize them for the crevasses they might become. It's what I did for almost two decades before Chicxulub, and what I've continued to do these past months as unofficial mayor. That fact alone is a reason to elect me. But another is this: Liberty is my home. It has been my home since I was born in the hospital right down the road. Our family has roots here, although that may not seem like a big deal to some." He chose wording that wouldn't offend Liberty's transplants who would be voting too. "I realize that we're an amalgamation of local folks and nonlocal folks. Texans, Nebraskans, Arizonans, even a Californian. But this land is in my blood; always has been, always will be. I know what the weather is like here, I know the properties of the soil and water, I know the indigenous flora and fauna, which are safe and which are harmful. Kansas is in my blood. Engineering is in my blood too, whether it's constructing windmills or putting the pieces of civilization back together.

"Elect me and let me continue the progress we've been enjoying these past months. I promise I will not let you down."

Thunderous applause filled the room. Steven smiled. It was a damn good speech.

When the clamor quieted, Marilyn drew the last folded paper from the bowl and called out the name; a superfluous gesture but a necessary one.

The town's religious leader patted Steven on the back as he passed. Steven sat down in his previous spot, resisting the urge to chew a finger-nail.

Calvin allowed a few moments for the audience to go silent.

He wore the same immaculate white shirt as he did on Sunday morn-ings behind the church's lectern. Thick, dark hair had been brushed back from the wide brow. Golden lantern light reflected off the angles of the etched, clean-shaven jawline.

Steven hated the man more at that moment than ever before.

"Friends, there's not one thing about that speech I can refute. Steven has done a great job. He has a wealth of knowledge. He knows the area. I believe he has the interest of everyone in this room at heart. I won't waste your time trying to one-up him. I'm no politician, after all. I'm just a preacher."

The southern accent seemed less pronounced. Perhaps intentionally so, to appeal to the Midwesterners.

"Every single thing he said is true. That's why he's a valuable asset to our town. He might be the most important asset we have, in terms of keeping us alive and reasonably comfortable. And he will continue to be a valuable asset, no matter which way this election goes."

With one sentence, the man had blunted the entire thrust of Steven's speech: Steven didn't have to be mayor for the town to benefit from his intellect and expertise. His stomach lurched.

"But when it comes to leading men and women on their journey through these times, we must shift focus. Let's put aside the nuts and bolts of the material world and think about the bigger picture. What if the plague wasn't a natural event? What if our Heavenly Father brought it about as a way of testing those who remain? It's a wonderful thought, isn't it? All our loved ones already up in heaven, enjoying the purest form of love and happiness there is, while watching the show that we're putting on down here. With all my heart, this is what I believe to be true." He paused, letting the words sink in.

"I've heard about the Hays incident, and while I know a few people were saved from a bad situation, it was not justification to commit murder."

A significant number of Liberty's residents nodded in agreement. Steven clenched his teeth against the acid that was building in his belly.

"And I weep when I think about our loved ones and our Heavenly Father seeing that carnage from above and knowing it was a choice...a conscious decision to take human lives. I worry that no matter how much we might pray for forgiveness, it might not be enough.

"As your spiritual counselor, I can only do so much. I can recommend, I can advise, I can comfort. But I can't legislate. I can't make the tough decisions that a leader, who is profoundly concerned for your immortal soul, should make. If I'd been here during that time, I would have done everything within my power to stop it. I know many of you feel the same way, since the majority vote not to intervene was ignored by those conducting the raid."

Steven gripped the bench below his knees, willing himself not to jump up and defend his actions.

"But I can assure you, that as your mayor, my decisions will be influenced by what our Lord would have us do. Because this span of years we call a lifetime is but a tiny drop in the ocean of our immortal, spiritual sojourn. It isn't something to survive; it's a brief interval, during which we must prove our worth. We must show God that we are deserving of His blessings, deserving of His love. Vote for me and we'll make this journey together. A pilgrimage of sorts, safeguarding each other while traveling this treacherous path toward the glory of our afterlife in heaven."

Sweat glistening on the handsome face reflected the lamplight, creating an almost otherworldly effect – a glowing messenger of God in their midst. Steven studied the enthralled expression of many in the crowd.

When he listened to the explosion of applause that was louder than that for his own speech, he had the gut-wrenching realization that he would likely lose the election.

"Everyone can come back in now," Marilyn shouted over the din of chatter and movement. "We've tallied the votes. Please, everyone get seated and we'll make the announcement." She stood with four others at a long folding table near the judge's bench – the voting station. Five surrogates had been chosen, one by each of the candidates, to help count and oversee the results. Marilyn had been Steven's choice; Natalie had been Calvin's. Pablo, the representative for the Kennedy brothers, held a piece of notebook paper in his hand.

"The sooner you all settle down, the sooner we can get this finished and get home to our beds," Pablo said, raising his voice to be heard. Finally the residents of Liberty – well over a hundred people now – found seats on the crowded benches and waited with an air of excited anticipation.

"The results of the vote for Mayor of Liberty are as follows: Isabel Fioretti, seven votes."

Steven turned his head to see the woman's frown from where she sat behind him. She was not pleased but also not surprised.

"Billy Ray Davis, four votes." Four was also the number of people in the fuel crew, including Billy Ray himself. Steven gave the man beside him a respectful nod.

"Bobby and Jack Kennedy, seventeen votes." A spattering of applause broke out, punctuated by a few shrill whistles; the twins were popular with the younger segment of Liberty's population.

Pablo paused before continuing, glancing up at the crowded room full of people who hadn't experienced this much excitement in a long time.

"Calvin Whitfield...forty-three votes."

He had barely gotten the last word out before it was greeted with a vigorous round of applause. A few *whoops* echoed off the walls of the building.

Steven was doing the math in his head. If every single person in the courtroom voted, he knew the precise number of votes he needed to win. A wave of nausea washed over him.

"Steven Berkstrom," Pablo smiled again before reading the number, targeting Steven's face among those of the other candidates. "Also forty-three votes. Folks, we have ourselves a tie. What's it going to be, gentlemen? A run-off election or a co-mayorship?"

"Look, Steven, I'm not going to, as you so eloquently phrased it, fuck with what you've accomplished in this town." The preacher sat four feet away in an office down the corridor from the courtroom, where everyone was awaiting their decision. "I think you have formed an erroneous opinion of me, and I don't know how I earned it, nor what I can do to fix it. But I believe that together we can do amazing things. Why take a chance on a run-off election which you very well may lose?"

The southern accent was back, all stretched-taffy vowels and languishing consonants; Steven could almost feel the breeze from an antebellum fan and taste sweet tea on his lips. The man had dialed it down for the sake of the Midwesterners during his speech. A clever tactic, and another reason not to trust him.

"Or I very well might win," Steven replied, "then wouldn't be forced into this diminished role. Do you actually believe the two of us can agree on a damn thing? Our views of the situation...hell, our views on everything...are as polarized as they could possibly be."

"But we both want what's best for the people. 'What's best' is of course the sticking point. But I believe that two people who are similarly motivated will be able to come together in the end. I'm concerned for their immortal souls, you're concerned for their corporeal existence. These two things are not mutually exclusive...at least they don't have to be. Let's give it a shot. One year. Let's see what monumental things we can accomplish together."

Steven almost believed the man meant what he was saying. Hell, maybe on some level, he did. The best liars bought some of their own bullshit.

But Steven knew better. He imagined dozens of scenarios that ended in disagreement, frustration, and no progress. The question was whether to take a chance with a run-off election, then watch their town turn into some goddamned theocracy if he lost. The alternative was to work with the preacher.

He locked eyes with the man who sat across from him. He saw keen intelligence there and a surprising lack of self-satisfaction in the tranquil smile. The man was either a sociopathic liar or a religious zealot.

Whatever he was, Steven couldn't risk letting him have all the power in Liberty.

Chapter 27

"What happens if you don't agree on something? Who gets to make the final decision?"

Natalie looked beautiful, as usual. She wore a thin nightgown and was keenly aware of how fetching she was as she posed on the bed she had been sharing with Calvin for several weeks now. There were frown lines between her eyebrows that had become more pronounced in the last year. Botox injections and other vanity indulgences were no longer an option. But she knew she was still the most attractive female in Liberty over the age of thirty.

"We'll cross that bridge when we come to it. As I explained to Steven, we both want what's best for the town and its citizens. And while I suspect compromises will have to be made, perhaps there will be less butting of heads than everyone thinks," Calvin said, drinking in the sight of his new 'wife,' proclaimed as such moments before their first coupling. This made everything they did in bed acceptable in the eyes of the Lord.

"That sounds watered down to me. Not at all what we discussed."

"It is His will. We'll make it work. Now slide that nightie down so I can see those magnificent breasts."

Natalie smiled. When she saw desire in a man's eyes, she knew she was in control.

"It seems to me His will would have been to make you sole mayor. Then we...you...could do what you want."

"Who are we to question our Lord?" he replied as he began kissing her slender neck, then worked his way down.

Just as every other man she had ever known, he was obsessed with her breasts and fixated on her vagina. With her beautiful face as the perfect bait, she was a walking man trap. She realized at fourteen that these physical attributes gave her power, and she began using them to her advantage soon after she had gotten her first period.

"You're His representative here on earth. He should want you in a position to do the most good," she said, navigating through the religious rhetoric.

"That's why I got forty-three votes, my dear. I'm in a vastly more improved position today than I was yesterday. All our hard work has paid off. Oh, these are delightful, but off they go!" he said, tugging her lace panties down her legs and off her feet.

"Yes, darling. Certainly it's an improvement. But I think we can do better, don't you?"

"All in good time." A moan escaped his lips as he parted the silky thighs, then paused to soak in the erotic splendor before him. "You are superb...a testament to His handiwork. Something tells me you know this already," he murmured into her ear as his fingers entered her. "Oh, you're ready for me, aren't you, sweetheart?"

She had taken a few minutes in the bathroom to prepare herself. Calvin was handsome, but she still carried a torch for Steven. It was a fact that vexed her daily, especially when she had to watch him carrying on with one of the least beautiful women in town. Before Chicxulub, she knew he was married, as was she, and rumor had it he was hopelessly in love with his wife. The few sexual overtures she attempted had ended in ego-bruising failure, confirming his fidelity. Then the plague happened, and Steven became more than just an obsession; he was a meal ticket. She had handled the situation badly though, and there would be no going back. She would have to make do with the man who was grunting and grinding away on top of her.

At least until she gained more leverage and could find a way to get rid of the woman who currently shared Steven's bed.

Chapter 28

"Pablo, do not start that. Please." Maddie pleaded as much with her eyes as she did with her words.

She removed her feet from the medical stirrups and gripped Pablo's hands in her own. He barely heard the click of the door behind the departing Cate.

"She said you're 'high risk.' Those were her words," he whispered.

"Yes, I know. But that isn't a death sentence. Cate and Amelia will take care of me and the baby, and everything will be fine. Don't get hysterical on me."

Despite the wave of apprehension, Pablo felt stung by the words. Enough so that he forced himself to get control of the panic before it gained a foothold.

"Okay. I won't." He took a deep breath. "But you're not raising a finger until the baby arrives. Is that clear?"

Maddie smiled. "At least the preeclampsia explains the headaches. I was worried it might be because of the visions."

"Yes, or the bullet that's still lodged in your beautiful skull," he added, careful to maintain a shred of composure.

"You got the short end of the stick with me and my misshapen womb, didn't you, Poet Fellow? Too bad you're just now finding this out after my warranty has expired. Sucks to be you."

"No, it doesn't. As long as I have you, no matter what shape you're in, I'm the luckiest man on earth."

"In light of how few of you dudes are still around, that's not the grandiose testament it should be. I promise I will be a lazy slug for the next few months, if you promise to stop being such a drama queen about me and my health. Seriously, Pablo, it doesn't do any good. It affects your emotional well-being and it affects my blood pressure. Do we have a deal? Pinky swear?" She extended a slender finger with an expectant look.

He ignored it, planting a soft kiss on her lips instead. "We have a deal. But only under the condition that you relinquish veto power of the name."

"No way. I know how your poet brain works. I don't want my child answering to Edgar or Rudyard. He'll get beaten up on the playground every day of his life."

"What about Dylan or William or Henry? There are plenty of poet names that don't evoke violence. And what if it's a girl? Almost all the female poets have lovely names. Maya, Emily, Sylvia."

"Not Sylvia. It sounds like a woman who plays bridge and drinks too much gin on weekday afternoons. I like Emily though. And I like Dylan."

"Agreed." He kissed her again, gripping the examination table with bloodless fingers.

Hecate, shortened to 'Cate' now as a way of fitting in with the townsfolk, hummed a strange, discordant tune as she crushed the dried herbs with an ancient mortar and pestle. It had been handed down to her from her mother before she died of a burst appendix shortly after Chicxulub. Her grandmother had given it to her mother before she passed of natural causes a decade earlier. According to family folklore, it had been chiseled out of a rare type of black granite sourced from a quarry in Wales some eight hundred years ago. Cate didn't know if the legend were true, but it pleased her to believe it was. She enjoyed thinking about what her life might have been like as the village Wise Woman in pagan pre-Roman Britannia or Gaul. Back then, before the damn Christians took over, women like her were respected...revered. How wonderful that must have been, not having to hide what they were from people who didn't understand their gifts. Even now, despite her knowledge of anatomy, disease, and mainstream medicine, she still raised eyebrows when resorting to one of her natural herbal treatments. There was also the time a couple of months ago when Natalie had caught her using her healing hands on one of the Hays girls. The girl had recovered nicely from her chlamydia; and the burn scars, a side effect of her gift, were barely noticeable now.

Why couldn't people just let her do her job and leave her the hell alone? Hecate, the Greek goddess of witchcraft, was her namesake for good reason. She was exceptional; had been a shining star in a family of talented women. How dare these idiots in Liberty question her?

She sighed, then continued whistling the odd tune. She loved being in her basement where nobody could peer over her shoulder or give her one of those sideways judgmental glances. The townspeople knew better than to offend their only doctor, so they weren't obvious about their disdain. But she could feel it coming off most of Liberty's residents like a low frequency radio wave; like they had caught a whiff of something unpleasant when she smiled at them. Her mother always said she had a lovely smile, but a person's body language didn't lie. Not many people in town liked her, except maybe Steven. And Maddie, who probably was only nice to her because she was helping with her pregnancy. Pretty girls like Maddie had never given her the time of day before.

It was a shame Maddie would have to die in order for Cate to get the baby. The baby was everything. The baby, although not of her bloodline, would be her legacy. She would raise the child as her own and teach her everything she knew. While it wouldn't possess the healing gift, she could still share the repository of knowledge she had accumulated over the years: mountains of pathological information, a reservoir of obscure remedies which had fallen through the cracks of modern medicine, and a wealth of botanical expertise. Much had been taught to her growing up, but some added by herself. She was a tireless researcher.

The combination of flora she was even now crushing in the granite bowl was her own creation. She had tested it several times on pregnant animals before and after the plague, with brilliant results. The plan had been germinating for years; a last resort measure in case she never became pregnant herself. When taken in the correct dosage, it would bring about the slow decline and eventual death of the mother, while leaving the developing fetus unharmed.

The best part was, when the baby was extracted from the dead or near-dead mother, it would appear lifeless. But within a few minutes of birth, the seemingly dead baby, whose physiological functions had merely slowed to a near imperceptible state, would 'come back to life.'

That was why she had a litter of kittens crawling around the hard-packed dirt floor, all healthy, and even now mewling for their bottle feeding. The mother cat had been buried in the wooded area behind the house – the pet cemetery for all those other animals experimented on during the last thirty years.

The tricky part was dosage. A hundred and twenty-pound human needed more than a ten-pound cat. Maddie had complained of headaches and her blood pressure was higher than ideal, both symptoms of preeclampsia, which was the perfect cover for the effects of the elixir Cate had been giving her for a month now. She mixed in a bit of dried blueberry to mask the bitterness and make it more palatable, and Maddie had sworn she was drinking it daily, believing it to be an innocuous tincture of homeopathic vitamins and nutrients.

Just a few more months to go and she would finally hold the baby that would be her legacy; would be redemption in her own eyes and in those of the ghosts of her ancient family.

###

Jessie moaned in her sleep. Amelia was instantly awake. Her slumber these days was as shallow as a cat's grave.

Amelia frowned in the dark, puzzled by the macabre simile her own brain had manufactured.

Another moan from Jessie's bed demanded her attention.

Amelia cooed softly in her antediluvian language, brushing the child's messy hair from her forehead.

Jessie's eyes fluttered open. There was terror in their depths.

"Hello, my precious *dlynga.* You're safe now. I'm here with you and will never let anything or anyone hurt you. Can you speak of it yet, or do you need a minute to breathe?"

The cherub lips trembled as she took deep, calming breaths – an exercise learned from her mentor.

"I think the Smiling Man knows where we are now."

These were the words she had been dreading. "How do you know? Tell me everything, child."

"I think Lootinent Martin is in danger. There's a scary Spider Lady close to him all the time. I think she wants to kill him."

"Spider Lady? What does she look like? Wait, never mind. It doesn't matter. What about the Smiling Man?"

"He's looking into a fire. The Spider Lady is sitting next to him. Lootinent Martin is on the other side. He's looking into the fire too, but the Spider Lady only stares at the Smiling Man. I think she's in love with him. He's very bad. How could anyone be in love with a man who is so bad?"

"I have no idea, child, but I've seen it thousands of times. What else?"

"The Smiling Man told them about his dream. In the dream he saw many things. He saw a sign."

"Oh dear. Was it our sign?"

The singsong voice took on an ominous tone. "STOP. YOU ARE UNDER ARMED SURVEILANCE. PLACE ALL WEAPONS ON THE GROUND BEHIND YOU. WAIT. YOU WILL BE APPROACHED AND ASSESSED. IF WE LIKE YOU, YOU WILL BE ALLOWED TO STAY. IF YOU MEAN US HARM OR CAUSE TROUBLE, WE WILL KILL YOU. WELCOME TO LIBERTY, KANSAS. This is what the Smiling Man told the Spider Lady and Lootinent Martin that he saw on the sign. Is that our sign?"

"Yes, it is. What else did he say?"

"He said the sign smacks of that cunning clever...and then he said a terrible word. I'm not supposed to say words like that."

"No need. I can imagine what it was. Please continue."

"He said he could smell her. That he could see her parading around town like it was the...Palatine? I think that was the word. Then he looked at a map in the firelight. He put his finger on it and said, 'That's it, Lootinent Martin. There's our Rome.' That's when I got that feeling. The one I get when you said I should hide. Right before he turned around, I ran behind a tent. Someone was in there snoring. Anyway, I'm pretty sure he didn't see me."

Amelia felt a stab of alarm. "Are you positive he didn't see you?"

The child hesitated a second before answering. The vocabulary of a seven-year old made it difficult to articulate the nebulous world of astral travel. She forced herself to be patient, despite the trepidation that was beginning to take root in her soul.

"I think he knew someone was there, but I don't think he could see who. I'm positive he didn't see that it was me."

The confidence in the voice gave her only a modicum of relief. Perhaps the Smiling Man didn't know about Jessie, but he most certainly knew the location of their town.

"Was there anything else?"

"No. After that, I just woke up and you were there."

Amelia kissed the warm forehead; one of the side effects of *langthal* was increased body temperature. Healers, whether they were able to merely self-heal, or possessed the rare gift of healing others, always ran hotter than the average 98.6 degrees. It was one of the clues she had noticed upon her first encounter with Jessie all those months ago. The second clue was the curing of the arthritis in her right hand when Jessie had touched it in the back seat of the Highlander on their road trip from Arizona. The evidence continued to mount when the child saved Maddie after her head trauma, then left no doubt when she healed her beloved Fergus after the mortal injuries the Hays bullets had wrought on that ghastly day.

This little girl was the reason the love of her dilatant life was still making a pilgrimage to the Atlantic Ocean instead of going the way of her old friend Thoozy.

"The sun won't be up for another hour. Do you think you can go back to sleep?"

An enormous yawn erupted on the elfin face. "I think so. Will you stay here with me?"

"I'll be right next door in the kitchen, making coffee. Is that close enough?"

"Yes. I like to snuggle in bed and smell your coffee. It's a nice smell."

"It's heaven in a cup. You'll be smelling it a lot in the weeks to come. Go back to sleep now. A growing girl needs her rest."

Amelia tucked the covers up under the child's chin and closed the bedroom door behind her. A candle was burning in the kitchen.

"And why are you up so early, young lady? Don't you know that baby bump needs rest?"

"Good morning," Maddie yawned. "It's the headache again."

The small woman frowned. The headaches weren't surprising considering her former injury, and now the preeclampsia, but they were worrisome.

"I'll make some coffee. A little caffeine won't hurt the baby and may help with the headache."

"That sounds good. There's some cream in the cooler on the back porch. Bessie was in a generous mood yesterday."

The Holstein and her calf had been brought home in the HG trailer after the cannibal incident. While the cost in human lives would never be worth it, the fresh milk was a priceless boon to the town. The milk and subsequent cheese had to be rationed, but as Liberty's only pregnant resident, Maddie received the lion's share.

Amelia went about the business of making coffee. She stirred up the banked coals in the fireplace, then added kindling and wood to the growing flames. Clean water from one of the town's two functioning wells was put in plastic five-gallon Sparkletts bottles, then transported to homes via wagon or sled, depending on the weather. Everyone who was able-bodied fetched their own water. The elderly or infirm received weekly water deliveries courtesy of whomever had the extra time. This time of year, the chore had fallen to the greenhouse workers due to their lightened winter workload. In the spring, when less firewood was needed to keep the residents warm and the gardeners were busy with the business of farming, the task would go to the fuel crew. Everyone hated hauling water, and as soon as time allowed, more wells would be dug. But in the meantime, they made do. Fortunately for Amelia, Pablo had shouldered that burden along with the million other things he did for their blended family.

His surprise gift to her of five pounds of Maxwell House instant coffee had scored him an ardent kiss on the lips. Just like her sleep, Amelia treasured her morning coffee.

"Here you are, my dear," she said, handing a steaming frothy cup to Maddie and sitting down at the kitchen table. "Two sugars and one glug of cream, just like you like."

"Thank you. Have I told you lately how much I love you?"

"You don't have to. I already know." Amelia squeezed the pale slender fingers with her own smaller, darker ones.

"I had another dream." Maddie said in a low voice.

"About the man? The one Alfred warned you of?"

She nodded. "He's getting closer. I can feel him. He's coming."

"Tell me everything you can. Every detail. Leave nothing out."

"There are people around him. Lots of people. An army, even. That's the vibe I get...like he's leading an army of people right to our doorstep. If it weren't for feeling so shitty, I'd be more alarmed. There's only so much I can handle at one time...emotionally, physically. You know what I mean?"

"Yes, I do. There's nothing more important than taking care of that baby. Let others deal with this business. What else?"

"Everything is a bit foggy, not quite as clear as when I had the vision in Oklahoma, but I can tell you Alfred was right. That guy is one scary mother-effer. He seems to be gunning for someone in particular, but I don't know who. I keep hearing the word 'Rome,' but I get the sense he's heading this way. I think he's in the northern part of Oklahoma now, but they're moving slow. He rides a black horse, but his people...army or whatever...are on foot. I can't see how many there are but I think it's a lot. More than a hundred. Oh, and he has everyone branded when they join. The shape is a wheel with spokes and it's carved onto their forearms...like a tattoo, but it's actually a scar. Anyway, that's all I remember."

Amelia nodded. Of course she had no intention of sharing Jessie's visions with anyone. It was her job to keep the child's gifts hidden. Nobody knew about her extraordinary talents, except herself and Tung...and Fergus, wherever he was. So the more information she got from Maddie, the better the case she could build when she presented it to the town leaders. And if she embellished with details from Jessie, nobody would need to know.

Which she would do as soon as the sun came up and she had three more cups of coffee in her belly.

Chapter 29

"Let me get this straight. The pregnant girl had a dream and now we're going to drop everything we're doing, all the plans we've taken great pains to design and implement, just to fortify our defenses against a threat that may be imagined? A threat literally dreamed up by a hormonal young woman?"

If Calvin had been looking at Amelia instead of Steven when he spoke those words, he would have felt her animosity burn a hole in his face. An impromptu meeting had been called and the courthouse was still chilly. The few bodies in attendance weren't sufficient to heat up the space, but Calvin had insisted on employing the town crier so everyone would know what was going on. *Transparency*.

A few intrepid souls had shown up, but the dialogue was limited to Amelia and the two co-mayors. Dani was present but silent, and in a sour mood judging by the expression on her face.

"Calvin, you're new here," Steven said, "but I know you've heard the story of Maddie's visions. They proved to be accurate then, so they could be now as well."

"They are accurate," Amelia snapped. "Ignorance is a choice, gentle-men. There has been no greater peril than what we now face. I would expect better from our leaders than willful obtuseness, particularly as it applies to the safety of every person in this town."

Both men raised their eyebrows and looked at her.

"With all due respect, Miss Amelia, a dramatic shift in our priorities now will cause significant problems down the road. We have so many big projects planned for the spring, and all require elbow grease and man hours now...woman hours, too," he added quickly. "So if all that comes to a screeching halt to build a fortress and train an army, all those plans...the wheat crop, the power grid, and the hundred other improvements...vanish into thin air like so much smoke. I can tell you, the citizens won't be happy about that." The preacher seemed pleased with his argument. He felt confident the town would be on his side in the matter.

"You know what we need to do," Amelia said, turning her back on Calvin. Her arms were crossed as she sought to impale Steven with her eyes from a foot below.

"I tend to agree with you," Steven replied. "But we need more. He has a point, as much as I hate to admit it. What else can you give me?"

She would not reveal the true nature of the child under her protection, even if everyone in town were in danger. She had a better idea. Whether it had come from some subconscious part of her brain or her *scythen,* she didn't know and it didn't matter. She remembered the story Fergus had told her during one of their clandestine couplings about meeting Sam and Dani for the first time. She had already put the pieces together: the Smiling Man that Jessie and Maddie saw in their dreams was of course that nasty piece of business, Isaiah. The person he was 'gunning for' was Dani. All these facts she realized upon hearing Jessie's and Maddie's visions. But the crucial element that would win the support of the town's leaders and therefore the townspeople was something she learned just this morning.

She turned away and walked the ten feet to where Dani leaned against a wall. The young woman had yet to say a word, but there was an expression of keen interest on her face. She would understand better than anyone the danger that approached their town; she'd had a taste of it in Texas, according to Fergus. But first she must believe that Maddie's vision was more than a bad dream; must see it, not as some mumbo jumbo psychic nonsense, but as the remote viewing that it was.

"Maddie saw something on the arms of the dream soldiers. I'll tell you what it was and then you pull back your sleeve. Do we have a deal?"

Dani gave her a curt nod.

"She said it was a brand. Not burned, not tattooed, but carved into the skin. The shape is a wheel with spokes. All the members in the army are required to endure this torture as some sort of initiation. I've seen this type of behavior before in tribal cultures. Now, young lady, may we see your," she closed her eyes briefly, "left forearm, please. Come closer, gentlemen."

The young woman removed her leather jacket and slid up the thermal sleeves of her layered t-shirts. She grinned broadly now.

"Is this what you wanted them to see? It's a Dharmacakra, the Buddhist symbol for order. That's what the psychotic fucker told me right before he sliced and diced it into my arm." The scar was pink, raised, and ugly.

"Are you saying Dani is one of them?" Steven asked, alarmed.

"No, of course not. Steven, use that big brain of yours. Dani, perhaps you should explain now what we're facing. Something tells me you know better than anyone."

The next ten minutes were filled with a terse recap of Dani's adventure with Isaiah and his followers in Texas, followed by Steven's rapid fire questions.

"I don't see how this proves anything. Dani could have shown that scar to her before now," Calvin said. "Or told her about it, at least."

"But I didn't. The only person who's seen it is Sam. Isn't that right, Sam?" Dani's eyes were on the preacher, who hadn't been aware the young man had entered the room. Nobody else had either.

"That's right." Sam's honest smile was for everyone in the room.

"So Maddie saw Dani's scar in her vision as well as the scars on the soldiers?" Steven asked.

"Yes," Amelia lied smoothly. "I'm sorry, I forgot to mention that earlier. That's how I was aware of it, of course." No surface dwellers had known about her relationship with the odd red-haired man. He had been the only person besides Sam and Dani themselves who knew about the brands, and he had 'died' before he could have had told anyone else.

"Why haven't you mentioned this person as a threat before now?" Steven was beginning to get angry.

Dani shrugged. "How was I to know he'd follow us? It doesn't make sense that he would pack up his little army and head north just to seek revenge. He didn't know where we were going. Hell, *we* didn't know where we were going. There's another motivation: Liberty. He seems to know a lot about what we have here. It would be much easier to take over our town, his new 'Rome in the Midwest,' than build it himself from scratch like we've done."

"Can you all hear yourselves? We're making decisions and legislating action based on dreams. And not just dreams of one of our own, but now we believe this supposed psychopath has psychic visions too? Visions of our town and the very sign that tells him our location? This is beyond absurd!" Calvin paraded about the room, gesticulating with his hands like he was giving a hellfire sermon.

Steven sighed. "If what Dani and Sam are saying is true, then the other sticking point is the validity of the visions. Amelia, I hate to ask this and please know that I believe that *you* believe everything you've told us, but before making such an important decision, we need to hear from Maddie herself. Is she well enough to come talk to us?"

"No, she's not. But I guess she'll have to be, if that's what it takes. I'll go fetch her."

"No, we'll send someone else. Sam?"

"I'll be back in two wags of a donkey's tail."

Amelia's mind raced. She wouldn't have time alone with Maddie beforehand to explain the situation. She would have to resort to other measures.

An uncomfortable twenty minutes later, Sam reappeared with Maddie and Pablo in tow. In the meantime, a few more citizens had wandered in to catch the last part of the unscheduled meeting. A biting northerly wind kept most people at home.

"Can we make this quick, please?" Pablo said, his voice low and angry. "She isn't feeling well. She should be in bed." He shot Steven a venomous look.

Steven nodded. "Amelia has told us about your visions, Maddie. We would like to hear it from you directly. A lot is riding on this as you must know, so please be as detailed as possible."

For the next five minutes, Maddie spoke of her dreams while rubbing pale fingers against her temples.

"Is that all? Anything else? What about the sign?"

Everyone's attention was focused on Maddie, not on Amelia who had become motionless where she stood next to Dani. Her eyes were closed and furrows of intense concentration appeared between her brows.

Maddie frowned. Her lashes fluttered, then the china blue eyes took on a dreamy quality.

"Yes, I'm sorry. I left that part out. The man saw our sign, the one posted outside one of the barricades. He talked about it to the other people who were around him. He told them the name of our town."

Calvin made a non-verbal sound of disgust.

Steven ignored it and nodded. "Anything else? It's important."

"Yes, the scars. I saw them on the soldiers and," she paused, frowning, "and on her too." She pointed to Dani.

Amelia sat down abruptly on the bench behind her.

"Very good, Maddie. Thank you." Steven addressed everyone now. "I'm convinced, but I think we need something more tangible to go on."

"Like what, tarot cards? Chicken bones? Should we conduct a séance to communicate with these figments?" Calvin drawled.

"I find it ironic that a person whose mission in life is to convince others to believe in some invisible all-powerful, all-knowing supernatural being can't accept a little psychic phenomenon," Steven replied.

Calvin opened his mouth to respond, but wasn't given the chance. "We're going to send out a scouting party," Steven continued. "We need visual confirmation."

"I'll go," Dani said. "The douchebag is after me, so I should be the one to go. Sam can stay here. He'll handle the security crew while I'm gone. And we don't need a party. Just me. I can travel faster and lighter by myself."

"No. You'll take two others with you, for reasons of safety, and also so multiple people can validate what they've witnessed. One person can be doubted, discredited. But I will let you pick the other two members of the scouting party. Do you agree, Calvin?"

"Agreed. But until they return, we don't change anything we're doing."

Steven arched an eyebrow. "I'm sure there are some steps we can begin taking that won't have an adverse effect on our productivity," he said, clapping the preacher on the back. "We don't know how long the scouts will be gone. Worst case, the actions we take will strengthen the town against any threat, whether it comes from this Isaiah person or someone else."

Before Calvin could respond, Steven directed his next question to Dani. "You'll be traveling south on I35, I assume?"

She nodded. "Yes. We'll take motorcycles. More fuel efficient and better for off-roading."

"Good idea. How long do you think it will take?"

"No more than three days. Fewer if we don't have any problems. It's less than two hundred miles to the Oklahoma border from here."

"Yes, but who knows what you'll encounter. Who will you take?"

"I'll take the Creeper – Logan – and Pablo. His experience from the supply forays will be helpful. And he proved that he can be a bad ass when he wants to be," she added with an evil grin. "I don't want to pull anyone else off the security crew. You're gonna need us more than ever."

"What a minute," Pablo said. "I don't agree to this. I need to stay here with my family."

"Sorry, dude. You make the most sense. If you truly want to protect your family, help me prove this threat is real."

Amelia saw the internal struggle play out on the young man's face. She watched as Maddie whispered something into Pablo's ear. He frowned, nodded. "Fine. Let's get this over with."

She was exhausted from utilizing her *scythen* to influence Maddie's testimony, but there would be no time for even a cat nap today.

Chapter 30

"Amelia, I don't have to tell you that what you did was against just about every rule there is," Tung said in their singular language. Now that Thoozy was gone, the pink walls and frilly curtains seemed more depressing than ironic.

"I know, I know. Trust me, the headache I have now may be the death of me. I had to do something though. This Isaiah person is the second biggest threat the people face."

"I realize that, but it's not our place to interfere. Manipulating Maddie's memory could count against them in the end."

"I don't regret it. They have to prepare for the coming battle. If they don't survive it, it won't make a difference whether the Ancient Ones decide to bring the floods. Or the pestilence. Or ignite the super volcano under Yellowstone. Or whatever earth cleansing they have in mind."

Amelia had been recruited before the last great flood, as had Tung. There were others, though, who had seen several apocalypses. She knew of these events through their memories; her *scythen* showed them to her when she was in their proximity. Not that she rubbed elbows with them much. Each generation of recruits gravitated to their own kind, those whose DNA was similarly engineered and who had been 'harvested' during the same ten or twenty-thousand year period. It was usually the youngest recruits who chose to go above most often, especially after a recent culling; to mentor, to watch, to report. Through their observations sent via *scythen* or the occasional in-person summons to disclose more detail, the *Cthor* would decide whether the current batch of humans was worthy of proliferation.

They were exceptional in many ways, as they had been designed to be. They were the elite – all carrying the same DNA molecule that had kept them from succumbing to the disease. They were the culmination of genetic engineering combining the most desirable, evolved traits of the all those humans who had come before; those who had lived during one or more of the many rises and falls of civilization on planet Earth and whose very existence had been removed from the fossil record by the *Cthor*. Evolution wasn't the ongoing linear event contemporary scholars believed it to be, nor was technology. Before the supercontinent Pangea had broken apart, there had existed a small populace profoundly more advanced than that annihilated by the recent plague. The *Cthor* had orchestrated the creation and genocide of every hominid species since they had first unlocked the secrets of genetics. Those discoveries and others had effectively extended their own lives to a degree that, while not eternal, was nearly so.

But not all the survivors were shining examples of human exceptionalism. Engineering humanity tens of thousands of years into the future didn't result in consummate perfection every time. Within the current population there were evident glitches. There always were.

If Amelia, Tung, and the others could convince the *Cthor* there were more positive results than negative – that there was more good clay to be shaped and formed than bad – humanity might have another twenty thousand years to live and evolve. But if they decided to wash the slate clean and start over, which was not unprecedented, new qualifying recruits would be brought below for genetic harvesting, and the rest of humankind would be destroyed.

The *Cthor* would begin their work anew, seeding the world with fresh, improved bloodlines as they had done countless times before.

Amelia was invested in the current population. She had been making pilgrimages above ground for millennia. She could still remember her first journey to Sumer, where she had almost gotten herself killed, a common problem with neophytes on their inaugural sojourns. Two thousand years ago, she was a hand maiden to Cleopatra, covertly observing her for months and nearly recruiting her before deciding the beautiful, clever, extraordinary woman was also a sociopath. Amelia had dwelled among the aboriginal humans in Australia. Watched in tears while the Aztecs engaged in human sacrifice. As an adopted member of the Mohawk tribe, she witnessed America's Revolutionary War as seen through the eyes of the indigenous people.

She had been on the surface for five years now, much longer than at any other time. She had known that Chicxulub, as these new humans had dubbed the genetic genocide, was imminent. She wanted to witness it for herself. It was the reason she had gray strands in her dark braids. Those who dwelled below only aged while they were on the surface; that physiological process didn't occur while living underground in what was essentially a massive hyperbaric chamber. Her devotion to the newest members of her family – family because they shared her own harvested DNA, but also because she had grown to love them – was the reason she came back to Liberty, even though her body wept for restorative sleep.

To her knowledge, the only human who qualified for recruitment was Jessie. The child would be safe if she survived long enough to meet the *Cthor's* age criteria. There was a place for her when she was old enough. And because of her exceptionalism, she would be allowed in sooner if there was to be a cleansing. Others who were exceptional, but not enough so, would not be spared. As long as she had breath left in her body, she would do everything in her power to get Pablo and Maddie and Steven and Julia and Sam and even the abrasive Dani...all the other good people...a fighting chance.

She had stayed too long and gotten too close. And Tung knew it.

He studied her with an air of annoyance mingled with affection. To a small degree, he empathized with her. He felt a kindred spirit with these people who also shared his harvested DNA, but he hadn't lived among them as long as she had. His *scythen* was stronger than hers, so much of his observation had been done remotely, below ground. He had only come to the surface this past year after Chicxulub had ravaged the planet. Now that Thoozy was gone – losing the last member of the first generation had been a devastating blow to everyone – Tung's burden was weightier. Thoozy's vast experience was their greatest treasure. His accumulated knowledge had been acquired during a prodigious lifetime that had begun a hundred million years ago in what now-dead scientists termed the Cretaceous period. Humans, and the giant reptile-mammal hybrids modern paleontologists called dinosaurs, had actually lived to-gether for a time, but that evidence had been removed per standard *Cthor* protocol. Amelia loved hearing his dinosaur stories, some of which had likely been embellished purely for entertainment value. Having Thoozy taken away by one such as Logan had been nearly unbearable, and it was one of the reasons Tung's assessment was less compassionate than hers.

The *Cthor* expected reports to be accurate and unbiased, not tainted with one's personal feelings. But when your *scythen* was as well-controlled as Tung's, certain events might be shrouded...cloaked...hidden among other images and thoughts. The question was, would he choose to do so? Amelia's *scythen* wasn't as sophisticated. They would find out what she had done, but not until she appeared before them in person. However, Tung could send news of her violation to them immediately. Or he could deem it low priority, able to wait for an in-person communique.

She would never ask him to do so; not with words, at least. Her expressive, old soul eyes were a different matter though.

Tung smiled at the small woman whose empathy and love was so strong it almost felt like a force field surrounding her.

He sighed. "We'll keep your indiscretion between us for now."

She launched her small body into his arms, kissing him with passion born of great relief.

"Thank you, my friend."

Chapter 31

"You know he will torture you. He will do some kind of horrible Apple Anguish thing to you."

Dani barked a laugh. "It's Pear of Anguish, Sam. You're adorable. I don't know if I've mentioned that lately."

He wouldn't be mollified so easily. "He wants to skin you alive. You know that. Maddie's dreams proved it."

She nodded, now convinced the clairvoyant business was straight-up legit. Freaky stuff, that. Sometimes she got a little déjà vu, but she suspected not one ounce of psychic ability flowed through her veins. She was all about the here and now...the corporeal world that she could touch and smell and see with her own eyes. All that dream shit was somebody else's problem.

Except for Isaiah. He was very much her problem and she would deal with him personally.

She was cramming weapons and MREs into motorcycle saddlebags in the living room of their home. Ammo disappeared into the interior pockets of a new quilted parka. It was the hard-core type mountain climbers used to scale Everest. A ghost of vanity whispered that the bulkiness of it made her look fat, but she dismissed the thought as soon as it surfaced; the former chubby insecure girl rarely haunted the lithe and lethal weapon standing before Sam.

"I'll be super careful. He'll never see me or what hit him."

Sam's eyes flew open in alarm. "You're not supposed to get near him. You just need visual confirmation of the army. That's it. Then you come home."

She smiled at the dismay on the handsome face.

"Think about it. If I take this guy out, the army falls apart, like flicking over that first domino in a chain. They'll probably just go back to Texas where it's warmer. I bet none of those people want to be marching north in the dead of winter. They have to be miserable. Once the leader is gone, the whole thing will crumble, like chopping the head off a snake. I guarantee it."

He frowned. "If you get close enough to kill him, you're close enough for him to get you."

"That's why I'm bringing the Creeper and his favorite toy. That weirdo can hit a fly off the ass of a donkey at a hundred yards. We won't have to get close, we just have to get close enough."

"Now I'm even more worried. I don't trust Logan. There's something wrong about his story of the night he killed that guy that had you pinned. The timeline doesn't add up."

"Come on, Sam. You love everybody. I know Logan is creepy, but he's harmless. He hero-worships both of us, I think. That's why he's always staring at us."

She kissed the unhappy mouth; just a brushing of lips at first, then a mingling of tongues that escalated to clothes on the floor and a quick coupling on the sofa in the chilly room.

"That didn't make me less worried," he said afterward, his dreamy expression belying the statement.

"No, but it distracted you for a few minutes. I love you. I'll be careful. I promise. I'll see you in three days at the most."

The next moment she was out the door. He heard the sound of the Yamaha rev to life, then fade away.

He sighed. "I would have to fall in love with a thrill looker."

"Julia, I have to go. They're waiting for me." Logan shifted from one foot to the other, like a four-year-old who needed to find a bathroom.

"Did you put the extra jacket in your pack? The water resistant one?"

"Yes. I don't like it though. It's loud. I don't think I can be invisible in it."

She gave him a worried smile. "No, but it will keep you dry if it rains or snows. Promise me you'll wear it if that happens, okay?"

"Yes, I promise. I have to go now. I'll see you in three days. That's what Dani said. Love you, Julia!"

The next moment he was out the bedroom, down the stairs and

through the front door. At the second-story window, she followed his progress from the porch to the street, then as he hopped on the motorcycle behind Dani. The rifle strapped behind his backpack looked cumbersome and awkward, but they seemed to manage just fine. Even with another person and the added weight, Dani maneuvered her bike with more skill than Pablo managed solo.

A minute later, the scouting party was gone.

She sat down on the neatly-made bed of what had been her nephew's bedroom but was now Logan's. She smiled at the verbal slip-up. He probably said those words to his mother every time he had left their house. An affectionate habit, nothing more. She wouldn't read too much into it, despite knowing how attached he was to her. And she had to admit she also felt an attachment to the boy-in-the-man's-body. She surveyed the bedroom, wondering if Jeff resented giving up his room despite his assertion to the contrary. Young boys need their space and privacy to do all the gross things young boys do when they're alone. But her nephew seemed fine about sharing his dad's bedroom. Neither he nor Logan were home much these days anyway; their shifts on the security crew, plus the ongoing training sessions, demanded most of their time. The nights Steven spent at Marilyn's house, Jeff got the bed all to himself, so she guessed it was working out pretty well under the circumstances.

She thought about her 'boys' and how they were growing up too fast. They had both been exposed to so much violence and bloodshed these past months; even been responsible for some of that bloodshed. How well were they handling that onus? How would it shape them? What long-term impact would it have on the men they would one day became?

And then there was Dani. She felt the familiar knot in the pit of her stomach – the one associated with the cold-shoulder rejection she still received from the young woman who was almost certainly her daughter. It was a crazy situation. The odds should have been astronomical that they would ever have crossed paths. Yet knowing what she did about the genetic nature of the Lexi molecule made it less crazy and the odds not so remote; they both shared the rare gene that had saved their lives when billions of others perished. It had taken the end of the world to reunite her with the baby girl she gave up all those years ago, only now to be despised by her. Had it been a mistake telling her? Perhaps. But she couldn't have lived with the ambiguity. Julia liked things as cut and dried and above board as possible. She would have fretted herself into an early grave if she hadn't talked to Dani. It was her burden to accept that disdain and resentment, which felt like a dagger plunging into her heart.

The melodramatic thought evoked a derisive snort. She brushed at the tears that trickled down the sides of her face. That was happening way too often these days.

Something poking out of a dresser drawer caught her eye. Logan wasn't clean, but he was tidy. Everything was orderly; all his belongings had their place. He made his bed every morning without being told, and the room was more immaculate now than when they had first arrived.

That's why she had noticed the pencil sticking out of the dresser.

She crossed the room and slid open the bottom drawer. Inside were three neat piles of threadbare but clean (she hoped) boxer shorts. Under the third stack she could see the corner of a spiral notebook. Below it, she discovered several more. Underneath those, was a different type of tablet with the words *Strathmore Drawing Pad, 400 pages* printed on its cover.

Julia gathered them all up and sat back on the bed, feeling like she had stumbled upon the secret location of an older sister's diary. Her curiosity got the best of her, and she dismissed the niggling, voyeuristic shame. She lifted the well-worn cover. What greeted her on the first page was astonishing.

It was a portrait of a woman, sitting in a chair watching television. The detail was exquisite. The scene looked so real she could almost hear the laugh track of the *Friends* sitcom on the TV screen, drawn so finely that she could identify Jennifer Anniston and the periwinkle walls of the shabby chic apartment set.

This must be Logan's mother. She could see a strong resemblance on the attractive but haggard face. The blond hair was pulled back in a messy up-do, revealing care-worn lines and a jawline just beginning to sag. She appeared to be in her forties. There was a gentleness about her face...a kindness that Logan had managed to capture with his colored pencils. Confirming her suspicion were the letters "Mom" printed discreetly in one corner.

Next came another remarkable drawing, but this time it was a landscape of a semi-urban neighborhood. The houses were small and un-kempt; residences that had probably been built in the sixties. The careful articulation showed low income housing of a type occupied by single moms and broke college students. That made sense. His mother had struggled to support the two of them without any financial help from the absent father, and without benefit of higher education.

The thought made her feel ashamed. She had put herself and her career before everything else, including her baby. For the last two decades she had lived a life of privilege. What sacrifices had this woman made to care for her special-needs child? How much more difficult had it been to raise a child such as Logan than it might have been raising a gifted one, like Dani?

She flipped the page quickly.

The next three drawings were also stunning. One was a beautiful wooded scene bursting with orange, gold, and red; the vibrant colors of autumn. The next two were more renditions of the dilapidated neighborhood. One was drawn in the dismal tones of winter, and another showed the pale greens of early spring.

She turned to the next page. It was another portrait, but it had been rendered in charcoal. The stark black-and-white color scheme might be the reason the heavy-lidded eyes staring up at her from the thick vellum felt vaguely malevolent. Maybe she was overreacting, but it seemed to exude an ominous vibe. Or maybe her first impression was correct and the man was what had popped into her mind: a predator. It was silly to attribute such characteristics to a drawing, but she couldn't shake it. She studied the slick-backed dark hair that was shot with streaks of gray, and the baleful smile that played about the corners of the thin lips.

That is one scary son of a bitch.

She shifted focus away from the face and to the background. A windowless cinderblock wall filled most of the page. A basement perhaps? She looked closer still at the intricate details. Hanging on the wall to the left was a pegboard with hooks, upon which were hung an assortment of tools. Strange tools that didn't look like they were meant for anything as innocuous as gardening or carpentry.

And knives. Knives of all shapes and sizes.

On the right side, positioned halfway out of the picture, sat a wooden chair. Leather manacles dangled from the armrest and a spindle leg.

Tiny letters had been scrawled at the bottom: "Mister C." Below that was the shape of a valentine heart.

A wave of nausea washed over her. The sinister eyes seemed to bore into her. She remembered Logan mentioning a Mr. Cheney, the neighbor who had helped Logan's mother start her car by *popping-the-clutch* and who seemed to have taken an interest in the young boy.

She also recalled a conversation with Thoozy on the drive to Kansas. It was a discussion about the pathology of a sociopath: *If his childhood development had been influenced in a negative way, or if he'd experienced unhealthy urges that weren't dealt with professionally and in a timely manner, the result could be bad...*

With a trembling hand, she turned the page.

The next moment she ran to the bathroom, barely making it to the toilet in time to vomit every spoonful of the powdered scrambled eggs she had eaten for breakfast.

"I can't just give you something like that without knowing what it's for."

Julia sat on a doily-covered sofa in Cate's living room. Julia didn't like the woman, but because her brother did and because she was such a valuable asset to their community, she kept her opinion to herself. Still, there was something off-putting about her.

And she hated that she needed to ask for her help now.

"I know you're knowledgeable about homeopathic medicine. I've seen you administer witch hazel and slippery elm and Echinacea...and belladonna as a sedative for the Hays girls who were so traumatized."

"That's not an explanation."

Julia blew out a measured breath. She needed Cate's help and she needed it now.

"I can't say what I need it for. Can't you just trust that I wouldn't ask if the situation weren't dire?"

"You're Steven's sister. I barely know him, and I know you even less. What part of that should inspire my trust?"

"What if I told you that lives are at risk?"

"I'd tell you that lives are at risk every minute. And that by giving you an herbal compound which, if taken in the wrong dosage, could be fatal, even more lives are at risk."

Julia studied the round face and the intelligent glint in the small, close-set eyes. She decided to take a leap of faith. For the next five minutes, she spoke in a low, urgent voice. When she was finished, Cate's familiar amused grin had vanished, replaced by a thin-lipped line that gave away nothing of what was going on in the head of the strange woman.

"You don't want belladonna. You want castor bean seeds. Ever heard of ricin? That's where it comes from."

"Do you have them?"

"Of course. What witch would be caught without a supply of caster bean seeds?" There was a smirk on the round face, but one that was tinged with sadness.

"It won't be painful, right?"

Cate didn't meet her eyes when she replied. "No. He'll just go to sleep."

Chapter 32

Steven had picked the worst possible morning to sleep in at Marilyn's. He read through Julia's note for the third time, sitting down suddenly in one of his kitchen chairs.

He knew his sister better than anyone on the planet. She was an emotional basket case at the moment. She could hold things together under extremely stressful situations...as long as her heart wasn't involved. He remembered her behavior at their mother's funeral, then two years later at their father's: debilitated by grief and sadness, barely able to drag herself to the services. Now here she was, venturing out of the relative safety of their town to go after Logan to stop him from hurting Dani. How she intended to do that was unclear since her note didn't offer any details, but the drawing pads left on the kitchen table explained everything else. Steven felt a fleeting vindication when he scanned the first of the drawings – he always knew the young man was trouble – then the petty satisfaction was chased away by dawning horror.

Scene after scene depicted in exquisite detail with colored pencils: torture, mutilations, dissections, and what appeared to be a flayed cat next to a dead girl with reddish-orange hair. He could tell she was dead because there was a circular hole in the center of her forehead.

He also knew that Logan was very good with his guns.

As grisly as the majority of the pictures were, two stood out. Julia had removed them from one of the college-ruled spiral notebooks – poor substitutes for the older vellum pad – which contained numerous scenes from Liberty and were therefore the most recent of Logan's artwork. She had torn them from the topmost notebook, left open with tattered paper remnants clinging to its corkscrew spine.

The first was an image rendered in charcoal of someone being stabbed. There was no color in the night scene; but every line, every wrinkle on Thoozy's face was perfectly captured. The mystery of the old man's disappearance had just been solved. The second picture was even more disturbing. It showed a carefully articulated drawing of Dani in her black leather jacket and the familiar *GIRL POWER* t-shirt. A miasma of color encircled her; a swirling fog of purple and green shading. Around her throat was a pair of hands. Around the wrist of one of the choking hands was a braided bracelet Logan always wore. An impossibly long tongue extended out of one side of Dani's mouth. Her eyes bulged, cartoonish in their distress.

This wasn't a depiction of a past event, as many of the other drawings likely were. It was a projection, a tableau of intent; a Dickensian ghost of a killing yet to come.

Dani had ridden out of town on a dangerous mission, saddled – literally – with the deranged young man who planned to murder her.

And Julia had followed in a stolen vehicle to save her.

The morning, begun in a delicious afterglow, had just turned into an epic clusterfuck.

There was something bothering Logan. He had been so excited to go on the adventure with Dani and Pablo that he was a little frazzled just before they left. That was a word his mother used all the time. And she usually said it after she had been at work all day and had come home to something bad that he had done.

He loved the way the cold air exploded against his face when he peered around Dani's helmet. When he turned his head to see if Pablo was still behind them, he always was. Logan thought it would have been better if Pablo hadn't come with them. This would be a great time to do what he had been thinking about, but he would need to be careful with a third person around. Maybe he should kill Pablo too. Then there wouldn't be anyone left to tell on him, and everybody in town would still like him. Thoozy was wrong. The perfect place to be was in the middle of the pretty meadow and the cold river. It was kind of like being invisible. He could still have fun and do all the things Mister Cheney had shown him, just as long as nobody found out. The Bad Thoughts weren't very loud anymore, but he realized that was because he had been listening to them again and not trying to ignore them. They didn't have to yell if he was already paying attention.

Even though he had started to like Dani a little ever since she had started acting like she liked him too, he knew she had to die. He couldn't stand that she had the same colors as his Julia. More importantly, he hated that Julia was beginning to think of her as a daughter, which kind of made Dani his sister. He had never had a sister his whole life, and he didn't want one now. Julia only had so-many-hours-in-a-day, and he wanted them all for himself. His mother had always said he wasn't good at sharing, which was a bad thing. Maybe that was true. But like Thoozy's...what was the word again?...parable?...there was a third option: he could be selfish and not share stuff and nobody needed to know. He could keep it hidden just like the drawings under his underwear.

They were going fast and expected to make-good-time because the roads were mostly clear. According to Dani, the fucking wheat farmers knew how to maintain their highways. It seemed like they had been on the motorcycle for about two hours when she signaled to Pablo to stop. Logan was glad because he needed to pee. He had forgotten to do that before they left. Thinking about Julia sitting there on his bed made him realize what had been bothering him.

Had he put the drawing pads and pencils back in their hiding place? Mister Cheney said he should hide his artwork. After showing the one of the dead puppy to his mother and seeing the unhappy look on her face instead of the happy one she usually made when he showed her pictures of trees or houses, Mister Cheney said he should just keep them private. Other people wouldn't understand them, and some artwork wasn't meant for anyone but the artist.

He felt worried for a long minute as he thought about everything he'd done before leaving. Then when he remembered putting the drawings back under his underwear (that always cracked him up...he thought *under underwear* was a great hiding place and it also sounded funny), he felt better. Yes, he had definitely put them back in the drawer. If someone were to open that drawer, all they would see is underwear. He couldn't imagine anyone would want to move a bunch of boxer shorts around...some of them weren't even clean. The drawings were safe. The thought made him smile.

"Why did we stop?" Pablo asked, standing next to his motorcycle, taking the opportunity to stretch his muscles. Why had these two-wheeled Roman candles been so popular? Sure, you could go fast, but they were uncomfortable. And cold.

"We're less than a half hour away from the state line," Dani replied.

They had taken I70 east to I35 south, then skirted the worst of the Wichita exodus by utilizing the I235 loop. The green highway sign under which they had stopped read *South Haven, next exit.* A frigid north wind pummeled them, whipping the chartreuse scarf wrapped around Pablo's neck. It was perhaps the ugliest item he had ever owned; a parting gift from Maddie, knitted by her own hands and therefore priceless. He just hoped her knitting skills improved with time.

"That isn't an answer."

"You're not going to like the answer." An evil grin uncoiled on the pretty face.

At that moment, Pablo could have punched the orthodontic perfection down the attached throat. For the life of him, he could not see why people liked this woman. Yes, she was attractive. Stunning, actually. But her cold, austere beauty was diametrically opposed to the warm, delicate loveliness that was Maddie. Dani was a snow-capped mountain range unveiled by an arctic sunrise. Maddie was a balmy, languorous sunset over turquoise waters. Dani was insufferable. And abrupt. And condescending. Personality traits he also shared, but felt obliged to stifle on a daily basis. Not so for Dani. She left them unchecked and unfettered. Hell, she basked in them.

"What am I not going to like?"

"We need to ditch the bikes. They'll hear them coming a mile away."

"You're joking. Please tell me you're joking."

"I'm not. Think about it, Pablo. You're a smart guy. The key to the success of this venture is stealth. There's nothing stealthy about two revving motorcycle engines."

He had no answer.

"We'll leave the bikes here and continue on foot. Stuff your backpack with water from the saddlebags. We can go without food if we have to. I hope you're wearing comfortable walking shoes," she added over her shoulder as she wheeled the Yamaha down into the drainage culvert which flanked the highway. When she tipped it over on its side, it was no longer visible from above.

He gritted his teeth, biting off the words he wanted to say, and followed the next moment. He had hated the discomfort of the bike not five minutes earlier. Now, contemplating the distance they would be walking, he realized something, as he had many times during his life and especially after Chicxulub: things can always get worse.

After he loaded his pack with supplies – water *and* food...this wasn't his first rodeo and he would carry whatever the hell he wanted in his pack – he returned to the blacktop where Logan and Dani waited.

"I think we can make ten more miles today," she said, pulling out a tattered Rand McNally road map. "That'll put us almost into Oklahoma. We know they're north of Guthrie, according to Amelia and courtesy of your psychic girlfriend. So they could be anywhere in this area." A gloved finger circled a small section.

Pablo studied the map with a frown. "It's eighty miles to Guthrie."

"Yes, but as I just explained, they're no longer in Guthrie," she replied with exaggerated patience. "They could be fifty miles north of Guthrie now. They could be five miles away from us even as we speak. We don't know, so we have to assume the worst."

Blue eyes locked with golden. Logan stood off to the side, watching the exchange with a slack-jawed expression. Pablo barely registered his presence. He was in a stand-off with this creature; a non-verbalized battle of wills...

...which he knew he would lose, because she was absolutely right.

###

Pablo's Journal Entry #452

Arrogance has a face, and it belongs to the woman who holds my fate in her wretched hands. She is a puto arrogante on steroids. She is the antithesis of all that is gentle and compassionate and kind. I suppose we need such as her – the chemotherapy that almost kills the patient – but good lord she's unbearable. How does Sam love this vile creature? She's all sharp edges and jagged corners. If I survive this mission, I shall refuse to embark on any venture with her again.

Some might say that when I look at her, it's like looking into a mirror. I realize now how others felt when I talked down to them. She assumes she's always the most intelligent person in every discussion. I behaved that way too, once upon a time. My humble parents almost seemed apologetic of their extraordinary son. It was awkward enough for them that my skin and eyes were lighter than those of all the other immigrant children. Despite being proud of my intellect and talent, I think they felt it aroused unwanted attention (never a good thing when one has entered the country illegally), and my youthful braggadocio was an affront to the collective humility of our people. White Americans want to shout their genius from the highest mountaintop, and Dani is the quintessential white American. For most of my adult life, I've tried to resist that inclination; and I admit it hasn't always been easy. Being smart doesn't give one carte blanche to treat others with disdain or disrespect. I know this now. But is this woman self-aware enough to see that? Does she know how awful she is? Probably. Does she care? Clearly not.

Enough on that subject.

We're bedded down under an overpass in northern Oklahoma. Of course we couldn't build a fire that might be seen by Isaiah – evil has a name now – so I'm writing by LED light on the lowest setting of my flashlight. I'm thankful the tempest has diminished to mere thirty mile-per-hour gusts. The scent of snow, a dreadful harbinger earlier in the day, proved toothless, manifesting in only a few capricious flakes. We also receive a modicum of relief from the buffering concrete overhead and behind our miserable camp.

Completing this horrific Hat Trick, this Perfect Storm of suffering, is the presence of Logan.

I could fill my journal with colorful descriptions of his strange behavior, his odd verbiage, his unsettling smile. He is one for the books. And by 'books,' I mean case studies of eminent oddballs. I don't expect to get any sleep tonight between the cold, the cement mattress, and the fear of what Logan might do when I close my eyes.

Chapter 33

.

"You were wrong, Lieutenant. Nothing came of that blizzard you forecasted. If I had listened to you, we would still be in Perry. Fortunate for everyone that I didn't take your advice." Isaiah's gesture astride the Friesian indicated the marching army spread out on foot around them. "We would have delayed reaching our New Rome."

The overcast sky provided the perfect backdrop for the magnificence that was Isaiah and his war horse. Lily, who 'refused to ride any beast that had a will of its own,' could barely keep her eyes off their general from where she walked beside him.

Martin got that sickening feeling again. How could Isaiah expect him to accurately predict the weather? It had been an impossible situation earlier, and when his opinion had been sought, he had taken the softer position: that of staying another day or two in the relative comfort of the Holiday Inn Express in Perry, Oklahoma. Nothing had come from what felt like a snow-laden artic front, and he had ended up on the losing side of the daily game of 'advising their general.'

Lily had been the winner. As a native Oklahoman, she was more knowledgeable on the local weather than he was. In Texas it was rare to see more than one snow event in a winter. But nothing mattered other than who gave the best advice when it was asked for, and she was beating him at almost every turn these days. He had noticed Isaiah studying him recently; a sideways, smile-less, calculating inspection. He knew he was being measured with a yardstick as long as it was daunting. What rational, reasonable, sane person could pass muster? The answer was Lily, because she was none of those things. She was as bat-shit crazy as Isaiah, and she loved him unconditionally...a hell hound devoted to a single master.

"I'm sorry, sir." He wanted to add: *I'm not a fucking meteorologist.* But of course he didn't. He preferred to stay alive. He knew that he teetered on the thinnest of tightropes, and all he could do was apologize, work on his escape plan, and hope that he could implement it before he was hanged from the nearest tree.

"If I didn't know better, I'd say you were distracted. What could be occupying your mind these days? It better not be a woman. Or worse, a man. You know that nonsense is forbidden until we've achieved our goal and vanquished our foes. Sex is such a waste of one's energy. It serves a purpose, of course. We must be fruitful and multiply!" The rich laughter was unexpected and welcome. It was usually a good sign. Usually. "But now is not the time nor place for it."

Martin responded with a careful smile. "No, sir. It's nothing like that. I guess I'm just tired. I know that's no excuse, and I'll try to be less distracted."

Isaiah glanced down at the woman trudging along beside him. "What do you think, Lieutenant Lily? Is our Martin merely fatigued or is he having thoughts of a more subversive nature? Rebellious, reckless ruminations?"

Lily had added more layers of rags to her wardrobe during the last week. Underneath all those tattered garments was probably a lithe, muscular body, but they made her appear bulky. God only knew what she carried in all those pockets and pouches.

Her gaze glided from Isaiah to him; her eyes were so black it was difficult to tell where the pupils ended and the irises began. She scanned him from top to bottom without blinking and without missing a step.

Finally she spoke. "I can't decide what's going on in his head. Sometimes I think he is committed to our mission, and other times I think he would prefer to be someplace else."

"Sir, I admit I'm no fan of the cold," Martin replied quickly. "Can I be blamed for an occasional daydream? Thoughts of, as you yourself mentioned, a warm comfortable bed and a place to call home? Yes, I'd prefer to be someplace else, but that someplace is our New Rome. I share your vision as much as she does."

After a long moment, Isaiah nodded. He had bought it. This time.

"You shall have your warm bed soon enough. At our current pace, we'll be in Kansas in two days. Now focus! No more distracted, diverted dithering. The only thoughts filling your head should be those which benefit our noble quest. Are we clear?"

"Yes, sir." Martin's mouth was so dry he could barely get the words out. He glanced at Lily once Isaiah's attention had moved away from him. He expected to see an expression of smug satisfaction at having prevailed, again, over her rival. Instead, the pallid, nondescript face was thoughtful.

The next moment he almost fell off his horse in surprise when one of the black eyes winked at him. It was followed by a widening of the thin-lipped mouth. With her pasty skin stretched tightly across the underlying scaffold of bone, she looked like a cadaver who had heard an amusing joke.

What the wink and smile meant would be the subject of much speculation during the cold dark night to follow.

Chapter 34

"Natalie, I appreciate the offer, but I rarely need help. And on the occasion that I do, Julia is kind enough to lend a hand."

Marilyn the Librarian was looking almost pretty these days. No, that was hyperbole. She was less unattractive. She had put on a few pounds, as had Natalie herself; an improvement for both women. There was some color to her cheeks, which highlighted the underlying bone structure; nowhere near the perfection of her own, but adequate. And was the woman wearing lipstick or were the thin lips naturally pink? Natalie grudgingly admitted to herself that when Marilyn smiled, it transformed her face.

And the smile happened often these days. Getting laid must agree with her.

Natalie felt a nauseating wave of jealousy.

"Please. You would be doing me such a favor. Working at the hospital is mind-numbingly boring. And Cate makes my skin crawl. I think she's a lesbian. I catch her staring at my ass and boobs several times a day."

"You should be used to that," Marilyn said with a grin.

"True. But it's different coming from a woman. I'm not interested in women…in that way. I don't want to be her sexual fantasy."

"That seems like a leap. Who cares what her sexual preference is? Has she made advances? Touched you inappropriately?"

"No, no. Of course not. She's not stupid. Just odd and creepy."

"Well, there's plenty of odd and creepy in town these days."

"So true."

Having regular access to Marilyn would make it easier to get rid of her. Natalie's objective was to remove all obstacles blocking her path back to Steven. Something would have to be done about Calvin too, but that shouldn't be difficult. She was fucking him, which meant she had complete control over him.

"Maybe just a few hours a couple of times a week. Let's say Tuesday and Friday afternoons. Those are your distribution days, right? It must get hectic sorting the supplies and handing them out to everyone. I'll still be putting in my fifty work hours, but some of them will be helping you instead of Cate."

"I don't know. Of course I'd need to check with Steven first. Did you run it by Calvin?"

"Yes. He's perfectly fine with it."

Marilyn hesitated. She seemed to be giving serious consideration to the request while studying the woman who'd made it.

"We can talk about books while we work," Natalie said. "I'm a bibliophile, just like you. My degree is in English Literature." She leaned in and continued in a conspiratorial tone, "I have an early Brontë edition. I'll bring it next time I come."

Marilyn's eyes gleamed. "*Jane Eyre*?"

"Much rarer. *Wuthering Heights.*"

When she saw the wide grin on the plain face of Liberty's former librarian, she knew the bait had been taken...every wriggling, tantalizing bit of it.

Chapter 35

Every few seconds, Julia took her eyes off the windshield and the unfurling ribbon of blacktop beyond so she could scrutinize the drainage ditches that ran parallel to the highway. The sun had almost set and even with the headlights on, visibility was poor. The knuckles that gripped the steering wheel of the stolen truck were fish-belly white. It had taken immense patience to drive slowly enough so she wouldn't overlook any evidence of the scouting mission's presence, or their passing through. They would have hidden the motorcycles and be on foot by now. That's what she would have done this close to the Oklahoma border. Isaiah's army could be near enough to hear the motorcycles' engines, and Dani would never have compromised the mission for the sake of comfort.

The next moment the headlights reflected off something in the drainage ditch. She pulled the truck over to the shoulder, then got out to investigate. The reflection had come from the rearview mirror of a motorcycle. She recognized both bikes from the glimpse through Steven's upstairs window. Other than a handlebar sticking up slightly, they wouldn't be visible from the highway. If she hadn't had the headlights on to see the reflection in a tiny section of exposed mirror, she would have missed them.

It was time for her to go on foot.

Two hours later, her feet were killing her and she was chilled to the core. She hadn't taken the time to put on decent walking shoes before she had hauled ass out of Liberty, and her parka was barely adequate. There would be hell to pay for stealing the vehicle; or more accurately, for using gas in a non-sanctioned endeavor.

Her mind didn't fully register the discomfort nor indulge in worry over the consequences of her actions. She had to get to Logan and Dani.

Nothing else mattered.

The next moment, her tenacity was rewarded. Fifty yards ahead she could see the glow of an LED flashlight. Then it vanished. Her eyes had adjusted to full darkness and she could make out the concrete overpass under which the threesome must be camped. If she had seen them, it was likely they had seen her too. Covert motility was not her forte.

She called out in the cold night air.

"Logan, it's me!"

A shadowy form materialized out of the darkness ten feet beside her.

"Julia, what are you doing here?"

"Where is Dani?"

"She's behind me somewhere. Why are you here?"

He stood next to her now, close enough for her to see confusion on the handsome face. An invisible icy hand twisted her guts, but she had her story ready.

"We got more information from Maddie about Isaiah's location. Someone needed to deliver it to Dani and I volunteered. Is she under the bridge?"

"No, I'm right here." Another shadow detached itself from the gloom.

She thought she might faint from relief.

"Good. You have a camp up ahead? I've been walking for hours. I'd like to sit down and have something to drink. I brought some hot chocolate for you, Logan. It's special just for you. I put lots of sugar in it."

"Why would they send you? You seem like an odd choice," Dani demanded.

Mother and daughter locked eyes. Julia felt something pass between them; a frisson of connectivity, or more specifically, a message had been sent and received. Dani knew she was up to something, but she wouldn't press her now. Not yet.

"Let's just sit down and I'll go over everything."

The young woman nodded, turned her back, and walked toward the overpass. Logan trudged along noiselessly beside her. Her own movements must have sounded like an elephant passing compared to theirs.

Dani got a fire going in under a minute. It was small and contained, but it was putting out a surprising amount of heat. The hot chocolate in the stainless steel thermos would be warm in no time.

"I thought you said no fire?" Pablo said, warming his hands.

"For some reason, it's important. It will probably get us killed though, even though we're on the north side of the overpass. Hope it's worth it to you, Julia," Dani said. The words didn't carry much sting though. She could see the girl was intrigued, wondering what she could be up to.

"I'm sorry I only brought enough for Logan. It's just that he loves it so and I left in such a hurry that it didn't occur to me to bring more, and I didn't have time to heat it. Here, Logan. I think it's ready now."

She lifted the thermos from the fire with a gloved hand, unscrewed the lid and filled the metal mug.

"Must be nice to have hot chocolate delivery service in the middle of nowhere. You have impressive connections, Creeper."

Julia looked at the young woman whom she believed to be her daughter. Eyes so similar to hers, dilated in the firelight, stared right back at her.

Julia shifted her attention back to the young man who was already sipping at the mug and wearing a smug expression. She knew what that look meant. He was getting something nobody else was. Her stomach was so knotted she thought it might never feel normal again. *She* would never feel normal again, that was a given.

"It tastes a little funny. Not like the stuff we usually have."

"It's a different brand. It's Godiva instead of Swiss Miss," she said, blinking rapidly to keep the tears in check. "Now drink it all before it gets cold. It'll warm you up nicely."

"Your colors are weird, Julia. I wonder why you're gray and brown, and not purple and green." He finished the dregs of the hot chocolate with a loud slurp.

"I don't know, dear. I can't see them like you can."

She could no longer keep the dam from breaking. Tears coursed down her cheeks.

"Why are you crying? Is it like that time at the lake in Yellowstone? When you felt sad and we thought it was because of the princess who lived in the rock castles?"

"Yes. I think it's something like that. I'm feeling very sad."

He scrambled over to sit next to her, wrapping his arm around her shoulders.

"I'm sorry. I hope you don't stay sad for long."

Dani and Pablo watched the scene from across the fire. They were both exceptionally intelligent people. They may have figured out what was happening.

"Creeper, tell me about your life," Dani said, her voice a ghost of the normal brazen, impatient version; kind, almost. "Before everyone died. I don't think we've ever talked about it."

"Oh, okay. My mom was really nice. She always said I was a handful, but she sure did love me a lot. She had the same colors that Julia does. Well, the ones she usually does. Anyway, I was sad when she died. I wrapped her in her favorite blanket and buried her in the backyard."

"What about your dad?"

"I never knew him. When I was little, my mom told me he was the captain of a big ship and was lost at sea. But one time, after she drank a lot of *vodka medicine,* she said he was a golden-eyed devil. And that he was living in Arizona now and *probably-screwing-everything-in-sight.* I'm not stupid. I know that means s-e-x. I like thinking that he was a ship captain better."

Pablo spoke then, kindness also evident in his voice. "Arizona is where I'm from. It's a very nice place. There are mountains and a beautiful desert near Prescott, where I grew up."

"Prescott? I think that's where my mom said my dad had moved to when she was drinking her vodka medicine. I remember the name of the town started with a P and ended with a T. I bet that was it! Did you ever meet a golden-eyed devil?"

Pablo laughed. "Not that I recall. I think someone like that would have made an impression on me."

"She told me I got his eyes. Hey, yours are like mine! Your eyes are gold but your color is blue. Lots of blues. I think boys should be blue. It just makes sense. Sam's are the prettiest colors I've ever seen. They look like girl colors, because they're so pretty. Like a rainbow."

"Is that why I always see you staring at Sam?" Dani asked with a smile. "I thought you had a crush on him."

"No! I don't like boys. I had a girlfriend once. It was a long time ago, back in the eighth grade. But then my mom made us move to a different house and I had to go to a different school. Are you feeling better now, Julia? Not so sad?" Logan took his arm from her shoulders and hugged his stomach. "My tummy hurts."

"Go lie down. Where is your sleeping bag?"

"It's over there. Ouch! My tummy hurts bad!"

"I'm sorry your tummy hurts. Just lie down and maybe it will stop hurting."

"You're still crying! You must be really, really sad."

Logan squirmed into the sleeping bag. His face was that of an unhappy six-year old. Julia stroked his hair.

"Would you like me to sing that song you like?" She refused to look at Dani. This was Logan's time. All her attention belonged to him.

"Yes. But I don't think it will help. I may need to go *do-my-business*. Oh! It hurts so bad! I must be *coming-down-with-a-bug.*"

"You might be. Just try to rest. It will pass soon."

Hours slunk by with torturous slowness. The campfire burned down to embers, yet no one seemed inclined to sleep. Julia was vaguely aware they were being watched by the other two; a macabre, unscripted tragedy where both actors could barely speak their lines, being crippled by either guilt or agony.

"I've never felt so bad ever in my entire life. I don't think this is a bug. I think it's something worse."

"Hush, now. What else could it possibly be? I'm sure you'll be fine by morning."

Another spasm of pain wracked the body of the young man. He could no longer be contained by the sleeping bag. After casting it aside, he alternated between rolling on the ground, clutching his stomach then pacing between their camp and the culvert where he would squat every so often to relieve his bowels.

This was not the reaction to the poison that Cate described it would be. It would have been kinder to put a bullet in his brain.

Logan's pacing stopped. The golden eyes stared at her. All traces of the unsettling grin were long gone.

"This all started after I drank that hot chocolate. Maybe there was something in it."

"There was nothing in it but cocoa powder, sugar, and water. I made it myself."

His eyes narrowed. "You're black and gray, just like all those bad people I saw in Fisherman's Wharf before I met you. Are you like them now?"

"That's nonsense."

The young man convulsed again, doubling over and holding his stomach. When the spasm passed, he stared at her accusingly.

"Did you see my pictures? Did you find them under-the-underwear? Was that hot chocolate an evil potion you made with your magic?"

She gazed back at the boy-in-a-man's-body who had wormed his way into her heart. What was the point of lying? Did this wretched creature deserve to be comforted and coddled, or should he hear the truth?

"Yes, I saw the drawings. Oh, Logan. Why did you do all those horrible things to people? Why did you kill Thoozy? He was always so kind to you. Why do you want to kill Dani?"

Another wave of pain washed over the boyish face. He fell to the ground, rolling from side to side, moaning in agony.

"Because she has your colors, Julia," he whispered. "Because you think she's your daughter and I think she is too because of the colors. I didn't want to share you. I shouldn't have to share *YOU!*" Another cramp made him cry out the word. It would be the last one he would ever speak and it would resonate in Julia's nightmares for the rest of her life, a final condemnation.

You. You. You.

It took four more hours for Logan to die.

Julia stayed by his side the entire time, even when his bowels turned to bloody water. The seizures at the end were excruciating to witness, but she wouldn't turn away.

Did it help to know she was doing the world a favor, putting down a rabid animal before it could harm anyone else? No. If she hadn't discovered his plan to murder Dani, she would never have been able to do it, even knowing he had killed others and would continue doing so. A good mother will sacrifice her own life or sell her soul to save her child. And that's what Julia had done. A piece of her died with Logan; she would never be whole again.

She was standing next to the shallow grave Pablo and Dani had dug, when she felt a hand on her shoulder. The eastern sky had begun to change from indigo to gray. Dani's touch jolted her from her reverie, the one she would replay in her mind for the rest of her life: placing Logan in the ground and covering him up with dirt. *You. You. You.*

"When you're ready, let's talk," Dani said. "I have a lot of questions about Logan, but even more about your life. And I want to tell you about mine."

Chapter 36

"I'm sure he's fine. You don't need to worry about Pablo, my dear. That young man can take care of himself, even though he may not realize how strong he is. You just focus on getting well and keeping that baby bump healthy. Did you drink your milk yesterday? And Cate's tonic?"

Amelia had hoped Maddie would be better today. She had waited until the sun was up before checking on her. She was careful to keep her concern about the preeclampsia to herself, but every day that Maddie didn't improve, the apprehension grew. This did not feel like a normal pregnancy. Something was wrong; Amelia could feel it in her bones.

"Yes to both," Maddie replied. She was still in bed even though the winter sun shone through the bedroom window. That in itself was alarming. Maddie was an early riser; one of those people who felt energized early in the day and gets droopy-eyed by eight o'clock in the evening.

"And the headache is better or worse?"

"Worse, I think."

"Let's take your blood pressure."

"We just took it last night. Let me sleep a bit longer, okay?

I'm just so tired."

Amelia made a clucking sound of disapproval but didn't argue. She closed the door behind her, resolving to get to the library later and research preeclampsia. She was no midwife as she told Pablo and Maddie when she first met them. She only claimed that title because her *scythen* revealed that Pablo was eager to have a family and she had wanted to travel with them. The lie was necessary and she didn't regret it. Besides, with her intellect and unparalleled experience of humans, she knew far more than most about their biology and its physiological processes. She knew more than the average non-medical person about pregnancy and childbirth as well.

But she didn't know enough to get a handle on Maddie's decline. She hoped to today, though. Something must be done or Maddie would not survive the next few months. Perhaps she would pay a visit to Cate at the hospital too. She had put off having a one-on-one conversation with Liberty's 'doctor' for fear that her own deception might be uncovered. But Maddie's health and that of her unborn child superseded everything else.

"What's wrong? Is Maddie okay?" Jessie asked from the kitchen table where she sat eating hominy with sugar for breakfast.

"Not really. I'm worried about her." She made herself another cup of instant coffee and slid into a chair across from the child.

"Do you want me to touch her? Like I did before when she got shot in the head?"

Amelia studied her protégé, pondering the question and the consequences of taking such action. It was one thing to utilize the girl when she was still in the process of being evaluated, but quite another when she did so to affect the natural course of events. Breaking that rule would get her a lifetime ban on ever returning home. She and Tung and the others were here to observe and report; nothing more. There had only been one case of expulsion that she knew of and she desperately did not want to be the second.

"Not yet, child. Let's hope she gets better on her own."

"When will it be time to go below? Can't we just take Maddie and Pablo with us so they'll be safe?"

Amelia smiled at the anxious face. "Remember what I told you? Only very, *very* special people get to go below. Pablo and Maddie aren't special enough."

"But Maddie can do math without a calculator and Pablo writes all that poetry and stuff. Plus, Maddie has the dreams like me."

"There are a lot of special people now. That's why the sickness happened, so that all the people left would be special. But out of all those, there is a scintilla...a tiny number...of infinitely more exceptional people. Maddie and Pablo are like red emeralds or black opals, somewhat rare and certainly beautiful. But you, my dear, are jadeite; the rarest gemstone in the world. It's an interesting coincidence that your eyes are the exact color of that elusive mineral."

Jessie frowned. "I wish they could come with us. And Bruno and Curly

Sue and Gandalf the Grey too. Maybe we should just stay here?"

It was Amelia's turn to frown. "That's what we're doing. For the time being, at least. I can't leave until we accomplish two very important tasks."

"Annihilate the Smiling Man and show the Ancients that humanity deserves a chance to evolve?" Jessie parroted the words as if reciting the multiplication table, and she understood their meaning.

Amelia laughed at the serious expression on the child's face and her somber tone. "Yes. Those are our tasks. Once we've taken care of business and you've grown more, we shall go below and have a lovely nap."

"I don't like to take naps. I'm a little old for them, don't you think?"

"Not for these kinds of naps, child. Now hurry and finish your breakfast. We're going to the library!"

Chapter 37

"So the sperm donor was just a cute guy? Not a world-renowned physicist or Nobel prize-winning chemist? He was just so hot that you forgot to use a condom? Good grief. I can't believe someone as smart as you could have been so stupid."

Dani had allowed Julia two hours to grieve Logan's death before beginning the question and answer session. If she were going to allow this woman into her life, she would make her earn the privilege. She had twenty years' worth of questions bottled up inside, and the person who could answer them walked right beside her. She no longer tried to deny the fact that the woman was her biological mother; the evidence was too compelling.

"Well it's a damn good thing I didn't use a condom. We wouldn't be having this conversation if I had."

Dani snorted. "Touché."

"When you two are finished with this tender moment, I have some questions of my own," Pablo said. "Also, I don't think we should be walking so brazenly in the open. Katniss Everdeen would have us trudging through the fields where there's cover."

Dani shot him a poisonous glance, but didn't respond. He was right...annoyingly so. She had been hugely distracted by her conversation with Julia; she was finally getting answers to a lifetime of questions. They were walking three abreast, south on I35, alert for the sounds of an approaching army, or anything else that wasn't just a harmless byproduct of Mother Nature and the skeletal remains of a near-extinct civilization. The day had dawned gray and sunless, but the wind had died down. The temperature was in the forties, not miserably cold when they kept moving.

"Like what kind of questions, Pablo?" Dani asked. She hadn't yet decided how she felt about the guy. He was clearly intelligent, and more articulate than anyone she had ever met. But he was also one of those sensitive, angst-ridden types...the type that would slice off an ear and send it to some chick he was pining over. Still, there was something else going on behind those unusual eyes, and she had yet to get a handle on it.

"Like why are there so many odd and extraordinary people these days?" Pablo replied. "I want to hear about your research, Julia. I'd like to know what you were studying before and after Chicxulub. You mentioned something last night. You said, 'considering the pathology of so many survivors, I should have anticipated this.' You were talking to yourself, I realize, but I couldn't help hearing it. Would you explain that statement, please?"

They had paused in their progress. Pablo's focus was on their surroundings, and wisely so. They needed to get off the highway pronto. Dani was about to say as much when she caught an expression on Julia's face before it was stifled and replaced with careful indifference. Dani knew that look: it was guilt.

"The ramblings of a distressed person," Julia said. "I don't even remember saying that. I had just poisoned someone I cared about, for god's sake."

"Oh, what do we have here?" Dani said. "You're hiding something. You look like Woody Allen at a Sweet Sixteen party. Spill it, Julia. We have a right to know. What nasty little cooties did you see squirming in your microscope when the end of the world came?"

Julia shook her head. "I told Steven that I wouldn't discuss that subject. Not yet. Not until things are more stable in our town."

"What? The poison-wielding assassin won't break a promise?"

"That was a low blow."

Dani thought for a moment. "You're right. Sorry. Still, I'm not letting this slide. I've been called a honey badger, and if you know anything about that adorably tenacious creature, you know I won't give up. You might as well tell us what you know and save yourself a boatload of irritation. If it makes you feel better, we won't share with the class. Agreed, Pablo?"

Pablo raised an eyebrow. "I won't agree to that beforehand. My silence is dependent on the content of Julia's revelation."

"Ugh. Thanks for nothing, Voltaire. Come on, Julia. Just tell us."

Julia sighed. Dani could see she was emotionally tapped out. The woman would talk...she could feel it.

Julia opened her mouth to speak, but before she could get the first words out, the heavy metallic click of a bullet being chambered in a rifle came from behind them.

"Don't make any sudden moves," a man's voice said. "Arms in the air. Now, before I take the top of your pretty skull off."

"Shit," Dani said under her breath. She moved her hands from where they were placed on her weapons, lifted them skyward, then turned in slow motion to face the threat.

What she saw made her heart sink. Three men were fanned out across the highway. Each held a firearm, all pointed at them. A quick assessment extinguished any thoughts of a Rambo-style response. All three appeared watchful, grim, and competent.

She had allowed herself to be distracted and had just committed the worst fuck-up in the history of fuck-ups.

"Tie 'em up," the leader told one of the other men. "The girl first...I can see she's trouble."

If it hadn't been for the presence of Julia beside her, or if Sam had been on her other side instead of Pablo, she would have taken the chance. But the remarkable brain that could interpret data with the speed of a supercomputer and convert it into battlefield strategies and logistics with ease, knew the odds weren't good of surviving the situation if she reacted aggressively now. The brain said: *wait...bide your time...a better opportunity will present itself when these guys lower their guard...and they will.*

She gritted her teeth as one of the men yanked both arms behind her and expertly wrapped several loops of paracord around her wrists. Then he began plucking all her weapons from their hiding places.

When he found the K-bar in its calf sheath under her heavyweight cargo pants, she felt the first stirrings of rage. That K-bar had been with her through everything.

"This little hellcat is armed for bear," the man said, grudging admiration in his tone.

The next moment he located the final weapon: a small claw-shaped blade strapped to her triceps. Its bulge barely showed under her clothing, but the pat down had been thorough. He pushed up the sleeve of her jacket and then the underlying layers of tee-shirts to get to it.

"Captain, you need to see this. I think we caught ourselves a deserter."

Chapter 38

"There's a run on belladonna these days," Cate said to the beautiful woman sitting across from her on her grandmother's sofa.

"What do you mean?" Natalie asked.

"Never mind. What do you want it for?"

"I'm having trouble sleeping. I was on Ambien before Chicxulub and lately I'm lucky to get four hours each night. I find myself waking up and worrying about everything, then I can't go back to sleep."

Cate sighed. The collective ignorance of Liberty's citizens regarding homeopathic medicine was irritating, but not surprising. Few people had taken the time to learn the old ways...*any* old ways...whether it was natural remedies, blacksmithing, spinning fiber into yarn then weaving it into cloth, or making serviceable shoes out of animal hides. People had been obsessed with shiny technology and demanded instant gratification in all things. It was funny that someone like herself, whose skill set was anachronistic before, was now in great demand.

"Your boyfriend is supposedly a former pharmacology major. He should have known belladonna wouldn't be the best choice for insomnia."

Natalie made a dismissive gesture. "Oh, I didn't mention it to Calvin. He has so much on his mind these days dealing with Steven and everyone else. I didn't want him to worry about me." The gray eyes were as guileless as they were beautiful.

Cate would have been suspicious if she hadn't been so captivated.

"So why not just ask me for it at the hospital?"

"You know how people talk. I prefer that nobody knows my personal business. I'd like to keep this between us girls." Natalie smiled, then placed her slender fingers on Cate's plump hand. "Can we do that?"

Cate felt flustered suddenly. "Y-yes. I suppose we can. You don't want belladonna," she said, forgetting that she had spoken those very words two days earlier. "You want aconite...wolfsbane. It's a sedative, but be careful with the dosage. Too much and you'll never wake up."

"That sounds perfect." Natalie removed her fingers and sat back, her dazzling smile framed by delicate crocheted snowflakes.

Cate's head was swimming. The woman was stunningly beautiful, but had always been so reserved and cold to her at the hospital. People like Natalie didn't have anything to do with the likes of her before the plague. But now, sitting in her own living room with this gorgeous creature smiling just for her, she almost felt under her sway. Nobody knew better than she that there was no such thing as a love potion, but good grief this woman's magnetism...her allure was not to be denied. She wanted to lose herself in those radiant gray eyes and kiss the exquisite lips.

The expectant look on the lovely face gave Cate an idea.

"I assume you'll be wanting the aconite soon?"

"Well, yes. I'm hoping to get a good night's sleep tonight. Do you have some ready?"

It was Cate's turn to smile. "Perhaps, perhaps. But there's something you can do for me first."

"Oh. I'm happy to trade services or barter goods. I'm the best laundress in town. I can get whites whiter than anyone." She glanced at Cate's girth and added, "I have a stash of Ghirardelli chocolate I've been saving for a special occasion."

Cate stood, then moved to sit beside Natalie on the sofa. She encircled the pale fingers with her own ruddy ones.

The gray eyes opened wide briefly, surprise evident on the exquisite face. Then it was gone, replaced with a calculating expression that did nothing to diminish the beauty.

"Oh, I think I understand what you want," Natalie purred.

Chapter 39

"Shouldn't we go after her?" Jeffrey said to his father. "It's been three days now."

Steven was having similar thoughts, but the logical thing to do was not chase after his sister on her ill-conceived mission, thereby leaving Calvin at Liberty's helm. Was this a selfish thought? Perhaps. But it was rooted in a valid concern. The preacher could stage a coup in his absence, and if Calvin controlled the town, it would become a mecca for religious zealotry rather than a secular haven for the continuation of civilization.

"I could go, Dad. You don't have to come too," Jeffrey said, reading his father's mind, as usual. Dark hair was beginning to usurp the peach fuzz on the chin and upper lip of the eager face on the other side of the kitchen table.

"Not a chance. We need you here," Steven replied. That was partly true.

"We could send a couple of other people from the security crew," Marilyn suggested. "Older, more seasoned folks. Sorry, Jeff," she added when she saw disappointment on the youthful face.

"When are you people going to understand that being fifteen these days is different than what it was two years ago?"

"You're right about that. Don't you think I know how grown up you are?"

"No, I don't. Come on, Dad. After Logan, I'm the best shot in town."

"And that's why we need you here, son."

"You're so frustrating! There will come a time when you can't tell me what to do."

Jeffrey pushed his chair back from the table and stormed upstairs.

Steven sighed. "I didn't handle that well, did I?"

"Nope," Marilyn said. "And he does have a point."

"What does that mean?"

"Well, he is the best shot. Who better to go against Logan if Julia doesn't have him under control?"

"I don't think shooting prowess is what will be needed in that situation."

"That sounds like a rationalization."

"Whose side are you on here?"

"I'm just playing Devil's advocate. Don't get your boxers in a wad." She stood, walked around the table to Steven and gave him a lingering kiss on the lips. "I need to get going. It's distribution day and Natalie is helping me out. Should be interesting."

"I'll see you later tonight then?"

"You shall."

There was the transformative smile. Steven realized at that moment that he was as smitten as a lovesick teenager; the notion took him completely by surprise.

A minute later Marilyn was gone and Steven was left to his own thoughts. Julia and the scouts had been gone for three days, and the scenarios as to what might have befallen them were endless. Maybe they had run into trouble. Maybe Logan had killed Dani before Julia got to them. Maybe everyone was fine and they were just gathering information. Maybe, maybe, maybe.

He wouldn't allow fear to dictate his actions. It was too soon to risk sending more people into harm's way. In the meantime, he had his hands full keeping Sam on task shoring up Liberty's defenses. All the young man wanted to do was chase after Dani. Steven didn't have much time left before their de facto head of security would go rogue. Frankly, he was surprised it hadn't happened already. At the impromptu meeting with Calvin and Sam, Steven had only shared an abbreviated and sanitized version of the news about Logan. Despite playing down the danger, Sam had almost flown out the door then, but Steven had wrangled a promise from him to stay put...for now. Give Julia, who could control Logan, enough time to do so. Otherwise, sending more people after them might further endanger everyone.

The sound of a vehicle interrupted his reverie. A quick look out the window confirmed the return of the HG crew's Dodge Ram...the one his sister had stolen. He flew out the front door. By the time he reached the street, Pablo and Julia were getting out of the pickup truck. Her face was a mask of anguish.

"What happened?" Steven demanded.

"They have Dani," Julia said. "They have my daughter!"

"Who? Who has her? What about Logan?"

"He's dead, thankfully," Pablo said, slamming the driver's door shut. "Isaiah has Dani. He's holding her captive as a bargaining chip to get us to do his bidding when he arrives with his army. We are royally fucked."

"Drink this," Steven said to Julia as he handed her a glass of water.

"I need to get home and check on Maddie," Pablo said as he headed for Steven's front door.

"Please, Pablo. Just a few more minutes. I want to hear the story from both of you, in detail. I don't know how coherent or thorough my sister will be in her version. She doesn't handle this sort of thing well."

"*This sort of thing*?" Pablo spat. "Who the hell has been through something like this before?"

"I meant traumatic family situations."

"I'll give you five minutes, then I'm gone. I have my own family to worry about." Pablo stood next to the sofa where Julia sat, his arms crossed, his bearing hostile toward Steven, and protective of Julia.

Steven wouldn't have thought his sister would need protecting from her own brother.

"Let's start from the beginning," Steven said.

Absent was the lively lilt and pleasing cadence Pablo used when telling a story or reciting poetry at one of their gatherings. His tone was terse and his words were clipped as he recounted the details of the past three days.

"When they saw Dani's scar, they assumed she was a deserter. Until then, we didn't know they were a scouting party for Isaiah. They tied us up and made us hike back to their camp which was five miles to the south of our position. From there, we were put on the backs of their motorcycles with our hands still bound behind us. Shortly after we encountered the spear tip of their army..."

"How many?" Steven interrupted.

"Perhaps two hundred. That's an estimate, of course. May I continue?"

"Yes, sorry."

"We were taken to Isaiah. I believe a runner was sent to notify him of our arrival because when we were presented to him, he was mounted on an enormous black horse...posing, it seemed to me. That's the impression I got."

Julia nodded in agreement. "Yes, I think so too. Classic narcissist with delusions of grandeur. Which fits with what we know about the survivors."

Steven felt a stab of alarm. "Julia, you didn't..."

"Yes, I did," she said, deadpan. "Of course I did. Keeping that secret is no longer an option. Deal with it."

He ignored the challenge. "What happened then?"

Pablo continued, "We watched him dismount and come toward us. It all felt staged, like he'd choreographed the scene. He wanted to evoke fear in his captives. When he saw Dani, he became apoplectic for a moment, then regained his composure. There was a caustic exchange of words between the two, which Isaiah seemed to enjoy. Dani was her usual belligerent self, and at one point I think she might have gotten to him, but it came to nothing. We were separated then. She was taken off somewhere by herself, and Julia and I were put in a tent and given food and water. He may be a power-hungry psychopath, but he has a distorted sense of honor, for lack of a better word."

"What then?"

"Nothing. Guards were posted outside. We were still bound. Escape was not an option. The next morning, we were given more food and water, then brought before Isaiah. I've tried to remember his speech verbatim because it was fascinating, despite the circumstances. He has a gift for language and his grasp of alliteration is remarkable."

Steven fought the urge to roll his eyes. Of course this young poet would be interested in language, but these details weren't the type he needed.

"He said he had plans for our town. That he'd seen it in a vision and it would be his Rome in the Great Plains."

"So his plan is to invade or conquer?"

"Interesting that you perceive the difference," Pablo replied.

Steven ignored what he hoped was an unintentional insult.

"He said, 'Like a tsunami, we will roll over your town, claiming every square inch of real estate. You decide whether the tide is tumultuous and terrible, or temperate and tranquil.' So he's offering us a choice."

"And he'll use Dani as leverage," Julia said. "So help me god, Steven, you will not dismiss her as collateral damage."

Steven raised an eyebrow. At some point, he may need to reassess his reputation. "What else, Pablo?"

"He said he expected his army to arrive at his Rome in the Great Plains within a fortnight. Yes, he used that word. Then he said that when he arrives we will have two choices: 'we can simply and serenely hand over the keys to the kingdom and there will be no superfluous bloodshed, or we can resist, thereby incurring abhorrent acrimonious annihilation.' That was it. If he weren't such a psychopath, I would enjoy having a conversation with him. He's charming when he's not terrifying. After that, we were placed on the motorcycles again and taken to the truck that Julia had abandoned earlier. The rest you know."

Steven rubbed his temples, already working on the logistics of defending his town.

"I'll leave you to it then," Pablo said, heading for the door. "Just so you know, I intend to make sure everyone is aware of what they're facing. No positive spin will be put on the situation in hopes of getting people to stay. And I will tell you this too: if Maddie is physically able, we're leaving. Staying here isn't worth jeopardizing our lives."

"Pablo, it's not just about that," Julia said as she stood. "There's Dani to consider too. And transporting a pregnant woman in a weakened state is risky."

"Exactly," Steven said quickly. "Pablo, just promise me you won't make any decisions until I've had time to think this through. Please."

Pablo was at the front door. He paused. "I'll give you twenty-four hours. After that, I'm going to get my family the hell out of town."

"What, on foot?" Steven said before he thought better of it.

Pablo turned slowly to face Steven. "No, of course not on foot. I will use a vehicle. Probably the one we arrived in."

Steven hesitated, then decided to finish. Pablo had pushed him into a corner.

"You'll need gasoline to run that vehicle, Pablo. As mayor, gas allocations are under my jurisdiction."

"You would do that? Keep people here, endangering lives, just to preserve your little utopia? Good god, I had no idea you were so coldblooded."

Steven blew out a measured breath, choosing his words carefully.

"I agree. That sounded harsh. Just give me some time to work this all out. Please."

The golden eyes studied Steven for a long moment.

"Twenty-four hours. That's it. And by the way, I'm going to find Sam. I want him to hear the unsterilized version of what happened to Dani."

Chapter 40

Dani refused to give Isaiah the satisfaction of letting him know she was scared. Of course she was scared. Only an idiot wouldn't be.

"Lily, what do you think of our guest? Does she look like the bogeyman you imagined her to be?"

Isaiah's rich voice flowed over her like poisoned honey. She was terribly uncomfortable with her hands tied behind her back, but she wouldn't squirm. The cold was seeping up from the earth into her bones, chilling her bottom as well as the legs that were crossed in front of her. From that vantage, she was forced to look up at the man who intended to kill her...if she didn't kill him first.

For the moment she had value, which she would exploit. She was leverage, and utilizing her could save him and his army in resources and lives. Ultimately, he would torture and kill her. But now that he knew about their town and all it had to offer, he would bide his time. He was one deranged motherfucker, but he was no idiot.

The bundle of rags standing next to Isaiah replied, "I think she's going to die a slow and painful death, dearest General." The black eyes staring from within the pale face seemed soulless; the eyes of a creature that lived in caves or under rocks with no spark of humanity in their depths. Dani had encountered a number of crazies since Chicxulub, but this broad took the cake.

The man standing on Isaiah's other side was a different matter entirely. Dani could see reason, sanity, and fear in his light-colored eyes, and also weakness in his bearing. He was a Yes Man, but perhaps there was wiggle room with him. He was clearly terrified of both Isaiah and Lily, and terror could be exploited.

"What about you, Lieutenant? You weren't there during my dealings with this vexatious, venomous vixen. Does she measure up?"

Dani studied Lieutenant Martin, careful to keep her interest from showing. Nobody would have noticed, though. Isaiah and Lily scrutinized the man while waiting for his reply. The question seemed to be some kind of test.

When he spoke, his voice was reedy with a slight quaver. "I think capturing her was quite a boon. Perhaps the men responsible should be given extra rations as a reward?"

Isaiah's eyes glittered.

Martin quickly continued, "I also think that when we arrive at your Rome in the Great Plains, she will be an enormous asset, *if* her life has value to the citizens. It could save us a tremendous amount of trouble if we don't have to fight, but that would mean giving up your prize in exchange for their surrender. You won't have your reckoning, which is more important than anything else." He added the closing words hastily.

"Very true, Lieutenant. So what do you propose?"

The man took a deep breath, locked eyes with Dani and said, "Perhaps a reckoning needn't involve killing her. Aren't there better ways to inflict intense, abiding pain? What about marring her beauty...disfiguring her ...then giving her back to her people – a hideous shadow of the former woman. We're honoring our agreement by returning her, and you get your reckoning in a slightly different form. Win, win."

All thoughts of subverting this little weasel flew from Dani's mind.

"Oh you may be onto something there," Isaiah said with a chuckle. "Well done. I shall ruminate on it overnight." He gave the man a hearty slap on the back, then shifted his attention back to Dani. "I've dreamed about this often, you know."

"Starring in your fucked-up wet dreams doesn't flatter me."

Isaiah's smile broadened. "Something tells me you would rather die than be physically repugnant. A ghastly, ghoulish ghost of the vainglorious girl."

"You're slipping, Isaiah. Your alliteration was flawed, you pernicious, pestiferous, puerile prick."

Obsidian eyes flashed and the smile vanished. He lunged a step toward her before catching himself, suddenly aware of the soldiers who had gathered to watch. She witnessed the physical transformation on the chiseled face, from poised and controlled to explosive rage, then back again.

She had gotten to him. She had pierced his armor of composure. It was a small victory but one she would analyze later...if she lived long enough. The problem was he had gotten to her too; or rather his lieutenant had. She wasn't free from the trappings of female vanity. After transforming the pudgy nerd into the primo goods that Sam had fallen in love with, the thought of being ugly was gut-wrenching. Would he still love her if she were mutilated and repulsive?

"I'm done with you for now," Isaiah said, turning his back on her with a dramatic flourish. "Lieutenant Martin, you and two others will guard her tonight. If anything happens to her, your life is forfeit. Understood? Lily, come with me."

Dani released the breath she didn't realize she had been holding. Martin grabbed her by the arm and pulled her off the ground.

"This way," he said, then lowered his voice so only she could hear. "You better not give me any grief. I'm on thin ice as it is."

Interesting. Despite his idea of disfiguring her, Martin just might be worth pursuing as a hostile ally. *The enemy of my enemy is my friend.* She would spend the next few hours conducting a subtle mining operation of the man...poking and prospecting, looking for promising veins that might lead to an alliance. Something told her that the best chance of escaping with her face intact would channel through this man. A rescue mission from Liberty was unlikely; they would have their hands full as it was. But Sam would come for her, and she had to get out of this mess before he risked his life to save her.

He may already be on the way.

Chapter 41

"We can't just ignore the summons," Tung said in their archaic tongue.

He and Amelia sat on the twin beds in the pink frilly bedroom of Thoozy's former home. They had both attended the emergency meeting Steven had called late in the day. Everyone had been there, and the news was grim. Not only was an army headed their way, bent on taking over their town, but Dani was their hostage. Steven hadn't had time to formulate a plan, but had asked that people remain calm. Yes, there was an imminent threat, but there was also time to thoroughly analyze the situation. Nobody should make panic-fueled snap decisions. When the meeting was over, Pablo had told Amelia to be prepared to leave town; that if Steven couldn't provide a viable solution to keep them safe, their blended family would flee, using whatever mode of transportation they could arrange. On foot, if need be.

Amelia looked at Tung. When she replied, there was a hint of annoyance in her tone.

"I know we can't ignore the summons, but the *Cthor's* timing could not be worse. I can't leave now. Maddie is ill and Jessie is not ready for harvesting. She won't meet the criteria for several more years and I can't just abandon her. My fear is that our report at this point will result in an immediate earth cleansing once the *Cthor* are fully informed."

Tung nodded. Amelia knew he wasn't as invested in these humans as she was, but he wasn't heartless either. He didn't want to see them destroyed, but to ignore a summons was a grave matter.

"I'm certain they would make an exception for Jessie at this point," he said.

"Yes, I'm sure they would, but still. Something tells me if we stay a bit longer...let this situation play out...we may be able to return with evidence that is compelling enough to grant these people a reprieve, if the *Cthor* are contemplating an earth cleansing as we believe them to be."

"So you're asking me to stall for you? Is that it?" Tung replied, his almond eyes glittering in the candlelight. Amelia thought she detected the tiniest twitch at the corner of his mouth.

"Yes, that's what I'm asking. You know my *scythen* isn't strong enough to convey the message with the necessary...nuance."

Tung laughed. "I think by 'nuance' you mean what the local folks would call 'spin.'"

"Tomato, tomahto," she said with a grin.

Amelia watched Tung's face as he pondered her request, contemplating the angles and possible consequences if the *Cthor* deemed their behavior dissident. She had already made the decision to jeopardize her own future if it meant saving those she loved, but for Tung to do so must be his choice. She would not coax further.

"Oh, Amelia. This is not a minor thing you ask of me."

"I know, dear friend. I will understand if you can't do it."

He sighed. "I'll tell them the situation is fluid and that we are on the brink of something quite extraordinary. I will ask if we might be given some extra time. Others who are farther away will require time to get there anyway. I don't see that it would be terribly impudent just to ask."

Amelia nodded.

"Okay, you rascal. I'll do it. If we're both booted out of our home and forced to live our newly-shortened lives here on the surface, I will exact some sort of revenge. I'll have you rub my feet every day...serve me peeled grapes...make you listen to me sing karaoke...and whatever else I can think of."

"I will happily do all those things and more."

Tung's expression became serious. "It's quite possible we will lose our lives along with these people you love."

"I know. I'm prepared for that."

"And this adopted family of yours is worth that price?"

"Yes," she said simply. Then again, "Yes."

Chapter 42

"Sam is gone, which isn't surprising," Chuck said to Steven and Calvin. They were meeting with the remaining members of the security crew at Steven's home. It was warmer and more comfortable there, and it also provided Steven a sort of home field advantage in the power struggle with his co-mayor.

"Right. We figured that would happen," Steven said. "Did he take one of your vehicles?"

"No. There are none missing. He probably took his bicycle. He's fast as hell on that thing."

Calvin broke his silence. "Do you accept the burden of temporary head of the security crew?" he said to Chuck. "It's an onerous job which will almost certainly require that you make decisions that result in the loss of human lives. Do you realize making those decisions and issuing such weighty orders may jeopardize your immortal soul?"

"You're barking up the wrong tree, preacher," Chuck replied. "Peddle your hellfire and snake oil to someone else. I'm not interested."

Steven stifled a grin.

Calvin didn't appear offended. He merely raised his palms in a gesture of acquiescence, then continued, "The question must be asked: Why risk the lives of all these people just to preserve the machinery of the town? Why not just pack up and move somewhere else? Start over? Yes, it would be difficult, but it's not an insurmountable task."

"That's a good question, and one many people are asking," Steven replied, aware that his next words would be shared through Liberty's grapevine. "Let me outline things first. We are flourishing here. All the steps we've taken that have brought us back from the brink of obliteration, all the systems we've put in place to ensure our future, all the hard work we've done planting the seeds of a society that isn't just scraping by but actually thriving, cannot just be walked away from for two important reasons. First, if it were even possible to duplicate what we've achieved, what's to stop this exact situation from happening again? We do all the work and somebody else decides they want what we have, so they threaten us, and we just walk away to avoid a fight? I guarantee this will happen again. It is human nature at its most primitive level to take what someone else has because it's easier than creating it from scratch. It's easier to utilize violence and piracy – which provide instant gratification – than it is to painstakingly build something or patiently grow something. We stop it here and now, or we accept the ultimatum, thereby sealing our fate." He paused to let his words sink in.

"And now to the next issue, which is more immediate and pressing. We have exactly seventeen gallons of non-oxidized gasoline. It's become the most valuable commodity these days, and there hasn't been time to implement an alternative fuel system. We simply don't have enough gas to transport everyone out of town."

"So people could walk or ride bicycles," Calvin replied.

"Yes, they could. They could put on all their heavy clothes and pack up as much food and water from their stores as they could carry, which probably won't last them more than a week, and they could venture out into the Kansas plains in February when temperatures stay below freezing even during the day. What are their chances of surviving under those conditions? The fifty mile perimeter of our town has been picked clean. I know this for a fact because the HG crew has to go farther and farther out to find anything worthwhile. So which is the bigger risk? Embarking on an ill-conceived, poorly planned mass exodus during the dead of winter out into the unknown? Or staying put, defending what we've built, fighting for our lives and our future?"

"I understand what you're saying," Calvin said, "but I'm visualizing a bloody battle where many or even all our citizens perish. Surely, knowing what approaches, they're wiser to take their chances out there than face this...this legion of evil."

Steven smiled. "That might be true if we didn't have a plan. A plan which, if executed properly, will eliminate the threat while keeping our losses to a minimum."

"You have such a plan?"

"I do," Steven said. "And it will work." He took the next five minutes to outline his strategy to his co-mayor and the security crew. When he finished, the room had gone completely quiet.

Steven took a deep breath and continued. "It's us or them. We are in the right, the approaching army is in the wrong. We're fighting for our lives."

"But as I've mentioned before, these physical bodies which house our souls are temporary. Once they're dead, our true selves will either progress to heaven or descend to hell as a direct result of our actions here on Earth."

"And as I've said before, I don't believe in that nonsense."

"It's not relevant that you do; it simply is."

"I won't have you muddying the waters with this kind of talk. We need people to be clear-minded and focused."

Calvin smiled. "On that we agree. All I'm asking is that you allow me to present your plan to the town as interpreted by a man of God. You will have the chair first. Then they can make their own decisions."

Steven was backed into a corner. He didn't see how he could reasonably refuse the request.

"Fine," he said finally. He glanced at Tung, who'd been summoned for his explosives expertise.

Tung was his usual serene and calm self, but the normal half-smile was gone. He didn't seem swayed or impressed by Calvin's religious rhetoric, but there was a hesitation in his demeanor; he had frowned at the part where Steven explained how the approaching army would be dealt with.

"Are we on the same page, Tung?" Steven asked. "It's like the Hays problem all over again, but this time they're bringing the war to us. We're not seeking it out."

"Yes, I remember our conversation then. We talked about the justification for murder."

"Right. Nothing has changed. What justification is more compelling than self-defense? They mean to kill us."

"I realize that, but it seems they have given us an option to avoid that. Not everyone sees the situation as the dichotomy you do. Maybe there are individual solutions that lie somewhere in the middle. I think Calvin is wise in at least offering an alternative. There are many kinds of leaders and many ways to lead. For what it's worth, I think your reasoning is sound, Steven. I do believe that taking lives is justified in this instance. I'm not thrilled with building explosives knowing how they're to be used, but I will, providing they're employed in such a way that only the most barbarous and malevolent, the most *inhuman* of these humans are destroyed. I suspect there are members of this army who have been conscripted and serve Isaiah against their will. I don't want to see them killed along with those who truly deserve to be."

"I don't know how I could possibly guarantee that, Tung."

"Hear me out. Let's assume that those who lead this invasion, those who are positioned in the front ranks are the worst of the worst. Perhaps there are camp followers, families...children even. People who aren't actively engaging in violence. They would be at the rear. So if the threat to us can be removed only by eliminating those leading the attack, you must promise to allow their survivors to leave in peace...unscathed. In other words, I don't support complete annihilation, which I believe is what you have in mind."

"Pablo and Julia didn't mention seeing anything like what you've described."

"Doesn't mean they don't exist. Those are my terms, Steven. Take it or leave it."

His plan would need to be modified, but he didn't have a choice. They needed Tung to succeed. "Very well. You have my word."

"Excellent. Okay, let's get this party started," Tung replied with a grimness that belied the words.

Chapter 43

The emergency town hall meeting that evening would have been pleasant if not for the subject matter. Steven had gone to great lengths to make the setting as cozy and appealing as possible. He had brought in extra oil lamps and food from his own personal stores for everyone to enjoy while he and Calvin presented their positions. He wanted to underscore their relative comfort and prosperity here in Liberty. According to Marilyn's recent tally, their population had grown to nearly two hundred. It was a significant number because it mirrored that of the approaching army.

Steven insisted his co-mayor speak first. He wanted to have the final words before everyone left to sleep on their decisions, which would be required the following morning.

Calvin took his place in the center of the court room. The concentric benches were filled to capacity. Those left standing crushed together behind and between the benches, overflowing into the outer corridor. Generated heat from so many bodies warmed the space, providing the exact type of ambiance Steven had strived for: protected, safe, comfortable.

"Good evening, friends," Calvin said in the southern elocution normally reserved for his sermons. "We all know why we're here, so I'll talk immediately about the issues that, as God's shepherd, I'm compelled to elucidate for the benefit of my flock. For those of you who attend the Sunday service, you've heard me speak many times about our immortal souls. For those of us who choose to stay and fight, this is a weighty choice indeed…"

For the next ten minutes, the preacher droned on. Facial expressions in the crowd were a mixed bag of rapt attention, wide-eyed contemplation, and impatient annoyance. A few older citizens nodded off from the combination of a full belly and the warm environment.

Finally, the preacher relinquished his place with an elegant gesture to Steven. His departure wasn't punctuated with the applause it had been in the past; he couldn't guarantee their well-being in this earthly plane. Even the more devout members seemed worried by the notion of venturing away from their safe haven in the middle of winter.

As well they should.

Steven didn't have the experience at public speaking that Calvin did. But he had conviction in his chosen path. He had clear-sighted vision. He had profound concern for the town, and he was invested in its people. All this he conveyed in the intelligent, level-headed delivery of what was his ace in the hole: a comprehensive plan to beat the marauding army, explained in such detail that Liberty's victory seemed assured.

When his speech was over, it was met with a thunderous standing ovation.

"Before we leave, there's that other issue we need to discuss," Pablo raised his voice to be heard above the din.

Steven shot him a hostile glance. The last thing they needed at the moment was to worry about that business.

"Sorry," Pablo continued, "People need to know. It may impact their decision about staying. Some might conclude they're safer alone."

All eyes shifted back to Steven, curiosities piqued now.

"Very well," Steven said, struggling to keep the annoyance from his tone and demeanor. "Julia, are you up to this?"

His sister sat on the opposite side of the room from Pablo. A stranger was next to her in what would have been Logan's place. They were obligated to reveal what had happened to the deranged young man, but he hoped she wouldn't do so now.

Julia nodded. She looked like she had aged ten years since her return; there was more gray in her hair than brown now, and a kind of frailty clung to her. It broke his heart to see her so distraught.

All eyes followed her to the center of the room.

"Most of you know me as Steven's sister," she began, "and some of you know that I was a scientist before. My field of study was molecular genetics. What nobody except my brother, and now Pablo, knows is the subject of my work before and after the pandemic." She paused. "The disease that killed most of the people on the planet isn't what I want to talk about tonight. The survivors...me, you, everyone here, is what I want to discuss. We're more special than you realize, and not just because we didn't succumb to the disease that killed everyone else. There are traits we survivors all share to varying degrees. Have you wondered why so many of us are so smart, or talented or proficient in a specific area?"

More than a few people nodded.

"That's because we are all quite gifted, in one way or another. Average people did not survive the disease."

She waited for the crowd's sudden clamor to subside before continuing.

"Some of us have very high IQs, like my brother for instance. I suspect many of you do, from what I've seen and heard...Marilyn and Pablo are two names that come to mind. I don't know everyone, but I'm certain there are many more. In addition to those types, there are others who are especially good at certain things: math and music, for example. Maddie's knack for doing numbers in her head like a human calculator, and Natalie's daughter Brittany who is a musical prodigy. These are instances of typical savant-type abilities.

"Another interesting and less typical paradigm I've observed is targeted mechanical talent in a specialized area. Firearms, for instance. Our sharpshooters on the security crew are examples of this manifestation."

She took a shaky breath. Steven knew she was thinking of Logan.

"None of this sounds like a bad thing," Calvin said, taking advantage of the hesitation. "Why do I feel that the other shoe has yet to fall? And more importantly, why were we not informed of this until now?" He addressed the last question to Steven who stood several feet away, arms crossed.

"Let her finish. We'll get to that," Steven said. "Julia, please continue."

She nodded.

"Calvin is right. This is not a bad thing at all. It's quite remarkable that the people who are left to pick up the pieces of our world are all so ex ceptional...so special. It's almost like the genetic disease that killed most of our families and friends was orchestrated somehow. But of course that's not possible. Anyway, Calvin is also right about the other shoe. There is a dark side to this. About half of the survivors will struggle with some neurosis, like anxiety and depression. Some will have obsessive compulsive issues."

More people in the crowd became animated now; a wave of nodding heads and excited whispers flowed through the room.

Steven gritted his teeth, dreading what was about to come out of his sister's mouth.

"The serotonin levels in a percentage of these people, roughly ten percent, will indicate psychosis. Bi-polar disorder, schizophrenia, those kinds of problems."

"Julia," Steven interjected.

"They need to know."

"What are you saying?" Calvin said. "We're not scientists like you. Please speak in layman's terms."

"I'm saying that some will have cognitive disorders, difficulty separating reality from fantasy. They may suffer from paranoid delusions...even hallucinations. They might hear 'voices' in their heads."

"What do the voices tell them?"

She frowned. "How the hell would I know that? I'm sure it's different for everyone who suffers from the disorder."

Calvin arched an eyebrow. "Where is Logan, Julia?" he asked.

Her frown turned into a grimace. "I'm getting to that. Now go sit down and be quiet. If you have questions when I'm finished, I'll answer them then."

Steven didn't bother to cover his grin.

The next moment it was wiped off his face.

"You too, Steven. Go sit down. I don't need either of you hovering around me like a couple of hounds eyeballing a bone. Go!"

He followed Calvin to a bench on the front row where smirking people made room for them. He liked to think his exit was dignified, but he suspected they both looked like chastised school boys. The preacher seemed more amused than embarrassed.

"As I was saying, these people may not be fully in touch with reality. They might imagine their neighbors to be demons or believe themselves to possess super powers. Or magic," she added, brushing at her eyes. "These fantasies don't always manifest in dangerous behavior, but they can. You've heard those awful news stories of mothers drowning their children, believing them to be possessed by evil spirits, or teenaged boys going on shooting rampages at neighborhood elementary schools. These kinds of behaviors stem from the type of severe psychosis I'm speaking of."

She took a shaky breath, then continued. "There's more...an even more virulent pathology. I call it the 'mentored serial killer.' This begins with a person who is predisposed to some of the problems I've mentioned. Added to that predisposition is direct interaction with someone, an older, mature someone usually, who channels the child's unhealthy urges into horrific behaviors. This is what happened to Logan and why he isn't here tonight." She shot an angry look at Calvin.

"Where is he?" The person who spoke was Steven's son. He was sitting with the other members of the security crew rather than with his father. Julia sought his face in the crowd.

"I killed him," she said simply.

The room erupted with raised voices. The security people were especially agitated. Logan had been a weirdo, but he was *their* weirdo.

Steven stood from the bench. "Give her a chance to explain," he said. "Please! Everyone, calm down." He was furious at his sister for her lack of finesse in presenting the truth. There were better ways to handle this, but she was too emotionally wrung out to care about her own future. If they survived the attack on their town, she would have to face some kind of legal action. People couldn't be allowed to get away with premeditated murder without due process. Not even his sister.

"Why, Julia?" Calvin's cultured voice cut through the din. "What happened?" The amused expression was gone, replaced with something that might have been compassion.

Steven took the floor. "Because he was the monster she just described: a mentored serial killer. We discovered this through his artwork. He killed a child before Julia met him. Of course she didn't know that at the time. We have evidence that he murdered Thoozy, and we know he intended to kill Dani. He was a danger to everyone in this town. Julia's act was heroic but also deeply upsetting to her, as you can see. She cared for Logan, but she knew he had to be put down."

"Like a rabid animal," Calvin said in a thoughtful tone, rising to stand near Steven.

"Exactly," Steven replied.

"Yet he wasn't an animal. He was a person. And your sister killed him."

"Yes, she did, but she was justified in doing so. Just as we are justified in killing the people who are on our doorstep whose intent is to kill us."

"That's enough, both of you." Julia stepped between the men who stood in the center of the room with barely a foot between their chests. "If we survive the next two weeks, then you can put me on trial. I don't care about that now. All I care about is Dani. Steven you damn well better make sure she survives this."

With that, Julia walked away from both men, pushed her way through the packed bodies, and out into the night.

Everyone watched her go. When the door slammed behind her, the room exploded in a cacophony of shouting.

Chapter 44

"Wake up," Martin said in a harsh whisper. He kicked at Dani's boots. She was curled up on the ground near one of the campfires, but she was not sleeping. The flickering flames revealed a fresh laceration on her cheek. The one on the opposite side was beginning to scab over. Neither were terribly deep, but they would scar without proper care. Her wounds were treated with peroxide, nothing more. Isaiah didn't want his captive to die from infection and deny him his reckoning. Even a bandage was not allowed. The goal was to open the skin and keep it exposed, allowing it to heal with as much scar tissue as possible.

"Fuck you," was the muffled reply.

Martin squatted down next her. Through her eyelashes, she watched him scan the immediate vicinity, then lean in close to her head.

"The other guards are on a pee break. Listen up...we don't have much time."

Dani's eyes flew open, but she didn't move. She studied the face of Isaiah's weasely lieutenant with new interest.

"I want out. You help me and I'll help you." The words were spoken so quietly that Dani barely heard them.

But hear them she did. They were as sweet as an angels' choir.

When she smiled, the sudden pain reminded her of the wounds on her face. They had more than a week to go before they would reach their destination. Isaiah's intent was to draw out his ridiculous reckoning until the very last moment, giving her a disfiguring injury every day. He planned to escalate their severity so by the time she was handed over to whatever was waiting for them in Liberty, she would be hideous. The thought of Sam's reaction made bile rise in her throat.

It was a pretty damn good strategy for exacting revenge, and she had the weasel to thank for it. But at least she wasn't dead. She supposed she had him to thank for that too.

"What's your plan?" she whispered.

"We need to get rid of Lily. That comes first. If we don't, we haven't got a chance. That bitch is as deadly as she is crazy."

"The same could be said about me."

"She makes you look like a fucking debutante."

Dani snorted softly.

"Here's the thing...I think she may finally trust me. For a long time she didn't, so that gives us an edge. She won't be watching our every move, but she's like a goddamn tarantula. You never hear her or see her until she's right up your ass."

"The Brazilian Wandering Spider would be a better metaphor. They're fast, highly venomous, and aggressive. Tarantulas are bigger, which means they're easier to spot; plus, their venom isn't strong."

Martin blinked once, then continued.

"She carries a shitload of knives, and god only knows what else. And I've noticed that the most likely time to catch her asleep is around three in the morning."

Dani studied the man who might be the salvation of her remaining beauty. Fleshy dark half-moons bulged beneath dilated orbs that were ringed with gray. One of the eyelids ticked spasmodically, and there was a slight palsy in the slender hands. She imagined him wearing a straightjacket and being wheeled into the local nuthouse. Could she trust him? All she needed him for was to cut her bonds. Isiah had learned from his past mistake; her hands remained lashed with para cord behind her back, and when she wasn't taking a leak, her ankles were bound as well. She had been under constant surveillance every moment of her captivity. There had been no opportunities to find a sharp rock or filch a blade or tool from her handlers.

She would be forced to trust him.

"What's the plan, Renfield?"

"My name's Martin."

"You're Renfield to me. Ever read *Dracula*?"

Another slow blink of both eyelids before the single eye commenced twitching.

"We'll wait for three in the morning. I'll slice the throats of the other two guards, then I'll free you. It's your job to kill Lily and get us out of here. I'm no strategist. I haven't been able to come up with a way to get myself out of this mess for months. That's why I need you."

Dani nodded. "I'll need some information."

"Come on, Renfield. Suck it up. Do you even own a ball sack?"

"You don't know what he's capable of."

"Oh, I think I do," Dani whispered, with a delicate touch to her most recent laceration.

"Those are nothing. If I'm caught deserting, he'll have me drawn and quartered. Literally. Like with four horses and everything."

"Interesting. He certainly likes the medieval stuff."

The fire had burned down to embers, and it was damn cold. Their whispered conversation created a tell-tale vapor cloud in the twelve inches of space between them. The other two people assigned to guard her appeared to be sleeping, which according to Martin was a catastrophic mistake if they were caught by Isaiah or Lily. Awake or asleep, the first order of business was for Martin to kill them. It was the witching hour, and Dani was ready for their escape. The dwindling campfires barely illuminated the army bedded down around them. People slumbered in a hodgepodge of bed rolls and sleeping bags; some were tucked away in tents of various sizes, and a few unlucky new recruits huddled under nothing more than thin blankets.

All she needed was for this cream puff to cut her loose. But first he must kill the other guards. Then they would wait for the roving night watch to make the rounds on the farthest side of the camp. The sticking point was their silhouettes; or rather the number thereof. Two people being seen by themselves was a big no-no. At first it had been only singles. If a person were seen alone doing anything, he would be shot on sight. Then it had become couples. Why? Because two people could form a bond...might develop loyalties to each other which surpassed their loyalty to Isaiah. So if you wanted to take a shit, you had to grab two others and make them go with you.

Delightful.

They needed someone to be their third silhouette in the night. She figured the best candidate would be a newbie. Martin would show her which one, then she would wake him with her hand over his mouth and a knife at his throat. She would hold it there until they were at least a mile away from Camp Crazy Ass.

But first she must dispatch Lily. Martin said they didn't stand a chance of escape unless Soulless Eyes was dead. And she always slept close to Isaiah, even when she wasn't on 'slumber duty.' Apparently he had become a raging paranoid since their last meeting; he even had a food taster now. Dani wasn't impressed. A strong leader would inspire devotion without using fear and intimidation tactics.

"Renfield, seriously dude. Get a fucking grip. Now is not the time to get stage fright."

The right eye was on twitch overdrive.

"You're probably dead either way, whether you get caught deserting or killed in the battle." The words were out before she realized how little comfort they offered.

"There might not be a battle." His whisper was all tremble and petulance. "They may just leave after they get you."

"That isn't going to happen. Steven will never just hand over his baby. Trust me. I know him."

"The woman, his sister, promised they would. That other guy said so too."

"Of course they would say that. Think about it. They would say anything to get away from Isaiah."

"But the town can't possibly stand against him...us."

Dani made a small clucking sound with her tongue. "Maybe not. Not without me there," she conceded. "But either way, it won't be pretty. Or easy. And you'll probably die in the battle."

"That would be quick at least."

Now the left eye began to twitch.

"Look, this is your best chance, Ren...uh, Martin. I'm telling you, I know my shit. I've done the logistics in my head and figured the odds of surviving seven different possible scenarios. This, what we're doing right now, is your best bet to escape that psycho fuckwad with your ass intact."

She could see he still wasn't convinced.

Movement in her peripheral vision caught her attention. When she turned her head, she saw only tents and blankets lumpy with sleeping bodies underneath. Then one of the blanket lumps inched in her direction.

If she hadn't been watching it, she wouldn't have noticed, so slow was the movement. She felt a frisson of excitement one moment, then alarm the next.

The last place she wanted Sam was here.

She kept an eye on the creeping blanket lump for a few moments before continuing her whispered campaign of persuasion.

"Where do you want to be, Martin?" Her words hung in the chill air. It must be in the thirties; cold as hell and miserable for anyone that wasn't acclimated to it. "If you could be anywhere in the world, where would you be at this moment?"

The eye twitching stopped, replaced now with a dreamy expression.

"On a beach. The sun is shining on my skin. There's not another person for miles. Just me with my feet in the sand. The ocean is turquoise blue and warm as bathwater. Crystal clear too, not like shitty Galveston. I can see tropical fish in it and sometimes a shark. There are a lot of sharks in the Keys."

"Ah. You're in Florida. Nice choice. Well, if you really want to be there, go kill those two guards. Do it now or I guarantee you'll never get to your happy place."

The dangling carrot was more effective than the stick. The strange man blinked once, then half-stood from his squatting position and moved toward the other two guards. Moonlight gleamed off a blade in his right hand.

Thirty seconds later, the deed was done. There'd been no resistance from either, so they must have been asleep – a lucky break.

The next moment, Martin sliced the cording at her wrists and ankles.

Once Isaiah's lieutenant made up his mind to do something, he got the job done quickly and quietly.

She squatted on the ground, rubbing the feeling back into her hands and arms while scanning the surrounding area. The blanket lump was only ten yards away now. A gauzy layer of vapor hung over the camp, the product of dozens of sleepers exhaling into the cold air. Above it, the cloudless night sky glittered with stars, creating a perfect backdrop against which moving figures would be easily seen.

It couldn't be helped.

The blanket lump, having witnessed the dispatching of the two guards, cast off its camouflage and covered the remaining distance to Dani's side in no time.

"Oh, Sam. I wish you hadn't come."

He reached for her face, holding it between his hands, then kissed her protesting mouth before she could get another word out. Then he pulled away and studied her wounds with the unhappy expression she knew so well.

"Pretty ugly, huh?" She had been dreading this moment, but at least Isaiah hadn't had more than a couple of days to play.

"How can you say that? You're the most beautiful person I've ever known. Do you think it matters what your face looks like?"

Dani snorted softly.

"I'm just mad at myself," he continued. "If I'd let you kill Isaiah back in Texas, we wouldn't be in this can of worms."

She smiled. "Yes, but that isn't you, is it Sam? You're the most beautiful person I've ever known too, and not because you're so handsome. It's because you have the kindest heart on the planet. Now, let's get the fuck out of here."

"Not so fast." The voice, a haunted house door creaking open in the night, came from behind Martin.

The next moment the throat of Isaiah's lieutenant was smiling. Blood, glistening black oil in the moonlight, rushed to flee its fleshy prison.

Martin slumped to the ground. His eyes no longer twitched but remained open and unblinking. Perhaps they were finally seeing that Florida beach.

"Well, fuck me," Dani whispered.

Lily's grin stretched unnaturally far, clown-like and utterly disconcerting. Dani's mind raced, formulating then dismissing several plans to address this new development. Two heartbeats later, she decided her next move, but before she could launch herself at the strange, rag-clad woman, Lily spoke.

"Not so fast, I said. You didn't want Martin. He's a spineless fool and a murderer of innocents. I'm your golden ticket."

"What the fuck does that mean?"

"It means that I'll help you escape."

"Why would you do that? Your Isaiah's weird little minion, plus you have a huge hard-on for him."

The noise that came from Lily sounded like air leaking from a balloon. It took Dani a few seconds to identify the bizarre squeaking as laughter.

"That's what I want him and everyone else to think." Moonlight glittered off a toothy, macabre grin.

Dani shivered from the cold, but also because this broad creeped the living shit out of her.

"You're her boyfriend," Lily continued in her low, raspy voice, shifting the focus of those dilated pupils from her to Sam. It was a statement, not a question. Dani had the sudden urge to stand in front of him, blocking him from the woman's spooky mojo.

Pale fingers sprouted from the tattered rags, like unquiet bones escaping a shallow grave. Even the normally friendly Sam seemed hesitant to shake the hand extended in his direction.

"I know people find me off-putting. I don't mind. Actually, I'm happiest when it's just me and my baby." A doll with corkscrew curls and bobbing eyelashes appeared in the other hand, was kissed, then tucked back into the rags.

Some vague memory scratched at the inside of Dani's brain. She ignored it, focusing all her attention on the woman in front of her.

"But before I can be alone with my baby, I have an important job to do. And you are going to help me. It's our shared destiny. I knew it when I saw you again here in Isaiah's camp."

"Again? I've never seen you before in my life. Trust me. I'd remember."

More of the escaping balloon air.

"You didn't see me. I saw you. You were in my house before the tornado hit. You and him, and that other man with the red hair. The house fell down on top of you, and my baby too. I'd left her there to keep an eye on things while I was out looking for food. Fortunately, she survived. And so did the two of you."

Dani remembered now. The doll had been propped up in the entryway of the house in which they had sought shelter. Sam had been wounded and the storm had been bearing down on them.

"I saw you all go in. I was about to come and get my baby, but the tornado happened too fast. Afterward, I watched you drive away in the blue truck. When I saw you again, I knew you must be important to the plan."

"What plan is that?"

"To corral all the evil ones. The murderers of innocents, the pedophiles and child abusers. Gather them all together, then kill them. Kill every last one of them."

Dani shot Sam a look that said, *We have a live one here.* He gave her the barest hint of a nod.

"And how are we going to do that?"

"That's why I need you. In exchange for allowing you to escape, you must agree to help purge the world of these monstrosities. You and your boyfriend, if he's agreeable...he feels like one of the rare good ones. It is God's will."

"By 'monstrosities,' who do you mean?"

"After almost everyone died, I realized that many of those still alive were vile, loathsome creatures. There was a group that had set up a barricade on the highway. I was with them briefly, until I discovered how terrible they were. Then I left with my baby and lived in the house that you people found. When the tornado happened, I had hoped it also struck the area near the barricade where so many awful people were concentrated. That's when I had the epiphany, which was God whispering in my ear: gather up all these evil ones and destroy them. It was soon after that when I joined Isaiah's army. So many terrible people brought together by the very worst of them...it seemed the perfect opportunity to do God's work. I was prepared to begin the task when Isaiah set his sights on your town, when again, I had an epiphany. God said I should wait until we've reached it and kill two birds with one stone."

Lily winked. "Of course, he didn't use those words, but that's what he meant."

"Let me get this straight. Your plan is to kill everyone? Not just Isaiah and his army, but the people in Liberty too?"

"I can only assume the people that live there are monstrosities too. That seems to be all that's left these days. So you'll have to stay with the army until we've reached the town. I'll make sure you're freed so you can help me."

"I'm free now. What's to stop me and Sam from making a run for it?"

The strange high-pitched titter again.

"You won't get far. I'd make sure of that. I'm too fast for either of you to keep me from sounding the alarm."

Dani shook her head. She looked into the black orbs of the woman and saw not one shred of sanity in their depths.

"Of course that means you'll have to suffer Isaiah's ridiculous reckoning for a few more days. That can't be helped."

Dani sighed. She scanned the sleeping camp, estimating where the night watch should be, plotting their best escape route through the slumbering bodies and calculating their odds of making it out while Lily screamed the alarm.

The probability of success was minimal. If it had been just herself, she would take the chance. But Sam was with her and she would not put him at risk.

"If I agree to this, Sam gets to leave now."

"I suppose that's okay. He doesn't seem like the type that has the stomach for this kind of wet work anyway."

"That's not going to happen, Dani," Sam whispered, his face a portrait of anguish. "If the tabletops were turned over, would you walk away from me?"

"You know I've already done the logistics. It's our best chance. You can shadow the army for the rest of the journey, but you have to promise not to get too close. Some of these soldiers have ninja moves too. Then when we reach Liberty, we'll be together."

"After we purge the monstrosities," Lily interjected.

"Right, after we purge the monstrosities."

"Because if you betray me, your boyfriend will be the first to die. I promise you that."

The words were spoken casually, but Dani understood the utter conviction behind them. This crazy bitch would go for Sam the second she caught a whiff of dissent.

"Got it. We kill everyone," Dani said.

"Good. Now tell your boyfriend to bugger off and let me replace your restraints. It has to look like you're still an unwilling prisoner."

Sam shook his head. "No. I won't leave you here."

"It's the only way, Sam. Please leave before someone wakes up. Go now. It will make me very unhappy if you don't."

"I'm not going."

Dani gritted her teeth. It was a damn inconvenient time for him to be immune to her ace in the hole. She thought of another approach that might work, but it would be painful for both of them.

"Sam, there's something you should know. I realize this isn't the best time to tell you, but I need to get it off my chest. I've fallen in love with someone else."

The heartbreak in his eyes was instantaneous. Seeing it felt like a fist slamming into her belly. She had to continue though or he might not take the bait.

"He's very smart. We share a love of books."

It was the cruelest thing she could say to someone who had a learning disability. He had always been aware of the disparity in their intellects; he loved seeing her happy, but she knew it bothered him to see her curled up with a book – a joy they could never share.

"Who is it? It must be that Pablo guy. He's a reader and you picked him to go on the scouting mission instead of me."

"Yes, it's Pablo. I'm sorry. It just happened."

The imagined fist in her belly grew claws.

"Okay, Dani. I understand. I think you're better off with someone smarter than me anyway. I always knew I wasn't good enough for you. I'll go, but I'll be nearby to keep an eyeball on things. Just because you don't love me anymore doesn't mean I don't love you."

The next moment he was gone from her side. She watched him glide through the tents and sleeping bags like a phantom, then lost him in the infinite shades of gray and indigo that colored the night. She was good, but she would never have moves like that. Nobody but Sam could have infiltrated the camp in the first place.

Nobody but Sam would ever love her so unconditionally.

And she had just broken his heart.

"Listen to me, Annie Wilkes," she hissed the next moment, pivoting to face Lily. "When I give my word, it means something. You hurt one hair on that man's head and I will crucify you. Are we clear?"

Twin black orbs blinked in the gloom, then came the odd squeak of laughter.

"Annie Wilkes. That's funny. Yes, we're clear," Lily replied. "I know what you did just now. I hope he still loves you after your face is ruined. Now turn around so I can tie you back up."

Chapter 45

"**A**ren't you supposed to be working on the perimeter defenses?" Maddie said in a weak voice. Any reserve strength she had was used for fighting the headaches and keeping food from coming back up. The tonics Cate gave her didn't seem to be helping with either of those ailments, but she continued to drink them under the watchful eye of Pablo. And her blood pressure wasn't improving, a fact that kept him in a constant state of alarm.

"Yes, but that can wait. There's nothing more important than you." Pablo kissed her forehead, noting the clammy feel of her skin. She was lying in her 'day bed,' the third bedroom of their tiny home. She liked the view from that room and the light was better for reading.

She was still months away from her due date and at the rate she was declining, she wouldn't make it. Both Amelia and Cate said there was nothing more that could be done. Maddie would just have to ride it out, get as much bed rest as possible, take the prenatal vitamins and drink Cate's tonic unfailingly, and hope for the best. A premature birth was likely, Cate said. Considering Maddie's health, it was even preferable. The baby may be underweight, but able to live outside the mother's womb as early as eight months; possibly less, with the help of the hospital's neonatal intensive care unit which would be powered by a backup generator and a ration of gasoline reserved for that purpose. The gas had been a blatant bribe from Steven to convince them to stay. Pablo still hadn't decided whether to hate the man or admire him. Usually he ended up doing both.

Maddie frowned.

"What? What's wrong?" he asked.

"You. You look like someone just told you Santa Claus isn't real."

He took a deep breath and forced a smile. "Wait. What are you saying?

Of course Santa Claus is real. Who do you think eats the cookies and drinks the milk on Christmas Eve? Next you'll be telling me the Easter Bunny isn't real either."

"Oh, that dude is legit but he's not the original bunny, you know. He's like the thousandth generation Easter Bunny. Bunnies don't live long and they like to screw like, well, bunnies."

"I didn't realize that. What about the Tooth Fairy?"

"The Tooth Fairy is real but he's no longer doing that pillow gig. He's got his own cabaret show in Vegas."

"You're an adorable little bigot."

Maddie chuckled. "I'm no bigot. I'm Irreverentia, the anti-angel of political correctness."

"I see."

She sighed. "Please try to not be so worried, Pablo. I know it's hard for you, but worrying does no good. It only sucks energy that could be spent on more important activities. Like helping with the perimeter defense. So go. Be gone with you. I'm fine."

"You probably have some stud coming over the second I leave."

Maddie chuckled weakly. "You're the only stud I need in my life. I love you, Poet Fellow. Now get the hell out."

"I love you, Angel Girl. I'll see you tonight."

He closed the door softly behind him. Amelia was waiting for him in the living room.

"She's only getting worse," he said. He didn't bother hiding his misery from her.

"I know," she replied. "I wish there was more we could do."

"Cate wants to move her to the hospital, so she can keep an eye on her."

Amelia shook her head. "Not yet. There's nothing she can do for her there that we can't do here. It would only make her unhappy to be away from home, and that is not in her best interest."

"I agree. I just feel so helpless."

Amelia pulled him into a bear hug. The top of her braided head only came to his collar bones.

"She's going to make it, Pablo," she said with an intensity that had become commonplace these days. Gone was the tranquil, unflappable Amelia, replaced by this fierce, grim, resolute version.

"I hope so. I won't be able to live without her."

Small hands pushed against his chest suddenly, surprising in their strength. Amelia shoved him again, knocking him off-balance and onto the sofa.

The old-soul eyes were blazing. "Don't talk like that. I won't have it. Life is the most precious thing there is, and you will not marginalize it by saying yours is dependent on the existence of someone else. If the worst happens and Maddie doesn't make it, you will live, damn it. You will bear the pain and you will heal. You will spend the rest of your life nurturing your soul, writing beautiful poetry, being kind, and watching spectacular sunrises. You won't waste a moment on regret or self-pity because those ugly indulgences will destroy you like a carcinoma, from the inside out. You will mourn because sadness and loss are part of life. For a while. But then a day will come when you will feel less sad and you will begin to again embrace all those simple joys that make being human on this planet – living in this world – the most wondrous experience any sentient creature may ever have.

"You will not piss that away. I won't let you."

Pablo had never experienced such vehemence from Amelia. He felt cowed by this person who was a foot shorter and half his weight. He didn't know what to say as she loomed over him from where he sat on the sofa.

"It's okay, Pablo," Jessie said from the kitchen. "She gets pretty riled up these days. I think she's been drinking too much coffee." She giggled, breaking the spell Amelia's outburst had cast.

"You may be right, young lady," Amelia said with a grin. "Just don't forget what I said, Pablo. Now get going. I'm sure Steven is wondering if you've decided to take Maddie and head for the hills."

"Yes, ma'am. Please watch over her. I promise I will think about what you said," he added hastily. "Let's just hope it doesn't come to that."

Amelia nodded and shooed him out the front door.

When he was gone, Jessie said, "Is it time to use my *langthal* on Maddie?"

Amelia was exhausted. The ferocity from moments before drained away as quickly as it had arrived. She sat down on the same spot Pablo had been. Jessie plopped down next to her, taking a dark-skinned hand in her own small dimpled one.

"Do we have to tell the Ancient Ones? Can't it just be our secret?" Jessie asked.

Amelia's smile was sad but determined.

"They will know, child. Something that disobedient can't be hidden from them. Tung won't go that far. So here's what's going to happen. When Maddie is asleep, you'll use your *langthal* on her. Then you're going to go with Tung to your new home, before the Smiling Man and his army arrive."

"I'm not going without you!"

"Hush now. Yes, you will. After we heal Maddie, there will no longer be a place for me there and it will be time to get you out of danger."

The sea-green eyes glistened with unshed tears. "I thought you said I wasn't ready?"

"Time is a luxury we don't have now. Remember what I said? About how rare you are? I can't keep you in harm's way even one more day. I've waited too long as it is."

"You waited so long because of Maddie and Pablo?"

Amelia nodded. "Yes. I love them as much as I love you. But it's time for me to put you first."

"What will happen to you? After Tung and I go below?"

"With luck, I'll survive the ordeal, along with the rest of the people here."

"I mean after that. Will you get old and die?" The tears could no longer be contained, spilling over the cherub cheeks.

Amelia nodded again. "Yes. The sacrifice is necessary, Jessie. Do you understand why?"

"No. I don't understand why you have to get old and die. It's stupid!"

Amelia smiled. "No, it's not stupid. It serves two purposes: first, Maddie will be well. She'll have the baby that she and Pablo created and they will have a beautiful life. Don't you want that? But even more importantly, the Ancient Ones will see my sacrifice and perhaps understand that humanity should be given more time. That many of those who remain are so extraordinary that I'm willing to exchange my own longevity – you know that word, yes? – so that not only Maddie will live, but that humankind...these people who are part of me, who share my blood...may develop and grow and someday create miracles. Does this make sense to you?"

Jessie nodded slowly. "I guess so. Will I get to come visit you at least?"

"Perhaps. It might be the *Cthor* will allow that. At some point they will want you to get a little older, which can't be done down below, so you'll need to come up again for a while. We'll just have to see what happens."

"I'd still rather stay here with you. Tung is nice, but I feel like he sees into my head too much. I think he knows what I'm thinking sometimes."

Amelia smiled. "He might hear some of your thoughts, as many of our people do. Some of the survivors here do as well, you know. I hear some of your thoughts too when we're holding hands."

"I don't mind if you hear them. You're my best friend."

"And you are my favorite of all the surface dwellers."

"Are Maddie and Pablo your next favorites?"

"Yes. I love you all very much. So you understand why we must do this?"

Jessie nodded again, but her frown was so exaggerated she looked cartoonish. Amelia was careful not to laugh.

"Should we go check on Maddie now and see if she's asleep?" Amelia asked.

"Okay. Do I get to tell her and Pablo goodbye?"

"You can tell Maddie if she's asleep, but I'll have to tell Pablo goodbye for you. They can't know you're leaving, nor about where you're going and with whom. That's the one secret nobody can know. Understand?"

"I guess. I'm just not very happy about this. I'm not very happy at all."

Amelia couldn't contain her laughter any longer.

"You are so precious, child. I know you're not happy, but you will be again soon. I promise. Now let's get to work. Think how ecstatic Pablo will be when he sees Maddie all better. Doesn't that make you happier?"

The elfin grin took Amelia's breath away.

Chapter 46

"Tung is gone again?" Steven said to Chuck, Liberty's ad interim head of security in the absence of Dani and Sam.

"Yep. After he built the IEDs you requested, he disappeared. Nobody can find him."

"Damn it."

"Yeah, well that's not even the worst part. That little girl, the one that lives with Pablo, is missing too."

Steven felt bile rising in his throat.

"My god. You think Tung took her?"

"Yes, I do, although I never would have pegged him for a pedophile. What's weird is how calmly that Native American woman is acting about the whole thing."

"How is Amelia acting?"

"Not unconcerned exactly, but not as hysterical as she should be. Know what I mean?"

Steven nodded. Something was wrong about that, but he didn't have time to investigate it further. Not with Isaiah and his army breathing down their necks.

"How is Pablo taking it?"

"He's so happy that his girlfriend is better that he's not talking about much else. I saw him this morning. He seemed worried about the little girl but not totally freaked out."

"Good grief. This is crazy. I know Amelia and Pablo both love the child. It'll have to wait, though. We'll do a thorough investigation later."

"Later, as in if we survive the battle?" Chuck said with a grim smile.

"We'll survive. Or at least most of us will."

"Yes. There are going to be casualties no matter what."

"I realize that," Steven snapped.

"Whoa, back off. I'm on your side, remember?"

It was amazing how dramatically the man had changed since the plague. The former plump grocery store manager was skinnier than just about anyone else these days, all sinew and scrawny muscle with a covering of pallid skin. Why he continued to decline when everyone else was improving wasn't much of a mystery; he was giving much of his food rations to his son, the brutish Bradley with the untreated bi-polar disorder. After they defeated Isaiah that would have to be addressed, as would all the other unresolved problems.

Like the fact that his sister had committed first degree murder.

"I'm sorry, Chuck. I'm just a little tense at the moment."

"Understandable. I wouldn't want to be in your shoes."

"No sensible person would."

"Except your co-mayor. He sure would like to have the reins."

"Yeah, well, maybe if we all survive this, I'll let him have them."

"Don't say that. You're the right man for the job and you know it. All that religious nonsense is for fools...people who want to believe in fairy tales because the truth is too hard to bear. It's bullshit and we both know it. No more talk of abdicating. Now let's get back to business. Almost all the Punji traps are in place. We're positioning Tung's IEDs where you said to put them. And the basement in the municipal building has been secured and supplied."

"Did the drone work?"

"Nah. The range was too far and the battery only ran for about twelve minutes before the thing crashed. It was a good idea, but it just didn't pan out. We'll have to risk real people on a scouting mission if you really want to find out how close they are. Or we can just wait for them to arrive."

Steven nodded, processing the information. He knew the amateur drone plan had been unlikely to prove successful, but it was Calvin's suggestion and had to be tested for appearances sake.

"How many volunteers are we up to?"

Only about ten percent of Liberty's population had left town ahead of the arrival of Isaiah's army. Those citizens who'd chosen to remain had been given the option to join in the fight or hole up in the basement of the municipal building until the battle was over. Children, the infirm, and the elderly got an automatic pass. Everyone else was strongly encouraged to fight, but weren't forced to do so. Steven had stopped short of conscription, but only just; a reluctant soldier makes an unreliable soldier, and they needed full commitment from those who volunteered. Firearms training had been an ongoing process for several days but ammunition was precious, so practice at the hastily constructed shooting range was limited to twenty rounds per person.

Winning a battle came down to numbers. The number of soldiers, the number of guns, the number of bullets, and the number of enemies those bullets found and eliminated from the equation.

If Steven's plan worked, very few of their precious bullets would have to be used at all. If the invading army breached the inner perimeter, their numbers would be diminished and therefore manageable; they would have to circumvent dozens of Punji traps and survive Tung's IEDs first.

If Isaiah proved reasonable, they could avoid bloodshed altogether. But Steven knew better. Everything Dani had told him about the man screamed delusional psychopath. On the day when they would parley on the outskirts of town per Isaiah's demand, he expected to gaze into the eyes of a charming monster. The tricky part would be to collect Dani before Isaiah realized they had no intention of surrendering. It would require a flawless performance if he wanted to keep his balls intact.

Julia had vowed to cut them off if anything happened to her daughter.

Fortunately the strategy played into his plan anyway. Lure the invaders into a false sense of complacency, then spring the trap.

Or rather *traps*.

The Punji pits were non-mechanical, simplistic versions of the pivoting leg trap he had constructed at his house all those months ago. These types of traps were used extensively and effectively by the Vietcong. They were nothing more than sharpened sticks set in a hole in the ground, covered with latticework then camouflaged with leaves or trash; whatever debris was indigenous to the area. Oftentimes the Vietcong applied human excrement to the tips to insure infection and a lengthy delay before the victim could return to battle. They weren't designed to kill American soldiers, just take them out of action, which is what Steven intended for the invaders with his sixteen-penny nail versions.

Any that managed to avoid the dozens of pits set up on either side of the barricades at the four main thoroughfares leading into town would then face Tung's IEDs. There were eight in all, placed in innocuous containers like refrigerator boxes and abandoned cars approximately a half mile from the town square. Inside the bombs were more nails and bits of broken glass that served as shrapnel. They were armed with detonators controlled remotely by a person who would be hiding nearby and waiting for the perfect moment to press the button. These devices were designed with more in mind than to disable. They were meant to kill.

Whatever invaders survived both the traps and the bombs would then face Liberty's armed citizens, including Jeff, who was deadly accurate with his Springfield, and the other sharpshooters, who made up a good percentage of the security crew. Steven's stomach did flips when he thought about his son exposed to the invading army, but he would be in sniper mode...perched at a second story window of the municipal building. The other sharpshooters would be similarly positioned throughout town. Everyone else who wasn't hiding in the basement of the municipal building would be near the greenhouse – their redoubt location since all avenues of ingress were blocked with razor wire that spanned Main Street on both ends as well as the alleyways between buildings.

Steven hoped very few of the enemy made it that far. The defenders positioned here were the least skilled and had received less training than those who would be manning the detonators and the sniper positions.

It was a good defensive plan. He doubted Dani could have come up with anything better.

"Seventy-eight volunteers total, not counting the security crew. That's not too bad actually," Chuck replied. "More than I thought we'd get."

Steven shook his head. They would have gotten more if Calvin hadn't spouted off about murder and their immortal souls. Everyone was scared about the approaching army, but some were actually more afraid of what they might face in the afterlife. If there was an all-knowing deity, surely he would understand the concept of self-defense.

"Yeah, maybe we'll get a few more between now and D-Day. We could use more bodies by the greenhouse," Steven said.

"Hmmm...no offense, but your word choice sucks. So what do you think about another scouting mission?"

"I think it's a superfluous endeavor. We have the cameras set up, so as long as someone is manning them twenty-four seven as usual, we'll know when they arrive. We can expect it to be within three or four days from now. Why risk another hostage situation like we're already facing?"

"Agreed. Just wanted to make sure we're on the same page, boss. Who are you taking with you for the parley?"

"I haven't decided. I won't risk you. Worst case, if my 'second' and I are both killed, someone with leadership skills needs to follow through on the plan."

Chuck nodded. "True. Who is our least valuable person? He should be your second."

In unison, both men said, "Calvin."

Steven couldn't remember the last time he had belly laughed. It felt good.

Chapter 47

"**S**teven must be quite pleased with himself at the moment," Natalie said to Marilyn with an ingratiating smile. It was Natalie's second day of helping in the commissary. She had wrangled the position by bribing Marilyn with the loan of several rare books from her own collection; a price happily paid since it got Natalie close to the competition she intended to eliminate. Despite the fact that almost everyone's job was now focused on defending the town, people still needed food and supply distribution. Marilyn had been working long days and appreciated the help.

There was Marilyn's return smile, transforming the unremarkable face into one which was rather pretty. Still, the former librarian was no beauty queen and never would be. Yes, she was intelligent and even interesting in a bookish way, but she wasn't beautiful, charismatic, magnetic, nor sexy...all qualities that Natalie possessed and which had served her well her entire life.

Qualities which Steven would admire again once she got this unlovely woman out of the way.

"Yes, almost everyone has decided to stay," Marilyn said. "I think he did a brilliant job with the speech. Of course, I may be a little biased."

Marilyn was blushing now. Good grief, what woman in her forties blushed? Natalie felt a wave of nausea as she considered the relationship this woman shared with Steven. Her Steven.

"Yes, I suppose. I don't think Calvin was trying too hard to sway people to leave, so that helped Steven's cause."

"He certainly seems to believe his own religious rhetoric."

"He does believe. At first I wasn't sure. I thought he might be one of those Benny Hinn or Joel Osteen types...you know, in it for personal gain. From what he's said, his ministry was gaining ground when Chicxulub happened. He has conviction in himself and his message. But the choice was a terrible one: stay and fight or leave town on foot in the dead of winter."

"Yes, it's an appalling predicament, but tough decisions have to be made. Steven is very good at cutting to the heart of the matter. It's one of the things I love about him."

"I imagine so." Natalie forced another smile. "Let's take a break, shall we? I brought some hot tea from home. It's my little indulgence these days, and this is the last of my chamomile stash. I want to share it as a way of saying thanks for letting me work with you. Getting away from Cate and the hospital two times a week is wonderful. I'd so much rather be here in the library with you where I'm surrounded by books instead of sick people, and can have an intelligent conversation. That Cate woman is frightful."

Natalie pulled a thermos out of her bag and set two delicate bone china mugs next to it on one of the reading tables.

"Oh, that's so thoughtful. I'd love some tea."

Natalie handed a steaming cup to her rival, thinking how satisfying it would be never to see the woman smile again.

Chapter 48

"What do you mean? How is that possible? I just saw her this morning. She was perfectly fine."

Cate wouldn't meet Steven's eyes, a fact that would have made him suspicious if he had been clear-headed enough to notice.

"I can't explain it, Steven. It may be that she has some underlying condition we didn't know about."

The woman's close-set eyes glanced toward the hospital bed where Marilyn lay. She wasn't dead. Not yet. But according to Cate her blood pressure was alarmingly low and her heart rate was only forty beats per minute. She hadn't regained consciousness since Natalie had found her on the floor in the library commissary an hour ago.

"Does she have any signs of trauma? Maybe she fell and bumped her head."

"Nothing that I could find. I'm sorry. There's just nothing that can be done right now. We'll continue to monitor her vitals. If the blood pressure continues to decline, she may slip away. I believe she may be in a coma, but that can be a good thing. It allows the patient's body to rest and heal itself."

"But sometimes they don't wake up. Right?" Steven's jaw was clenched so tightly the words could barely escape. He would not break down in front of this woman. The anguish he felt surprised himself. He knew he had developed feelings for Marilyn, but hadn't realized how deep they were. He thought he would never feel that way about anyone after he lost his wife to the plague. It was somehow fitting that he had fallen in love with her former friend.

A wave of misery washed over him as he gazed at her in the bed.

"Yes. Sometimes they don't wake up."

Cate patted his shoulder and left the room. He thought he might have a few minutes alone, but the next moment he smelled perfume. When he turned, Natalie was standing behind him.

"I'm so sorry, Steven. I couldn't believe it when I found her sprawled out on the floor. I ran straight to the hospital, and we got her transported here right away."

She moved beside him, encircling his bicep in one arm and draping the other around his shoulders.

"I just don't understand," he said.

"I know, I know. It's not something you expect from someone who seems healthy. Did you know she had a heart murmur? She mentioned it to me just recently."

"No, I didn't know that. She didn't tell me."

"Well, she probably didn't want to worry you," Natalie replied with a squeeze to Steven's shoulder. "Let's just hope for the best."

Jeffrey's voice came from the doorway.

"Dad. They need you over at the southern barricade. There's some arguing about where the detonator should be positioned. Calvin is being a jerk and Chuck is about to punch him, I think."

"Go Steven," Natalie said. "I'll keep an eye on Marilyn. If anything changes, I'll let you know right away."

###

The next moment Steven was out the door. Jeffrey started to follow his father when Natalie said, "Jeff, may I have a word with you? It's about Brittany."

The boy stopped, then pivoted in slow motion to face the mother of the girl he may or may not be in love with. A small voice in his head suggested it was more lust than love. Brittany could actually be pretty annoying; all she ever wanted to talk about was dead celebrities, clothes, and makeup. But when they were doing other stuff besides talking, he liked her very much.

"Come in. I promise I won't bite," Natalie said with a smile.

Jeffrey walked the few steps toward the woman, marveling at how different her beauty was compared to Brittany's. The mother was Hollywood gorgeous, but there was no warmth...no sweetness...just cold beauty glittering like the night sky in winter.

"I know you two are having sex."

The abrupt statement caught him off guard. He had no ready answer, so he said nothing. Better to see where this was going then self-incriminate.

"And while I don't condone it, I understand what it's like to be a fifteen-year old with raging hormones. All I ask is that you treat her with respect and use condoms. Not when it's convenient, but every single time. If you don't have a condom, then do oral. She's much too young to be a mother, and she has my narrow hips. Having her almost killed me, and that was with access to the best doctors and hospitals."

Jeffrey's mouth fell open.

"What? Too blunt?" she said with a leering grin. "I'm a realist. I know you kids are going to do what you want no matter what your parents say. So just be smart about it, okay?"

She reached for his hand and gave it a squeeze. He glanced down at the slender fingers wrapped around his grubby ones, then looked back up at the lovely face. He frowned, struggling to process the disturbing images that came flooding into his mind.

Natalie released her grip, then said, "Now, run along. I'm sure they need you out there somewhere doing something to get ready for this epic battle that's about to happen."

Jeffrey bolted.

"Like a hare from a fox," Natalie said to herself, then went to the doorway and peeked both directions down the long hospital corridor. Nobody was in sight.

Her strides to Marilyn's bedside were purposeful and unhesitating. The next moment she was pinching the nose of the unconscious woman with one hand and covering the thin lips firmly with the other.

Chapter 49

"Oh, dear. Such a lovely face. Well, it *was*."

Isaiah's grin was magnificent. Three days had passed since Dani and Lily's nocturnal pact. There were two fresh vertical lacerations on her forehead, done so as to look like lightning bolts coming up from her eyes. Isaiah's idea, of course. He thought the resulting scars would be a hoot. For now, the wounds just looked ghastly. Forehead skin wasn't thick, so the pain wasn't too bad at least.

The fifth and freshest knife wound, which began from the corner of the right side of her mouth and extended to her ear, was the one to worry about. She didn't have access to a mirror, but her mind summoned visions of Heath Ledger in one of the Batman movies. Tomorrow, on the other side of her face, she would have a second one to match.

The silver lining was that Lily was the designated butcher or surgeon, as it were, being so capable with her knives. The blades were always razor-sharp and sterilized prior to the daily 'reckoning.' She sliced as shallowly as she could get away with...just enough to draw a sufficient amount of blood to satisfy Isaiah, but not so deep that muscle was involved.

Thank god. Surface scarring was one thing. Looking like a stroke victim was something else.

"Fuck you," she muttered. She would never give him the satisfaction of appearing cowed or beaten.

"Tsk, tsk," the dulcet voice said. He gazed down at her from his position astride the black horse. "Now that you're no longer beautiful, that coarse language won't be so readily tolerated. Nor that discourteous, distasteful demeanor of yours. It's human nature, you know. We love beauty and will abide much to be in its presence. Who would put up with your arrogance when they have to look at that ruined face? I wonder if your young man will still be so captivated by the frightful, feckless freak you have become."

Of course this was the source of Dani's personal hell; the thorn in her paw that vexed her every moment that she wasn't thinking about how satisfying killing Isaiah would be. The last time Sam had seen her, there were only two lacerations on her face. Now there were five and they had three more days to go before reaching Liberty.

"Dearest general, I think it's time for your dinner. Let me tend to this girl and I'll join you shortly. Let's go with," she paused, the black eyes studied the leaden, winter sky, "Luther for your taster tonight."

"Luther? He's a good fighter. Brilliant with that mace of his. Why risk such as him?"

Isaiah preferred his food tasters be the least valuable members of his army, but Lily contended all should be put into the rotation. It would keep everyone on their toes and less likely to commit treason.

And now that Martin was out of the picture, she was Isaiah's only advisor. He trusted her like no other, especially after hearing the story of how his former lieutenant murdered Dani's guards then attempted to assassinate Isaiah in his sleep. Thankfully, Lily had been awake and watchful.

She and her knives.

"Because Luther is getting a little big for his britches, I think. It sends a message, yes?"

"Ah. Good point. Very well. Have him sent. As for you, Dani the Disfigured, sleep well tonight. I know I will!"

Both women watched the man on the horse as he trotted away.

Lily dug through her ragged clothing for the bottle of hydrogen peroxide and a clean cloth to treat Dani's wounds.

"The best we can do is keep them sanitary and moist," she whispered as she worked. Everyone in the camp was busy setting up tents and starting cooking fires. The two new guards assigned to watch Dani looked as tired as she felt after the long day of marching. The hope had been that they would sleep inside that night at a Motel 6 just east of Lyons on Highway 56. The scouts had found it earlier in the day and advised Isaiah that it would make an adequate refuge for the night. But the general rejected the idea. Camping under the stars in frigid temperatures hardened his soldiers. Made them stronger, like forged steel.

It was an unpopular edict but nobody would complain. Not out loud, at least.

Dani was so exhausted from the day's march, she barely noticed the growling of her own stomach.

"I'll bring you some food," Lily said, then leaned in closer to whisper in her ear, "I have a tube of petroleum jelly. I'll put a dab on the wounds. It'll help keep the germs out and the flesh moist."

Even if someone had been watching, they wouldn't have seen anything suspicious in Lily's movements. She was like a magician doing sleight of hand. Objects appeared and disappeared from within the ragged clothing faster than Dani could follow.

"Do you happen to have a mirror in one of your magic pockets?" It was a strange paradigm to be receiving kindness from the very person who had inflicted the injuries.

"Trust me. You don't want to see," Lily replied without a moment's hesitation.

No sugarcoating there.

A sudden spike in the ambient noise level came from the direction Isaiah had gone. Crowd sounds, raised voices that escalated in pitch and volume, then diminished as suddenly as they had begun.

Dani noticed Lily frown.

"What? What is it?"

"I don't know," Lily replied, turning her head owl-like toward the ruckus.

The next moment Isaiah reemerged on foot fifty yards away with his three-man escort in tow, plus a fourth person whose silhouette looked vaguely familiar in the fading light of dusk.

Dani was more alarmed by Lily's demeanor than the sight of a returning Isaiah. She seemed nervous; unsure of herself for the first time.

"What's going on?" she repeated, but Lily ignored her, standing to face the advancing group which was growing in numbers with every step. The soldiers sensed, as she did, that something out of the ordinary was happening.

The fourth silhouette was female. The wave of relief she felt that it wasn't Sam was replaced the next moment by a rush of apprehension.

She knew that face. How could anyone who'd seen it once ever forget the eyes and nose which defied symmetry? She remembered those taxicab door ears that stuck out from matted hair at diverse latitudes.

The one useless emaciated arm, woolen-covered now in the winter chill, and the other that ended in pincer-like fingers.

She recognized that ghastly, hygiene-challenged mouth and the smirk of satisfaction it now wore.

"Bet you never thought you'd see me again, huh, Dani?"

Dolores's voice was as lovely as her face was hideous.

"I've been filling Isaiah in on all your doings back in Hays. Remember? When you murdered my brother and your boyfriend killed my pa? Anyway, I've also been following the army...doing a little covert operation of my own. Been watching you and Isaiah's number-one-girl getting all chummy."

Dani remembered how the creature moved. *Like a ghost*, she remembered thinking in the foul hotel room repurposed as a bordello. Like Sam, Dolores could easily have been moving in and around the marching army without being noticed.

Dani looked at Isaiah walking next to the girl. His composure was gone. Betrayal was etched into the downturned mouth, and lash-fringed onyx marbles glowed in the gloom like white-hot coals.

Lily darted behind Dani where she still sat on the cold ground and pressed one of her many knife blades against Dani's throat.

"Don't take another step, Isaiah, or I'll slaughter your little prize like a spring lamb."

"You ungrateful bitch!" he roared.

The strange squeaking laughter came from behind.

"You are a fool," Lily said. "A fustian, flamboyant flatulent fool. I can confirm the flatulence too. A little FYI...just because they're silent doesn't mean they don't smell."

Dani realized two things at that moment. First: Lily was crazier than she had previously thought. The woman might have escaped if she had hauled ass when she first saw the look on Isaiah's face, but soldiers were already beginning to encircle them now. Second: there was going to be bloodshed and the smartest thing Dani could do was to stay perfectly still.

"I will have you drawn and quartered! But first, I'll pluck those black eyeballs out of your skull and rip that serpent's tongue from your lying mouth."

"You want to be careful, silly man. I know the importance you've placed on this woman whose carotid artery is under my blade. I can nick it quicker than a shake of that lamb's tail I mentioned."

Dani didn't move. She watched the emotions play out on Isaiah's face. He was fuming, breathing in and out through flared nostrils and clenched teeth like he was facing a Spanish matador, *espadas* sticking out from his bloodied hide.

"What do you want then, Lily?" he spat.

Dani felt the pressure of the blade lessen. Her brain processed that development, calculating various escape options and the maneuvers they would require.

"I want all of you to die. You especially, Isaiah. You're the worst of the worst. I was going to save you for last, so you would witness the crumbling of your monstrous so-called empire."

The pressure lessened further. Lily was distracted by her verbal sparring.

Just a little more...

"Do you know why? Because all the people that are left...all of you," she gestured to the silent, watchful crowd with the hand that wasn't holding the knife, "are monsters. People like you killed my baby's big sister. Right after the end came. You brutalized her virginal body and then you took her life."

The last part came out as a sob. The revelation that Lily's child had been raped and murdered explained much about the woman's mental state and the transferred affection for the doll she always carried. Under different circumstances, Dani would have felt compassion for the woman. But it was difficult to feel sorry for the person who had ravaged her face and held a knife at her throat.

"It is God's will that you be destroyed and the earth cleansed of your pestilence!"

A bitter laugh erupted from Isaiah.

"You're insane, Lily. Do you know that? I always knew you were a bit off, but now I realize you're delusional and deranged. You're a treacherous, traitorous troglodyte."

"And you are Satan incarnate! You are all child-killing demons from hell!"

There it was. Just enough slack in the tension of the blade against her throat to allow an evasive maneuver with reduced risk and a higher expectation of avoiding death than a moment earlier.

All this went through Dani's mind in a microsecond. In an explosion of movement, she reverse head-butted Lily while spinning the opposite direction from the hand with the knife. It would never have worked if Lily hadn't been distracted. It worked now, though. At least enough to get her out from under Lily's blade and several feet away from the woman who was twirling like a like a rag-clad dervish, knives now in both hands. Dani saw lucidity in the eyes – understanding that Lily realized she was about to die.

And something else: acceptance. Perhaps even relief.

Five soldiers approached the woman from different directions, closing in on her but leery of getting too close. Everyone knew how lethal Lily was with her knives.

The sharp crack of gunfire came from Isaiah's direction.

Lily fell to the ground next to the campfire, like a rag doll dropped from the hand of a sleeping child.

A dime-sized hole in her forehead began to ooze, startlingly red against the backdrop of the pallid face.

The black irises gazed up at the winter sky, unblinking.

Dani's gaze shifted from Lily to the person who'd shot her.

"Been practicing a lot since I saw you last. 'Course my left hand isn't much use." Dolores lifted the arm with the pincers. "But my right hand seems to get the job done." She held the revolver between the only two fingers she had on that hand.

"Excellent, Dolores. I believe you just proved your loyalty as well as your ability. Luther, take two people and bury this wretch." He kicked at Lily's boots. "Deep. I don't want to smell her betrayal in my dreams tonight. You two, not one wink of sleep," he said to Dani's guards. "If my prize lamb escapes, you'll know pain like you've never known before. Dolores, come with me. We shall dine together. I'm certain there's more information in that unfortunate skull that can be useful."

Dani watched Dolores's back as they began to walk away, trying to identify something vaguely bothersome.

'I've also been following the army...doing a little covert operation of my own.'

She felt a stab of apprehension. The words implied Dolores was not the only person shadowing the army. Had she spotted Sam? As if reading her thoughts, the girl turned her head to say something over her shoulder.

"Oh, by the way. I ran into your boyfriend out there. He's got some moves for sure...but so do I. Let's just say you won't have to worry now whether he'll still love you with your messed-up face. I left him by the road with a knife in his gut. You know, the kind of injury that is super painful and slowly, inevitably lethal? That's what I gave him. Payback for my pa. I figure by now the crows and the buzzards have gotten to him. Good night, Dani!"

She had been sitting on the cold ground, her wrists still tied behind her back, her ankles bound in front of her. She collapsed onto her side, not feeling the chill of the earth, not feeling the pressure of the rocks against her body, not feeling the sting of the burning ash flying from the fire and brushing against her wounded face.

Not feeling anything but despair.

Chapter 50

"I don't know, Pablo. I can't explain it. She was doing so well," Cate said.

Pablo wanted to scream at the ruddy-faced woman who wouldn't meet his gaze: *YOU FAT PATHETIC MORON!*

Instead, he asked through clenched teeth, "How high is her blood pressure?" It took every ounce of self-control not to punch one of his balled-up fists into the face of Liberty's nurse practitioner.

"One fifty over a hundred and ten."

He stood in the hospital corridor outside of Maddie's room. He had agreed to move her there so Cate could keep an eye on her. Maddie fought it at first, but after collapsing in their living room the evening before, she acquiesced. The headaches were back, the high blood pressure was back, and Pablo's anguish was back after a two-day reprieve during which time Maddie had been the picture of health. He had been so deliriously happy that the loss of Jessie and the mystery surrounding her disappearance didn't penetrated as deeply as it otherwise would have. Of course Maddie had been beside herself with worry. It was an uncomfortable juxtaposition seeing a healthy Maddie so distraught.

Now that she was ill again and Jessie was still gone, he felt like the world was imploding all around him.

"We'll have to move her to the basement when the time comes."

What Cate meant was when the town's security cameras revealed the invading army was at their doorstep.

Pablo wouldn't be down there with her. Steven had insinuated that any able-bodied person who chose the basement option was a cowa rd...especially any of the young men, even though his official position said otherwise. Steven had been a mechanical engineer in his old life, but he was the consummate politician these days. He gave great lip service to the unwashed masses, then engaged in backdoor deals and manipulation to achieve his ends.

"I'll be down there with her, Pablo. I promise I won't leave her side," Cate continued.

"Did you leave Marilyn's side?" he said.

Marilyn's death would have made bigger headlines if the entire town hadn't been so consumed with preparing for the invasion and worrying about their own survival.

Cate had been shifting from one foot to the other, looking everywhere but into Pablo's eyes. The offhand remark snapped her focus back to him.

"That was a low blow. I'm not a miracle worker, young man. Nobody could have done anything for the woman."

"Sorry. I shouldn't have said that. I'm sure you're doing the best you can."

Cate gave him a curt nod. "I'll watch over her every second when we're in the basement. You have my word."

"I appreciate that. I have to go, but I'll be back this evening."

He peered into Maddie's darkened room, looking for the rise and fall of her chest beneath the blanket. There it was. Perhaps a little faster than it should be, but that was a good thing. Better too fast than nothing at all. When he turned back, Cate was walking away down the corridor. He watched the diminishing blue hospital scrubs stretched tightly across the round shoulders and plump torso.

He thought of Steven again and what he must be going through now, having just lost the woman whom he had been courting. It wasn't possible that Steven could have cared for Marilyn as much as Pablo did for Maddie. People like Steven didn't experience emotions on the same level as people like himself. It was a theory he had never shared with anyone, but he believed it utterly. There was a reason creative types...the artists, the writers, the poets...were less emotionally stable than the mathematicians, scientists, and engineers of the world. It was because they were more sensitive. They felt emotions more intensely, both good and bad.

Steven was also juggling Liberty's governance and the town's defense on top of the loss of his girlfriend. It was a lot for one man to bear and Pablo did feel empathy for him. But Steven signed up for the job...campaigned for it, actually. Burdens came with the territory.

He felt a hand on his shoulder, startling him from his dark thoughts.

"Amelia, you scared the crap out of me."

"Any change?"

"No."

She frowned and shook her head.

"Still no news about Jessie?" he asked.

Another shake of the braided head.

"It's crazy, you know. Tung seemed like such a good guy. I can't stand to think what he might be doing to her." The last few words caught in Pablo's throat.

Amelia took both of his hands in her own, forcing his attention from Maddie's hospital bed down to her.

"I'm going to tell you something that will make you feel better. You'll want to ask a lot of questions that I won't answer. You may want to talk to Maddie about it or perhaps share it with others. You can't do that. Now, do you want to hear it?"

"Something that will make me feel better? Of course."

Amelia took a deep breath, then said, "Tung is not a monster. He's no pedophile. He has taken Jessie somewhere safe. I know this because I know Tung well, and have for many years. You have much to worry about, Pablo, but Jessie should not be among those worries. I promise she is in no danger."

"How could you possibly know Tung for many years? You came here with us. He showed up later and he's from this area. You're from Arizona. This doesn't make any sense."

"What did I say about no questions?"

A memory surfaced suddenly; floated to the top of Pablo's conscious thoughts. It had been a minor event that resonated as odd at the time, then was buried under a mountain of more immediate and pressing issues.

Months ago, Amelia had disappeared for a short time and so had Tung. Pablo remembered one of their early town hall meetings when the man had mysteriously reappeared. He remembered that upon Amelia's return at roughly the same time, she had been uncharacteristically silent about her whereabouts.

He released the small hands and took a step back from the woman he had grown to love almost like a mother. He recalled those occasions when the Amelia mask had slipped and he had seen glimpses of something else...nothing malevolent or distressing, but something that didn't fit with the veneer of the Amelia he knew.

"I know that look and you can stop right now. We had a deal. No questions," she said before he could begin an interrogation.

"Come on. You can't expect me just to accept what you're telling me without even a semblance of an explanation."

"Of course I can. Why wouldn't you? What have I ever done that would make you question my honesty? My loyalty? My devotion? My integrity?"

"It's not about questioning you so much as needing to understand what the hell is going on."

"When you and Maddie came across me in the cabin in Arizona, do you remember our conversation over tequila about whether we would live our lives differently if we knew how and why the plague happened? This is part of that. It's something you will never know and don't need to. It serves no purpose for you to pull back the curtain searching for the wizard. Some things are just not meant for you to know. Accept it. Be strong. Live your life, with or without Maddie, because in the end the whys don't matter. All that matters is that you lived and lived beautifully and generously and kindly for the years you were given in this world."

Pablo opened his mouth again to argue, but was cut off by a noise he had heard several times since their arrival in Liberty and only twice during his life in Prescott. If the Four Horsemen of the apocalypse had a harbinger of their own, it would sound exactly like Liberty's emergency siren. As the speaker rotated on its pole in the center of town, powered by windmill energy stored in a lithium ion battery, its dreadful song waxed and waned. One moment it might have been broadcasting its eerie resonance outward, to some other town full of frightened people; the next moment, it seemed to be calling to him personally.

Something wicked this way comes...

He locked eyes with Amelia, sharing a moment of mutual fear and dismay, then said, "It's time."

"Go," she replied. "I'll see to Maddie before I join you. Blessings on you, Pablo. Blessings on all of us. Be careful, young man. I want to see your handsome face across my breakfast table in the morning."

He kissed her cheek and was gone the next moment.

A million thoughts flew through Amelia's mind as she listened to the emergency siren and watched Cate double-timing it back up the corridor toward Maddie's room. A gurney was set up next to the hospital bed for easy transportation to the basement in the municipal building. She would help the woman get Maddie situated down there, then regroup with those who planned to fight for their world, their lives, and their tenuous grasp on this fledgling civilization.

She would participate in defending the town, despite the persistent nausea she felt at the sight of a sick Maddie; the nausea having sprung from the bottomless reality of what she had sacrificed in order to assure the health of Maddie and her unborn child.

At least Jessie was safe. And Tung. And Fergus, wherever that lascivious rascal might be. She would focus on those happy thoughts, rather than think about how soon her own life might be over.

During the act of moving the unconscious Maddie from the bed to the gurney, Amelia's hand brushed Cate's. Something passed between them; a minor one-way missive of which Cate seemed unaware. The message was incomplete yet bothersome on some level. If the emergency siren hadn't been blaring, Amelia would have insisted on further investigation, but delaying Maddie's move to relative safety was not an option at the moment.

If she survived the ordeal, she vowed to get to the bottom of the mystery that was Cate. At least to the best of her *scythen's* ability...

Chapter 51

"That's not going to happen, Calvin. Don't waste my time. Not now. Not when everything is on the line," Steven said to his co-mayor.

A small group of Liberty's citizens stood behind the town's southern barricade – a seemingly haphazard pile of debris built a mile from the town proper months ago and reinforced days ago. It was positioned on state highway 281, which ran north and south. Isaiah had opted to approach Liberty on this smaller two-lane highway rather than the wider Interstate 35, which ran east and west.

Steven had anticipated that decision after a thorough analysis of all possible routes and current weather conditions, thus the extra time spent securing this particular pile of ramshackle junk that housed a number of deadly surprises for the would-be invaders. More Punji traps had been dug in this vicinity than elsewhere. It seemed that Steven's reasoned crapshoot had paid off. According to the security camera placed a half mile south of the barricade, the first of Isaiah's army were coming from that direction. Some on horseback, as Steven had also anticipated. He regretted the injuries the traps would inflict on the horses, but he didn't feel even a twinge of dismay about the human suffering. People had free will. They had chosen to be there.

He expected the parley group to break away from the advancing line, which consisted mostly of infantry with a smattering of cavalry. When that happened, he and his 'second' would circumvent the barricade on foot – carefully – and meet them, looking as beaten down, weak, and helpless as possible; looking like people who'd given up and were resigned to their fate.

He had chosen Ed to be his second for a number of reasons, but mostly because he trusted him. If something happened to the man, the loss to the town would be significant – he was brilliant at designing effective, efficient plans for infrastructures of all types – but his awkward social demeanor would mask any deception Isaiah might sniff out. He had a quick mind that could process unexpected deviations from Steven's plan. Most importantly he was motivated to succeed. There was a pretty blond Ed wanted to keep safe; she was armed to the teeth and positioned by the greenhouse. It was appropriate that Lisa would be included in the last line of defense near the lifesaving crops for which she was largely responsible. Steven knew she would die before walking away from that greenhouse. It was a thought he did not share with Ed.

"Please, just hear me out," Calvin was saying.

"Yes, Steven. Just listen to him." Natalie added with a squeeze of Steven's bicep. He glanced down at the hand on his arm, then to the woman herself, wondering again why in the hell Calvin had brought her. She should be down in the basement with her daughter or standing by with one of the armed groups in the town square.

"They are expecting Liberty's leader. Does this Isaiah demon know there are two? Probably. He's most likely tortured the girl and extracted all the town's details. But we're still abiding by his mandate, sending out a person of 'supreme authority' to collect Dani in exchange for relinquishing the town and all its bounty."

"Get to the point, Calvin."

"Yes, yes. My point is this: why should we risk you?"

Steven didn't know what he had been expecting to come out of the mouth of his rival, but it wasn't this.

"Let's face it. Your value to this community exceeds mine, at least on a corporeal level. Whoever goes out there is walking right into the lion's den. If the worst happens and the emissaries are killed, the town won't have lost its keystone...its life's blood."

"See, Steven? He's right. You can't argue with that kind of logic," Natalie said. Steven brushed away the slender hand that still held his arm.

He pondered Calvin's words while studying the man's face, looking for any hint of duplicity in the intense eyes or in the mouth that wore a relaxed smile. As for all important events, Calvin had dressed in a pristine white shirt, and even though he wasn't freshly-shaven as was his norm, the five-o'clock shadow didn't detract from the image Steven suspected the preacher always tried to project: *I have the ear of God...you can trust me and believe everything I say.*

When he put aside the hostility he had felt upon Calvin's arrival in town, he could understand why the man inspired such a loyal following. He imagined the crowds his sermons must have drawn before the plague. Calvin was charismatic and suave, and passionate about his message. Steven had always assumed he was a just another hypocritical, bible-thumping, evangelical phony. So the sincerity he now saw caught him by surprise.

Could it be possible the man was truly willing to sacrifice his own life for the greater good?

"What's your angle, Calvin?"

The preacher gave a hearty laugh. There was no enmity in the rich sound nor the kindly expression.

"Steven, you'll just have to take this on faith. I know that isn't your nature, but it is mine. Let me do this. Let me be God's emissary in this dangerous undertaking. He doesn't want to risk you. I know this. He has important plans for you. As for me." He was grinning now, "I've done all I can do. I know I have a place in heaven, so I'm not afraid to die. You on the other hand, you'll probably want to stick around down here as long as possible." The wink was playful and unaffected.

Steven found himself convinced. He hated the flood of relief he felt at not having to venture out there, knowing that whomever did may not survive the encounter. He would have done it, but Calvin's plan made sense. Why risk the person who could do so much for the town and its people when an acceptable proxy had volunteered? And happily so. Hell, was downright insistent.

Steven turned to his second. "What do you think?"

Ed didn't hesitate before answering. "He's absolutely right. And if he pulls any shenanigans, I'll kill him."

Calvin's chuckle was slightly less enthusiastic, but there was no trace of animosity in his bearing.

Steven gazed at each individual in the small group as he considered the change to his plan. Julia was frowning at him with big-sister disapproval written all over her face. Seeking her opinion was pointless; all she cared about was getting Dani back, so of course she would want Steven to handle the prisoner retrieval himself.

Natalie stood uncomfortably close, staring at him with a come-hither smile. He wanted to slap it off her face. The loss of Marilyn was newborn pain; still in the early stages of developing, mushrooming inside the emotional compartment to which he had banished it. His wife always said he could compartmentalize better than anyone. That talent was serving him well now. There wasn't time to wonder what motivated Natalie to encourage Calvin, her lover, to take on the risk Steven had intended for himself.

His focus came to rest on Amelia, who stood off to the side with her eyes closed and a frown of concentration between her dark brows. With her braids and knee-length leather moccasins, she looked like a doll he had seen years ago at a souvenir shop in Colorado. Her lips moved like she was talking to someone. Was she praying? He had never seen her attend any of Calvin's sermons; she treated the preacher with disdain rather than reverence. Maybe she was praying to some Native American god.

He shook his head, clearing his wandering thoughts.

Pablo stood next to her, a death grip on the ancient shotgun he always carried and a grim, disconsolate expression on his face. The golden eyes locked onto Steven's, projecting vague disapproval. Or perhaps it was disgust. Whatever Pablo felt for him, Steven knew it wasn't good will. He burned a bridge with the young man when he had used Liberty's gasoline as leverage to get him to stay.

Steven moved on to the next face.

Now that Logan was gone, the security crew's best shooters were Jeff and the eighteen-year-old standing near the barricade, ready to scramble into her sniper's lair. If the girl known as Annie Oakley – a nickname she liked so much she wouldn't answer to her former name – could get a clear shot at Isaiah's head (she would not risk anything lower which would probably be protected by Kevlar), the invading army might immediately fall apart without their charismatic and terrifying leader.

Steven estimated the odds of that happening were less than fifty-fifty. It depended on how far away from the sniper-hiding barricade the parley group stopped. It depended on where the members of the parley group stood and how still they were – a moving target was exponentially more difficult to hit. It depended on the wind, the curvature of the earth, whether the bullet had been manufactured identically to all the others Annie Oakley had been practicing with.

The most important ingredient in the mix was whether Isaiah would be anticipating what they had planned.

Steven figured he would be, which is why the girl would not take a chance on anything less than the perfect kill shot. He had drilled that directive into her head, made her repeat back to him all the conditions under which the shot would be taken, over and over again.

Because if she missed, the emissaries would die. Of that Steven had no doubt. And besides, they had a backup plan. It was just a hell of a lot bloodier.

"I know. We've been over this a hundred times," the girl said when she felt his gaze upon her. "The Kestrel 4000 is telling me everything I need to know – wind speed, density altitude – I'm on it. I won't take the shot unless it's a lock. You want me to get into position now?"

Steven studied the plain, eager young face. She should be holding a clarinet instead of a Remington Long Action; should be marching onto a high school football field rather than crawling into a sniper hole. That such a monstrous burden was placed on those round shoulders evoked a wave of self-loathing; a familiar emotion these past months. At that moment he realized Pablo didn't feel mere disapproval when he looked at Steven. He felt revulsion.

And understandably so.

Delegating this looming task to Calvin would only add a layer of contempt to already unfavorable opinions of him. He had made a lot of tough decisions in the process of preparing their town for the coming invasion; he could only hope he would have the opportunity to address those sentiments later, when and if they all survived.

"Yes, please. I know it's not comfortable in there, and I don't know how long this will take. Stay frosty, Annie. There's a lot riding on you."

The girl rolled her eyes but didn't respond. Instead, she placed her portable weather station in front of a decades-old Kenmore top-loading freezer and crawled inside with her rifle. Through the drilled hole in the south-facing end, she would be able to see the digital numbers of the Kestrel 4000 and beyond to the long, flat stretch of highway 281. The hole was large enough to accommodate the barrel and scope of the Remington. She could see for almost two miles with the scope, but she wouldn't risk a shot on anything farther than half of that distance. At least that was the plan.

"What's your answer, Steven?" Calvin prompted.

He turned to face the preacher.

"We'll do it your way. I appreciate the offer and hope you don't regret making it."

"Regret is a destructive emotion and one in which I don't engage. It was the right decision. I know it wasn't an easy one." He clapped Steven on the back, turned to Natalie and pulled her into his arms, kissing her with the passion and abandon more befitting a randy schoolboy than a man of God. She broke it off after a few seconds.

"Okay, then. Good luck," she said with an embarrassed glance at Steven.

"Ed, my good man! Are we ready for this great adventure?"

"Ready as I'll ever be. Don't forget, preacher. You make any fishy moves and I'll take you out."

"Understood. Steven, one more thing. I haven't had a chance to tell you how sorry I am for your loss. Marilyn was a fine woman. Also, if something should happen to me, please promise that you'll look after my lady and her daughter. Such pretty girls need looking after," he said with a wink.

Calvin turned on his heels and began maneuvering through the traps set around the barricade. Ed kept a distance of several yards between them when he caught up to the preacher.

They wouldn't have too far to walk. Through his binoculars, Steven could make out two people on horseback and one person shuffling between them. They weren't close enough to see minute details, but he saw enough to make his stomach lurch.

He lowered the field glasses.

"Do you see her?" Julia demanded.

"Yes," he replied.

"What? What's wrong?"

"She's alive. That's all that matters."

"What the hell is it, Steven?"

When she pushed against his chest, he was surprised by how much strength was behind the aggression. Julia was almost as tall as him and even though her thinness bordered on gaunt, the shove felt plenty solid. Back when they were kids, she kicked his ass on a regular basis.

There would be no dissembling with his sister. She knew him better than anyone.

"It looks like her face has been cut."

"Just a cut? Is it bad? Give me those binoculars."

"No. You don't want to see. Not now. Let's get through this, Julia, then we'll take care of her. I promise."

They stood mere inches apart now. Julia's wide eyes held his narrowed ones in a flinty tractor beam; her expression was a mixed bag of challenge and fragility. Finally she broke.

"Fine. Do what you need to do. I'm telling you, though, all I care about is getting her back safely. I don't care about this town or your precious greenhouse or your 'fledgling civilization.'"

"Yes, I get that. Now please either go to the basement if you're not up to your assignment or get into position."

She blinked once, then turned her back on him and headed toward town. She wasn't a great shot, but she would not hide out with old people and children. She would stand by in their redoubt location with all the others whose skill set didn't include sharpshooting and hand-to-hand combat.

He breathed a sigh of relief. "Natalie, you too. Get to the basement."

"I'm going. Please be safe, Steven!"

She wrapped her slender arms around his neck and planted a lingering kiss on his lips before he could stop her. The next moment she was peddling away. He worked up some saliva and spat on the cracked pavement.

"Amelia?"

The tiny woman had opened her eyes and was studying him.

"Yes, Steven?"

"Why are you here?"

A smile played about the corners of her mouth.

"I had something to do. I'm leaving now."

He watched the enormous knife in its sheath strapped to the child-sized back as she walked away. It always amused him to see it; the barbaric weapon was half as tall as she was. Still, when he considered the ferocity the diminutive woman seemed to barely hold in check these days, he wouldn't want to tangle with her and her giant knife.

Steven glanced at Pablo, who stood beside him now. He had asked the young man to be there because Chuck was positioned at the western barricade in anticipation of a flanking maneuver. Pablo's mind was one of the quickest in town, and if something happened to Steven, he hadn't wanted Calvin left to his own devices at this critical location. Since Steven was no longer the emissary, he would observe the parley from a distance, in the presence of this brilliant young man who despised him.

Pablo didn't look at him. He was gazing through his own binoculars; the corners of his mouth were turned down in concentration or perhaps abhorrence. Maybe both.

"They're almost there," he mumbled.

Steven peered through his own binoculars. There were contrived holes in the debris barricade through which they could watch the action without being exposed to any snipers the approaching invaders may have in their ranks.

"I see them. Did you look at Dani?"

"Yes. Her face is a travesty, but her body language doesn't harmonize with it. I don't think her spirit has been broken."

"Oh my god. What is wrong with that woman on the horse?"

"Genetic birth defects would be my guess."

"Annie, how are you doing in there?"

"Fine. No shot yet," was the muffled reply. "Please don't lecture me again. I know what I'm doing."

It was the price one paid for being a controlling micromanager, and it glanced off him like a well-thrown stone on a placid lake.

"Isaiah isn't what I pictured in my mind," Steven said. "He's holding back a bit...keeping that woman in front of him."

"Too bad we didn't have a sniper we could place at their flank," Pablo replied.

It was an admonition, of course. Jeffrey had been positioned at the much safer sniper location in town.

Steven ignored it.

"Looks like they're talking now," he said. "Calvin is making that hand gesture he uses when he's proselytizing. Damn, I wish we could hear what they're saying."

If he had known someone other than himself would be meeting Isaiah, he would have planted a two-way radio on them, turned to the squelch setting. He watched as Calvin, his shirt dazzlingly white against the drab, dirty pigments of a broken world, glided about in front of the riders; his movements so graceful they seemed choreographed. He could imagine the man on stage at one of those mega churches, preaching the Word to millions through syndicated Sunday morning television. He strode from one side of the highway to the other, gesticulating as he walked. Steven realized suddenly what he was doing. He was drawing Isaiah out...enticing him away from the safer position behind the other rider. Was he trying to give Annie Oakley a clean shot? That would fly in the face of everything Calvin had been saying about the sanctity of life for months. Had he had a last-minute change of heart?

Whether he was doing it intentionally or not, it was working. Isaiah's horse was taking small steps forward, giving its master a better view of Calvin's performance. Steven almost felt mesmerized by the lithe movements of the preacher. He didn't realize he was holding his breath until the moment was shattered by the explosive report of rifle fire.

Annie Oakley had taken the shot.

The horses reared and pranced about, barely held in check. Calvin stood facing the animals and their riders, frozen in place, his arms pointing skyward. Ed began to run back to the barricade.

Isaiah still sat astride the enormous black horse.

The next moment, the back of Calvin's head exploded, spraying blood, brains, and skull fragments onto the blacktop. Then the same scenario in reverse with Ed, his forehead bursting open in a crimson fountain.

"Annie, let's go!" Steven yelled.

The girl was already out of the ancient freezer. She scrambled to the edge of the rubble pile, exposing herself, to line up a second shot.

"Annie, *now!*"

The rifle's discharge pushed the youthful shoulder back but the girl knew how to absorb the energy. She was lining up a third shot, crying.

"Goddamn it!" she screamed in frustration.

Steven began running toward her, intent on grabbing her arm and pulling her out of harm's way.

Instead, he watched the gray woolen cap covering the girl's head jerk backward. Just like in the movies, the world slowed to a crawl. Her body crumpled to the ground at quarter speed so he wouldn't miss a single detail. By the time he skidded to a stop, the lifeless eyes stared at him from below, blood oozing from her temple and trailing down the round cheek, then dripping onto the winter-dead grass.

He turned away and vomited.

"Come on, Steven. We have to go."

It was Pablo's voice. He looked up into the young man's face and saw nothing but frozen tundra in the depths of those golden eyes.

"My fault," he muttered.

"Probably. Let's go, Steven."

Steven allowed his compartmentalization talent to take over. The horrors he had just witnessed – for which he was largely responsible – were delegated to the same part of his consciousness where grief for Marilyn was being stored.

"Okay."

The two men jogged back to the scooters waiting for them. There was no need for stealth at this point. Both engines fired up simultaneously.

From her hiding place, Amelia watched them motor back toward the direction of town. She closed her eyes and forced the calm state necessary to maximize her *scythen's* reach.

Chapter 52

"A pitiful, pathetic ploy. Did they think we wouldn't be expecting this?" Isaiah said as he urged his horse forward from the ranks of more than a hundred wiry, road-weary soldiers. He stopped next to his body double from the parley group, who wasn't controlling the strong-willed Friesian nearly as well as Isaiah himself did. The similarity between the men was uncanny until they were side by side. Still, Isaiah's doppelganger had been good enough.

"I'm sure they have more tricks up their sleeve, asshole."

Even in her miserable state, Dani wouldn't let him intimidate her.

"Your insults are becoming tiresome in their crudeness. *You* are becoming tiresome. And since the gentleman's agreement has been broken, I'm no longer under any obligation to release you. I can kill you whenever I want. I think that time has come. I have accomplished my reckoning, and now you simply bore me. I'm ready to wash my hands of you and begin the next chapter in my glorious life."

Dani noted the lack of excessive alliteration as she watched him dismount the gray gelding. He must be distracted, which was good. She had to admit that using the decoy had been clever, and Steven had taken the bait. It was another reason she knew she couldn't count on help from him and the townspeople to get her out of this mess.

She held her arms behind her, just as if they were still tied. During the pandemonium the night Lily had wandered off the reservation, she managed to snatch a sharp-edged rock before anybody noticed. It had taken her the next twenty-four hours to covertly hack through the paracord which bound her wrists. The hardest part had been to allow the mutilation of her face to continue when she could have escaped. It had been necessary to stay in place, feigning constraint, to remain close to Isaiah and kill him when the moment was right. She wouldn't have had a chance before now; he had doubled his personal guard to six soldiers. They surrounded him everywhere he went, even when he used the latrine.

But she had gambled that during the excitement and chaos of approaching Liberty and preparing for battle, there would be an opening...a chink in his armor. And once she killed him, that circus freak Dolores would be next. She wasn't doing it to save the town or to impress Steven or even Julia. She was doing it for herself and the sublime gratification their deaths would bring her.

After that, she didn't care what happened. Her face looked like Lon Chaney in Phantom of the Opera, and Sam was surely dead by now, courtesy of Dolores. There wasn't a whole lot about living that appealed to her anymore.

As she watched Isaiah walk toward her wearing that bat-shit crazy grin and carrying her beloved K-bar in his right hand, she slowed her breathing down, then did the same to her heart rate. She began to enter the state of consciousness that allowed her to perform feats that seemed to defy the laws of physics. This ability had come naturally to Sam – she had to learn it.

Sam.

An invisible knife plunged into her chest.

Twenty more feet...come on you psycho fucktard...I want to be rid of you once and for all...then I'm going to take a bit more time with Dolores the Disgusting...

She continued making minor adjustments to the mentally choreographed movements which would be necessary to knock the knife out of Isaiah's hand, retrieve it from where it would land seventeen inches from where he would be standing at that point, then in a rapid pivoting motion plunge it into the exposed throat.

Or perhaps the right eyeball...whichever option was most expedient. She hoped the throat would win out. She had an intense desire to hear that rich honeyed voice gurgling with blood.

"General, be careful. She's a wily one. I should know!" Dolores said.

Dani ignored her, but registered her location by the vocalization, and plugged the coordinates into her mental logistics. She knew the girl was still astride the chestnut mare she had been riding since arriving at their camp and winning Isaiah's favor. It was a strange twist of fate that Lily, the woman who had mutilated her face, was dead as a result of that nasty bit of business sitting on the mare. Dani placed the mare fifteen feet behind her at a five 'o clock position.

Dolores wasn't long for this world, but Isaiah first.

The maniacally charming smile was only ten feet away now. Dani's quadriceps tensed for the spring without being told by her brain to do so. She had written the code, now it was up to the cerebrum to execute the program.

Dani smiled in return, wondering for a fleeting moment how macabre her face must look, engaged in what would be a pleasing human expression on a non-disfigured face.

The heels of her boots hovered an inch above the cold earth.

Isaiah was a mere five feet away, raising up the K-Bar like it was fucking Excalibur. Her grin broadened. He was so preoccupied with visions of glory and whatever else was going on in that mincemeat he called a brain, that he was leaving his vulnerable bits wide open.

Yes...it could well be the throat.

Suddenly a blur of movement registered on the right side of her peripheral vision, originating from the grassy stretch just past the shoulder of the highway.

The next moment Sam flew head-first into Isaiah, knocking him to the ground and snatching the knife from his hand. Before anyone could react, he had grabbed Dani by her arm and was dragging her with him, back to the tall grass next to the road. He was moving so fast, she thought her shoulder might pop out of its socket any second. When they reached the motorcycle hidden behind an ancient pickup truck, the bullets had started to fly.

"You're not tied up anymore?" he hollered as he straddled the machine.

"You're not dead anymore?" she yelled back as she jumped on the seat behind him.

"I almost was. I'm a fast healer!"

"Where are you going?" she screamed above the thundering of the motorcycle's engine and the bullets that zipped around them.

"I cut a hole in the fence. We have to go through this field. There are traps near the road."

Sam zig-zagged the motorcycle as they plowed through the fallow corn, the withered stalks making it difficult for Isaiah's people to draw a bead on them. The rough terrain caused the beetle-green Kawasaki to bounce and twist mid-air, a mechanical salmon swimming upstream through a pale ocean of dead vegetation. It was working though. The rifle fire was diminishing with every furrow they navigated.

Dani gripped the motorcycle seat with her thighs and Sam with her arms. She closed her eyes and held on tight, breathing in the smell of him.

When the bullets stopped flying, she turned her head to get a visual of their enemy.

"They must be conserving their ammo!"

The back of Sam's golden head nodded. He didn't let off the throttle.

They were a football field away from Isaiah and his army. Sam kept going, and soon nobody was shooting at them.

Ten minutes later they skidded to a halt under a copse of cottonwoods near a desolate farmhouse. She couldn't even see the highway from there, which meant they couldn't be seen from the highway either.

The world was preternaturally quiet after the insanity of what had just transpired.

Sam was alive!

"Dani, you have to let go of me. You're safe. Let's take a breather."

She held on, her arms encircling him with a death grip.

"I'm still a little tender there. Dolores got me pretty good."

She lessened her grip, but wouldn't let go. Because the sooner she did, the sooner Sam would turn around and get a clear look at her face.

"It's okay. We got away."

He gently disentangled himself from the one-sided bear hug and stepped off the motorcycle. She stayed perfectly still, following his movements, resisting the urge to cover her face with her hands, dreading when he would turn around. What would she see on his face? Shock? Horror? Revulsion? Or worse, pity?

Instead, there was the beautiful Sam smile, like March sunlight shining on winter-pale skin.

"I knew you made that stuff up about being in love with Pablo just to get me to leave. I knew it the moment you said it, but I figured it was best to play along. Then when I was shadowing the army, Dolores got me when I was resting. Anyway, it took me some time to heal well enough to catch up. Then I went on ahead of the army and scouted the perimeter of the town. Steven's done a good job locking things down, but you would have done better."

As she watched Sam talk, her hand fluttered up to her face, ignoring the directive of her brain to *Stay Away!* Her fingertips told a horrific Brothers Grimm tale of what they found there.

"Sam," the word came out a croak; a fitting vocalization for someone so hideous.

"I know you're worried about your face. I told you before that you're beautiful no matter how bad the cuts are."

"It's so much worse now." She had to break eye contact. It was too painful looking at that handsome face from the vantage of Ugly Girl.

"You're smart. You should know that it doesn't matter what's on the outside. All that matters is what's on the inside. We are soul mates, Dani. Nothing will ever change that. You could have warts and a bald head and I wouldn't care. How can you not know that?"

He kissed her lips, being careful to hold her face in a way that didn't cause pain.

"I love you so much, and I always will. No matter what. You are my forever and always," he said.

She didn't realize she was crying until the salty tears began to sting her wounds.

"Now, we have to get going," he continued. "We have about ten minutes to get through all the booby traps. Steven will need our help, for sure. Are you ready?"

She nodded. His smile was a watery distortion through the tears she couldn't stop.

"Suck it up, daffodil! We have work to do."

Chapter 53

"How did you get through?" Steven's tone was a mixture of frustration and relief.

"We came through the north, just like half of Isaiah's army is going to do," Dani replied.

Pablo found it difficult to look at her face. It was much worse in person than seen through the binoculars from a mile away. It didn't seem to diminish her confidence, though. She was still overbearing, but there was something new in her demeanor; the jagged edges and sharp corners had been smoothed down a bit. She seemed almost...respectful.

He was relieved that she and Sam stood with them near the southern barricade. Isaiah's army was less than a half mile away now. According to Dani, a faction would also be approaching from the north, not the east as Steven had anticipated.

"Did you see them?" Steven demanded.

"We didn't have to. That's what I would have done. No offense, Steven, but Isaiah is better at this shit than you. Fortunately, he's not as good as me. That's why these guys," she indicated the army advancing toward the southern barricade, "are going so slowly. They're giving the flanking group time to get into position in the north."

"We didn't secure that perimeter as well. There wasn't time."

"That's why you need to pull all your shooters from the east and west and send them north."

"That will leave us exposed on those sides."

"Yes, but it won't matter since the bad guys won't be coming from those directions."

She might have been speaking to a slow-witted child. Pablo got the sense she wasn't even doing it as an intentional insult. She was genuinely trying to be patient with a slower thinker.

With a smirk he said, "We're running out of time."

Steven nodded and pulled a walkie-talkie from its belt holster.

"Alpha and Gamma teams, fall back and rendezvous with Zeta at their location."

"What? Why?" Chuck's static-filled reply was immediate.

"That's an order. We have new intel." Then to Dani, "You better be right."

"I'm right."

Almost as an afterthought, he pressed the button again. "Lisa, tell my sister I didn't fail her. She'll know what that means."

"Roger that. Take care of my man down there."

Pablo actually felt sorry for Steven when he saw the anguish wash over his face. Lisa's man Ed, along with Calvin and Annie Oakley, were the first casualties of a battle that hadn't even begun yet but was just moments away now.

"Everyone into position!" Steven yelled.

As Pablo stood on the cracked blacktop with a cold wind blowing across the back of his neck, he felt weirdly calm and not wholly...*there*. A strange detachment took the place of the adrenaline-fueled anxiety from moments before. A sudden notion occurred to him: he had been placed in that specific location at that precise moment in time to observe a chain of events that were imminent and far-reaching in their significance. Perhaps that's how Homer felt those last fifty-three days of the Trojan War.

Unlike Homer, he didn't have the luxury of being merely an observer, a fact that was underscored by the sound of the approaching army just beyond the southern barricade.

Pablo jogged to the Toyota sedan parked seventy yards from the debris pile and slid in behind the steering wheel. On the passenger seat lay his allotment of shells for his shotgun and the extra clips for the Glock that was strapped to his hip. None of the firepower would be necessary if everyone did their job perfectly and the invaders behaved exactly as Steven anticipated.

And nobody but Steven thought that was even a remote possibility.

He reached for the detonator that had also been placed in the passenger seat and peered through the windshield, waiting for the first figures to come around the barricade. The windows of the Toyota were lowered; he could hear the screams of horses and humans alike as they encountered the Punji traps. He watched Dani and Sam take up positions on either side of the barricade, a bit too close to the IEDs for his liking, but it was too late to worry about that.

His walkie-talkie squawked.

"In position at Zeta. We have a visual." Chuck's voice. "They're coming."

"Told you." Dani's voice, casual and calm. "Chuck, give me a number."

"Forty or fifty. Shit! We were not expecting this."

"Steven, pull your snipers out of downtown and send them north." Dani's voice again.

Silence on the walkie-talkie. Pablo heard more screams, closer now.

"Steven!"

"No. We need them at the redoubt location." Steven's voice was deadpan.

"Fuck that. If they get through, we're screwed and you know it." Dani hadn't lost her cool, but she was getting close.

Pablo pressed the talk button. "He doesn't want to send his son into danger," he said into the Motorola, then watched through the windshield as Dani shook her head. She was crouched beside a feed store, peering south around the brick corner.

"That's bullshit, Steven. Everyone is making sacrifices. Jeff, you roger me?"

"Roger that, Dani. We're on the way."

Pablo smiled at the rebellious tone he heard in the boy's voice. He imagined the dismay the father must be feeling and the smile vanished.

"Pablo, fingers on those buttons." Dani again.

"Roger," Pablo said into the walkie-talkie. "You're kind of close," he added.

"Don't worry about that."

"If you say so." He set the walkie-talkie next to the shotgun. "Amelia, what are you doing back there?" he said to the rearview mirror.

"Just backing you up, my dear."

"You're supposed to be at the greenhouse."

"We both know that was never going to happen."

He smiled at the tranquil face with the old-soul eyes.

The next moment, all hell broke loose.

Chapter 54

Pablo found himself mesmerized by the sight of the handsome man astride the gleaming horseflesh. The spectacular beast used its hooves like fists, attacking anyone who came near its master.

Isaiah was smiling, an exquisite fallen angel with obsidian eyes so full of manic joy they seemed lit from within. The poet could imagine sooty wings sprouting from the muscular back and demons jockeying for position at his boot heels. His movements were fluid, graceful, and lethal. Somehow he was evading all the bullets whizzing around him while brandishing a sword in one hand and the reins of the horse and a pistol in the other. Everyone he targeted became a casualty. Three, four, five of Liberty's defenders who had emerged from their hiding places and gotten too close fell to his blade or his bullets.

Pablo thought he might vomit.

The walkie-talkie squawked. Steven's voice came through the static.

"I'm going north. I'll grab the IEDs from the eastern location on the way. Dani, Sam, Pablo, you know what to do here."

Not only had Steven forgotten to use their code words, but he was relinquishing control of the defense of the critical southern barricade when Isaiah was in their very midst.

Of course there was good reason. Jeffrey was also heading north to fight the flanking threat there. Steven would be with his son, in victory or defeat. The town and its safekeeping were now secondary.

Pablo decided there might be hope for Steven after all.

"Get ready," Amelia said from the backseat, snapping him to attention.

"Do you see how close Sam is? I can't detonate yet."

He grabbed the walkie-talkie from the passenger seat.

"Sam, you're too close to the IED in the red Taurus. Fall back so I can blow it!"

The golden head vanished from his field of vision. He had no idea what direction it had even gone.

"Do you see Dani?" Pablo asked Amelia, yelling to be heard over the gunfire which exploded nonstop from multiple directions. He watched as a handful of invaders breached the razor wire stringing outward from the barricade, like tentacles of a junkyard octopus. They scrambled toward him and their town, Dermestid beetles scuttling to a freshly-dead body. Just a handful though...not hundreds nor even dozens. How many had fallen to the Punji traps? How many more were coming? He needed to maximize the IEDs, making sure they killed as many attackers as possible, because the rest would have to be dealt with in a more hands-on fashion.

"No. Wait, yes. She's at your eleven o'clock."

"That's too close!"

"Pablo, you have your orders. Think of Maddie and all the others in the basement. Do what needs to be done." Amelia's voice was emotionless.

He nodded. She was right.

The moment before he hit the first detonator button, he saw Dani's lithe form leap onto the black stallion behind their would-be conqueror.

Still too close...

He pressed the red button.

Dani held the K-Bar to Isaiah's throat. The Friesian was agitated by the unfamiliar weight of the stranger on its back, but wasn't panicking...yet. Isaiah's firm hand on the reins seemed to keep the massive animal from bolting away from the rattle-pop of gunfire, the oppressive stench of spilt blood and bowels letting loose in terror or death, and the incessant screams of humans and horses.

Dani blocked all that stimuli from conscious thought to focus on the task at hand.

The explosion happened the next moment, almost knocking her off the huge beast when it reared up in fright. While ash, gravel, and chunks of red steel rained down on them, she held firm to Isaiah's waist with one arm. With the other she gripped the knife, never allowing it to budge from the muscled throat of her nemesis.

"Are you ready to die now?" she murmured into his ear like a lover.

For once, he had no glib response. Instead, he released the sword he held in his right hand, letting it fall to the ground. The pistol dropped from the other hand the next moment. Both arms extended skyward, holding only the horse's reins now. All weapons had been relinquished.

This was not the reaction she expected.

"No, I surrender. I'm your willing captive, and it would be in violation of all honorable warfare conduct to harm a prisoner. You there," he yelled, pointing to a Liberty defender who was rounding the corner of the feed store where Dani had just been. The man's sudden sliding stop and his shocked expression were almost comical. He forgot to point his gun at the man on the horse.

"Be my witness! I'm surrendering myself to you, but this woman wants to cut my throat. I'm unarmed! Do you see? I'm going to dismount now. See that this creature doesn't harm the most valuable prisoner you'll capture today! Don't let her steal your glory!"

Incredibly, the man's gun swiveled up to point at Dani rather than Isaiah, as he slid out of the saddle with his arms still raised in supplication.

Isaiah stood next to the horse now, wearing a shark's grin. The leather reins were still held loosely with one upraised hand.

What kind of bullshit is this?

With the instinct of a mongoose anticipating the cobra's strike, Dani sensed Isaiah's next move just before it happened: he was going to jerk the reins, causing the horse to make a sudden move and disrupt the barely controlled situation. That split second was all she needed to deliver a perfect Taekwondo side kick to his skull from atop the stallion.

The next moment she stood next to his unconscious body on the ground, while chaos continued all around her.

Tung knew how to build a bomb. The roof of the red Taurus convulsed a half second before it exploded in all directions, hurling chunks of metallic flesh in a rough circular pattern twenty yards in diameter. The shrapnel placed inside the vehicle was devastating. The broken glass and jagged rocks cut through the scuttling soldiers like they had been flung from the invisible hand of an angry god.

Pablo let out an involuntary cheer, but the next moment it stuck in his throat.

More invaders still scrambled around the barricade, part of which had been destroyed by the first bomb, allowing them easier access now.

"Pablo, get ready." Amelia's voice was calm. She might have been telling him to rinse out his coffee mug.

The second IED was planted on the other side of the road in an ancient pickup truck, ten yards closer to Pablo's Toyota than the red Taurus had been. If the invaders got too close, he would hand the detonator to Amelia and make use of his allotment of ammunition. The driver's window was all the way down now and the stock of his shotgun rested doglike in his lap, the business end placed on the rearview mirror. The Toyota was not a camouflaged position. If the attackers got close, Pablo and Amelia would be seen.

His finger hovered over the detonator's second button. "Just a little closer..." he muttered.

The walkie-talkie squawked again. Steven's voice.

"Zeta, get ready. Here they come."

With the driver's window all the way down now, Pablo clearly heard the sound of two explosions in quick succession coming from the north, then rapid gunfire that sounded like children's air rifles from so far away. Pablo knew the northern barricade must hold even though less time and energy had been spent on the fortifications there; there was no way the southern defenders could fight a threat coming from in front as well as behind.

More figures were approaching the Toyota now through the dust and smoke. He could discern features, expressions. Rather than sinister, they appeared terrified. Their movements also seemed strange...evasive and reckless somehow; not aggressive. There was one man and three women. One of the women was holding her arms up and yelling something.

Sanctuary?

Was this a trick? Something wasn't right, but in those fleeting moments, there wasn't time to figure out what it was.

He thought of Maddie and the baby.

When the crouching, huddling group was five feet from the rusted pickup, Pablo pressed the second button.

From this IED's location closer to the Toyota, he felt the invisible force of the blast in the airwaves. A piece of rusted tailgate soared fifty feet into the air next to a severed hand. Everything on the ground was obscured now by the aftermath of the explosion; a dusty, screaming, writhing miasma of confusion and pain and smoke. He had no idea how many people had been killed or injured in the blast, nor if the casualties were limited to only the invaders.

There wasn't time to ponder such questions, because more figures were beginning to emerge from the fog of war even now, and there was one final red button to press.

His hand floated above it. He was relieved to see that his finger barely shook at all.

"Something is amiss," Amelia said from the back seat. "Do you see how those people are acting?"

"Yes, but I don't know what it means."

Amelia's tranquility had finally slipped. The braided head pivoted left to right and back again, trying to see all around her at once. There was an urgency to her movements and something different about her voice…she sounded surprised.

"Pablo, I think these people – some of these people, at least – are surrendering."

"We can't take that chance. It could just be a trick."

A larger group was approaching the final IED now. It was nesting in a pile of asphalt chunks. Under the road construction debris lay thousands of ball bearings and dozens of sections of razor wire cut for the purpose of transforming into airborne shrapnel.

This was the most powerful of Tung's IEDs and intended to be the most lethal. Those that managed to get that far into their town were going to die a painful death.

"What if they're defecting? That group to the left, they all have their arms raised. Maybe they're giving themselves up? Maybe they don't want to hurt anyone."

"And maybe that's what they want us to think!"

His finger began applying pressure to the final blast button.

"Think carefully about what you're about to do. Killing people who are trying to kill us is one thing. Killing people who are throwing themselves at your mercy is something else."

Pablo watched the group close the distance between themselves and the final IED. Close the distance to the Toyota. Close the distance to Maddie lying in a hospital bed.

Wait...was that a child in the middle of the human cluster scrambling toward them?

The radio squawked again, startling him.

His finger involuntarily pressed the button.

The force from the blast felt like an invisible giant's fist pressing into his chest, sucking out all the air in his lungs and pinning his skull against the driver's head rest.

The previous explosions had been an amateur fireworks display by comparison. This one ripped through everyone in a fifty yard radius. The scene through the cracked windshield looked like some nameless devastated Syrian town on the news before Chicxulub.

"Are you okay, Amelia?" he hollered to the backseat when he could get some air in his lungs.

"Yes, I think so," came the reply.

The radio squawked again. Chuck's voice now. "I can't fucking believe it! They're surrendering here too! We've got fifteen in custody."

"Twenty-nine here." Steven's voice. "Pablo, do you read? We heard the blast. What's happening there? Dani, do you read? Sam? People, check in!"

He felt a small hand squeezing his shoulder.

"You didn't know."

"I didn't mean to do it. It was an accident."

Amelia reached over the passenger seat to retrieve the walkie-talkie that Pablo ignored.

"Amelia here. I'm with Pablo. We just blew the final bomb...an armed group was targeting us. Nobody else is coming through now. What's happening out there?"

More static, then Steven's voice again.

"The bulk of the invaders from the north surrendered. The others are dead. Has anyone seen Isaiah? Dani, check in!"

Seconds ticked by as Pablo continued to watch the tiny, finer pieces of death and destruction drift down from the heavens.

Finally, Dani's voice. "Roger. I got the bastard."

"You killed Isaiah?" Steven demanded through the static.

"Negative. I have him contained. And he's all mine. Is that clear? Sam, where are you?"

Ten heartbeats passed with no response.

"Sam!" Dani's voice again, urgent now.

"Roger!" Sam said. "I'm at the western barricade."

"What the fuck are you doing there?"

"I have someone who wants to talk to you."

Chapter 55

A bedraggled, exhausted subdued gathering of Liberty's citizens filled most of the benches of the courtroom, which had served as the location for all the town's business since Steven, a far-thinking planner-prepper-genius, had taken on the unofficial mantle of 'leader.' The room wasn't overflowing because there had been casualties. More than expected.

Lisa sat on a row in the middle of the room. The invaders hadn't gotten near their precious greenhouse. She was thinking about the spring planting and what new crops she might try to coax from the sandy soil in the fallow fields on the outskirts of town. The absence of Ed, who was usually at her side gazing down at her with those smitten puppy dog eyes, was a telling pictorial. She didn't seem to be aware of the tears streaming down her cheeks.

Jack Kennedy, the stoic half of the popular twin brothers, stood by the back wall. His face was streaked with grime and tears. His brother's body had been found covering a woman knocked unconscious by one of the IED blasts. She told the remaining twin that his brother had died saving her life. Jack knew he would never recover from the loss of half of himself. Having an arm or a leg amputated would be a cakewalk compared to the incompleteness he felt now. He knew he could not remain in the place where his brother had died. Tomorrow he would leave town, even though he had no idea what direction he would go.

On the row in front of him sat the father of an eighteen-year-old girl named Lorilee. The father hated that his daughter had cast aside her real name in lieu of one that defined her solely by her prowess with a gun. He was the only remaining survivor of their family now that his child was gone, and his pain was too enormous for mere tears to express its magnitude. He was pondering by what method he would end his own life in the morning.

A dozen other empty places on the benches told similar stories of loss.

Pablo sat next to Amelia at the back of the room. His face was a picture of anguish after seeing Maddie at the hospital minutes earlier. Her condition was stable but worsening. He hadn't wanted to leave her side, but Steven had demanded the attendance of everyone who was physically able. Pablo thought if Maddie died while he was sitting at this town hall meeting, he might have to kill the mayor.

Only Amelia knew the full extent of Pablo's misery. Neither of them had mentioned those people who might have been surrendering at the southern barricade, but whom Pablo had killed instead with the involuntary movement of his finger on the third detonator. Two tiny shreds of redemption sat next to him on the opposite side from Amelia. Rebecca and Tiffany, the children Pablo had rescued from the cannibals, had been flourishing since their arrival in Liberty. The older girl, Tiffany, had even begun to speak again. Rebecca, the younger, spunkier of the two, had become a common sight around town, asking questions and learning everything she could from anyone who would teach her. She was a special girl with one of the quickest minds Pablo had ever seen. She just might become mayor someday. The knowledge that without his intervention those two little girls wouldn't be alive was something Pablo clung to when his memory wanted to obsess on the moment he accidentally pressed that final IED button.

Julia sat a few rows back from where her brother was pacing, gathering his thoughts and waiting for people to settle down so he could get started on the meeting. She was smiling for the first time in days. *Dani was alive. Her daughter was alive.* She knew her happiness was inappropriate, but she couldn't stop feeling it. Didn't really want to try. More than twenty years of guilt was melting away, and for just this moment in time, she would let herself be at peace. Her nephew sat next to her rather than with the remaining members of the security crew. She held his hand, which was still trembling hours later. Her smile faded when she thought of her own recent murderous act and knew he struggled with similar internal conflicts. His sniper rifle had found nine targets, and no matter how justified the taking of lives, in the end, human beings had been killed by his hand. It was a burden many people in the town now shared.

Natalie perched on one of the front rows. On her right sat her daughter, who was just as lovely as the mother. They had both been in the basement during the battle, so their tidiness – their clean clothes and neat hair – stood out among the disheveled gathering. The empty place on the bench to Natalie's left was earmarked for Steven when he finished his speech. She tried to appear sad, as people would expect her to be. She had lost her man, after all. It was difficult to contain the giddiness she felt now that Marilyn and Calvin were both gone. The road to Steven was obstacle-free. She was wondering what would be a seemly waiting period before she initiated her campaign of seduction.

A voice rose above the din.

"You have me to thank. If I hadn't orchestrated the whole thing, we'd have annihilated you all."

The woman who spoke, or perhaps she was just a girl...it was difficult to tell because of the grime covering the asymmetrical features; the rat's nest hair might have contained some gray strands, or it could have been streaked with ash fallout. Woman or girl, she was in custody, of sorts. Because of her deformities, the zip ties around her wrists weren't secure, but the ones around her ankles were doing an adequate job for the moment. Sam stood beside and just behind her. He gently held one of the skinny biceps in his hand. Because Sam was Sam, there was no animosity in his face, even though the girl-woman he was guarding had stuck a five-inch blade into his belly days earlier. He wore the beautiful smile he always did when he looked at Dani, who was in the center of the room with her own captive.

Dani had taken great pains to secure Isaiah. Steven had wanted to put him behind bars along with the other prisoners in Liberty's jail cells, both the hostile soldiers and the ones who had surrendered with claims of seeking sanctuary. The two factions had been separated so the hostiles wouldn't kill the others. But Dani knew better than to let Isaiah out of her sight even for a moment. He sat on the floor in the center of the converted courtroom. His wrists were tied to each other, then bound again to his bare ankles with commercial-grade zip ties and lots of them. As she stood over him, she pressed the point of her K-Bar below his ear. Minutes earlier, she had allowed Julia to take a peroxide-soaked cloth to her face, followed by what seemed like an entire tube of Neosporin. The discomfort of the doctoring had been secondary to seeing the pained expression on the face of the woman who looked so much like her. Well, *used* to look, she thought when she studied the older woman's scar-free skin during her ministrations. She had resisted the urge to ask for a mirror and pointedly ignored any reflective surface since the battle had ended. More important issues than her vanity were at hand.

"I made this happen!" Dolores squeaked, her lovely voice pitched high from distress. "If I hadn't converted all those people, they would have been killing you instead of surrendering. Don't you idiots get that? You have me to thank! You didn't win this war, I delivered the victory to you. Me! I did that!"

"She has a point," Sam said looking at Steven who stood with his arms crossed a few feet away from Dani's prize prisoner.

"Yes, and she stuck that point in your belly, Sam," Dani said.

"She only stuck me once. She probably could have gotten me a couple more times, but she didn't."

"That's right!" Dolores said, excited to have an ally. "I only wanted to disable him, not kill him. I didn't want anything to ruin my plans. I'd been surveilling Isaiah and his army for days and formulating my strategy. I knew there was dissension, and I intended to exploit it. I couldn't have you two messing it all up."

"This is a steaming pile of horseshit," Dani deadpanned to Steven. "I hope you're not buying into it."

"There's some truth to her claims," Steven replied, his eyes on Dolores. "Dozens of people at the northern barricade surrendered to us."

"You can't be considering letting this bitch go free," Dani said.

"I am," Steven replied. "Along with all those who didn't raise arms against us."

"Oh for fuck's sake. That's just peachy. We're going to release them like we did those others? So they can gather another army and come at us again? What the fuck is wrong with you people?"

Despite her agitation, she was careful to keep the blade pressed firmly against Isaiah's neck. He was gagged too; unable to contribute to the discussion. Maybe it was time to allow him to do so. Maybe she should let Steven and Liberty's residents see the kind of monsters they would be dealing with for the rest of their pathetic, bleeding-heart lives.

With a quick flick of her wrist, she sliced through the bandana that was holding the gag in place. When she did so, she allowed the blade to also slice a sizeable portion of his cheek. She contemplated all the tender bits her K-Bar would find before she killed him once and for all.

"What do you have to say about that, Isaiah, you pedantic, pernicious prick?"

He grinned. The perfect teeth were crimson from the fresh wound, but when he spoke, his voice was rich and dulcet as always, a gentle, loving father counseling his frightened children. It made Dani want to slice out those vocal chords on the spot.

"I think all people deserve a second chance. Even such as myself. I see now how wrong I was…how hurtful…and how misguided was my scheme to seize this lovely town and displace all you good people. I only wanted to provide my followers…my children, as it were…with a safe haven. A home where we could start over, rebuild civilization in a moral, ethical, humane way. Our intel – that the town was overrun with debauchery and horrible people committing unspeakable acts – was sadly inaccurate. That vile creature over there," he indicated Dolores with a nod, "told us as much. She spoke of rape and torture, misogyny and brutality. You can see how I would feel justified in my desire to end such as that."

"You lying piece of shit," said Dani.

The rich laughter took her back to Texas, to that first time she heard the beautiful sound in her backyard. She felt the tight scarred tissue of Isaiah's 'brand' twinge under her layers of clothing. She thought of her ruined face and the misery she had endured for the sake of his absurd reckoning.

She scanned the benches, noting the exhaustion, the sadness, the resignation – and something else – in many of the faces that were looking at Isaiah as he laughed. And it caught her completely by surprise.

They believed him.

She pivoted, still pressing her blade against Isaiah's throat, to look at Steven. He was wearing that expression she had grown to hate; that calculating one, like he was trying to decide if Dani had outlived her usefulness.

Next, she found Julia's face in the crowd. The older woman gazed steadily back at her. Something passed between them – a frisson of understanding and something else: accord. Encouragement, perhaps. She remembered having a similar experience with her the night Logan had died. Was it because they were of the same blood? Mother and daughter, as Julia believed them to be? She knew exactly what Dani was contemplating.

Julia gave her daughter the barest hint of a nod.

That was all Dani needed.

As she reversed the pivot, she slid the razor-sharp K-Bar from Isaiah's earlobe across his throat to the other ear.

Chapter 56

"I'm sorry, Pablo. There's nothing more I can do for her. She might live but it's not likely," Cate said. "But we can save the baby. I'm convinced of it, if we induce labor now. If we don't, we'll probably lose them both."

Pablo might have strangled the woman if he had been capable of any kind of movement. As it was, all he could do was stand by Maddie's hospital bed and hold her cold, pale hand in his. He desperately didn't want Maddie to hear those words because he knew what her choice would be.

Her beautiful blue eyes were open. She had heard every word.

He leaned in close to hear what she was saying.

"I love you, Pablo. I'm sorry to cause you so much pain, but there is nothing more important to me than bringing this baby into the world. This tiny miracle that we created. Don't be selfish. I know that sounds harsh, but I know how you are. You'd rather risk the life of the baby for the barest sliver of a chance at saving me. That is not what I want. Do you understand me? Tell Cate to induce labor. That's my decision."

"What is she saying?" the stout woman hovered too close. With his free hand he pushed away her intrusive bulk.

Amelia, who had been standing by the door, stepped up to the woman and tugged her away.

"I can't bear it, Maddie."

"You can and you will. Do it for me."

A sob escaped him.

"I know. It's so hard," she breathed into his ear, "but you can do it. For me, Poet Fellow."

"I love you, Angel Girl," he said. Tears streamed down his face, dripping onto the blanket that covered his Maddie. He watched the moisture being channeled away by the wool fibers as Maddie's chest rose and fell. Tiny, salty rivers coursed down either side of the chest that still rose and fell. Still rose and fell. For now.

It was the ultimate sacrifice she asked him to make. And he must do it because even though it was not what he wanted, it was what she wanted.

He wrenched his face away from hers, prepared to pass on Maddie's directive to Cate, despite the agony it would cause him to say the words.

When he turned, both women stood behind him.

Amelia wore an unidentifiable expression as she looked at Cate; one he had never seen before. She held the pudgy hand in her own tiny one, despite the larger woman's attempts to release herself from the steely grip. Seconds ticked by as Pablo tried to make sense of what was happening through his mental fog of anguish.

Something was passing between the two of them, but what it could be, Pablo had no clue.

Finally, the spell cast between the two women vanished. Abruptly, Amelia released Cate's hand, like it was burning her skin. Then with the same continuous motion, she reached behind her back and slid her knife from its sheath. Her next movement was to plunge the blade under the heavy, shelf-like bosom of Liberty's nurse practitioner.

Chapter 57

One Week Later

"The jury finds the defendant guilty," Steven read from the piece of paper that had been handed to him. "Per the new legislation which prohibits capital punishment in any form, we sentence the defendant to banishment from our town as well as the surrounding hundred mile radius." His voice echoed throughout the half-filled courtroom.

He locked eyes with his sister across the room. Whatever emotions she was feeling at the moment were hidden by that cloak of icy reserve she wrapped herself in when it served her purpose. They weren't in the room used for the town hall meetings, but rather one newly designated for trials and sentencing. He felt it important to keep the two rooms separate. One signified progress and hope, while the other dealt with crime and punishment.

He shifted his focus to Natalie, who sat in the defendant's chair. He saw fear in those lovely gray eyes. The shapely lips trembled.

"This is a mockery of justice," she said, her voice husky and strained. "You're convicting me on the basis of a telepathic message? Do you hear how ridiculous you people sound? Don't you think it's a coincidence that Steven's son is the one who is making these allegations against me? Can't you see what's going on? He wants me out, and you people are too stupid to know you're being manipulated." She was yelling now, gaining courage from her defiance.

"There was more evidence that you murdered Marilyn besides Jeff's testimony, and you know it, Natalie. We're not going to go over it again. You've been found guilty by a jury of your peers. Your punishment begins immediately. You'll be escorted back to your house so you can pack, then you'll be taken a hundred miles out. You can pick which direction. We'll give you enough food and water to last a month."

"You can all go to hell," she spat, then stood and walked past the jury box. Only half of the twelve chairs were filled, also per the recently passed legislation. Maybe a few years from now they would increase that number, but for now six jurors were all they had deemed necessary for a trial. There was too much work to be done to take any more people away from their jobs.

"Come on, Brittany," she said to her crying daughter who had watched the legal proceedings from the gallery. "Let's go."

The young girl sniffed, dabbing a handkerchief at her pretty face.

"I'm not leaving," she said, her voice a whisper. "I'm staying here. I want to stay here." She shot a sideways glance at Jeffrey.

Jeffrey's face could have been carved in stone, but the flushing cheeks gave away his discomfort. It had been his testimony that was largely responsible for the conviction of his girlfriend's mother. When Natalie had touched his arm in the hospital at the bedside of the unconscious Marilyn, Jeffrey saw the murder in his mind's eye. Saw the tea that Natalie gave to the librarian. Received the knowledge from Natalie herself, telepathically, that it was poisoned. After the chaos of the battle, he told his father everything. A search of Natalie's house uncovered the wolfsbane. The rest had been left up to the jury.

"Don't you want me to be safe?"

"I want you to come with me!" Natalie shouted, grabbing the slender arm of the fifteen-year old girl.

"That's enough, Natalie. Brittany is old enough to decide what she wants to do. Leave her be. Sam, please escort Natalie to her house."

"She's my daughter!"

"Yes, but she's not your property. Sam, please."

The golden head nodded, but the handsome face was a picture of dismay; Steven felt on the inside as wretched as Sam showed on the outside.

Nobody wanted this, but the law was the law. He and everyone else would abide by their new laws no matter how unpleasant. Dani's, Julia's, and Amelia's trials had gone differently. They had been found guilty of murder, but the acts themselves had been deemed justifiable. It was to be a new legal distinction in these extraordinary times.

All the jurors had to do was look at Dani's face to decide Isaiah's murder had been justified. The jury deliberation had only taken five minutes.

Logan was a sociopath; there had been no question. After his drawings were presented as evidence – the murder of Thoozy along with all the rest – the jury had commended Julia for her bravery in eliminating him. She had dismissed the praise with obvious disdain.

Cate had been something more difficult to identify. After Amelia had killed her and explained why she had done so, evidence had been found in the woman's basement to corroborate Amelia's claim that she had been poisoning Maddie. If Amelia's reputation hadn't preceded the event, the sentencing might not have gone the way it did.

It was a moot point. Amelia had chosen to leave town after her trial. The last anyone knew, she had been heading east.

The members of Isaiah's army that had surrendered had been allowed to stay, including Dolores. The vote had been put to the entire town, and it had been close. Steven had voted to banish them with the rest of the prisoners, but in hindsight, he was glad they were here now. People were a commodity these days, and there were skill sets among the newest citizens that would benefit everyone. Two of the newcomers would be helpful in getting the power back on. Also among their number was a Yale-educated psychiatrist to help Julia, which would be more necessary than ever as unprecedented mental and emotional pathologies – both good and bad – were coming to light.

It was a new world. New polices, new rules, new laws must be tailored to fit it. When considering the talents, abilities, limitations, and proclivities of those who had survived Chicxsulub, the old ways would never work. Steven knew that; perhaps better than anyone except his sister. And with her help, they would steer their tiny pocket of civilization through the uncharted waters of this altered reality.

A reality where people could process information with the speed of a super computer, share thoughts telepathically, and heal themselves of mortal wounds.

Steven found the prospect both terrifying and thrilling.

Chapter 58

Three Months Later

"You're kind of scaring me," Sam whispered into the ear he was currently nuzzling.

Dani smiled in the dark. "Good. You should be scared. I'm a scary bitch now."

"No, you've always been scary. Long before this happened."

He touched her face, feeling the contours of the cheekbones and the curve of the lips with appreciative fingertips. She could sense him smiling too.

She felt more at ease at night; less conspicuous when her face was in shadows. Sam swore he loved her still, despite the scars.

And she chose to believe him.

The first time she had gotten a good look at herself in a mirror, it took her breath away. But even though she didn't have the super-healing ability that Sam seemed to possess, Isaiah's reckoning was fading and would continue to do so with time. She kind of dug the menacing vibe she could project more effectively now; the scars gave her an edge when she needed to intimidate someone.

So there was that.

"I mean that you used to be a thrill-looker, and now you're not. At least not so much. Don't get me wrong...I like that you're not that way anymore. But because it's new and different, it's a little scary to me. And it makes me wonder about something."

"What's that?"

"It makes me wonder if now that you're settling down a little, maybe we could think about having some, uh, kids."

She heard the nervous note in his voice, and she could feel him holding his breath.

After a long minute, she said, "You want to have a pack of ankle biters? Do you realize how much work those little fuckers are?"

They knew each other so well. She hadn't flat-out put the kibosh on the idea of having children. She felt his smile in the dark.

Then she let him feel hers with his fingertips.

###

"Pablo, put her down before she throws up all over you."

He grinned at the indulgent look on Maddie's face as he held their baby aloft with outstretched arms.

"Emily says she wants to be a pilot when she grows up." He made vrooming sounds as he twirled their daughter carefully in the air.

"She'll be disappointed then. I'm pretty sure planes will be grounded for at least a generation."

"True. Better rethink that career choice, young lady," he said to the baby who was gurgling with delight, breast milk dribbling from the corners of the cherub lips.

Maddie sighed happily. "She's beautiful, isn't she?"

The effects of Cate's poison seemed to be out of her system. The only reminder was an occasional migraine, but she'd had those before; before Cate, and before a bullet had found its way into her head. They had always been a part of her life. Pablo often wondered if they weren't a side-effect of her remarkable mathematical talent. She still received visions sometimes too. Nothing terrible at this point, but it distressed him to hear her moan in her sleep, knowing it might be something worse than just a bad dream.

"She's perfect," he replied. "Every inch of her."

"Let's hope she gets the best of both of us."

"You mean my brilliant wordplay and your gift with numbers? Good grief, she could take over the world!"

"Let's hope she gets my humility then," Maddie said with a kiss to Pablo's cheek.

"She is Subliminia...the Angel of Perfection," Pablo cooed.

Maddie laughed, then was suddenly serious. "She is Serendipity...the Angel of Everything That Fell into Place and Defied the Odds. She's a miracle, this one. And she has your beautiful golden eyes instead of my boring blue ones. Those eyes that must have come from a gringo in the woodpile."

He smiled, then placed their baby back at her mother's breast. The greedy lips quickly found the nipple they sought.

He looked at his Maddie holding their child. Both alive. Both healthy. Both perfect. The larger chest and the tiny chest rose and fell in unison.

Rose and fell.

Pablo thought he would never be able to close his eyes and sleep when that beautiful sight was before him.

###

Minutes later, Maddie smiled at Pablo's snores. She sat up in bed, cradling the milk-drunk baby in her arms, then crossed the few feet of carpet to the bassinet. She laid the warm bundle in a mound of blankets, her fingers brushing the colorful, freshly-washed serape that had belonged to Pablo's mother. It was important to him to have it near his child; a kind of proxy for his parents. He had plans to teach his daughter Spanish in their honor, and to share with her the same bedtime stories they had told him as a child.

Maddie's fingertips burrowed deeper into the woven cotton stripes, drawn into the fibers now, as if compelled by some invisible force. She didn't realize it, but her eyelids were half-closed, and her face had taken on the dreamy expression Pablo dreaded.

A man stood in the open front door of an old, ramshackle house. The scrape of his boots drew the woman's attention from the clean laundry on the sofa she had been folding. A hot, dry breeze wafted through an open window, lifting the yellowed shade with an invisible ghost hand, revealing a mountainous desert landscape beyond. Alarmed, she darted toward the back of the house, but he was too quick. The next instant her back was pinned to the braided rug by the man who straddled her now. Blue-black hair fanned out around her beautiful, heart-shaped face. The delicate chin trembled.

The man wore a lecherous smile; his golden eyes never left the pretty face as he pulled up her dress and thrust himself inside her. When it was done and he was gone, she remained on the floor. Fear and shame kept her from running down the street to the federales building. Instead, she reached up to the sofa, grabbed the colorful blanket folded neatly there, and pulled it over her body and face. She stayed there for hours, heaving herself up just before her husband was due home.

Maddie removed her fingers from the bassinet where they had been entangled in the serape. The blanket had belonged to Pablo's mother, who, according to Pablo, had been the most perfect woman in the world. Maddie felt a wave of sadness; not only because her daughter would never get to meet her grandmother, but also because Maddie would not be able tell anyone the reason why both Pablo and his child had such unusual golden eyes.

It didn't matter. It was ancient history and no good would come from Pablo knowing his beloved *Papa* was not his biological father.

Maddie watched her baby sleeping, the tiny miracle who had squirmed into their ravaged world and who healthily remained there, having been gifted a double set of the genetic code that allowed her to do so. Maddie knew this child would be more special than any of them. She knew this not because she was a proud mother, but because her *scythen* told her as much. Finally, the word for all those images she saw in her head had a name. It had come to her recently. And somehow, the word felt perfect.

Epilogue

D r. Harold Clarke crouched on the foyer floor of the BISI section of the British Academy in London. After all this time being alone, all the months of solitude and the increasingly erratic conversations with himself, another human...a reasonable-sounding human...was on the other side of the massive mahogany door. A mere four inches of wood separated them. Harold didn't know whether to be excited or terrified.

"Sir, I mean you no harm. I have food! Please, just let me in."

The voice was male, and there was a compelling tone to it; a subharmonic that resonated...spoke to him on a level that couldn't be heard, but rather felt, like the vibrating notes of a bass violin.

His mind did a quick calculation, while his eyes absently scanned the walls of the foyer of the British Academy. The building had begun to feel less like a knowledge-filled sanctuary and more like a prison.

With shaking hands, he unbolted the three sturdy locks, then opened the massive door a crack to peer at the man on the stoop. He breathed a sigh of relief.

"It's you, then?" Harold said.

A wide grin revealed perfect teeth in the dark-skinned face.

"Yes, it's me." The brown eyes were kind. Loving, almost. Harold felt an instant kinship with the man; an immediate bond like he had never experienced with anyone before.

Harold said, "It took me a while to decipher your journal. Then longer still to establish the...connection. I'm sorry. I don't know what you people call it."

"It's called *scythen.*"

"Ah, yes. That feels right. Come in, come in. I have many questions."

"I'm sure you do, but they'll have to wait. We must be on our way."

Harold frowned. "Where are we going?"

The man's smile turned mysterious. He reached for Harold's hand, and said simply, "We're going home."

###

"Oh, you sexy vixen. Come to papa!"

Amelia laughed at the expression of pure lust on the face of her beloved Fergus. After weeks of travel – some on foot, some on bicycle, some in an abandoned Ford Focus she had found on the road with a full tank of miraculously good gasoline (yes, she could drive an automobile, but hated every moment) – she had arrived at the specific dot on the map where the Atlantic Ocean met the sandy beach known as Jupiter, Florida.

It was the place her *scythen* told her she would find Fergus. Tung had helped with that. Even though he was below with Jessie, his *scythen* was needed to help boost the signal.

"How many more times do you intend to bed me, you lascivious creature? I'm getting a little sore in the nether regions, and this sand is making it worse."

They lay on a blanket on the beach, watching the scuttling clouds dance above the turquoise water. The sun at their backs painted the sky in swaths of lavender and tangerine. The warm, salty breeze felt delicious on her skin after the long months in the cold Midwest; felt like being fondled by a benevolent, lustful god.

"As many beddings as you'll allow me. We have lost time to make up for."

At the mention of time, her smile faded.

When he noticed, he quickly added, "Let's not think about it right now. We'll think about it tomorrow."

"You sound like Scarlett O'Hara," she replied. She knew how he loved those silly movies. She had never seen the appeal. Life itself held plenty of fascination for her without capturing it on film and projecting it onto a screen or broadcasting it from an electronic box.

"We can't keep putting it off," she said.

He sighed.

She continued, "Before you say anything, I don't want to see sympathy. I don't want to hear chastisements. I don't want to feel disappointment. I knew the price I would pay for my choices. Is it possible that we could just leave it at that?"

He kissed her lips.

"Not bloody likely. Amelia, my love," he said, suddenly serious, "how can I lose you? How can I just pack up and go home, knowing that you're going to get old and die in the blink of an eye?"

It was rare to see such solemnity on the face of the man with the bright blue eyes and the flaming red hair. The somber tone was at odds with everything about him, from the vivid colors of his physical body to the larger-than-life personality. It didn't suit him.

"I don't know. But you'll do it and you'll survive it somehow, and probably do so in the arms of the first female you meet on the road home."

They both laughed, breaking the tension.

That lightness of being was how she wanted to spend her last days or months (maybe even a year, if she were lucky) with the love of her life, before she shooed him away and back to his virtual immortality. Because of her transmissions, which had revealed all the goodness she had witnessed during and after the battle at Liberty...the *worthiness* of the survivors, and the sacrifices they had made for each other...the *Cthor* had decided to delay an earth cleansing, pending further research and observation.

She had bought everyone on the planet some time, and they would never know how close they had come to death. They didn't need to. It was her burden and her gift.

Forfeiting not only her longevity but her home below wasn't a terrible price to pay, actually. She was in paradise. There were worse ways to spend the next thirty or forty years than a place like this, and she would cherish every second.

Besides, when her time came – the end of a life longer than most humans could fathom – she knew she had a friend waiting on the other side to greet her.

When she thought of Thoozy, she smiled again.

That lightness she felt was partly due to being with Fergus, here in this beautiful place after surviving months of discomfort, fear, stress, and disgusting food. (*Spaghettio Stew!*) But the lightness was also because an obscenely long life no longer loomed before her, weighing on her with its appalling unendingness. She had never realized until now how tired it made her knowing she might live forever.

We all make sacrifices, she thought. Indeed, every one of us.

She turned back to Fergus. He held her hand; she knew he was feeling all her emotions through their physical contact, and was accepting them with equal measures of sorrow and joy.

She was happy to know he understood, even if his own path would eventually take him away from her. Just as there can be no light without darkness, there can be no joy without sorrow. But the sorrow could be delayed for a time. For now, this sunset, this ocean, and this man were all that mattered.

THE END

Excerpt from Moving with the Sun

Moving with the Sun, Book 3 in the Troop of Shadows Chronicles

*D*ear Diary,

We destroyed the bridges today in an effort to make us 'safer.' Acquiring the explosives was no small task, but the placement and detonation was child's play. Bridges are easily demolished, unlike larger structures, such as skyscrapers and athletic stadiums. When it came time to topple them, it was over in less than five seconds. Rather anti-climactic, but still more interesting than anything else that happened today.

I admit, I have mixed feelings about being cut off from the continent. Of course, there will still be access via boat, or for those so inclined, an invigorating swim, but removing the bridge roads felt a bit like severing an umbilical cord. It's an appropriate metaphor; all the necessities of life for this baby island formerly came from the mother mainland.

Now we're truly on our own.

You have to see the irony, Diary. You do, don't you? They went to such extreme measures to secure their safety and well-being, blissfully unaware that already in their straw-hut midst is one who intends them more harm than any huffing-puffing wolf.

CHAPTER 1

"Little dude, that is not the way to do it. You can't rush these things. Pretend there's a school of mermaids swimming around out there. You don't want to fling that hook into a mermaid face or a mermaid breast. You want to lob it gently into the water so she'll notice it. She'll see the bait and swim up to it, all sexy and gorgeous with her long red hair streaming around her, then her luscious lips will latch on to it. When you feel that tug, that's when you go Rambo on her. Jerk the rod to set the hook. Got it?"

Tyler spoke to the fourteen-year-old standing next to him on the beach. The water looked like celadon silk, the late morning sky was an azure canvass painted with wispy horse-tail clouds, and the temperature was already a balmy ninety degrees.

"You just described The Little Mermaid. You want me to set a hook in the mouth of Disney's most beloved princess? What kind of monster are you? And a *Rambo* reference? Are you eighty?"

Tyler laughed. During college at the University of Florida, the movie star smile in the handsome face had compelled most members of the Zeta Tau Alpha sorority to drop their lacy panties. He doubted that many of those nubile young ladies were alive now. The Zetas were known for their blond hair and long legs, not their brains, and the scattering of survivors seemed to register very high on the intelligence scale.

"Never mind about Rambo," he said to the boy. "Just remember what I told you. You're smart. You can do this."

"For sure. But I'm a lover, not a fisherman," Kenny said, slipping into Tyler's surfer-dude accent. Tyler wasn't sure if the kid did that without thinking or if he were being made fun of. Kenny was one intelligent kid. And it was

hilarious to hear a short, nerdy black teen emulating his speech pattern.

"Lover? Really? Have you even kissed a girl yet?"

Kenny smirked and waggled his eyebrows. "I'm not the kiss-and-tell type, pervert. Go bag your own woman."

"For sure, man. Just know that if you have any questions about...that kind of stuff...I'm here for you."

He had become attached to the orphaned teenager these past few months. There were a lot of brainy people in the Colony — himself included — but Tyler often wondered if Kenny weren't the smartest of all. When the boy had wandered onto the island while the bridges were still intact, he had been near-starving and suffering from PTSD. God knew what he must have witnessed out there in Mad Max Land. Tyler had offered up one of his bedrooms with the understanding that his fostering was temporary; at twenty-six, he wasn't ready to be a parent. But in the process of getting some meat on the kid's bones, the two had bonded.

There would be no need to pass him onto any of the other Colonists at this stage.

"Dude, I know about sex. I'm fourteen, not four."

"Right. Sorry. But I'm just saying, I'm here for you if you have any questions. There's a lot more to relationships and romance than just the sexual act."

Kenny rolled his eyes. "Seriously. Stop talking."

"Okay, okay." Tyler smiled. "I think you have an interested mermaid. Do you feel it? Look at your line skittering as you reel in. See how it's darting a little to the left and right? That's what you're looking for."

"I think I do feel something," Kenny said, too excited to resume surfer-dude speak. His normal voice often carried a post-puberty break — much to his dismay — and the accent was pure Brooklyn. "Fuckbucket! I think I caught one!"

"Hey, that kind of language will not cut it. You know Rosemary's etiquette law. Nothing worse than 'shit' or 'damn.'"

"I can't help it. I have Tourette's."

"Horseshit. That Tourette's business might work on the others, but not on me. You're such a weirdo for doing that."

"Not a weirdo. Fake Tourette's allows me to say shit I wouldn't otherwise get away with."

"Yeah, there's nothing weird about that at all."

"It's brilliant, actually," Kenny replied, reeling in what might be a decent-sized fish, judging by the sweat glistening on the kid's face as he struggled with the rod. "The benefits are twofold: I get to make snarky comments with

impunity, and I also get sympathy because I have a 'condition.' With sympathy comes cookies. It's simple causation theory. Oh wait...let me dumb that down for you, blondie. That means cause and effect. Ladies feel sorry for me, I get cookies. Holy crap! I think I hooked Moby Dick!"

"Amberjack, subspecies crevalle, more likely. Let me dumb that down for you, Moriarty. You snagged a jack. That's what you usually get in the surf. They're decent eating when smoked or diced up in corn fritters."

"Why did you call me Moriarty? Isn't that the bad guy in *Sherlock Holmes*? I'm not a villain. I'm delightful."

"I called you that because you're an evil genius."

"Let's keep that between the two of us for now, shall we?" Kenny said with a grunt, pulling the fish out of the water and flinging it onto the sand.

"You got it, little dude. Yep, it's a jack, all right. Good job," Tyler said, removing the lure. "This is a small one. They'll get three times that size a half mile out. Let's take it up to the Love Shack and have them put it on ice. Maybe

you can use your fake Tourette's to score some cookies for us both."

It was a five-minute walk from the shore to the Colony's common house, aka The Love Shack. In its former life, the building had hosted parties and social functions for those locals willing to pay the hefty annual membership fee; it was a beach version of a country club, but without the golf or tennis courts. And it didn't need them. The 180-degree views of the ocean to the east and the inlet channel to the south were magnificent. The second story wrap-around balcony was one of the best places on the island to catch a cool breeze. Inside the first-floor great room lay the nucleus of the Colony. Two commercial freezers, three refrigerators, a six-burner stove, several microwave ovens, and anything else that required electricity and was necessary for comfort and survival, including a serviceable collection of books. Nobody had power at their houses, not after the Solar Harvest when every panel in the area had been collected and installed here. Outside, a herd of 12-volt deep-cycle marine batteries stored the sun's energy captured by the panels; a dozen nearby inverters transformed it from DC to AC. Everything was connected — panels to batteries, batteries to inverters, inverters to the Love Shack. The result was a miniature power plant, and it was vastly more efficient than the meager electricity formerly produced at individual homes.

The decision to create the Love Shack had been a pivotal moment in the evolution of their cooperative community. They would all fare better if they worked together, just like those hundreds of solar panels that lined the roof and grounds of the communal building.

There was strength in numbers.

"Hello, gorgeous," Tyler said to one of the people standing at the stove. The kitchen folks usually did the cooking in the early morning or at night, when it was cooler. All the windows were open and the temperature wasn't unpleasant at the moment. By late afternoon it would be sweltering, just like everywhere else on the island.

"Howdy, handsome. Hello, little boy," the woman replied without turning. Charlotte hadn't seen the kid, but she knew he was there. The woman was a hillbilly ninja, with her partially toothless grin and her innate ability to know everything that was going on around her. It was a bonus that she was the best cook this side of Appalachia.

"How do you do that?" Kenny said to the woman's skinny backside. "And why do you call me a little boy? I ain't little where it counts. *Huge cock!*"

The combination of the fake Tourette's done in Charlotte's Kentucky accent was almost too much. He bit his lip and punched Kenny in the arm.

"Sorry about that, Charlotte. You know how it is with him."

The woman turned around while stirring the large stock pot. Thin lips twitched at the corners. Tyler could picture a corn cob pipe poking out of that mouth and a ramshackle cabin in the background. She might look like a country bumpkin, but that wasn't a euphemism for stupid. And while he suspected Charlotte might have been a deep-south racist in her former life, she had grown as attached to the nerdy black teenager as had Tyler himself.

"You brung me a fish, I see. Not a big 'un, but it'll do. Gut it, scale it, put it in a baggie with some water, then stick it in the freezer on the right. Not the other one...that's for everything that didn't come from the ocean. When you done that, come back and I'll give you boys some cookies. I baked a fresh batch this morning."

"Whoop!" Kenny said, darting a pointed glance at Tyler. He was out the door the next moment.

"He know how to gut and scale?"

"Yep. I let him do that string of pompano I caught two days ago. He did a good job."

Charlotte nodded. Whatever bubbled on the stove smelled delicious. Tyler thought again how fortunate their community was to have her. She could make seagull edible.

"He doing okay? I fret 'bout that boy. Ain't right for a child to go through all that by hisself." She waved the soup ladle in the direction of the mainland and the aftermath of the plague. "He ever talk about it?"

"Nah. I've tried to get him to, but he clams right up. Maybe sometimes it's best to leave sleeping dogs lie. Know what I mean?" he said, maneuvering to get a spoon into the pot.

"You're lucky I like you. Otherwise, you'd be missing some fingers right about now. Go ahead. Tell me what you think."

He could see okra and bell pepper floating in the rich broth, and something else that might have been looking right back at him. The spoon paused on its trajectory.

"Don't worry. Thems frozen oysters from the spring. I know better than to serve summer oysters, even though I never seen seafood until I come here. If you'd hurry up and get that oyster farm going, we'd have a lot more. You marine biologists sure do move slow."

Tyler smiled, then sipped the liquid heaven. "Oh my god. You're a culinary sorceress. As for the oyster farm, these things can take a couple of years. It took weeks just to get the cages repaired and in place, then seeded with the...let's call them 'baby oysters'...from the aquaponics tank. They'll still take another year or two to reach maturity. In the mean-time, we'll still have wild oysters during the winter months. Patience, my dear." He kissed the bony cheek before heading out to check on Kenny.

As he stepped back through the main door of the Love Shack, he heard a popping sound, then shouts coming from the side of the island that faced the Intracoastal Waterway and the continental land mass beyond. The western side of their diminutive paradise had been secured in sev-eral ways. The first line of defense was staying out of sight. Colonists were discouraged from going to the west side where they might be seen from the mainland — if there were no visible inhabitants, there was no one from whom to steal food. Second, a discreet watchtower had been constructed in a copse of royal palm trees in which a sentry stood guard twenty-four hours a day. Third, a series of cadavers, long dead and past the smelly stage, dangled from wooden crosses near the shoreline, signaling a clear warning: stay away or this will happen to you. Their fourth line of defense for the persistent would-be intruder: a percussion tripwire installed near the water's edge. Anyone who swam or boated across the waterway and trudged upon the sandy beach of Jupiter Inlet Colony would encounter it. The
tripwire wouldn't kill; its purpose was to announce a breach of their perimeter. The ball bearings from the shotgun shells had been removed, leaving the harmless caps that would explode with a loud pop when triggered.

"Come on, but stay behind me!" Tyler said, sprinting past the boy, who had already dropped the half-gutted fish.

"Should I arm my dart gun?" Kenny reached into the back pocket of his baggy cut-off shorts as he ran.

"No! I told you to leave that stuff at home. You could accidently hurt yourself or someone else with those things." The two sprinted down residential streets on their way from the Atlantic side of the tiny island to the Intracoastal side.

"You never know when there might be a pirate invasion. My wolfsbane darts are ready for those eye-patched, parrot-shouldered bastards."

"Put them away. Now."

"Damn it, you're pissing in my Wheaties again." He slid the gun back into its pocket.

"Where are the darts?"

"They're in a Tupperware container. Don't trouble your pretty head about them."

"You're a scary little bastard," Tyler said, as they jogged around a corner.

"You don't know the half of it. Hey, you're not supposed to say that word!"

They reached the western shore moments later.

"That's no pirate," Kenny said, as they approached two Colonists huddled next to a young woman. "She might be the Little Mermaid all grown up."

You can continue reading here: https://www.amazon.com/Moving-Sun-Post-Apocalyptic-Thriller-Chronicles-ebook/dp/B07B8SRRMG

Your Opnion?

What Did You Think of the Beauty and Dread?

If you didn't like the book, please tell me... if you did like the book, please tell everyone. My email address is nicki@nickihuntsman-smith.com.

If you liked the book, please leave a review. Studies have shown that most readers say reviews (both the number of reviews as well as the rating) are an important factor in their buying decision. Please take 2-3 minutes to leave a review.

Here's a link to Amazons review page for Beauty and Dread. Direct book review link on Amazon. https://www.amazon.com/review/create-review?&asin=B01MSFIMI0

On a side note, if you've spotted a typo, please email me a nicki@nicki-huntsmansmith.com. I hate those insidious little buggers as much as the next reader.

You can follow me on Facebook at:
https://www.facebook.com/AuthorNickiHuntsmanSmith/
You can signup for my newsletter at:
https://nickihuntsmansmith.com/. My subscribers are the first to know of a new release.

I look forward to hearing from you!

Nicki Huntsman Smith

All My Books

All my books are enrolled in the Amazon Kindle Unlimited program. So if you are a Kindle Unlimited subscriber, like me, you can read all of my books for free.

DEMON CHASE- Book 1 in A Monstrous Dread Series
A nail-biting, supernatural suspense horror series begins with DEMON CHASE.

SUBLIME SEVEN Time Travel with a Transcendent Twist
Follow the evolution of a soul as told through seven incarnations on earth and beyond.

TROOP OF SHADOWS – Book 1 in the Troop of Shadows Chronicles
A riveting, multi-character post-apocalyptic journey starts here with Book One.

BEAUTY AND DREAD – Book 2 in the Troop of Shadows Chronicles Series
The second installment in the Troop of Shadows Chronicles follows the characters you loved (and hated) in Book One.

MOVING WITH THE SUN – Book 3 in the Troop of Shadows Chronicles Series
The third installment in the series takes place in Florida and introduces a new cast of characters, along with some old favorites.

WHAT BEFALLS THE CHILDREN – Book 4 in the Troop of Shadows

Chronicles Series
The fourth installment in the series takes place in Appalachia and introduces new characters to love and hate, along with an old favorite.

THOSE WHO COME THE LAST – Book 5 in the Troop of Shadows Chronicles Series
The fifth book in the series returns to Whitaker Holler where two adversarial clans finally determine the fate of their people once and for all.

DEAD LEAVES, DARK CORNERS – A collection of short stories
An eclectic assortment of nail-biting short stories and one spine-tingling novelette.

SECRETS UNDER THE MESA
A pinch of "X-Files" and a dash of "Stranger Things."

PERCEPTIONS
A short story